THE PARADISE COMPLEX

Douglas Lockhart was born in Scotland. His writing career started by accident in 1959 as features editor for a military magazine in Germany. After some years in advertising he published two novels, *Skirmish* and *Song of the Man Whom Came Through*. During the 1970s he also trained as personal assistant to Dr Maxwell Cade in the Biofeedback Department of the Franklin School of Contemporary Studies. Since moving to Australia in 1979 he has written radio scripts, his first play and *Jesus the Heretic*, his controversial study of Christianity's origins, published by Element in 1997.

by the same author

Jesus the Heretic
Skirmish
Song of the Man Who Came Through

The Paradise Complex

An Exploration of the Forbidden

Douglas Lockhart

ELEMENT
Shaftesbury, Dorset • Rockport, Massachusetts
Brisbane, Queensland

First published in Great Britain in 1997 by
Element Books Limited
Shaftesbury, Dorset SP7 8BP

Published in the USA in 1997 by
Element Books, Inc.
PO Box 830, Rockport, MA 01966

Published in Australia in 1997 by
Element Books Limited
for Jacaranda Wiley Limited
33 Park Road, Milton, Brisbane 4064

Cover design by Mark Slader
Design by Roger Lightfoot
Typeset by ABM Typographics Ltd, Hull
Printed and bound in the USA by
Edwards Brothers Inc.

British Library Cataloguing in Publication
data available

Library of Congress Cataloging in Publication
data available.

ISBN 1–85230–809–5

High on the dunes, watching eyes discern upon the naked body a sign they wished, and at the same time did not wish, to see: a blood-red cross between the shoulder blades.

(Carlos Fuentes *Terra Nostra*)

Rational argument can be conducted with some prospect of success only so long as the emotionality of a given situation does not exceed a certain critical degree. If the effective temperature rises above this level, the possibility of reason's having any effect ceases and its place is taken by slogans and chimerical wish-fantasies. This is to say, a sort of collective possession results which rapidly develops into a psychic epidemic.

(C G Jung *The Undiscovered Self*)

Acknowledgements

I wish to acknowledge my very great indebtedness to my partner Robin Mosley for her unstinting support, encouragement, and the many valuable suggestions she made during the writing of this book; Rob MacKenzie for his extraordinary patience in listening to many thousands of words being read aloud (not to mention his talents as an eagle-eyed editor); Jane and Damian Brown and Michael Powell for reading the final draft and making many useful comments; Richard Leigh for generosity of time, patience and learning; and the *Tasmanian Arts Advisory Board* for awarding me a grant to experiment with the book's initial drafts.

I would like to acknowledge the assistance afforded me from such works as *The Messianic Legacy* and *The Holy Blood and The Holy Grail* by Michael Baigent, Richard Leigh and Henry Lincoln; *Psychotherapy and Existentialism* by Viktor E Frankl; *The Passover Plot* by Hugh Schonfield; *A History of Religion East and West* by Trevor Ling; *The Dream and the Underworld* by James Hillman; *Inner Visions* by Nevil Drury; *The Imagination of an Insurrection* by William Irwin Thompson; *The Clowns of Good* by Morris West; *The Jesus Scroll* by Donovan Joyce; *The Weekend Australian* for such articles as 'Church Hesitant' and 'The Catholic Paradox'; and last but not least, John Baldock, my editor at Element, for his many pertinent and intelligent suggestions. I would also like to thank David Higham Associates for permission to reproduce an extract from 'Valediction', from *Collected Poems* by Louis MacNiece (Faber & Faber).

This book is dedicated to my daughter Jennifer.

DGL
Tasmania

PROLOGUE

THE AMBER sunset in his dream tinted the rooftops of the houses, softened their extravagantly carved and garishly painted exteriors. It even coloured the warm, silky air through which he seemed to glide, or swim; and there was the added illusion of this ambered light eating into the deepest recesses of gloom as it travelled, almost like a radiant acid, down the faces of the buildings and into the alleyways.

But interrupted, this dream, by a whitish sheen of light distantly apprehended. He stirred towards that light, hung for a moment in the balance between sleep and wakefulness, then sank back into that ambered landscape as if called to complete a pattern – a recurring pattern. He recognized the streets and the houses, knew in which direction his quarry lay, but was suddenly aware of certain differences which disturbed him, cautioned him. For on every other occasion there had been a howling wind, rain on his face, a black and boiling sky overhead – not this pantomime of an evening with its gentle claustrophobia and deserted streets.

The deserted streets bothered him, as did the shuttered windows and the silence. He was being scrutinized from behind those shuttered windows, his every movement relayed, perhaps with a nod, a raised eyebrow or the backward flick of a hand, to other interested parties. Of this he was certain. He could feel presences and detect infinitesimal changes in the density of the ambered air as he glided towards his objective.

They had betrayed themselves. He could smell their fear, their excitement, their breathless fascination.

But if they had betrayed themselves, he had not, would not. There would be nothing of note in his movements to alert them to the fact that he had penetrated their scheme and was now engaged in the task of outwitting them – and that in spite of their clear advantage. The deed would simply have to be accomplished in their very midst, deftly and swiftly executed without their even realizing that the blow had been struck, that their confidence was not only mistaken, but laughable. He moved on, exuding a complementary confidence to allay their fears and lull them into a less vigilant state.

The house was not far distant – but how to enter? There would be men in the house itself, waiting. He could almost see their shaded faces, feel the pressure of wall or post on their straightened backs. There would also be men on the roof, men at the rear, men stationed even at what would be considered the least likely point of entrance. He immediately chose the least likely point of entrance knowing that the men stationed there would be less in spirit. Courageous men they might be, men of comparable experience to the others, but that indescribable tension which so possessed the others would not be theirs in full.

The situation required a moment of magic, an illusion of powers released, a veritable disappearing act through which a momentary confusion could be sown. He stopped, stood for a moment, then began to spin slowly, but with gathering speed so that his monk's cloak might billow out, and out, to form a cone. And from out of this cone, having perfectly gauged angle and distance, he slipped, leaving the gyrating garment to fall flat and empty on the street's uneven surface.

Chapter One

He came up out of his dream as if physically hauled, opened his eyes and registered the familiar layout of his bedroom. The dream was still upon him, however, in the form of an immediate memory of events so full of incipient drama that his breath caught in his throat. Sucking air in, he lay for a moment and tried to reorient himself, rid himself of the quite overpowering desire to sink back into that ambered landscape. But he managed to hold on, managed to rally his senses and take control.

Not exactly a nightmare, but certainly the entrance to one, the beginning of a battling of his will against forces malevolent and cunning. That was the pattern. But he suspected that on this occasion the dream would have taken a more substantial turn – for although the insubstantial element had been there in the form of faceless individuals watching him, their insubstantiality had been due to an intervening brick and mortar, to shuttered windows and bolted doors, not to the insubstantiality of beings fleshless and bloodless in their own right. Compelled to rise, he got out of bed and padded naked and reeling into the kitchen in an attempt to shake off the dream's effect. But it went with him, and eased only slightly when he splashed his face with water and stepped back, his hands resting on the cool, shiny aluminium of the sink.

Head down, he drew breath and exhaled slowly. Then glancing around he smiled crookedly to himself and straightened. Everything looked so damned normal, so solid, so incapable of being anything other than what it was. Yet he suspected that with a little nudge everything perceived could undergo a transformation. Blinking that thought away, he turned and walked out of the kitchen, crossed the carpeted hallway and entered his study. There he stood for a moment, uncertain as to why he had done so. Then with an electrifying jolt he noticed the opened drawers in his desk, and the protruding papers. Everything did change in that moment, but not with a nudge. Even as his body turned, the blow aimed so expertly at the nape of his neck made vital contact and he dropped where he stood. An empty sleep this time, followed by a completely different kind of awakening some 20 minutes later.

He tried to get up but fell over on his side, causing a shock wave of pain throughout shoulders and neck. What the hell had happened? For a moment he could not fathom what had happened, could not understand why he was in so much pain, but it soon came back to him. Galvanized by the realization that his attacker might still be somewhere near, he listened, every nerve in his body acting as a receiver. But there was only an empty silence, an uninhabited stillness. Reassured that he was alone, he levered himself up, and with herculean effort got to his feet.

His priority was clothes. Only when he had clothes on would he be able to function properly, feel himself to be in control. With clothes on he would give full vent to his anger, investigate the other rooms, call the police, reinstate himself as Ian Drummond. But as he did not yet have clothes on, he moved gingerly into the hallway fully expecting a confrontation in spite of what his senses told him.

It was an unnerving experience for someone of his temperament; he felt belittled, reduced to the level of a frightened child. That annoyed him, made him ignore the pain and dress quickly and barge into the other rooms in a mood of savagery. For he was of the opinion that 'fear' had been eradicated from his system, expunged from his nature through head-on collisions with life. Obviously not so. He stopped in the doorway of the guestroom as that realization turned into a more pointed and exact definition of his earlier state: he had quite simply been afraid to die. The brutality of the attack, and its swiftness, had revealed a mind within which no quarter was given to the victim; he could just as easily have been killed in that moment. It made him shiver to think of his assailant standing behind him preparing to deliver that blow. And it was also fairly certain that his sudden awakening from such a powerful dream had been due to the intruder's standing in the bedroom itself . . . torch in hand? That, without doubt, was what had taken place. The bastard! Not once, but *twice* the sweep of the beam across his face. A moment of raw light interrupting the affair of his dream, then a more direct and pronounced blast of light dragging him back to full consciousness.

So how had his attacker got in? And what was missing? He speedily checked out the answers to both of those questions – they hadn't occurred to him during his rampage – and returned to his study both puzzled and uneasy. Nothing appeared to be missing; and the front door had not been forced. Whoever it was had had a key and a definite purpose in mind – to go through his private papers. Two hundred pounds' worth of crisp fivers had not been touched.

The silence of the apartment suddenly bore in on him. He broke that silence with an epithet, rang the police, was transferred to the CID and gave his story over again. Going through to the lounge, he then poured himself a large whisky in an attempt to reduce the pain in his neck. Nothing missing. A key used. His private papers sifted. He dismissed the idea of industrial espionage as too ridiculous, drank his whisky down, and turned back to the crystal decanter. But it was just after five in the morning and the police were about to arrive. What would they think if they found a half-inebriated Scot trying to convince them that he had been brutally attacked in his own home when there was virtually no evidence of any such thing? And as it didn't take much to put him under these days, and some of his neighbours already thought him a periodic drunk – a judgement they would be sure to pass on once the questioning started – sobriety was undoubtedly the best policy.

And all because his wife had left him a couple of months before, and he had taken to emptying the crystal decanter on a daily basis. But it was under control now, that urge toward oblivion. It was as if he had willed himself to overcome the problem against his will – a contradiction in terms that had not escaped his notice. Exactly seven weeks since that moment of mutual failure, that moment when the last tie was sundered, the umbilical cord of their union severed by the honed edge of rancour and a final truth.

Patricia taunting him, yelling at him, informing him icily that he lacked human feeling, that he was without soul and did not know what love meant. Of all the things she had said over the seven years of their marriage – and she had said plenty – that had hurt the most. He had shouted back that she was being unfair, turned away from her in disgust thinking it just another of those moments. But it wasn't. She had then rounded on him like a wildcat, and he had learned that there was someone else, that there had been someone else for months. A blistering anger had welled up amidst tears, an anger that would have swept her from the room, perhaps from the planet, if it had been released. Turning, he had suggested that she leave before he broke his vow never to strike a woman. She would have replied even to that but for the controlled ferocity of his tone, the visible stiffening of his frame. For if she understood anything, it was the latent violence in him, that East-End-of-Glasgow violence which ran through his nature like a seam of glittering metal. There was a limit. Only a fool disregarded that limit.

The drinking bouts had started almost immediately, and continued for some weeks. He had awakened one morning possessed not even of the desire to wash or dress himself. Aware of a terrible emptiness, of a suddenly magnified uselessness, he had wandered aimlessly around his sumptuous apartment in search of he knew not what.

You're without soul, Ian. You don't know what love means!

It was as if she were standing in the room on occasions: an invisible Patricia with whom he argued in his mind. But lessening now, this pointless dialogue with a ghost, for it was she who had had no idea of what love meant, and he who had pointlessly attempted to find it in the emptiness of their relating. There were only the dreams to contend with now: the disturbing, and sometimes horrifying, dreams.

One dream in particular had seared itself into his memory.

Suspended in an electric darkness he had hung, a target somehow singled out by a set of alien forces. A weight of evil, so great that he had felt it anvil the shape out of him, approaching and threatening the seams of his existence with an ultimate tearing, or buckling. An inky brightness surrounding him, closing in on him with the cunning of a disembodied mind whose sole purpose was the devouring of form. Arms outstretched, fingers spread wide like fans held by a dancing geisha, he had resisted the onslaught and stubbornly refused entry to that which he knew could suck him up like a liquid. An eternity of terror as he wrenched himself free, managed to rouse previously untested energies and fight his way back to consciousness. Then had come that breaking down of the fabric of his will that had frightened him more thoroughly than anything else he could remember. Touching on some self-annihilating edge deep within, he had staggered back bemused from his own image in the bathroom mirror as if slapped, aware for the first time that he was a stranger to himself, a stranger kept numb by the dictates of existence. Anaesthetized by the life he led, and by the frigidity of the woman he had tried to love, he had stared into that mirror as if into the mirror of existence and experienced his own intrinsic absence. But three weeks later he had returned to his old ways, and was now interpreting the reverberation of that slap as nothing more than a moment of weakness.

The anaesthetized stranger turned from the crystal decanter and headed for the kitchen, and amidst the empty desolation of immaculate surfaces and shining gadgetry noticed something distinctly out of place: a picture postcard of the *Arc de Triomphe* propped neatly and conspicuously against a salt-cellar. He stared at it for some seconds before grasping the fact that it had been put there by the intruder. It had probably been the intruder's last act before leaving the apartment. Lifting the card so that only its edges pressed into his fingers, he turned it over. On the back, neatly printed in black ink were the words *Quos Deus vult perdere, prius dementat.* Latin? The card also bore a stamp, a quite discernible Paris postmark, and was dated 12 November. Apart from that rather odd message, there was only one other unusual factor: the card was addressed to himself. So where had it come from? He had never seen it before. It was now the 16th of November. Which meant that the card had probably arrived on either the 14th or the 15th. He stopped right there. The postman would have pushed it into the letterbox along with the rest of his mail on either of those two dates – and that could only mean that the same man had been in his apartment twice within a few days. But why come back and run the risk of detection? And why do this with the card? Why intimate a previous entry and a predetermined return?

Not knowing what to make of it, he put the card with its incomprehensible message back where he had found it and turned with the intention of making himself coffee, but the door chime sounded in that same moment and he made to answer it. It was then that something quite astonishing occurred to him: the torch beam on his face had been an intentional act – he had been *meant* to wake up. The sole purpose of the intruder's visit had been to scare the wits out of him. He digested that as best he could, opened the front door, and ushered the two plain clothes policemen into the hallway without a word. The larger of the two men introduced himself as Detective Sergeant Gary Spencer, his partner as Detective Constable Morrison. Drummond nodded, led the two men down the hallway to the study, pointed at his desk, and watched as they looked around. Morrison asked if he had disturbed anything. He said he had not.

'I believe you were attacked,' said Spencer.

'Yes, but I didn't see the person who did it,' he replied, anticipating the man's next question. 'He took me from behind – chopped me as clean as you like.'

'Chopped?'

'I know when I've been chopped; I was a paratrooper 20 years ago.'

'Are you okay?'

'I think so.'

'Pity you didn't get in first.'

'You might have had something to cart away if I had.'

Both men smiled. 'Regular?' asked Morrison.

'National Service – long enough as far as I was concerned.' He realized immediately that they were too young to have done National Service, yet it seemed like only yesterday that he had walked into that camp in Hampshire and come face to face with discipline for the first time in his life. Discipline. Hard men brought under control, their energies schooled and channelled to a common purpose by other hard men.

Spencer nodded at him sagely. 'Nice place you've got here. What's missing?'

'Nothing – so far as I can tell.'

'Nothing?' said Morrison.

'I don't think the purpose of the exercise was to rob me.'

'What do you mean?' said Spencer, tilting his head slightly.

'I think the intention was to scare the shit out of me.' He explained quickly about the card and they asked to see it, followed him into the kitchen and stood staring at it.

'It was obviously put there for a reason.'

Lifting the card in the same manner as Drummond had lifted it,

Spencer said, 'You've got enemies?'
'Not that I know of.'
'What does this mean?' he asked, turning the card so that its strange message could be seen.
'Who knows?' said Drummond, laughing. 'They didn't teach Latin at the school I went to.'
'Nor mine,' said Morrison.
'It's obviously a joke,' said Drummond. 'I think I know who it's from.'
'So who's it from?' asked Spencer.
'A journalist friend of mine. A woman called Georgia Patton. She's quite often in Europe. Freelance. Writes for most of the top magazines.'
'Nice work if you can get it,' said Spencer, who had once tried to write something.
'She's very bright.'
Drummond had known Georgia for years. Patricia had introduced her to him not long after they got married – not exactly a raving beauty, but attractive in a strong kind of way, and able to turn on a delicious smile. He had seriously considered going to Georgia for help during his miniature breakdown, but had decided against it, having no wish for her to see that particular Ian Drummond, that unsure spectacle of a man who had stumbled upon emptiness in the bathroom mirror.
Detective Sergeant Spencer was suddenly a man who eschewed complexity. 'You could be reading more into this card business than is actually there,' he said in a flat tone. 'You may just have forgotten about the card. Maybe the blow –'
'The bastard put it there so that I'd work out that he'd been here before and taken the card with him. He also woke me up with the intention of clobbering me. No thief in his right mind shines a torch in a sleeping man's eyes. I'm almost certain he did it twice.'
'You're sure nothing's been taken?'
'As sure as I can be. He certainly didn't take the two hundred pounds in that drawer.'
'So what was he looking for?'
'I don't know. I'm beginning to think the drawers in my desk were left open just to confuse the issue.'
'Looks to me like he was hunting for something.'

'Probably a tactic to put you fellas off the scent. He wants you to think that.'

'Then why not take the money?'

Unable to answer that question, Drummond shrugged.

'The way I see it,' said Morrison, 'it was you who scared the shit out of him. That's why he scarpered without taking anything.'

'I don't think so,' said Drummond. 'You have to know what you're doing to deliver a blow like that. Which means he knew I'd be out for at least 15 minutes.'

'Might just have been a lucky blow,' said Spencer.

'There's no way I'll believe that,' said Drummond, adamant in his knowledge. 'It's not something you try for the first time. You either know what you're doing, or you don't. That's why I think what he did with that card is important.'

'*If* he did with the card what you say he did.'

'Don't you believe me?'

'– It's not that we don't believe you,' said Spencer, bringing ten years of experience to bear on the question. 'It's just that the criminal mind isn't generally sophisticated enough to go in for things like this. There are a lot of crims around who are handy with locks, and some of them are pretty tough customers, but they're basically thick, Mr Drummond.' The man laughed to himself. 'I could tell you –'

'You're projecting the wrong profile.'

Spencer's smile vanished. 'Look,' he said, trying to sound reasonable, 'it's just possible you forgot about the card.'

'With a message like that on the back?'

It was Spencer's turn to shrug. 'He could have a twisted sense of humour.'

First light and the sound of a bird whistling filtered in through the kitchen window, reminding Drummond of the hour. He glanced at the sky, then back at Spencer's face. Morrison came in at that point and drew the next response. 'So what was he after the first time?' he asked.

'I've got no idea.'

'Documents?'

'It's possible, but not probable.'

'What do you do for a living?' asked Spencer.

'I run my own advertising agency. Had it about six years.'

'Successful, is it?'

'In its own terms, yes. We're small, but moving up fast.'

'Someone maybe thinks you're moving up too fast.'

'I can't see how anyone could think of us as a threat.'

'Got some big clients?'

'A few.'

'Are you handling anything a competitor might want to get his hands on?'

'Nothing that I can think of.'

'You're sure about that?'

'Yes, I'm sure.'

'Then what you're suggesting about the card doesn't make sense. It's too complicated.' He smiled again. 'We'll send someone round to dust the place off. There may be a stray print.'

'I doubt that very much.'

'Would you chop someone with a gloved hand?'

It was a good point, Spencer was using his head. 'Make it late afternoon,' said Drummond. He added, 'Can I get you an envelope for the card.'

The big detective nodded.

'Anything on it is probably smudged to all hell,' said Morrison, his insinuation obvious.

'You won't find my prints on it,' said Drummond. 'I've handled that card just as carefully as yourselves – as carefully as I imagine the man who put it there handled it.'

'Point taken,' said Spencer.

They left after a quick look at the rest of the apartment. Both men were impressed with what they saw. Drummond had spent a small fortune on the place, to keep Patricia happy – Patricia of the unhappy countenance. The moment they were gone he ran a shower, stripped and stepped into it with relish, rubbed the hot water into his neck like a salve. Half an hour later he was frying bacon and eggs and spreading toast. At a quarter past seven he rang Bill Everton – his chief executive – and explained what had happened. The man was taken aback by the news and suggested immediately that he see a doctor in case of complications. Drummond agreed; it was sound advice. Then Everton said something purely logical considering the circumstances, something which halted Drummond in his mental tracks. He said, 'Hope everything's okay at the office.'

Pausing for a split second, Drummond said, 'I'm leaving right this very minute, Bill. Let's hope everything's as it ought to be.'

Everything, they soon discovered, was not as it ought to be. The principal upstairs offices of Drummond Advertising had been taken apart; the place was a shambles. Arriving first, Bill Everton stood among the debris staring, sick to his heart as he considered the clearing up that would have to be done. There were papers everywhere, mounds of files; the files had been emptied onto the floor, stirred and trampled on. But it was the sight of their computers that anguished Bill more than anything else – someone had taken a heavy hammer to them, pulverized them to make sure their memories were irretrievable. There were of course back-ups for everything, but it would take time to piece the whole show back together again, and the work of the last few days would be lost for ever. It was scary to think what would have happened if someone had decided to strike a match.

The executive offices were just as bad. The telephones had been ripped out and most of the furniture smashed or slashed. And there was the problem of replacing, at short notice, the large amount of commissioned artwork that had been wantonly destroyed.

It was all so meaningless.

It was the kind of mindless vandalism one read about daily in the newspapers and wondered at. But on this occasion it wasn't mindless. Ordinary vandals had no knowledge of sophisticated alarm systems. What had happened here was not the work of youths on the rampage. It was an operation planned to coincide with the attack on Drummond. It was a statement of some kind. Someone was saying in no uncertain terms *We have the ability to wipe you out, so be warned.* It was frightening.

By the time Drummond arrived, Bill Everton had assessed how long it would take to have the place functioning again – almost ten days, he reckoned. There were going to be a lot of angry clients clamouring for attention.

'It's unbelievable,' said Drummond, when he had seen everything for himself and compulsively attempted to rescue the odd undamaged piece of artwork. 'You would think an army had been through here.' Then, quite hopelessly, he added, 'Why, Bill? What have we done to deserve this?'

Chapter Two

One week of absolute chaos, then a semblance of sanity. But only a semblance. Bill Everton reached irritably for the yellow telephone on his desk as it bleeped for attention; he didn't like the new phones.

'Yes?' he said curtly. After a few seconds of listening he cut in. 'Why tell me?'

'Because Mr Drummond isn't in the building. He left about an hour ago and hasn't returned.' The receptionist grew more apologetic. 'I'm sorry to have to land you with this, Mr Everton, but it could be important. Can you fit him in?'

'I don't have much option, do I? What was the name again?'

'Edouard Duval – I think he's French.'

'You don't say,' said Everton, continuing to scribble notes about something quite different on his desk pad. 'Is he in the appointments book?'

'Yes.'

'Then hold onto him for a few minutes. Offer him coffee. Apologize. Say that Mr Drummond's been delayed.'

'Check.'

'I'll get back to you.'

Everton rang Ian's personal secretary, but she had no idea where her boss was. No, he hadn't left any telephone numbers. But there had been a call just before he left – on the direct line. Could have been a client he knew well.

'Damn!' said Everton. 'What can you tell me about a man called Edouard Duval?'

'Never heard of him,' said the woman. Then she said, 'I'll take a look in Ian's desk diary. There's generally a short note if he's seeing a new client.'

'As quickly as you can,' said Everton.

But there was nothing that made sense, just the word *Katharsis* next to the man's name.

'What's Katharsis?' he asked.

'A company?'

Everton sighed. 'Okay. Give me a buzz the moment Ian returns.' He replaced the receiver, waited for a moment, lifted it again and punched the buttons for reception. 'Sally? Give me a couple of minutes, then have Toby bring him up. And explain that he'll be seeing me instead of Mr Drummond. Push the delayed bit. Right?'

'Will do.'

He thrust the telephone back into its cradle, sat rock still for a moment, then quickly cleared his desk, put on his jacket and sat waiting for the Frenchman to appear, an image of the man already forming in his mind. That image did not conform to reality.

Edouard Duval turned out to be an exceptionally tall man, and lean with it. His hair was black and swept back close to his head from the brow. Everton estimated his age at around 70, and wondered if the hair had had dye put through it. But it was the man's eyes that fascinated him most – they were the most penetrating eyes he had ever seen, the darkest he had ever seen.

When everything that had to be said was said, and Duval was seated, Everton cautiously approached the reason for his being there. 'It's Katharsis, isn't it?' he said, testing the water. Before the Frenchman could reply, he added, 'I'm afraid I haven't been fully briefed. It was Mr Drummond's intention to handle your inquiry personally.'

'I understand,' said Duval, his accent almost undetectable. 'His delay is unfortunate.'

'But if I can be of any help –'

'You assuredly can,' replied Duval quaintly, 'even if it is only to convey our intentions.'

'Which are?'

'To make ourselves known. We wish you to mount an advertising campaign on our behalf.'

'On behalf of Katharsis.'

'Exactly.'

Bill Everton hesitated, smiled a professional smile. 'What exactly is Katharsis?' he asked.

'Ah! I am sorry,' said the Frenchman. 'There was no opportunity to go into detail with Mr Drummond on the telephone, merely time to make this appointment. I will explain, as best I can.'

'Would you care for some coffee?'

'No thank you. I do not drink coffee.'

'Tea?'

Duval shook his head, conveying dismissal of the idea rather than refusal. Then with hardly a break he launched into a complex definition of Katharsis and its rudimentary aims. Everton listened with growing amazement, and became decidely uneasy as Duval's vision unfolded.

'What we know of psychoanalysis,' said the Frenchman, lacing his fingers over a protruding knee, 'was first called *katharsis* by Sigmund Freud. Aristotle defines the word as meaning "intellectual and moral purgation". Freud chose the term because it accurately described what his patients experienced when they surfaced from a neurosis. We have chosen the term for similar reasons. Katharsis, as an organization, is composed of a group of individuals highly skilled and qualified in the fields of psychotherapy, philosophy and religious ideas, but no one individual is of a particular religious persuasion. Our group has synthesized all three departments of knowledge and experience into an overview that allows the *Zeitgeist* – the trend of thought and feeling in our period of history – to be accurately interpreted. It has taken over a decade for our group to put its ideas and observations in order. It is not, as you say in English, a . . . *fly-by-night* affair.' He unclasped his hands, smoothed his already smooth hair and continued. 'But you are of course mystified as to what all of this means. The question in your mind is *To what end has this thing been done?* I will attempt to answer your question.

'There has been a breakdown in personal responsibility throughout the Western world, Mr Everton. On the whole, mothers and fathers no longer feel responsible for their children, teachers no longer feel responsible for their pupils, politicians no longer feel responsible to those who elected them. The Church, in spite of its grand words and gestures, is virtually powerless. The authority of legitimate and necessary law is flouted at every turn. Terrorism flourishes. Vandalism is everywhere to be seen. Drug-taking has become a way of life. Assassination is almost the promised reward for high office. In a word, Mr Everton, Western society is *ill*. We are in a state of crisis. And a major component of that crisis is our personal and collective inability to properly fathom its cause. This is to say that life has been emptied of meaning and value to such an extent that we are in danger of psychic collapse and social upheaval.' He paused to let his words sink in, adding darkly, 'The first signs of mass psychosis are already with us. If we are to avert the collective epidemics that lie ahead, then we must act *now*.'

Dumbfounded by the man's quiet eloquence, Bill Everton fumbled within himself for a suitable question, or statement, but before he could formulate either the Frenchman said, 'I can assure you that we are not cranks, Mr Everton. Proof of our credentials can be furnished.'

'I'm sure they can,' he said back, his discomfort obvious. Then with a rush he said, 'True as many of the things you've said are, I can't help but feel a little uneasy when I hear someone talk the way you've just been talking. The Western world is certainly in trouble, but it isn't exactly falling to pieces as far as I can see.'

Duval's smile was sympathetic, his reply accommodating of Everton's scepticism. 'Things are breaking down more rapidly than we think. It's just that we find it difficult to face the facts and articulate back to ourselves what we sense to be happening. We are already in dire trouble, but cannot admit it because we are fundamentally afraid within ourselves. We know there is not a great deal of time before . . . the roof collapses in on us.'

'You have evidence that the roof is going to collapse in on us?'

'Yes.'

'And you believe you can stop it from happening?'

'No! But we do believe that the contribution we have to make *will* assist in general stability. That is all we have in mind. We do not think of ourselves as potential saviours of the Western world. *That* would be an idiotic notion.'

'I'm delighted to hear it,' said Everton with relief. 'So what would your contribution entail?'

'An advanced training programme for therapists.'

'That's what you want advertised?'

'Yes.'

'On what scale?'

'Nationally.'

Everton registered the magic word without comment or visible reaction. 'Where's your organization based?'

'In France. Our headquarters are in Paris.'

'Are you already well established there?'

'Yes.'

'May I ask why you're including Britain in your plans?'

'Because no country exists in isolation, Mr Everton. We are all part of a whole. What I described to you a moment ago is taking place throughout the Western world. Our separate governments are well aware of it, afraid of it. If social collapse occurred in this country, no country in Europe could avoid the repercussions – we are none of us an island unto ourselves.'

Stating the obvious, Everton said, 'I hate to remind you, but we are an island unto ourselves.'

'Yes, but you are not psychologically isolated from Europe. I'm afraid the few kilometres of water between our two countries would prove no safeguard. Fear is the most contagious disease of all. It knows no boundaries.'

Everton hesitated. 'Would this be purely a French affair?'

'It will be coordinated from France, and French people will certainly be involved in each country, but the Centres will be predominantly staffed by nationals. It is our hope that within a year of establishing a Centre we can withdraw our own therapists and move them on.'

'Are you saying that it's your intention to set up these – Centres – right across Europe?'

'In every accessible city.'

'Backed by national advertising?'

The Frenchman nodded.

An involuntary whistle escaped from Bill Everton's lips. 'It'll take a couple of kings' ransoms to pay for what you have in mind,' he said, astonished by the scope of the enterprise. 'You must be expecting a high return.'

'But of course.'

'You're talking millions – tens of millions.'

'So I have been informed.'

The question had to be asked and Everton asked it. 'How do you intend to finance such an operation?'

'That is something I cannot divulge at the moment.' Duval's smile was apologetic. 'I'm sure you can understand my position.'

Everton smiled back, sucked at his cheeks, and realized that he would have to present Ian with something a little more substantial than a resumé of Edouard Duval's idealistic vision. Although it was perhaps not as idealistic as it sounded. The man expected a handsome profit, and his backers must have worked the whole thing out pretty thoroughly. He asked for background materials, plus any available literature on Katharsis. He then tried to draw the Frenchman out on whether there had been any press coverage in France, asked for copies of articles or features, said that if they decided the account could be taken on without breaching medical ethics, banking references would have to be supplied.

'I'll have all you require posted to you within a few days.' Duval hesitated. 'You must understand that most of the materials do not concern Katharsis as such – more an evaluation of myself as spokesman for a set of ideas which are the foundation stones of Katharsis. Our policy over the last year has been merely to familiarize the requisite professions with our line of thinking, and, where possible, demonstrate our basic techniques.'

Everton frowned. 'You rather gave me the impression earlier that things were well under way in France.'

'They are. But we are not yet functioning anywhere near full capacity. We have already purchased properties in Paris, London, Amsterdam and Berlin, but only the Paris Centre could be said to be properly activated – that is, moving quickly toward fulfilling its generic purpose. The others are in varying states of renovation, but work of a therapeutic nature is going on.'

'I see,' said Everton. 'Would you say your ideas have been well received so far?'

'Most definitely.'

'You're confident of success?'

'As far as the training of therapists is concerned, yes. What we have to offer is quite unique.'

Everton nodded, asked if there was a number at which Duval could be contacted. Taking out his wallet, the Frenchman extracted a white card and handed it over. Glancing at the card, Everton said they would be in contact the moment a preliminary evaluation had been made, but that that depended on their receiving the materials asked for. He then apologized again for Ian's absence and indicated by his movements that the interview was over.

'We will meet soon enough,' said Duval, getting to his feet.

'You have been most helpful, most attentive.'

Bill Everton opened the door of his office expecting Duval to pass straight through, but the man stopped halfway and said, 'Are you familiar with the word *scotoma*?'

'Something to do with the eyes?'

'Correct. In ophthalmology, a scotoma is a partial blindness – a certain segment of the field of vision does not register on the retina because of some defect. There is also a psychological equivalent. Psychological scotoma is an inability to fully observe certain phenomena or recognize certain situations although they are perfectly obvious to others. That accurately describes our present condition, Mr Everton. We do not want to believe that Western society could collapse because we cannot allow ourselves to conceive of such a disaster taking place. How could such a thing happen after all this time? We are so powerful, so knowledgeable, so much in control of our destiny. Or are we? We are afraid to articulate that doubt to ourselves. So we direct our attention away from the inevitable anarchy staring us in the face and attempt to laugh it off. But it will not go away. The mounting violence and insanity is everywhere to be seen, torture and rape and senseless killings the core of every other newsflash, riots and unrest a continual threat. Such things are happening here in Britain, in France, in every other country in Europe. But what is happening, Mr Everton? What is the name of the thing we are facing but cannot face? I'll tell you what it is – it is our own meaninglessness. The Church tells us that we are created in the image of God, but we have long since destroyed that particular conception and re-fashioned ourselves in the image of our own societies – which is to say that we are hollow, and sterile, and afraid. And our fear grows by the minute as we enter ever more deeply into what Freud called *dunkle angst*, that dark anxiety that slowly undermines our ability to see clearly and reason effectively. We have now reached the point where the collective is beginning to dramatically experience that dark anxiety as a blanket effect. People are everywhere breaking down under the strain of a civilization at the end of its tether, of ideas wrenched out of a living context, of hopes and ambitions thwarted even as they arise because the future is so blatantly uncertain for everyone. And I do mean everyone, Mr Everton. We can no longer afford the luxury of a future, the luxury of things done slowly and methodically and for their own sake. Everything has been speeded up. All that is conceivable has to be fitted in before the end arrives. We are in a state of disguised panic. We know without question that *time* has virtually run out.'

'One big flash and it'll be all over, eh?'

'On the contrary, that is what in all probability will not happen. What will happen is the unbelievable and the unimaginable – massive psychic breakdown. We will quite literally tear ourselves to pieces in a paroxysm of despair.'

'I find what you're saying hard to believe.'

'But of course.'

'You could be wrong.'

'We would be delighted if we were wrong – that is, if pleasure in the alternative is sensible. But I fear that we are not wrong. You see what I have described to you is not mere speculation. What I have described is based on statistical evidence drawn from clinics right across Europe over the last 18 months. The figures are terrifying.'

'Statistics can be misinterpreted.'

'Assuredly. In fact it is the branch of science most likely to be distorted and manipulated. But not in this case. The finest analysts in more than one government have already declared our basic findings beyond dispute.'

'You're working in conjunction with government? The British government?'

Duval's reply was enigmatic. 'Let us just say that a certain department of the British government is aware of our findings. I cannot say any more than that.'

'When will you be able to say more?'

'When we have finalized procedures with Drummond Advertising.' Duval moved out into the corridor and turned. 'I would be obliged if you didn't mention this conversation to anyone except Mr Drummond.' He extended a bony hand. 'It would not do any of us any good if the press got hold of the story.'

'I understand,' said Everton, wondering why Duval had given such apparently explosive information to a perfect stranger.

At exactly that moment, and with a certain trepidation, Ian Drummond gripped the brass bell-pull of Georgia's flat in Willoughby Road, Hampstead, yanked at it, and stood listening for the sound of her feet on the stairs. She appeared, dressed in faded blue jeans and a white blouse, and stared at him as if at an apparition.

'Aren't you going to ask me in?'

'Should I?' Her eyes grew wide and questioning. 'I gave up trying to contact you weeks ago.'

'I rang you three times last week.'

'I've been in Paris for the last two weeks.'

'Ah,' he said.

'What've you been doing?'

'I've been in bed mostly.'

'Bed? You've been ill?'

'Flu,' he said, trying to grin some truth into the statement. 'Worst bout I've ever had.'

'Bill didn't mention anything about flu.' She was still standing her ground. 'I eventually came to the conclusion you'd got cold feet.'

'I had to work my arse off when I got back.' He smiled, decided to play at half-truths. 'But I have to admit to being a fraction unsure. Weren't you, afterwards?'

'You'd better come in,' she said, with a look. She closed the door and he followed her up the staircase to her tiny flat, her plant-infested flat. When they were safely closeted she said, 'I only rang the office twice, for obvious reasons. Did Bill tell you?'

'Yes, but not right away. As I said, it was a nasty bout.'

'Must have been. You didn't even answer your phone.'

'Look, I'm sorry. I really am.' He stepped towards her, but stopped. 'I didn't want you to catch it and I felt confused . . . I needed time to think.'

'You've lost quite a lot of weight.'

'A bit. Hardly ate anything for about ten days.'

'That bad?' She shook her head at him. 'Probably overwork, knowing you. Coffee?' She left him standing in the lounge and went into the kitchen. 'I don't want to marry you, if that's what you're afraid of. I'm not in the least interested in marriage.'

He was standing in the doorway now, watching her. 'Me neither,' he said.

She turned to look at him, stopped what she was doing. 'So what was the problem?'

'It just seemed odd – you and I going off to bed like that.'

'My randiness embarrassed you?'

'Surprised me.'

'I can't help being healthy, or being your wife's best friend. That's how things are.'

'I know that.'

'But that's what bothered you, isn't it?'

'A bit.'

'Didn't you enjoy my fresh young body?'

'You know I did.'

'And then you disappear on me. For weeks. I didn't know what to think.'

'It wasn't your fault.'

'I didn't think it was.' She laughed and went on with her coffee-making, rubbing salt into the wound by saying that she had had lunch with Patricia on arriving back from Paris; she was now attending the migraine clinic at Bart's Hospital. He stood leaning on the doorpost and remembered the darkened rooms, and the silence. God, how he had hated coming home to that silence, the sight of Patricia lying on top of the bed with her eyes covered. She had always lain so straight and prim – almost as if she were dead. He had wished her dead on a number of occasions, not consciously, but at some lower level of his mind.

'She used to get them every other day.'

'Pretty awful thing to be afflicted with,' said Georgia, sustaining the balance without thinking about it. 'Constant headaches must rob one of common sense at times.'

Drummond smiled. 'Her outbursts sometimes verged on the manic. I didn't know what to do when she got like that.'

'Well, you'll be pleased to know she didn't speak badly of you – not this time. In fact she virtually admitted that she sometimes drove you to extremes, that she couldn't help herself.'

'But she's still bitter.'

'At times.'

He concluded silently that he would never understand women. They worked on a different wavelength from men. Patricia had sometimes driven him mad with the illogicality of her logic, a form of logic against which it was impossible to fight without incurring the accusation of being a rabid intellectualist. He had often marvelled at her ability to ignore his point and simply restate her own as if he had uttered not a word, and had eventually realized that she was a literalist, and for that reason she couldn't see what he was getting at most of the time. So he had resorted to verbal abuse, the only alternative left to him on almost every occasion, and afterwards had appeared pathetic even to himself.

Handing him his cup of coffee, and remembering how Patricia had rabbited on and on about her 'failed' marriage, Georgia said, 'I have to admit to having felt just a little guilty while I was with her. I kept thinking of you naked in bed.'

'Hope you didn't let the cat out of the bag.'

'Of course not.' She was seated now in her favourite chair, her hands clasped behind her head, her small breasts stuck out towards him tantalizingly. 'It isn't as if we're serious,' she said, fighting down a smile.

He eased himself down onto the sofa, coffee mug in hand, and settled in knowing full well that he ought to be elsewhere. 'She'd never understand if she found out. She'd view our little arrangement as quite distasteful.'

'I didn't realize we had a – *little arrangement*?'

'You know what I mean.' He felt embarrassed and looked at the floor. 'She's terribly moral.'

'She doesn't really believe in anything, as far as I can tell. I've often wondered what it is exactly that holds her together.'

'What she believes or doesn't believe no longer concerns me,' he said quickly, his own bitterness surfacing. 'I spent too long trying to work out where she was at in herself. I still don't know. I don't think she knows either. I suspect the poor bugger she's with now must be asking himself the same question.'

'He's having an affair. She's at her wits' end.'

'Oh Christ!'

'At least you never did that, according to her. I think she's beginning to look back on your relationship with a kind of sad affection.'

'I should be so lucky.'

'Don't mention what I've just said to anyone. If it got back –'

Drummond's smile was a fraction crooked, almost mischievous in its droop. 'I have to admit,' he said, consciously avoiding a smug tone, 'there's a certain satisfaction in knowing that the man who stepped into my shoes has fallen from grace so quickly. And please don't misunderstand me, Georgia, I don't mean by that that I wish ill on Patricia. I don't. It's purely a personal thing between me and the man she said I could never be.' He let out a little laugh and continued. 'It's almost as if some part of me has been rescued.'

'She hopes it'll blow over.'

That astounded Drummond. Patricia was obviously afraid of losing face, afraid of being silently accused of not being able to hold her man, or of having chosen badly. 'Has she confronted him with it?'

'Not yet.'

'How long's it been going on?'

'About three weeks.'

'And she hasn't said anything?'

'She's lost confidence in herself, blames herself. She's now blaming herself more than you for the marriage failing.'

'How kind,' he replied stonily. Then with a touch of anger he said, 'Listen, Georgia, I've never known *anyone* who could play games like Patricia, or keep the truth from themselves like Patricia. She could argue black was white and admit six months later to knowing that she was wrong at the time without a blush. Or an apology. That used to infuriate me.'

'You're quite easily infuriated, Ian.'

'I can't stand dishonesty.' He felt the old anger return, the old tightness in his chest, and stomach. 'She almost did me in emotionally,' he said in an utterly flat voice, wanting Georgia to understand what her dear friend was really like. 'She was either frigid, or afraid, or both. I never quite worked out what was going on. I think she maybe wanted to be religious but didn't know how to go about it. She took my emotional system to the cleaners, succeeded in disabling me, then blamed me for not being able to perform – not in as many words, of course. Just gave me little sad smiles, and a pat occasionally. I did the rest to myself.'

'I'd never have guessed.'

'That's nice to know.'

'You hate her?'

'I did, sometimes. Not now. That doesn't mean that I like her very much.' He felt suddenly uncomfortable, as if time had been shoved into reverse and the gears had got stuck. 'I shouldn't have told you any of that.'

'I shouldn't have told you about her wayward boyfriend.'

'Her younger-than-I-am wayward boyfriend,' he replied,

repeating his crooked grin. 'Nothing's ever quite the answer to anything, is it?'

They sat in silence for a moment. Drummond stared at the plants, wondering why it was that some women could only hate the men they were supposed to love, the men they married or lived with for the sake of love. It was a conundrum. Maybe it was because they were afraid of love, afraid of what they might discover about themselves if they once allowed entrance to the love of a man. And not just up between their legs, as was the custom, or habit, but right into the centre of themselves, right into the darkness. The anaesthetized stranger smiled for a moment. Perhaps that was why some men murdered their wives, some wives their husbands. It was perhaps their final attempt to breach the gap and initiate a moment of infinite closeness. That was what Patricia had never allowed. She had always shown embarrassment when he drew genuinely close, camouflaged disgust when he made love to her and revealed his need. She had never understood the male capacity to be penetrated by a woman, the desire within men to flood their systems with femaleness. He had on only one occasion almost attained that rarefied state of mind through her, but she had managed to short-circuit it with a complaint. He had tried to explain afterwards, but failed, and had made the mistake of suggesting that fucking wasn't really all that important, and that physical orgasm in both male and female was often nothing more than a last-ditch stance because infinite closeness had yet again been denied. It was probably something Celtic in his blood that made him think this way, something old and mysterious that made him want to sacrifice himself to –

Georgia said suddenly that she didn't think Bill Everton liked her very much. He was always very cool and distant.

'He hardly knows you.'

'I never know what to say to him when we meet; it's even difficult talking to him on the telephone.'

'Knowing how to keep at a safe distance from people is part of his job, part of his nature.'

'Last time we met was at your place, at the party just before Patricia bailed out. I got stuck with him for ten whole minutes – it was excruciating.'

'Did you meet his wife?'

'We weren't introduced, but I saw her. She was the tubby little thing in the too-yellow dress.'

Drummond smiled. 'They've been together for almost 20 years. Got three grown-up kids.'

'Catholic?'

'Very much so. Why?'

'He had a tiny crucifix in the lapel of his jacket. I had to stare at it to make out what it was.'

'He belongs to some Catholic Society or other. Quite devout in his own way.'

'Do you realize how devoted he is to you?'

'Yes.'

'Have you told him about us?'

'Of course not! Too dangerous. He and his wife are still friendly with Patricia.'

'Would he say something if he knew?'

'I don't think so, but if his wife found out she probably would.'

'. . . I think his attitude towards me, even as far back as the party, was a bit icy because he suspected us of having an affair.'

'We weren't having an affair.'

'True, but it was on the cards, wasn't it?'

'Was it?' He stared at her. 'You would have had an affair with me while I was still with Patricia?'

'It crossed my mind; it must have crossed yours.'

'Yes, but –'

'Bill's a pretty sharp cookie.'

Drummond's frown conveyed his perplexity. 'You think someone's said something to Patricia?'

'I sensed that she knew, Ian. Guessed, perhaps. She was almost a bit too forthcoming, if you see what I mean. It was rather as if she were saying that she didn't want to lose my friendship, but that she nevertheless wanted me to feel guilty. Hence the admission that Mike was having an affair. I think I was being told not to be a silly bitch.'

'And?'

'And then we kissed each other on the cheek and parted. I felt like a female version of Judas Iscariot.'

Drummond could not get to grips with the scenario; there was something missing. Patricia was not the kind of women to let anyone off with anything, close friend or not. She was brittle. The slightest pressure made her crack all over and pour her vitriol on the most innocent of parties. He said this to Georgia, and waited for her reply.

'We go back a long way, as you know,' she said, trying to justify her own suspicions. 'She relies on me in the same way as Bill relies on you. I'm almost like a younger, but more experienced, sister.'

'She wouldn't have let you away with it, Georgia. Not Patricia. And if she had suspected us of having an affair as far back as the party, I'd have been the first to know about it, not you.'

'I don't think anything's been said about back then.'

'I don't think anything's been said at all. She didn't have to tell you about – Mike's – misdemeanour. She could have got at you in some other way.'

'Yes, but that would have been bitchy. As a close friend she simply wanted me on an equal footing; she didn't want me to feel put down. Telling me about Mike was her way of telling me that she knew about us.'

'Pretty subtle stuff, if it's true.'

'Women are subtle creatures.'

Drummond did not reply. He knew there was no arguing with that.

'We'll have to be careful.'

He glanced at his watch. 'I've got to go.'

They rose simultaneously, awkwardly, and stood for a moment facing one another knowing neither what to say or do. Drummond broke the impasse by blurting out about the office break-in, inaugurating what could have been a whole conversation but for his movement towards the door. He described the mess that had confronted them, the slashed furniture and ruined artwork, the ripped-out telephones and the video reels torn apart and used as decoration in the presentation room. And their many computers so carefully wrecked. It would take weeks for them to get back to normal, he said, opening the door. And then with a smile he thanked Georgia for the card with the rather unusual inscription.

'What card's that?' she asked.

'The one you sent from Paris. The one with the fancy Latin on it.'

Georgia blinked, frowned, said that she had thought of sending him a card, even a letter on one occasion, but had decided against it. 'I didn't quite know where we stood with one another,' she added, staring straight at him.

'I told the police it was from you.'

'The police? I wouldn't have sent a card to the office.'

He explained about the other break-in, about his being chopped, about how the card had been used to make a point.

'You could have been killed!'

'I think the purpose of the exercise was to frighten me,' he said back, remembering those moments of fear with distaste. 'It was done by a professional.'

'You don't sound very frightened.'

He huffed a laugh and dug his fists down into the pockets of his coat. 'I still can't take it in; it's unreal to me. And the fact that you didn't send that card makes the whole thing even more incomprehensible.'

'What was on it?'

'Something in Latin. Can't remember the words. I was so sure it was from you.'

'Quite a coincidence, me being in Paris at the time.'

'To say the least.' He touched her arm. 'Look, let's have dinner tomorrow night. Are you free?'

'Yes, I think so.'

'Fine. I'll pick you up at seven. Okay?'

'Aren't you going to kiss me?'

'I didn't know if you'd want me to or not.'

'I am not averse,' she replied with a smile.

He kissed her lightly at first, then more deeply. She disengaged her mouth suddenly and looked at him, held him away a little. 'Why did you think I wouldn't want you to kiss me?'

'I – don't rightly know why I thought that.'

'You are silly at times.'

'I think I'm just a little bit out of practice.'

'Is that why you were so slow on the uptake.'

'I didn't think you'd want to go to bed with me.'

'You aren't exactly one of the ancients.'

'There's at least ten years between us.'

'And Patricia, it would seem.'

'We've all known one another for a long time.'

'Too long?'

'. . . I think I still see you as forbidden territory.'

'Should be more exciting that way. Is it?'
'What do you think?'
She beamed a smile at him. 'But you want to go.'
'I have to get back. They'll be wondering where the hell I am.'
Her smile melted. 'Be careful. I didn't like the sound of what you told me a moment ago one little bit.'
'Don't worry about me,' he replied. 'Given half a chance I can look after myself.'

A metallic sky shrouded the city of London – another attack of meteorological anaemia that once again drained the streets of colour, reducing everything to the texture of a hard-grained black and white photograph. Carefully manoeuvring his new olive green BMW through the dense traffic at Marble Arch, Drummond circled John Nash's attempt to reproduce the Arch of Constantine in Rome, turned left onto the Bayswater Road and accelerated, annoyed that his usual short cut had been blocked off by roadworks. A soft, drizzly rain clouded the windscreen, causing him to punch on the wipers as he drew up behind a line of stationary vehicles. Through the arc of cleared glass he strained to detect what the hold-up was, but could see little of what lay ahead due to the bulky Leyland buses that dominated his immediate horizon. An accident? It would be just his luck to be stuck there for half an hour, or longer. He wound down the window, craned to see what was happening, but saw nothing except traffic, and more traffic. Then in muffled gusts of sound he heard music, the beating of drums, and voices caught up in song. Everything having ground to a halt, he shoved open the car door and stepped out into the fine rain. A march? Coal-miners lamenting the closure of yet another pit? Unionists demanding workers' rights? Something of that nature was going on, and they had chosen a fine time for it, whoever they were.

But as it turned out, it wasn't the coal-miners, and neither was it the Unionists. It was in fact a huge procession of militant Christians complete with banners and megaphones. They had taken up the centre of the Bayswater Road, stopping everything in both directions. There were hundreds of them, perhaps thousands, all soaking wet and singing their hearts out, their banners almost black with rain, their placards identifying a quite dizzying array of Churches and Missions, Gospel Halls and tiny backstreet sanctuaries. The stranded motorists greeted them stage by stage with cries of derision and a deafening barrage of depressed horns. The noise was unbelievable. It reminded Drummond of a disastrous 12th of July march in Glasgow when the Hibernians and Orangemen had met head-on in Argyle Street and attempted to demolish one another. But on this occasion it wasn't Catholic Christian facing Protestant Christian across the great divide of history and theology, it was Christians of every hue united against paganism and Darwinism and Eastern religions and alcohol and sex and just about everything else one could think of. The banners were explicit. They condemned in bold strokes a Godless society, and warned that Godless society that the hand of God was about to uproot it and throw it into the abyss. Getting back into his car to escape the din, he sat staring at that multitude of singing faces as it streamed by *en route* for Hyde Park and an eventual confrontation with the police. He would read later that the police, not knowing how to handle such a mass demonstration of piety, had underacted for a change and allowed chaos to result. Bands of banner-waving souls had eventually invaded and virtually paralysed the city centre.

It had gone five-thirty when he got back to the office on Holland Park Avenue. Bill listened patiently as he explained how he had had to dash out to Murchinsons Distributors in Hampstead to pacify the Board and give assurances. Everything was okay now, he said, but it had been touch and go for a few minutes. They would have to see to it that there were no more delays, no more unforeseen hold-ups if they wanted to keep the account. And then he got on to talking about the march, and took one of Everton's cigarettes from the packet on his desk.

'. . . Everything okay here?' said Drummond, at last.

'Just fine – except that you weren't around to interview a new client.'

'What new client?'

'Edouard Duval ring a bell?'

The arrangement by telephone came back to Drummond immediately; he contorted his face and apologized. 'I think I must have blocked it out,' he said, remembering Duval's voice on the line. 'Couldn't get anything out of the man.'

'It was in the appointments book, and in your desk diary.'

'Went out in such a rush I forgot to check. Sorry.'

'No harm done. It was an interesting one. If it's for real it could be the biggest thing we've ever handled.'

'How big?'

'From what I could make out, a national multi-media campaign.'

'Selling what, for Christ's sake?'

'Would you believe an advanced training programme for therapists?'

'That's what Katharsis is?'

'Yup. It's their intention to sell Katharsis right across the board in Europe. They've already acquired properties in Paris, London, Amsterdam and Berlin – at least, that's what he told me.'

'Easily checked.'

'Exactly.'

'Sounds like a consortium.'

'Most probably.'

'Any names?'

'None.'

'Are you thinking what I'm thinking?'

Everton nodded, leaned on his desk and looked up at the Scotsman. 'If the two things are related, then someone sure as hell doesn't want us to take on that account.'

'Presuming that that's the case, it also means that someone has excellent intelligence on what Duval's up to. And that either means we have a ruthless competitor on our hands, or someone very resourceful is out to ruin Duval's chances of getting this thing off the ground in the UK.'

'It stinks, whichever way you look at it.'

'It's intriguing.'

'I don't like what I sense.'

Drummond's response was immediate. 'And I don't like bullies, Bill. I saw hundreds of potential bullies less than an hour ago marching to a drum beat. I won't be frightened off.'

'Might be that Duval's not as lily-white as he paints himself. Could be a racket of some sort that someone else doesn't want to share.'

'Then we'll just have to check him out, won't we?' replied Drummond, stubbing his cigarette out.

Chapter Three

Another morning of rain, only this time with a hint of sleet. Drummond sat very still at his desk and stared out of the window, as if waiting for something, but the waited-upon thing did not show. It was perhaps a case of looking up too late, or of turning away too soon. He smiled to himself, and dragged his gaze back to Bill Everton's hastily written report. But the words drove his eyes away from the page and back to the window, back to the small rectangle of garden that fronted the Holland Park Avenue office of Drummond Advertising. Then quite suddenly he determined to do the thing he had to do in spite of its being problematic: he reached for the telephone and dialled John Eglington's number at *The Times*. When they were connected, he dealt with the pleasantries quickly and asked the man if he had ever heard of an organization called Katharsis.

'What's your interest?' asked Eglington.

Giving little away, Drummond explained about Edouard Duval's visit.

'He came in person?'

'You've heard of him?'

'He's a philosopher of some repute in Europe, but not taken much notice of over here. Made a big splash in the French newspapers about six months ago. He attacked the educational system. Said that the present system was churning out armies of desensitized souls. Those were his exact words. Went as far as to say that the people perpetrating the system's present values were nothing more than mindless automatons. The French public lapped it up.'

'What about the French Government?'

'They came out strongly on Duval's side, but not quite for the same reasons. Suarès – the French education minister – used

Duval's outburst to attack the liberal trends that have flooded into French education since the student riots in '68; it also gave him a chance to have a go at the country's largest teachers' union, the *Fédération de l'Education Nationale.* That's when things really began to hot up. Its head, Monsieur Bousset, accused the government of betrayal, and described Suarès' plans for education as a whiff of the past.'

'When you say he "used" Duval, what exactly do you mean?'

'Rode-on-the-back-of,' replied Eglington. 'Basically, Duval agrees with the liberals – that is, he doesn't want to see a return to the old three-Rs routine just for the sake of it. But he feels strongly that the present mode of teaching in French schools lacks any real sense of direction. This breakdown in standards – in combination with the blind acceptance of scientific materialism – is, to his way of thinking, undermining personal value systems. André Suarès, on the other hand, wants exactly what Sir John Bowen wants here in Britain, a set of agreed-upon educational objectives right across the board.'

'What was the outcome?' asked Drummond.

'Ten days of vitriolic exchange followed by a juicy scandal that eclipsed the whole thing.'

'You seem to be saying that it was all for nothing.'

'No. Not really. I'm just stating a fact of life.'

Drummond smiled into the telephone and asked about Katharsis.

'A therapy of some kind,' said Eglington. 'Duval's own pet creation, from what I've heard.'

'What's a philosopher doing getting mixed up in therapy?'

Eglington laughed, said that Duval was full of surprises, that it was his almost pure eclecticism which caused him to be ignored by his British counterparts. 'I think he makes most of them feel uncomfortable,' he added, 'he's for synthesis wherever possible.'

'Is that bad?'

'It seems to anger his peers this side of the water; I think they suspect him of being an advocate of synthesis at any price.'

'What's your opinion?'

'I don't really know enough about the man to have an opinion.'

'That's my problem too.'

'He's sometimes referred to by French journalists as "Don Quixote". Not terribly flattering.'

'. . . If I told you off the record that Duval's planning to advertise Katharsis nationally in Britain, would that make you dig a little?'

'Sure would.'

'I'd be very interested in what you came up with.'

'Worried?'

'Just being careful, that's all. Don't want to do anything stupid.'

They talked on, Eglington expressed his surprise at the fact that Katharsis had already been established in London without his being aware of it. Drummond passed on the address, and suggested that they have a meal together sometime soon. Then came the moment he had been dreading. 'How are the kids bearing up?' he asked.

'Oh, they're fine – as fine as can be expected. They're with their Aunt Paula in Epping.'

'And Sophie?'

'She's slowly coming round; at least that's what I keep telling myself. I suppose it could be months before she's anywhere near her old self.'

Her old self? She was only seven.

'I still can't take it in,' said Drummond, remembering how John's wife had sat talking with him over dinner. She had seemed quite normal, then. But he too had seemed quite normal to everyone before his own crack-up.

'You can never be sure of anything, or anyone,' the man replied. 'I keep expecting to see her walk in the door.'

Totally at a loss for what to say, Drummond again suggested that they have a meal together. 'Are you free any time next week?' he asked.

They agreed on a time, and on a place.

'If anything of interest comes up before then, I'll get back to you,' said Eglington.

Drummond replaced the receiver and sat back, unwillingly contemplating John's tragedy for a moment. Then, pushing it from his mind, he got back to work. So far so good. Now that Eglington was primed there was every chance of a speedy resolution without mistakes. He again scanned Bill Everton's report, halting at point eight. Why have a point eight? It was the first time Bill had ever offered a personality breakdown on a new client. And it was obvious from that breakdown that he had been unable to pigeonhole Duval. It wasn't his failure in this that bothered Drummond, more the fact that he had thought it necessary to try. Something about the Frenchman had patently disturbed his chief executive, and that something would have to be thoroughly investigated before any letter of acceptance changed hands. Pressing the intercom button, he summoned his private secretary and prepared to face the early morning ritual of the mail. The day had finally started. He presumed that it would end later that evening with Georgia Patton naked in bed. But that was not how the day would end, for the god who governs coincidence had other things in mind.

A few miles away, and at the same instant, the man around whom everything had begun to centre stood watching as two of his most highly trained therapists worked on a young woman; she was seated on a straight-backed chair in a large, empty room, her head tilted back slightly, her eyes wide open and hypnotically fixed on a solitary red bulb that hung almost directly overhead. The therapists – two male imports from Paris, brothers, and twins at that – stood behind her, each with a hand on her head, their colliding fingers forming a ribbed cap. From where Duval stood it looked as though the folds of the young woman's brain had been laid bare in some macabre operation.

The man's willowy body swayed fractionally due to a consciously produced systaltic action between pelvis and sternum – a snake-like contracting and dilating of the solar plexus of which the therapists were fully aware. In fact it was towards Duval that the therapists' gaze was directed, their intense concentration having been generated and brought to pitch through what they termed the Maestro's *gift*. For it was as if he conducted them with his stomach during each major session, somehow signalling with his body the exact emphasis of will necessary as they plied their unusual art. And in a way it was a form of art they were engaged in, an art neglected and replaced in the modern world by attitudes and rituals of another kind, but still in use elsewhere. The willowy man upon whom their attention was riveted had resuscitated this art, rediscovered and reintroduced it to the West as part of a therapy, an unorthodox series of techniques culled from direct shamanic experience in central and northern Asia.

During training, Duval demanded that his trainee therapists sit together in total silence for hours on end. He described this as an interiorization process. As little as a whisper was sufficient to have one removed from the training programme for a day or two. It was difficult for some trainees to fully grasp what it was all for. According to the Frenchman, the purpose of this rigorously enforced silence was the production of a 'laminated stillness', an almost claustrophobic collapsing of the silence into itself until the therapist, and eventually therapist and patient, became sandwiched between layers of stillness. The therapeutic results of each healing session depended on the degree to which this collapsing effect was consciously accomplished. Only later did the trainees discover Duval's contribution to the process as 'conductor'; and later still the fact that he was also a 'composer' in his own right, a creative artist whose very presence sculpted raw silence into a fully-formed stillness. The breakpoint was when the trembling started, a spontaneous eruption of trembling in the patient that heralded a healing.

It was as 'composer' that he now stood and watched as his two most promising therapists worked on the young woman; she was the daughter of one of Duval's oldest friends, and had come over specially from Paris for the treatment. After 15 or 20 minutes her eyes closed involuntarily and the trembling started. A few minutes later she underwent a minor seizure of the upper trunk followed by a loss of control in hands and face. The two young men standing behind her became as immobile as rock, their hands pressurelessly static on her head, their eyes reading the almost imperceptible movements of the Maestro's body. Breathing gently within their frozen frames, they once again found themselves perceiving the figure of Duval as if it were floating – it was as though the man's immensely tall figure were hanging, rather than standing, in space. Then quite suddenly their patient convulsed and pitched forward, leaving their cemented hands suspended in air. Two, perhaps three, minutes passed before Duval spoke; the sound of his voice broke the spell. But although released, both men remained stationary, the rhythm of their breathing only gradually returning to normal. Duval came towards them, delivered one of his rare smiles, congratulated them on a job well done, and assisted the young woman to sit upright. When she was fully recovered, and standing, he grasped her to him in an embrace and whispered

something that made her smile.
'Really?' she said.
'I have no doubt,' replied Duval.

The day wore on for Drummond at a snail's pace – and that in spite of the fact that he was extremely busy. Time seemed to stand still, elongate itself, and only under protest, proceed. Annoyed by this quantum drag in events, the Scotsman battled on, ineffectively willing time to pass. By five-thirty he had accomplished much, but felt unusually tired and flat. He left the office at six, drove back to his apartment in Camden Square, showered, changed, and left for Georgia's at quarter to seven. She was ready and waiting, and they drove in the direction of High Holborn, for it was Drummond's intention to take her to a small, but extremely popular Italian restaurant with one of the best house pâtés in London. A strangely distorted silence generated between them, devouring their ability and inclination to talk. Tired, but pleased to be away from the office and its incessant demands, Drummond decided to break that silence and talk of Duval. Georgia listened, but he sensed that her concentration was laboured.

'Anything the matter?' he asked.

She said that she had a bit of a headache, and that in one way or another it had been one of the most oppressive days she could remember.

'A glass of wine will put you right,' he said.

Using the backstreets – Drummond prided himself in his knowledge of the London backstreets – he talked on and cut through to Mount Pleasant. By the time they reached Rosebery Avenue and turned right, he had managed to convey some of the problems they faced.

All clients were automatically investigated; there was a computer index that could be consulted. But that index – specifically set up to service the advertising and public relations industry – could only speak the limited language of finance and affiliations. This was generally enough, even if the company under investigation were foreign, but Katharsis was an anomaly. A lot of digging would have to be done. Duval might have flipped his lid and be engaged in a fantasy exercise – the title 'Don Quixote' was not encouraging.

They drew up outside the restaurant; it was one of the beauties of the place that you could generally park at the door.

When they were seated, Drummond ordered a decent bottle of Italian wine and suggested to Georgia that she try the tournedos steak for a change. The sauce was delicious, he said.

'I didn't realize you had to be so careful with clients.'

'Standard practice if we don't know them – particularly when they have no business record. You have to keep your eyes skinned for bankrupts' surfacing under new names before they're halfway clear of old debts, political front organizations, and religious groups with more money than sense and the belief that they've got the truth-market cornered.' He laughed and added, 'You can sell God, but you daren't attempt to sell a particular religious denomination as better than any other.'

Their wine arrived; they watched it being uncorked and poured. When they were alone Georgia said, 'You still haven't told me what Katharsis is.'

Drummond explained as best he could, having only Bill Everton's report and what the man had told him to go by. He then mentioned the proposed extent of the organization's activities, the kind of money that would be involved.

'They obviously expect to make a killing.'

He laughed nervously. 'Heaven forbid that I should turn down the chance of making a quick million because of prejudice. Problem is, you don't find the kind of money they'll be dishing out under a bush.'

Flourishing menus, their waitress returned. They ordered, and she topped up their glasses.

'What's your first move?'

'John Eglington,' he replied. 'I've already set him in motion.'

'That should bring in results.'

'I'm banking on it. He's given me a few interesting snippets already. Duval's apparently some kind of philosopher and activist. When he hits, he hits hard. Had a go at the French educational system a few months ago; caused quite a stir. But I rather got the impression from what John said this morning that the man's a loner – that isn't true. He told Bill that his "group" had been formulating their ideas for over a decade. Now that's worth thinking about. Sounds to me like he's a conduit for the ideas of others.'

'You don't know that for certain.'

'No, but the signs are there. Remember Bertrand Russell and CND?'

'Russell had ideas of his own.'

'True. But he allowed himself to be used. Even philosophers can be naïve.'

'It's fascinating.'

Drummond nodded, smiled wryly. 'It would be the biggest thing we've ever handled if it came off.'

'But you think he's a screwball.'

'Doesn't really matter as long as he's a harmless screwball.'

'That still leaves the question of the people behind him and what they're up to. Not to mention the money.'

'It's got to be a consortium.'

After a pause, Georgia said, 'How is John?'

'Depressed.'

'I was shocked when I heard of his wife's suicide – and about one of his daughters finding her. Is that bit true?'

'It was the youngest who found the body. Sophie.' Drummond sighed. 'You didn't know Marjorie, did you?'

'I've only met John a couple of times – seemed a really nice person.'

'As was Marjorie. You'd never have guessed she was bothered about anything. Just a nice middle-class lady with three kids who kept up with what was going on in the world. I liked her a lot.'

He understood the woman better now than he had done then, having himself touched upon something of what she had obviously experienced in full. In fact he had communed with her at one point, communed with her sad, sad mind out of his own unutterable sadness.

'How is the child?' asked Georgia.

'John didn't spell it out, but I think she's in a bad way. All three kids are in Epping with an aunt.'

'Is she being treated by anyone?'

'I don't think so. Why?'

'– Just that I know someone who's particularly good at dealing with young children.'

'I'll keep that in mind.'

Two tournedos steaks arrived; they had decided to skip starters. Georgia said that she would be back in Paris within a couple of weeks on another story and would try to find out more about Duval. A journalist friend on *Paris Match* was bound to know something. And then quite suddenly she put down her knife and fork and stared at Drummond, the obvious having hit her. 'Dr Freeman!' she said. He waited for an explanation. She went on to say that Freeman was the person she had been referring to in connection with Sophie. He knew everything that was going on in the therapy scene. She had done a long article on Freeman some years before for one of the colour supplements because the man's story was so unusual.

'In what way?' he asked.

'He was a priest for some years, but had to bail out.'

'A Catholic priest?'

She nodded, gave a little giggle. 'He's quite a character. You'd probably think him a little odd.'

'Why?'

'Because he's more priest than therapist – a kind of religious psychiatrist, if you like.'

Drummond cut into his steak. 'I could put up with that if he's got the information I'm after.' He looked up. 'Is that likely?'

She said that she would put a small bet on it – very little escaped Dr Freeman's attention.

'Do you have a number? An address?'

'Not on me, but he's in the book.' She became animated for the first time that evening. 'There's a phone here,' she said, looking up the aisle towards the front door, then back at him. 'I could ring him now and fix something up. It would only take a minute.'

'Finish your meal first.'

But she wouldn't have that; she drained her glass instead, smiled at him, and eased herself out of the little wooden cubicle. 'Be back in a tick,' she said. But it took much longer than that. He looked around a couple of times expecting to see her walking towards him, but she was still on the telephone and quite obviously having a chinwag with Freeman. A few more customers drifted into the restaurant and settled themselves before she returned.

'Your food must be stone cold,' he said.

She waved his comment aside, slid into the bench seat, and said that they would have to see Freeman that evening; he was leaving the following morning for a conference in Germany and wouldn't be back for a few days.

'He doesn't mind?'

'Not in the least. He was delighted to hear from me. I told him we were having dinner and would be with him about nine, or just after.'

Drummond glanced at his watch; it was already eight-twenty. Smiling at Georgia he said, 'I thought you might come up with something, but this is more than I expected. Where does he live?'

'Moscow Road. It's off Queensway.'

'I know where it is,' he said, his mind already working on how long it would take them to get there. 'We've still got time for coffee. You had better eat *that* before it gets any colder.' Turning, he summoned a waitress, ordered coffee, and said that they would have to forgo sweets. When he turned back, Georgia surprised him by criticizing his manner, the abruptness of his summons. Not everyone was on his payroll, she said.

'Habit,' he replied.

'A bad habit,' she said back.

He watched her attack what remained of her steak. Freeman, she said between mouthfuls, had undergone a crisis of faith five years after taking Holy Orders. Convinced at first that his doubts were reversible, his superiors had attempted to deal with his questions behind closed doors, but to no avail. A few months later he had been temporarily suspended from duty and subjected to some rather inadequate argumentation by his bishop. When that didn't help either, a Jesuit friend of Freeman's had been brought in. When this approach also failed, and it became obvious that he was suffering dire mental stress, he had been put in the care of a kindly Benedictine analyst who was used to handling such cases – there were quite a few each month, it seemed. A year later he was granted a special dispensation from Rome and ceased to function as a priest.

'They have their own analysts?'

'Little you know,' she said, glancing up at him with surprise. 'You surely don't expect them to leave such a juicy subject totally in the hands of unbelievers!'

'And now he's in the game himself.'

'And still a good Catholic in spite of the problems he's had.'

'I wouldn't have thought that possible.'

Giving up on her meal, Georgia said, 'He didn't have any argument with the Christian faith, just with a particular doctrine – celibacy.'

Drummond grinned darkly.

'It wasn't like that,' said Georgia, fully aware of what was in his mind. 'It wasn't just a matter of wanting, or needing, sex. It was a matter of deciding whether celibacy was an authentic doctrine of the Church.' She paused, stared for a moment at the remains on her plate. 'The only way he could prove to himself that sex and the priesthood were compatible was by having sex. His problem was that he refused to do it behind anyone's back, if you see what I mean. He ended up marrying and blew any chance he might have had of going back into the priesthood.'

'Why didn't he just have an affair?'

'Because, as I've been trying to explain, he wasn't after the right of priests to have affairs, dummy! He believed – and still believes – that priests ought to be allowed to marry.'

'At least he proved the case to himself.'

'That's how it seemed, at the time. But his wife ran out on him six months later. She left a note saying that he ought never to have left the priesthood.'

Drummond tried to digest what that must have meant to the man. 'Oh boy,' he said. 'What happened then?'

'A second breakdown.'

'He obviously recovered.'

'And how. It suddenly dawned on him in the midst of it all that there was only one answer – become an analyst.'

'Tough old bugger.'

'Not so old. He's probably only about forty-seven now.' She watched him top up her glass, empting the bottle. 'He's of the opinion that the Church will eventually change its policy.'

'I suspect it won't in his lifetime.'

'Maybe. Maybe not. There's a lot of unrest in that establishment.'

'So I've heard. But they aren't going to give up on that one without a fight.'

'They may have to if the present intake of priests is anything to go by.' She smiled, and her face lit up for a moment. 'Liberationist theology's taken a few hard knocks recently, but if the present pope isn't careful he could end up with a general strike on his hands.'

'And all for the sake of a good lay,' said Drummond.

'No. Not for that. For the sake of being loved, the *right* to be loved physically. That's what it's all about.'

He nodded slowly, realizing that she was angry at his attitude. 'I'm glad I wasn't brought up Catholic,' he said, glancing at his watch, 'I'd never have been able to swallow what they dish out. I'd have been an instant heretic.'

'No, not a heretic,' said Georgia, staring at him. 'More likely a cardinal.'

Chapter Four

They were led down a monumental hallway and into a spacious, high-ceilinged room that obviously served Dr Freeman as lounge, kitchen and bedroom. It was a bleak room, badly lit and haphazardly furnished. An oak sideboard of gigantic proportions bulged out from one wall, its stubby wooden-framed mirror reflecting the empty expanse of wall opposite. There were no pictures. A single bed roughly disguised as a couch graced the room's far corner. An ugly Victorian fireplace with a surround of green tiles added to the bleakness. Apart from one antique chair in faded plum velvet, the only other redeeming feature was a fitted cord carpet, but it was steel grey in colour and hard underfoot. A kitchen table covered in green formica, four straight- backed chairs and an old television set completed the room's scanty furnishings.

What amazed Drummond most of all was a cooker cunningly housed in an asbestos-lined cupboard complete with panelled door. The door was open and a huge aluminium kettle burbled on the gas; there was no sink anywhere to be seen.

Dr Freeman stood in the middle of this gaunt assembly of things smiling, seemingly unaware of the oddity of it all. He was a small man, thin-bodied, angular-faced, with a shock of soft brown hair which he regularly swept back from his brow. Drummond tried to picture the man as he had once been: black-cassocked, Roman-collared and kneeling before some altar with sacred words on his lips. Those lips now moved to form a sentence.

'I finished packing just before you arrived.'

There was the trace of an accent, a subtle lyricism in Freeman's speech which made Drummond think he might be of Irish stock, one of the race chosen by the Church because it found bleak sanctity irresistible.

'Ian Drummond,' said Georgia.

Freeman had kissed Georgia lightly on the cheek as they entered, smiled at Drummond, but not waited for an introduction. Fussily ushering her down the hallway, he had gabbled non-stop, leaving Drummond to follow at will.

'The advertising man,' said Freeman.

A statement of fact which sometimes, depending on the company, made Drummond feel a fraction uncomfortable; but not on this occasion. There was no edge to Freeman's articulation of those words, no hint of judgement in his voice. Before Drummond could reply, the man moved away from them, stooped, opened a door at the end of his grotesque sideboard and produced a bottle of wine; it was a pale Sauterne with a pinkish label.

'All I have,' he said, holding up the bottle as if for inspection. 'I'll get some glasses.'

Drummond remarked that they ought to have brought wine with them, but Freeman said that he hardly touched the stuff himself, so there would be plenty for all. Inserting a simple kitchen corkscrew into the bottle, he started a wrestling match with the cork, talking to Georgia all the while about people unknown to Drummond. Sitting down on the floor next to a small electric fire, Georgia warmed herself and batted back her replies. Drummond remained standing, helplessly watching as the man struggled with the cork and it began to disintegrate under his inept touch. He offered assistance, but received no reply, and began to wonder if the analyst-cum-priest was playing some kind of game with him. Finally, the cork did budge.

'A tough one,' said Freeman, pouring the wine and bits of cork into the glasses. Before delivering them, he carefully removed the cork fragments and flicked them into the blind eye of the fireplace. He then handed them their wine and sat down beside Georgia, saying that he had only recently met so-and-so again after a number of years.

Put out by the oddity of Freeman's behaviour, Drummond seated himself on the antique chair, a move he immediately regretted. Beautiful to look at, the chair turned out to be ungiving and downright uncomfortable. Unable to lean forward easily, he sat back and stretched his legs out, sipped at his wine and waited for Freeman to properly recognize his existence. He watched the man talk while he waited, rapidly coming to the conclusion that Dr James Freeman's personality had undergone a distortion due to past pressures and the nature of his adopted profession. Highly intelligent he might be, but something deep in the man had snapped, rendering him almost incapable of normal conduct. Catching Georgia's eye, he signalled his growing discontent, his wish to engage Freeman in conversation.

Georgia said suddenly, 'Ian must be bored listening to us ramble on like this – we're being terribly rude!'

'Yes, but of course,' said Freeman. He turned to look at Drummond. 'I'm terribly sorry. It's just that I haven't seen this young lady for some time.'

'Not to worry,' said Drummond.

The ex-priest swivelled himself around, placed his glass of wine carefully on the carpet and got straight to the point. 'I believe you're interested in Edouard Duval,' he said.

Drummond nodded and said that he was trying to vet the man for professional reasons.

'The French invasion,' said Freeman, smiling to himself.

'You know about Duval?'

'Everyone knows about Monsieur Duval,' replied Freeman. 'He has already made quite an impact with this Katharsis thing of his. It's such a silly name, isn't it – but appropriate I suppose.'

'Have you met Duval?' asked Georgia.

'Only fleetingly, but I have heard him speak. He is an impressive lecturer.'

'I believe he's a philosopher of some kind,' said Drummond, delighted with Georgia for having thought of Freeman in spite of his oddities. 'Can you enlarge on that for me?'

Looking to the side for a moment, Freeman said that Duval belonged to the upper echelon of French philosophers; he was either the fourth or the fifth philosopher in his family. Imagine having four or five generations of philosophers in the one family! It was of course a very good family – from the Languedoc, he thought. He laughed and added that the Languedoc was a 'blessed area' as far as the Church was concerned. Then in a rush he said that the really unique thing about Duval was that he had consistently challenged French society on major issues since the war years. Whenever an issue of real importance had arisen, Duval had always been among the first to make a pronouncement and put his learning on the line. He was, in other words, a courageous man, a man who believed in total commitment.

'And now he's committed to Katharsis,' said Drummond.

'He founded Katharsis, almost single-handedly created it, from what I've heard.'

'You approve?'

'Yes. The man is theoretically sound.'

'That's reassuring.'

'You were concerned about something?'

'I was quite simply out of my depth – still am, for that matter. I couldn't just assume Duval to be on the level. He could have been into anything for all I knew.'

'Spurious therapy?'

'Exactly. That's why I'm asking around.'

Nodding sympathetically, Dr Freeman said, 'Katharsis is an experiment in therapeutic procedures – quite a daring experiment. In fact, I don't think I've come across anything quite like it before.'

'It's Duval's intention to loose that experiment on a grand scale,' said Drummond, watching the analyst's face for a reaction.

'Ah, I see,' said Freeman. 'I didn't realize that.'

Smiling down at the analyst, Drummond went on to say that in spite of what some people believed, he belonged to quite an ethical profession. There were strict codes to abide by, rules to be obeyed, categories of legitimate and illegitimate action. So he had to be very careful, particularly when dealing with a field he knew absolutely nothing about. There were oddballs everywhere these days, and some of them were dangerous.

Dr Freeman's reply puzzled him somewhat. 'All of us are dangerous in some way, Mr Drummond – even God is dangerous at times.'

'Would you classify Duval as being potentially dangerous?'

'He would have us plumb the depths. I imagine some people might consider that to be dangerous.'

'But you think he can be trusted.'

The analyst's 'Yes' was a little slower in coming this time, but it did come. He immediately began to explain that Duval had taken a body of unusual ideas and transformed them into a practical philosophy of interaction, a therapy based on materials known to the West, but not understood. Then in answer to Drummond's question he said, 'All I can say about that therapy by way of assurance, is that I am truly challenged by it – that is, challenged to reconsider the nature of the universe in which I live. I speak both as analyst and priest. I'm sure Georgia must have mentioned something of my past to you.'

Drummond nodded. 'You still think of yourself as a priest?'

'A priest "after the Order of Melchizedek" – an affiliation that cannot ever be annulled.' Freeman's smile was suddenly sympathetic. 'What I mean by that would take too long to explain. Suffice to say that I still consider myself a priest in spite of what others may think.'

There was a slightly awkward silence.

'You don't happen to have a paracetamol tablet, do you?' asked Georgia.

'Headache come back?' said Drummond.

'Never really went away.' She opened her eyes wide, blinked, forced a smile. 'I don't think the red wine we had with our meal helped very much.'

'I don't even have an aspirin,' said Freeman.

'Shall I take you home?' said Drummond, willing her to hang on.

'No, I think I'll survive.'

'If you'll put up with a little chicanery, I might be able to help,' said Freeman.

'Anything,' said Georgia.

What followed verged on the absurd. Making her sit very straight, Freeman placed his hands on her head and pressed down ever so slightly; he asked that she keep her neck straight, her eyes open, and visibly increased the pressure. Then he did something very strange. He took a deep breath, exhaled slowly until his lungs were completely empty, produced a sharp little sound at the back of his throat and breathed in again. He did this three times, sustaining pressure all the while, allowing his breath to become deep and rhythmical. Without being told, Georgia followed Freeman's pattern of breathing with her own, her expression conveying to Drummond that something was happening. After a few minutes of this, Freeman again produced that odd little sound in his throat, something akin to 'hic', and withdrew his hands. In that same moment a violent shudder ran through Georgia's body, forcing her eyes shut.

'I think that's it,' he said.

Not knowing what to think, Drummond waited for the verdict.

'It's gone!' said Georgia. She looked around fully expecting the throb to return, but it did not return. 'It really has gone!'

'Are you sure?' asked Drummond.

'It should be gone,' said Freeman, 'her system cleared beautifully.'

'How do you mean?'

'You saw it for yourself. The shudder.'

'It was like an electric shock,' said Georgia.

'You could make a fortune with that technique, if it's for real,' said Drummond, remembering the hours Patricia had spent in darkened rooms trying to get rid of her headaches.

'It really has gone, Ian. There isn't even a trace of it.'

Dr Freeman sat down on the floor again, looked up at Drummond and said, 'I learned how to do that in an hour from one of Duval's colleagues about three weeks ago. It hasn't failed me once so far.'

'How often have you done it?'

'Six, perhaps seven, times.'

'It's foolproof?'

'Certainly seems to be.'

'Can you explain why it works?'

'– Not really. I can only speculate.'

'I'm all ears.'

Dr Freeman smiled and wetted his lips. 'It was once thought that healers acted as relay systems for the power of God – that God poured His healing energies through the healer and into the sick person's body – but it seems that it's not at all like that.' The man paused, gathering his thoughts. 'What always bothered me about people who healed through the laying-on of hands was that they could belong to any madcap cult or religion. Didn't seem to matter. If the person had the *gift*, then it seemed to work in spite of any oddity of belief. In the old days, the Church coped with this problem theologically: they said it was the Devil at work if the healer was outside of the established Christian fold. Today it's a little different. Almost everything is interpreted in psychological terms, within the terms of energy flow.'

'Does that explain how you did that?'

'I'm not at all sure myself. All I know is that healing takes place as a result of something being released in the patient.' He laughed suddenly, almost nervously. 'I still feel a bit like a cheap magician when I do it – a sorcerer's apprentice.'

'This is the kind of stuff Duval's into?'

'Yes, and on a number of levels.'

'And they're willing to teach the techniques to anyone?'

'Not quite. They only take on those with the correct disposition – and I don't mean by that those who accept what they say without questioning. Questioning is welcomed, positively encouraged in fact. Where they draw the line is with what they call "antagonistic mediums". Duval's of the opinion that out-and-out sceptics aren't really governed by pragmatism at all but by a programmed need to destroy anything that threatens to upset their circumscribed and basically heartless appraisals of reality. They in other words go beyond their educational brief because they've mistaken the meaning of that brief. Or because the brief they received was totally inadequate in the first place.'

'Is that why Duval recently attacked the French educational system?'

'Yes, it is. You're better informed than I thought.'

'I know people whose job it is to keep their finger on the pulse, that's all.' Before Freeman could reply, Drummond said, 'Tell me more about those individuals Duval refers to as "antagonistic mediums".'

Submitting to Drummond's probing, the ex-priest said that it was important to realize that such people were not merely antagonists. The word 'medium' was also important. It was important because such individuals reflected the opposite side of the coin of possibility. Just as there were those who could provoke paranormal phenomena, so also were there those who could disrupt, or prevent, such phenomena from taking place. They weren't just super-sceptics, they were anti-mediums by nature of their personal energy field. In a sense, the whole of Western society exhibited such an energy field. And Duval wasn't attacking the role of 'reason' in Western culture, Freeman stressed, he was attacking reason in the service of limited values, values sometimes so distorted it was almost frightening. We seemed to progress in spite of this, but at the same time were being carried further and further away from our generic natures. The whole climate of scientific and philosophical opinion was negatively directed, and the offshoot of such negativity was collective despair, a despair detectable in three basic forms: bland indifference; violence without apparent motivation; and modern medievalism. A good example of modern medievalism could be seen in the argument that God had literally created the world in seven days. Creationism. Creationist ideas were a whiplash reaction to both the indifference and the violence in our society, a kind of last-ditch stand by a rapidly growing minority to again add meaning and value to existence on behalf of a dying race. It was a cry to stop; a cry of despair in exact proportion to the cry of hope uttered by those who had once thought that a thoroughly educated populace would automatically eradicate both violence and stupidity. That quite obviously had not happened, and we were on the point of losing even what we had gained.

'You don't believe God created the world?'

'Do you?'

'No.'

'I do. But that does not automatically make me a creationist. The Church continues to teach the creation myth, but it only does so because that myth has retained something of its archetypal energy – the energy that underlies our innocence and ability to be enchanted. That's what we've lost: the ability to be enchanted, the capacity to be confronted with wonder. We have become, in effect, satiated with technological and conceptual novelty to such an extent that we are no longer capable of a proper response to our own existence. That, Mr Drummond, is what underlies the breakdown in our civilization – a kind of rational gluttony.'

'An understandable reaction when you think of the crazy things we used to believe,' said Drummond, trying to hold his own. 'And it could be said that the Church more than anyone else has contributed to that craziness.'

Dr Freeman agreed, but suggested that human beings had become foolhardy and insensitive to their own needs. At one time, the average individual had looked to the Bible and to orthodox religious teaching for answers to important questions. That was no longer the case. Over the last hundred years the 'religious answer' had progressively lost its punch and been replaced by a faith in science which, although incomprehensible to many, could prove its worth in the shape of technological marvels. But in spite of its sophisticated gadgetry, science too had not contributed to a useful cosmological theory; the bulk of humanity could not assimilate its pronouncements, merely play with its toys. Science and present-day philosophy were currently obsessed with semantics and linguistics and were quite unwilling to offer practical help. And yes, Christianity still offered many outdated, time-worn and implausible concepts. Was it any wonder that human beings were coming apart at the seams? And on top of it all lay the threat – the very real threat – of nuclear war.

But there had of course been a reaction to science's arrogance and the Church's ineptitude: the cult fads and Christian splinter groups. Things spiritually and scientifically *avant-garde* were now being offered at every turn. Some people were of the opinion that these multifarious cults – and the new psychologies which sometimes indulged them – heralded a new age of scientific enlightenment and spiritual freedom. Others felt that they more clearly represented a sign of weakness among those who could not sustain the pace demanded by a highly technical civilization – a civilization bent on the eradication of 'soft options'. There was, Freeman said, an element of truth in both opinions, but the accumulating evidence strongly suggested a third possibility: a breakdown in Western consciousness. Duval agreed. Most analysts and therapists were aware of a dramatic increase in mental disorders, and an alarming number of those professionals had themselves succumbed to manic-depressive states because of what they could sense happening in the community at large. We were quite possibly on the verge of something catastrophic, and whatever could be done had to be done quickly.

'Hence your interest in Katharsis,' said Drummond.

'Exactly. I've attended a few of Duval's seminars – three of his experimental clinics for professional therapists. I've also been accepted for the training programme.'

'I'd already worked out that you were more involved than you were saying,' said Drummond, eyeing the man with interest. 'I'm lucky to have found you.'

'Perhaps.'

Drummond registered that 'perhaps' without comment, and chose a new tack to draw Freeman out. 'From what Georgia's told me,' he said, avoiding a tone of flattery, 'you're not exactly

lacking in courage or commitment yourself.'
'Are you speaking as a Protestant?'
'I no longer think of myself as a Protestant.'
'Accepted. But I think you would have to admit that your Protestant background makes it easier for you to accommodate the idea of a Catholic priest coming out against celibacy.'
'Yes – I suppose it does.'
Smiling, Dr Freeman said, 'I should thank Martin Luther for that, but I won't. Nietzsche said that Luther lacked intellectual acumen, that he was fatally short-sighted, superficial and imprudent. I find myself in agreement with Nietzsche.' The smile faded. 'What you have to understand, Mr Drummond, is that I am not against celibacy as such, merely against the idea that *all* priests must necessarily be celibate for them to function as priests. You see some people are quite capable of sustaining the celibate life without harming themselves. For reasons known only to God, I am not one of those people.'
'I wouldn't have thought there were many of those around. And who could say for sure?'
'Indeed. When it dawned on me that my vows were impossible to keep, I began to notice for the first time that a lot of other priests were having the same problem. Of course, none of us would admit to such a problem – that is, state it boldly and frankly. We joked about it. Alluded to it guardedly. Even discussed it on occasions. But at no time did anyone come right out and say what was on most of our minds – least of all myself. But we knew what was going on, and eventually I couldn't take any more of it.'
'Surprises me that more priests don't do what you did.'
'They do, Mr Drummond. My researches show that for 75 per cent of priests reduced to the lay state since 1967, it was their inability to remain celibate that drove them from the priesthood.'
'Must be nice to know you're not on your own.'
'A small comfort when the Church's very existence might be at stake.' He stared for a moment at the wine-glass in his hands. 'I have a strong feeling that the whole thing is going to come to a head fairly soon, much sooner than most people think.'
'Anarchy?' said Drummond, remembering what Georgia had said. 'You think it'll come to that?'
'It is the tenor of the age we live in,' replied Freeman. He

sighed, drank down the remains of his wine in one gulp, spun the stem of his glass between thumb and forefinger and stared at it. 'Why should the Church be exempt?'

Picking up on what he sensed was disillusionment, Drummond said, 'I'd have thought you would have been pleased to see things change, no matter how it was done.'

'I would prefer the Holy Father to initiate such change, not simply be overtaken by it. There is no spiritual merit in bludgeoning others into an acceptance of outdated doctrines because of fear, Mr Drummond. And there is equally no spiritual merit in being bludgeoned into reversing one's hysterical pronouncements because of fear. The Holy Spirit is not an extremist principle – never has been and never will be. It is the dove of compassion and reconciliation. Love. Love in thought and action. Love incarnate as the Holy Father when the Holy Father submits to the will of God fearlessly. Extremism, whether of the softly sentimental variety or of the savagely harsh, always indicates a faltering of love and its replacement with fear. Today we are faced with the latter. Fear of being viewed as weak. Fear of breaking with tradition. Fear of a future Church riddled with licence. Fear of being classified as revolutionary because the word has been indecently usurped by Marxist extremists, terrorists and religious fanatics. But it should be remembered that our Lord never once faltered in love, and He was the quintessential revolutionary living in an age of revolution. As his representative on Earth, the Vicar of Christ cannot afford to err on the side of fear too long. That would be to initiate disaster on all fronts.'

For a moment the man had burned like a flame, his vision obvious. But he checked himself and fell silent.

'Being a pope must be a pretty heady position,' said Drummond.

'I am reminded,' said Freeman, glancing at Georgia, 'of what John XXIII said when first carried aloft in the *sedia gestatoria*, the golden throne chair. He looked down on the heads of the people below and sadly remarked "It's windy up here".'

'He was quite a fella.'

'Fearless. As was Albino Luciani – Pope John Paul I. But alas, such men are feared because of that very fact – feared, and sometimes hated.'

Georgia broke in suddenly with something that made

Freeman's expression visibly tighten. 'Have you read Yallop's book?' she asked.

'Yes.'

'What did you think?'

Freeman shrugged his shoulders, gave her a knowing look and changed the subject. 'There is still hope in the world,' he said, turning his attention back to Drummond, 'the possibility of change on a wide scale. I think Monsieur Duval's contribution will be considerable.'

'I can't see anyone paying much attention to a handful of healers,' said Drummond, knowing instinctively that his interview was at an end.

'That rather depends.'

'On what?'

'What they set out to heal.'

'Meaning?'

'Exactly that.' The priest smiled up at Drummond with a look verging on innocence. Then all of a sudden he was on his feet and extending his hand. 'Perhaps you will see for yourself quite soon. I imagine they will have to take you into their confidence at some point.'

Drummond pushed himself up, smiled, shook the man's belatedly proffered hand. 'Don't be too surprised if you hear I've dropped the whole thing,' he said, the limp softness of the priest's grip surprising him. 'It'll probably prove too awkward an account to handle.'

Dr Freeman's reply was an oblique summation. 'I suspect we both have stubborn souls, Mr Drummond,' he said softly.

Edging the BMW out from between two cars, Drummond changed gear swiftly and accelerated to just under 60mph before applying the brakes and halting at the junction of Moscow Road and Queensway. Taken aback by the car's sudden surge of power – by the quite brutal sensation of being forced back into her seat – Georgia merely gasped.

'Had to break the spell somehow,' said Drummond grimly. 'I don't think I've ever had such an intense feeling of claustrophobia in all my life!'

'You really scared me doing that,' she replied, eyeing him. 'Please don't ever do it again.'

'You don't look half as scared as you did earlier.'

'That was different.'

'I thought you were going to faint.'

'It was a rather odd experience.'

'Looked like a convulsion.'

They turned into Queensway proper, engaged the traffic, stopped. Georgia sat with her hands in her lap, like a schoolgirl unconsciously shielding her sex from adult eyes. Her sitting like that maddened Drummond; it reminded him of Patricia. He squinted another look at her face and for a moment saw Patricia's profile. He looked again and could still see Patricia, but knew that he was reading, or projecting, Patricia onto Georgia. That angered him. He rammed the stubby gear stick into second and played the accelerator off against the clutch, angry with himself for being angry.

'What's the matter?' asked Georgia.

'Voodoo,' he replied.

She looked away from him out of the passenger window into the lighted shops and said that what Freeman had done could hardly be referred to as voodoo.

'You didn't see his face. I wouldn't have been surprised if he'd broken into a dance.'

'You're being unfair,' she said, turning. 'And whatever you might think, it helped.'

'Helped?' he said back. 'Are you telling me it wasn't an instant cure?'

'Is that what you want me to say?'

He straightened his arms on the steering-wheel. 'Was it or wasn't it?'

'It was.'

'Then it did more than *help*.'

She wanted to say that it had been an extraordinary experience, that she had felt something leap up from deep within her, but decided to hold her tongue. The man beside her was not in a receptive mood; she knew that mood. She also knew that Ian had disliked Freeman from the moment he set eyes on him, and that he would not listen to reason. It was one of Ian's failings. He sometimes judged people a little too quickly.

He caught the lights at the top of Queensway and swept round on to the Bayswater Road with a squeal of tyres. He was still angry. Angry with himself for being angry. Angry with Georgia because she obviously held Freeman in high esteem.

'What are you thinking about?' asked Georgia.

Drummond's laugh had a brittle ring, as he gunned the car a second time. 'I was thinking that Freeman's a man worth watching.'

'You didn't like him, did you?'

'I reserved judgement right up until he began to talk about celibacy and the priesthood.'

'I thought he was very reasonable about the whole thing.'

'Too damned reasonable.' A quick change into third allowed them to pass a stream of cars on the outside and nip back into line again. Georgia was not impressed. Drummond ignored her exaggerated reaction and repeated the move a few minutes later when they reached Park Lane. Up ahead, a pinkly lit Marble Arch softened the black silhouetted buildings above the hard, red glitter of tail lights. Aware suddenly of their faces reflected on the windscreen he said, 'Caring can become as much of a habit as killing, Georgia. Depends where you start.'

She stared at him.

'He's a professional carer, just as I'm a professional image-maker.'

'Then he's as necessary as you are.'

'Perhaps.'

'Won't you even allow him that?'

'I'm not sure. It might be that we'd all have been better off left to our own devices. The Church didn't invent love, and neither did it invent caring – although you'd bloody well think it had, the way they go on!' He chuckled to himself, drew up abruptly as a set of lights changed against him. 'Like any good business, they're experts at packaging, that's all.'

A fairly long silence followed.

When they were almost at the top of Wellington Road, Georgia said, 'Did you ever believe there was a good God up there looking after us all?'

'I suppose I must have done, sometime or other.'

'I did right up until I was seventeen.'

'What changed your mind?'

'Nothing, really. I just suddenly realized one day that I didn't believe it any longer – that the feeling had evaporated.'

'And you a Catholic too!'

'I was never a terribly good Catholic. My parents were liberal-minded types. Not into confession at all.'

'What about school?'

'Yes, they tried to instil it into me there, and I played along, but it never really stuck.' She smiled. 'I can remember an old bitch of a nun telling me that I had a reprobate soul.'

'What's that?'

'*A soul that cannot enjoy the things of God*,' she intoned, her expression exaggeratedly severe. 'That worried me for a time.'

'A nun said that to you?'

'More out of frustration than calculation; I was a very difficult child. Even my parents thought so.'

'You were lucky to escape,' he said, remembering how Patricia had always hedged her bets by calling herself an agnostic. 'Isn't there something about getting a child before the age of seven?'

She nodded, and surprised him by saying, 'I don't think people like myself ever fully escape. We're too conscious of it all. It's almost as if we're Christians in reverse, non-believers who have to rigorously keep on not believing because it's the only way of retaining some notion of a spiritual life. I've come to suspect that there's no such thing as neutral gear.'

'Freeman would lap that one up.'

'I'm sure he would.'

The car ate up Fitzjohn's Avenue. He began to fiddle with the radio, but could find nothing of interest and said, 'Do you really think that hocus-pocus cured your headache?'

'It was pretty bad.'

'Yes, but –'

'It went immediately, Ian.'

'Really bad?' he said, glancing at her.

'Have you ever known me to shut up for so long?'

'And afterwards?'

'– I just didn't feel like talking.'

A momentary shadow cut across his face, leaving one eye bright and glittering. He considered what he had witnessed, and came immediately to the conclusion that Freeman had been too damned confident, much too sure of that technique, considering he was a therapist of some experience. And that was odd, for he suspected Freeman of somehow lacking confidence in spite of his aura of calm academic certainty. The man was a mess inside, a mass of irreconcilable contradictions, a jumble of hopes and fears welded into an uneasy alliance. And Duval had further unsettled him, it seemed, challenged even his view of the universe. They turned right onto Hampstead High Street and came to a halt at the zebra crossing almost adjacent to Flask Walk. A string of youngsters meandered across the road. Two girls tailing on behind let out a howl of laughter, stopped, hung on to one another and began to speak animatedly. And then they suddenly realized that they were holding things up, and with an even greater hoot of laughter ran the last few paces hand in hand.

'Probably on the pill, both of them,' said Drummond, shaking his head. 'I really don't know what I'd do if I had a daughter their age to bring up.'

'I'm sure you'd cope.'

'I doubt it.'

A second string of youngsters appeared and he thought of the daughter he had had to leave behind in Scotland for reasons too complicated ever to explain sensibly. She was a young woman now, fully grown and no longer a child, but still a child in his imagination. He had been twenty-two years of age when he first married, when he walked back up the aisle with his bride on his arm. All white and glistening, like the cake soon to be cut into with a sharp knife. Twenty-nine years of age when he walked out on her, deserted her, abandoned her, dismissed her from his mind in a moment of cruel lucidity – but not the child. Frozen at the age of two in his imagination for ever, in a little red dressing-gown, standing mute in a doorway clutching a doll. Something of Sophie's frozen silence in that image. Images of himself in his daughter's mind beyond resuscitation, beyond recall. Existence in name only all that was left of him in the mind of another human being.

'Why are you waiting? It's clear!'

He slid automatically into the movements required, released the handbrake, allowed what he could see beyond the windscreen to flood his senses again. But the tenderness was still in him, the sense of loss, and shame. Another life in his eyes as he turned into Willoughby Road and drove slowly down to where Georgia lived, and stopped. Double-parked, and with the engine still running, they sat in silence for a moment. It was the kind of moment in which he would normally have lit a cigarette, but his pockets were empty, and the tension attached to his knowing that became immediately unbearable.

'I feel bushed,' he said.

She gave him a little smile, said that she felt the same, quickly kissed him on the cheek and turned away.

'I'll ring you soon. Okay?'

A tight little nod from Georgia as she opened the car door and slid her legs out. Cool air wafted into the car.

'And thanks for taking me to see Freeman – it was illuminating.'

'I have my uses,' she said back.

The door closed, leaving only her torso in view, her head and limbs curiously severed like that of a statue he had once seen.

Chapter Five

THE FILE OF news clippings on Katharsis arrived on the Friday morning. Drummond spread them out on his desk, checked their date order and slotted them into a dark blue snap-back folder. Of the 35 items enclosed, nine were in French and three in German; each print-out carried a translation. On ordering coffee, he settled down to read the folder's contents, knowing that it would take the rest of the morning to sift through the material and gain a general perspective. Within a few minutes he was totally engrossed.

What immediately surprised him (over and above content and the occasional dramatic heading) was the breadth of the market tapped. It ranged from newsy items in periodicals of popular taste to decently written articles of some depth in up-market magazines. There were also quite a few technical pieces from the professional journals, and two fairly long articles in the religious press discussing the impact of a seminar given by Duval to a mixed gathering of Salesian priests and Church of England clergy. Both of these groups had apparently responded well to his ideas, and there was mention of further seminars to be held. The other pieces had been culled mostly from the French and German national press, and were either in the form of interviews or features.

He made copious notes as he read, listing where given the names of the writers on a separate sheet of paper. By one-forty he had gleaned everything of importance from the clippings and was already on the telephone to John Eglington, having had to wait a minute or two as the journalist was in turn telephoned in some other department. What Eglington had to say added substantially to the growing picture. So much so in fact that half an hour later, complete with folder and notes, he was sitting in a nearby pub with Bill Everton discussing the situation over a pint of beer and a plate of lukewarm steak-and-kidney pie.

Passing on what he had learned about Duval and Katharsis from Dr Freeman, Drummond gave an assessment of what he had read earlier and added by way of summation what Eglington had only just found out – namely, that of a seven-man board of directors set up in Paris with Duval as chairman to oversee the Katharsis expansion, one held an important diplomatic post in the French Foreign Office, the others positions of note in academic institutions. The diplomat had been identified as Aretino Lefèbvre, his Foreign Office specialty Israel. As the diplomat's affiliation with Katharsis was on public record, albeit described as 'honorary', and neither the government nor the French press had seen fit to question that affiliation, it could only mean that Duval's group had been given a clean bill of health.

For it stood to reason that had there been the slightest impropriety in the diplomat's aligning himself with Katharsis and its aims, he would have been quickly brought to heel by government insistence and media pressure. This in turn seemed to support Duval's oblique contention that the French government was sympathetic to the group's statistical speculations concerning the future of Western society, and that the governments of those other countries within whose borders Katharsis operated, or intended to operate, were similarly sympathetic. This had caused Drummond to reassess his idea of a business consortium behind it all. It was just conceivable that Katharsis was being independently financed from the purse of more than one government in the European Union. And as Duval had shown himself to be uncertain as to the outcome of the whole incredible exercise (the promised reward for so much effort was 'stability', not 'cure'), government was the more probable source of revenue, a business consortium of any kind being ruled out by the fact that such an animal was too careful and too selfish in its tactics ever to innocently squander its resources on anything other than a mathematically assured financial return.

'Then it's all systems go,' said Everton.

'Perhaps.'

'You've still got reservations?'

Drummond nodded, pushing the remains of his pie aside. 'I'm

uneasy about only one thing, Bill,' he said, staring at the man. 'Why us? Why not one of the larger agencies? I know we've got an excellent track record in the industry, and that it's only a matter of a time before we join the big boys, but you would think an operation of this size would have automatically gone to one of the larger and more prestigious agencies. That's the only thing I don't understand.'

'Don't knock it.'

'I'm not. I'm just a little puzzled, that's all.'

'Could be that we've been chosen because there's less chance of a leak on the information level. Big companies have a lot of trouble with that one. Their very size makes them vulnerable.'

'We've already shown ourselves to be pretty vulnerable.'

'The new alarm systems here and in your apartment should take care of that.'

They talked on and he said that he wanted a preliminary meeting set up with Duval and some of his colleagues for early the following week. Might as well meet the whole thing head-on and lay down the basics. But under no circumstances was he to give the impression that everything was tied up with a bow. They would simply be engaged in a fact-finding mission, an informal probing of each other's minds for the sake of clarity. If there was anything to be seen it should be seen. If there was the possibility of a demonstration of some kind, it should be arranged.

'Got you,' said Bill.

'You should also know,' added Drummond more slowly, 'that their ... therapeutic procedure includes something akin to the laying-on of hands.'

'Where did you come across that titbit?'

'From Freeman,' he said, bending the truth a little. He made a wry face. 'Can't allow ourselves to be caught with our advertising trousers down, can we?'

'Doesn't make sense, that.'

'No, it doesn't.'

'No wonder you're edgy.'

'More intrigued than edgy. There's nothing in what I read this morning to suggest a religious slant, but that could just be them being careful. Or it might be that there's altogether another explanation for the laying-on of hands bit.'

'Duval described Katharsis as a synthesis of ideas drawn from psychotherapy, philosophy *and* religion. But I rather got the impression he was more interested in the psychological aspects.'

'The press material has the same emphasis.'

'Then there's probably nothing to worry about.'

'Probably not,' replied Drummond, wondering what a good Catholic like Bill would have made of Dr Freeman's little demonstration. 'Anyway, we'll know everything there is to know by the end of next week.'

Glancing at his watch, Everton said, 'I'll have to get back. Are you coming?'

'No. I'll hang on here for a few minutes.' He gestured towards the blue folder. 'I want to take another look at that stuff.'

When Everton was gone, Drummond made no move to touch the folder. He sat very still and stared at the bar, his fingers toying with the handle of the pint mug of beer he had hardly touched, the dream he had had in the early hours nudging at him with a kind of dumb insistence. Freeman had turned up in that dream in a not unexpected role, but with a twist. The man had looked fanatically inspired. Demonically possessed? And feeble attempts to unravel what the dream was about had fallen flat except for one small insight: he had an almost pathological dislike for religious people. They angered him quite unreasonably at times, and Freeman's particular brand of stuffy religious certainty angered him most of all. So he had built a dream around the man, it seemed, and successfully distorted his image. But what a dream. The vast nave of a cathedral lighted by torches and candles as a starting-point, its magnificently vaulted and buttressed roof visible almost to the apex. Endless rows of black-hooded men sitting with heads bowed, the peaks of their hoods sticking up like waves on a frozen black sea. A huge corona of yellow candlelight on each side of a distant altar infusing stone, wood, marble and gold-threaded fabric with what had seemed a heavenly impregnation. And before that altar the solitary figure of a man robed in glistening white, his hands raised high in adoration of a giant, empty cross. But all of this made as nothing by the electrifying jolt of a face recognized, a pale wedge of flesh revealed on his right that had caused his heart to batter insistently at his chest wall: the quickly withdrawn face of Dr James Freeman. This face, as pale as death, had knifed into him and caused such a moment of horror that he had been unable to shake off the memory of it. In fact he seemed to be compulsively resuscitating it for some reason, his mind turning back to it the moment he ceased to be engaged in thought or conversation.

A face recognized. Something recognized and understood? A demented face quite at odds with reality – or was it?

What was it Freeman had said after the healing? *I still feel a little bit like a cheap magician, a sorcerer's apprentice.* And he had also said something about Duval forcing him to *reconsider the nature of the universe.*

A Catholic priest turned therapist reconsidering the nature of the universe?

A whole series of inexplicable dreams, many with a religious content silently accusing him of things beyond his understanding. It was maddening and it was tantalizing – and it was a waste of his valuable time. Dreams were just dreams, and that was all there was to it. Once allow them meaning and relevance, and you were no better off than a primitive, a savage dressed up in 20th-century garb. The hatches had to be kept battened down on such rubbish. It was simply a matter of controlling one's self, of refusing point-blank to be drawn into the trap of considering such things real in any way.

A mouthful of beer helped quench the flame of his annoyance. Reaching for the blue folder, he opened it and began to read quite without retention, realized that he was taking nothing in, and closed it again. The memory of another pub swam into focus of its own volition, capturing him. Another pub and another time, and an elderly uncle saying that they had been pleased when they heard he was coming up from London. His mother dead. His step-father dead only a few weeks before, and his real father long dead and buried without a headstone. Only one visit to his father's grave that he could remember: a bunch of daffodils with their stalks wrapped in silver paper and a piece of wood with a number on it – his father had liked numbers. 'And all because his feet were too hot!' His mother speaking. The same words repeated time and time again as they travelled back into the past. 'Walked home most of the way with his dancing shoes tied together and strung round his neck.' Off dancing on his own because there was a child to look after. Competition stuff. Girls and women in big flouncy dresses. 'God knows what he got up to!' Had blamed Elizabeth Drummond for the blood he was spitting up, a badly cracked pot of jam with a shard of glass in it identified as the cause of his ailment. Pure carelessness. Damned thing ought to have been thrown out. His mother shaking her head and sighing at the memory of it all; but still a young woman and soon to be married again, to Frank. A dead wife in Frank's eyes and a load of well-worn furniture delivered to the door. Hairpins in the crevices of the bulbous couch. A treasure hunt. His hand rammed down into the seam behind the cushions. A tiny coin with a wren on it – a bloody farthing!

Eleven years of age when Alexander Drummond died; thirteen years of age when Elizabeth Drummond accepted the name Macdonald. Steak pie, peas and mashed potatoes at the reception. Held in the Masonic hall. Frank's face burnished bright from the inside, from the whisky he had consumed. And above his head a huge painted eye and a pair of compasses: the eye staring at nothing, at everything. His new father in a new suit, and his mother in a powder-blue two-piece costume with a little veil attached to her powder-blue hat. Off to Girvan for their honeymoon – dirty old bastard! A life of veritable misery from there on until her own death three weeks after his. A bizarre funeral; in fact no funeral at all. And before what was supposed to resemble a funeral, his first glimpse of the body still in bed all tucked up as nice as ninepence with that last expression of fear and bewilderment still etched into the face. Partly erased by death that expression of fear, by the slackening of facial muscle, by the fact that her eyes had been closed and had remained closed as she battled with death itself. But the residue of that fight still plain to see, still visible although lessened, made subtle and more haunting by the process of final exhalation and hardening. Then later that afternoon the Reverend Talbot talking quietly to the assembled relatives of his mother's sacrifice, of how she had so courageously donated her body to medical science and denied herself the dignity of a ritualized burial. And later, as if time and circumstance meant nothing at all, another dollop of mashed potatoes, peas, and a wedge of steak pie – the same damned meal as at the reception; the same as eaten after his father's funeral on New Year's day; the same as lay before him now, cold and unappetizing.

For what, all that living and battling, loving and hating? For what? She had gained nothing but degrees of distaste, a fear and loathing of the human body, a fatalistic emptiness that she had tried to fill with one last act of courage. And what a curious act of courage it was, living with the knowledge that she would be scalpelled into pieces and ignominiously buried 18 months after her death. A female version of that Egyptian god who got himself carved up, and scattered. A belated entry into university life with Dante's hell as a reward. Frozen with a tag on her toe. Wingless angels in attendance, their faces set hard against the recognition of her as a human being, a woman. Secondhand organs for the use of – a kind of farcical immortality. Or perhaps just a joke wrought in her unconscious, a hilariously macabre joke designed to smash the expected pattern of things when least expected. Revenge? He smilingly accepted that as a possibility, knowing all the while that he was doing her an injustice. For she too had had the wish to accomplish something, and could be said to have wrested accomplishment out of the most unlikely situation.

All of this, and more, sensed and opaquely seen as he sat there, the anaesthetized stranger stirring into momentary life. Then on his feet and heading for the door, blue folder in hand. Back into the real world, he supposed, his life as dream shrugged off and shelved. But like an old wound subjected to stress, soon to be prised open again, this need to forage in darkness and obscurity, for on his desk a note in Bill Everton's meticulous hand to say that he had been invited to attend one of Duval's lectures that very evening. They would however be unable to meet, the Frenchman having an engagement for immediately afterwards. That of course was a pity, but it was at least a chance to hear and see the supposed philosopher in action, arm oneself with impressions, familiarize oneself with his style of talking and thinking. Noting the address in his diary, Drummond plunged into what remained of the day, confident that he would be able to access this philosopher. He was good at that, being a kind of psychologist in his own right.

He was on his way over to Islington by six-thirty, having already showered and changed. At seven-fifteen he emerged from the King's Head pub on Upper Street and walked slowly up towards Highbury Corner. It was dark and the streets were glassy with rain, virtually empty of people. He knew exactly where he was going, having earlier checked out the old warehouse now functioning as Duval's temporary headquarters. Struck by the building's ugliness, by its squat solidity and obvious decay, he had stood looking at it for some seconds before walking back to the King's Head for a steak and a beer. The double-leafed entrance was now open, allowing yellow light to spill out onto the pavement as if from a square mouth. Just inside, a young man sat at a card table with a checklist of names. Drummond gave his name and watched as it was ticked off; it surprised him that his name was on the list at all. There was also a visitors' book. He signed it, and moved through another set of double doors and into a long, green-painted corridor. Some attempt had been made to clean the place up, but wash marks were still visible, and a whole section of skirting board was missing at one point. As he walked down that corridor it occurred to him that Duval had chosen a singularly depressing place in which to practise the art of psychotherapy, temporary or not.

The lecture hall turned out to be a partitioned-off section of a much larger room. There was a makeshift platform complete with lectern, a microphone, the compulsory jug of water and a tumbler. As he walked into that room, quite a few heads turned in his direction; he estimated that around 40 people were already seated. Choosing a seat on the outside aisle near to the back, he sat down, conscious of the fact that the others were probably a mixture of therapists and psychologists eager to hear what new tricks Edouard Duval had evolved. It amused Drummond to think that they might consider him a professional colleague, although unidentified, for the moment. Pushing his hands deep into the pockets of his coat, he sat back, and waited. It was 28 minutes past seven. At exactly seven-thirty Duval's towering figure appeared on the platform. Introducing neither himself nor his subject, he launched straight into a crisp analysis of the contention that human beings lacked freedom of will.

'Only two classes of people maintain that their will is not free: schizophrenics and deterministic philosophers.' A well-dressed woman in the front row smothered a giggle with the flat of her hand. Ignoring her, Duval carried on. 'Schizophrenic patients suffer from the delusion that their will is manipulated and their thoughts controlled by others, and deterministic philosophers suffer from the same malady – but with one important distinction. They insert the proviso that our experience of our will *as* free is self-deception. The exact point of disagreement between what they believe, and what I believe, lies in the question of whether or not human experience is conducive to truth. That is the crux of the matter.'

He then went on to speak of the conditions that curtailed human freedom – biological, psychological and sociological conditions – but maintained that human beings could express freedom of will in spite of those limiting factors through choice of attitude. It was through a conscious choice of attitude that human beings rose above the somatic and psychic determinants that threatened their existence. Captured by Duval's eloquence and presence, by the authority with which he spoke, an almost claustrophobic stillness generated within the audience. And then Duval enlarged on the issue by pointing out that human beings had the capacity to 'judge' themselves, that they could detach self from self and consciously enter the sphere of existential awareness: full awareness of their own existence. When that happened, the conditions curtailing human freedom were momentarily suspended. Change was possible. In fact almost anything was possible. And so we were confronted, moment by moment, not just with the threat of being automatons, but with the terror of being free; for true freedom initiated change beyond conception. That, he said, was the substance of the therapy he was engaged in, and it applied equally to therapist and patient.

And so the lecture progressed, the Frenchman delving ever more deeply and succinctly into the neurosis of the age, into the psychological sleight-of-hand we engage in when attempting to describe and define ourselves and our world.

According to modern scientific thought, we were merely a homunculus, a nonentity, nothing more than a series of automated reflexes, a bundle of drives, a psychic mechanism; or simply a blind product of environment.

Under constant professional attack, human beings were being forced consciously and unconsciously to consider themselves to be without meaning or value. Having devalued ourselves to a point verging on absurdity, we were now willing to describe humanity as nothing more than a complex biochemical mechanism, an adaptive control system whose values could be defined as homeostatic restraints in a stimulus-response process. In the realm of scientific thought, the human essence had all but evaporated. We were once again travelling insensibly towards the gas chambers of Auschwitz, the horrors of Treblinka and Maidenek in new guise. And we shouldn't scoff too quickly at such an idea, for in recent history the conception of man as *nothing but* the product of heredity and environment – or, as it was then termed, Blood and Soil – had pushed us as near to the abyss as it was possible to get. We were, in other words, creating an existence vacuum for ourselves, and one by one were disappearing into it without trace. But not without first undergoing a series of 'abyss experiences', moments of dark anxiety during which we had a foretaste of the hell to come.

He then talked of Europe as a seismographic station, saying that Europe was already registering warnings of an advancing spiritual earthquake because Europeans were more acutely endangered by collective neurotic traits. But it should be understood that in his scheme of things the word 'spiritual' referred not to anything specifically religious but to all things specifically human. The specifically human was a dimension of existence, and it was fast becoming a lost dimension. The spiritual dimension of our existence was therefore that dimension within which specifically human phenomena – love and compassion, tolerance, hope and perseverance – could be located. Preserving the humanness of human phenomena was therefore our highest priority. For only by consciously re-entering the dimension of the specifically human could we rediscover ourselves and our world.

But there was a problem, and the nature of the problem was that in our growing frenzy to escape the existence vacuum we were being drawn more and more into the destructive whirlpool of hyper-interpretation directed at the self. Psychiatrists and analysts were daily confronted by patients suffering from, and crippled by, the obsessive compulsion to analyse themselves, to observe and watch themselves, to reflect upon themselves endlessly: awareness of existence had been usurped by manic self-consciousness. And next to this lay the mirror-image compulsion towards what was commonly termed 'self-actualization': the desire to realize one's potential by making the self the supreme object of attention. Both paths, although different in many ways, were part of a collective obsessive neurosis.

There was a momentary break in the audience's concentration; it was as if some of them had been asleep and had suddenly awakened, as if the hypnotic verbal bubble created by the Frenchman had been clumsily pricked from within. When this restiveness abated, Duval addressed himself directly to its cause by saying that the concept of self-actualization had gone through many variations over the years. He gave examples, declaring that the search had been for an all-encompassing theory of life's ultimate goal with self-actualization as ultimate motive. That, in his opinion, was a mistake. Self-actualization was a side-effect of living in the world and should not be made the whole object of intention. Man's primary concern ought to be the realization of values and the fulfilment of meanings found in the world rather than within his own closed psychic system.

The Frenchman's thinking was obviously a blow to many present. Murmuring broke out, then died away. Drummond felt sorry for the man; he looked so alone, stranded as he was on the platform, his great height distancing him further still from his audience. And he couldn't quite understand what all the furore was about, for although many of the things said had gone over his head, much of it had sounded perfectly reasonable. But one thing was certain, the philosopher had thrown down some kind of gauntlet, and it was without doubt going to be picked up.

A summary brought the lecture to a close.

The woman who had earlier smothered a laugh sprang immediately to her feet, stood uncertainly for a moment as if surprised by the rapidity of her own response, and said, 'My name's Rosemary Waters. I'm a psychologist. And I have to admit to being greatly disturbed by some of the things I've heard this evening.' She was plumpish, quite devoid of make-up, and obviously rattled. 'I couldn't believe my ears when you said that self-actualization was not sufficient grounds for a motivational theory. Surely A H Maslow has furnished sufficient reason to accept self-actualization as being of primary motivational importance!'

Duval stared down at the woman. 'What is the exact nature of your question?' he asked.

'What I've just said!'

'And what have you just said?'

Rosemary Water's response was again immediate. 'Don't play games with *me*,' she replied haughtily, 'you know damned well what my question is!'

'Yes, but it would seem to be incomplete.'

Twice dumbfounded by the Frenchman's tack, the woman said,

‘What the hell do you mean?’

‘I mean that I can detect nothing of what I’ve laboured to say in your question. You have chosen to ignore what has been said because you cannot bear the thought that self-actualization ought not to be the central focus, goal, or target of life. Is that not so?’

‘I simply don’t agree with you!’

‘And so you take a stand to one side of true centre.’

‘Which is?’

‘Dialogue.’ Before the woman could reply, Duval added, ‘What you are engaged in at this moment is known as monologue.’

‘Huh!’ said Rosemary Waters. ‘Now I’ve heard everything!’

‘On the contrary,’ replied Duval, ‘you have quite obviously heard nothing at all.’

Spinning round, the woman said to the audience, ‘Well, I’ll leave you to it. Have a good day!’ She then stormed out, throwing one last remark at Duval before disappearing. ‘You’re nothing but a bloody dictator!’ she shouted.

Seemingly unaffected by the woman’s fiery summation, Duval went on to answer a number of highly technical questions with what seemed to Drummond immense intellectual dexterity. Even those who fundamentally disagreed with him accepted, in the end, at least some of his contentions. Some looked dumbfounded, their pet theories and opinions expertly scalpelled out of existence with a few well-chosen words. And then an elderly man again raised the issue of attempting to fully actualize one’s potential through self-development programmes.

Smiling almost benignly up at the Frenchman he said: ‘Allowing for your observations, there still seems to be a contradiction in your assertion that self-actualization cannot be directly intentional. Isn’t this just the problem facing most of the human race – that they are basically unaware of their potential ability to behave humanely and decently towards one another? How can they learn that they have the potential for empathy, and perhaps even love, unless they are made consciously aware of their secret resources in a direct fashion?’

It was a good question – so good, in fact, that some of the audience clapped quite loudly.

In reply, Duval said that he had nothing whatsoever against programmes designed to assist people towards greater awareness. What he wholeheartedly disapproved of was when such programmes turned into interminable processes of self-glorification. In many instances, he said, including the whole audience with a look, such programmes turned into narcissistic exercises. Those involved became so enamoured with the search for 'self' that everything outside of self became a mere tool mysteriously designed for the accomplishment of that rather dubious task. Awareness was sacrificed in that moment, cast aside as a secondary accomplishment as the shadow of 'self-perfection' loomed on the horizon as ultimate prize. Self-perfection, whether it appeared in psychology or religion, was however tantamount to a blasphemous exercise – blasphemous to the extent that it disregarded the world of pain and turned us into narcissistic seekers of a truth allied to the whims of individual advancement. That was ultimately an inhuman exercise, an exercise in futility almost brought to perfection by the Third Reich.

The elderly man seemed more than satisfied with the answer to his question; he smiled again at Duval, gave him a curt little nod, and said, 'I see.'

There was only one more question to follow, and Duval used it to bring the lecture to a close. Addressing the audience as a whole, he said that ultimate questions were on the lips of every man, and that these questions, scrambled almost beyond recognition in many cases, had to be descrambled and played back to the patient. When that was satisfactorily accomplished, the treatment proper could begin. What had to be clearly understood was that there existed a natural tension in all human beings, and this tension lay between their being in the world, and what being in the world meant to them personally. In other words, this tension lay sandwiched between 'being' and 'meaning'. Man was naturally oriented toward meaning. This orientation towards meaning was inherent, ineradicable, and therefore indispensable to both psychological and physical health. But as said earlier, this should not be confused with a 'drive' towards meaning; it was not some kind of mechanical process initiated by the manner in which our brains had evolved. On the contrary, it was what caused us to be regarded as human. However, this natural orientation towards meaning was confounded daily in Western society through an inadequate confrontation with meaning. Educated to believe that we were composed of nothing more than instinctual drives, reaction formations and defence mechanisms, we eventually succumbed to the notion that life was merely a series of automatic responses governed by blind forces. This was what the patient brought to the consulting room, to the doctor, the psychiatrist or therapist, and it was this deeply ingrained negative hypothesis concerning human existence that underlay his condition. He had for too long been devalued and demeaned, brought low and rendered impotent in his search for meaning; he was spiritually exhausted. So our first priority was the reorientation of the patient's mind towards the possibility of re-encountering meaning in a meaningful sense, and that in turn necessitated that we ourselves thoroughly identify with man and his world – our world – in a completely new way.

It was not at all the kind of thing Drummond had expected to hear from the Frenchman, and quite obviously not at all what his audience had expected to hear. And so impressively done, without notes or hesitation, and in a foreign tongue. Not that everyone had ended up agreeing with Duval; that without doubt had not been the case. But there was a sense in which all present had left the lecture hall – apart from the woman who stormed out – feeling that something of importance, perhaps great importance, had been communicated. Edouard Duval was deadly serious and more than capable of combating either complacency or prejudice among his peers. And on top of it all that electrifying moment when their eyes had met, and parted. A moment of recognition, almost, but not in any conventional sense. More a recognition of his existence.

A clear, sharp November evening, and only nine-fifteen according to his watch. He crossed the street and headed down Upper Street to where his car was parked, dialled Georgia's number on his mobile as he walked, and stopped adjacent to his car when her voice sounded in his ear. Rummaging for his keys, he said he was in Islington, and that he had just attended a lecture by Duval.

'Any good?'

'Fascinating – what I understood of it.'

'Are you coming round?'

'Did cross my mind. Okay with you?'

'Yes. Of course. But I should warn you, I've got company.' She laughed and said something to someone in the room, came back on the line and added, 'A mad Irishman by the name of Kevin

Murray dropped in. He's almost polished off my bottle of scotch.'

'– I don't want to intrude.'

'You wouldn't be.' She sounded genuine. 'I'd very much like you to meet him.'

Drummond hesitated.

'Say you'll come. Please!'

'I'll come,' he said back, his curiosity aroused. 'Be there in about twenty minutes.'

He pocketed the mobile and stood considering his decision, turned to insert his key, and froze. Two youths with closely cropped hair and pasty complexions were within a few feet of him, their expressions a curious mixture of feigned innocence and insolence; their intention was blatantly obvious. Drummond stepped back, bracing himself.

'What can I do for you lads?' he asked almost amiably.

There was no reply, just a sudden movement of bodies with the predetermined purpose of bringing him down – a purpose immediately and quite unexpectedly thwarted. For as the youths moved in, their quarry retaliated viciously, and with surprising speed for a man of his age. The larger of the two youths reeled back yelping, blood spurting from nose and mouth, his jaw all but dislocated by the downward curve of the blow delivered. His mate then emitted similar sounds of agony as a knee jabbed into his groin and the supposed victim butted him full in the face.

It was all over and done with in a matter of seconds.

Shocked and humiliated, his attackers made an at first faltering escape, then as best they could took to their heels as Drummond delivered the final insult by booting one of them up the backside. That, he knew from raw experience, would be remembered when all else was forgotten. But as he turned away, one of the youths began to shout face-saving obscenities, and rounded off his barrage of garbled abuse with a threat, but not a personal threat. 'They'll get you next time, no mistake!' he bawled out.

Drummond spun round, stood staring as the youths bolted, the truth of the situation slowly dawning on him.

Chapter Six

'It never leaves you,' said Kevin Murray when he heard about the fight, and saw the dark bruise on Drummond's brow. 'It's like learning to swim, it's always there when you need it.'

'I was lucky. If they'd been a fraction faster–'

'Yes, I know – it'd have taken you about a minute longer.'

Drummond grinned, eyed the stocky little Irishman with interest. 'Belfast?' The man nodded, watched as Georgia examined the bruise and headed for the kitchen. 'Glasgow,' said Drummond.

Kevin Murray reached for his glass of whisky, tasted it and said, 'Where else?' He laughed and added, 'Don't think I'll be driving anywhere tonight. It'll have to be a taxi.'

Georgia reappeared with a metal dish and a roll of cotton wool.

'The warrior returns carrying his shield,' intoned the Irishman, quoting from something. 'Jesus, I'd loved to have seen it!'

With mock sourness Georgia said, 'You're all the same, you Celts.'

'Just as well for him,' the man replied.

She pressed damp cotton wool onto the bruise, allowed her eyes to drift down and meet his, shook her head. 'This is the second time he's been in the wars.'

'Really?' said Kevin Murray.

Drummond explained, but did not go into detail.

'Do you generally attract so much trouble?'

'Not as a rule.'

Completing her act of mercy, Georgia suggested that he hold the wetted wool in place himself.

'How long have you been this side of the water?' asked Drummond.

'About . . . fifteen years.'

'Doing what?'

'Teaching.'

'He lectures in literature,' amplified Georgia.

Kevin Murray pulled a comic face. 'Which is another way of saying that I live off the creativity of others.'

'That's nonsense!' said Georgia.

'Nonsense, is it?' said the Irishman, staring at her. He looked back at Drummond and spoke rapidly. 'I'm one of the many who get paid handsomely for repeating what has already been said by those who were paid a pittance for having said it much better. I am, in other words, an arranger and classifier of things too fluid ever to be arranged or classified in any real sense. I think that makes me a parasite, or worse.'

'You don't believe that,' said Georgia.

'What don't I believe?'

'That you're a parasite.'

'An inescapable conclusion, dear lady; and that in spite of the fact that I function most of the time as if it weren't true. You see I have to, Ian – for the sake of the bairns.'

'He doesn't have any bairns!'

'For the money, then.'

'Don't listen to him, he always gets like this when he's had too much to drink.'

'Ah! The truth spurned,' said Kevin Murray, rolling his eyes idiotically.

'He's brilliant at what he does.'

'She means by that that I have evolved the knack of saying boring things in an interesting way. That's all.'

'And he of course writes beautifully.'

'But am seldom written, alas.'

'Nonsense.'

'An observation.'

'Not accepted.'

'Then I capitulate.'

Both amused and bemused by what he was hearing, Drummond said, 'Where are you lecturing at the moment?'

'University of London – for my sins. It keeps me out of trouble.' He chuckled to himself. 'It's been keeping me out of trouble and *away* from trouble for some years now.'

'Ireland,' said Drummond.

'Ireland,' said Kevin Murray.

Drummond felt no need to refer to the breakdown in the Peace Accord with the IRA, or to the bombs that had again gone off in London; it was in the man's voice and eyes that he was drowning his sorrows for that very reason.

'You'd be mad to even think of going back,' said Georgia.

'The mad belong together, I sometimes think,' he replied, smiling a crinkly smile. 'God knows what St Malachy's would make of me now that I've been infected with ideas various and subterranean.' He added quickly, 'My old college, Ian. Do you know Belfast at all?'

'I've been through it a couple of times. Had a week's holiday in Larne once, years ago. I remember the ten shilling notes were orange in colour.'

'All part of a Protestant plot,' said Keven Murray, beaming, 'if you'll allow the gibe.'

Drummond waved the remark aside. 'I'm not in the least religious,' he said, remembering how Dr Freeman had shown that even a lapsed Protestant could not altogether shake off the past. The memory of that prompted him to add, 'But I'm aware of having retained something of the Protestant value system in spite of that fact.'

'You are?' said Kevin Murray.

'I had an example of it thrust under my nose only recently.'

'By a Catholic priest,' said Georgia.

'By someone who had once been a priest,' said Drummond, annoyed with Georgia for having revealed the source of his enlightenment.

'You obviously bit the bullet.'

'I didn't have any choice.'

Kevin Murray sighed a sigh of exaggerated pleasure, looked at Georgia and said, 'Did you hear that? He didn't have any choice. Intelligence demanded immediate acceptance of the proposition!' He turned his head slowly back towards Drummond. 'You almost give me the confidence to complete something I'm working on.'

'The paper?' asked Georgia, who was seated in a little cane chair.

'I'm afraid the paper is rapidly turning into a book.' He screwed up his face. 'God knows what I'll end up saying!'

'That's marvellous news,' said Georgia. 'I always said you should write a book.'

'What's it about?' asked Drummond.

'Well may you ask. I'm beginning to wonder myself.'

'It's about Yeats and the present crisis in Northern Ireland,' said Georgia, frowning.

'It still about Yeats and the present crisis – but it's grown a bit, changed a bit.'

'In what way. What you read to me sounded fine.'

The man paused, sucked at his teeth. 'I'm now working completely outside of my field of expertise . . . Things suddenly came into focus that changed the whole direction of the piece.'

'Hope you haven't spoiled it.'

He looked at her. 'I hadn't grasped the nettle.'

'The nettle being?'

The Irishman was silent for a moment, then in a gravelly voice he began to quote something. 'I can say Ireland is hooey, Ireland is / A gallery of fake tapestries, / But I cannot deny my past to which myself is wed, / The woven figure cannot undo its thread. / On a cardboard lid when I was four / Was the trade-mark of a hound and a round tower, / And that was Irish glamour, and in the cemetery / Sham Celtic crosses claimed our individuality –'

'Louis MacNeice,' said Georgia.

'A good Protestant, Ian. And a fine poet.' He closed his eyes and delved back into MacNeice. '– I will exorcise my blood / And not to have baby clothes my shroud / I will acquire an attitude not yours / And become as one of your holiday visitors, / And however often I may come / Farewell, my country, and in perpetuum; / Whatever desire I catch when your wind scours my face / I will take home and put in a glass case / And merely look on / At each new fantasy of badge and gun –'

'Amazing images,' said Georgia.

'Split right down the middle,' said Kevin Murray. 'Yet whole, in a funny kind of way.' He added two more lines. 'Romantic Ireland's dead and gone, / It's with O'Leary in the grave.'

'Yeats,' said Georgia.

'I'm afraid I don't read poetry,' said Drummond, irritated by Georgia's continual punctuating of everything said.

'Few people do. It just happens to be part of my job.'

'So what have you come up with?' asked Georgia.

'A mistake, at best; or the best mistake I've ever made.'

She frowned again, felt Drummond's eyes on her and decided to wait for an explanation.

'I'm surprised the same thing hasn't happened in Glasgow,' said Drummond, remembering for a second time the banners and the bands and the bottle fights. 'All the ingredients are there.'

'Not quite all the ingredients,' said Kevin Murray. 'For a start, you're not an island.'

'You think that makes a difference?'

'I suspect it does.'

'Ireland's just one big Abbey Theatre,' said Georgia.

'Yes, it's become a stage,' the Irishman agreed, 'and we're squandering our gifts on it.' He sobered suddenly, became serious in a serious way. 'Yeats and Russell and Synge wouldn't give them the reality they wanted, Ian, the permission they craved to wreak holy vengeance on their masters, so they wrote their own poetry and took drama out onto the streets. Even O'Casey was pushed aside because he wouldn't give in to their gutter romanticism. In O'Casey's eyes, the Easter Rebellion wasn't a holy rising enkindled by St Pearse – why do you think they chose Easter, eh? – it was as someone has said, *a class struggle lit by a page torn from the book of Marx*. But they didn't want to hear that, to think about that. They wanted their artists to conform and reduce their vision to the size of a holy postcard with a mutilated Jesus on it. That's what they wanted! Do you know why? Because their symbol of victory was death. That was the kind of myth they were handling inside their heads. They objected to any form of art that didn't conform to that grotesque little image. Art in any real sense was redundant because it offered complexity instead of simplicity. And so also with the old Irish gods. They were too big, too demanding, too incomprehensible. So what did they do? They knee-capped them and brought them down to manageable size. Is it any wonder that Yeats roared at them from the stage of the Abbey Theatre? He knew what he was up against.'

'They should have listened to O'Casey; he was one of them.'

'They couldn't listen, Georgia. They didn't understand O'Casey for the same reason that they didn't understand Yeats – complexity. O'Casey's Marxist views were as incomprehensible as

Yeats' Platonic vision: it was all too civilized. Both Yeats and O'Casey were men of civilization, and that made them suspect in the eyes of those who eventually took to the streets. That's why Pearse could say in one of his revolutionary poems that he loved the folly of his actions more than the wise men their books or their counting-houses, or their quiet homes. It was no longer a case of polite argument – it was a case of raw action and to hell with the consequences.'

'Blind nationalism blended with religious bigotry,' ventured Drummond.

'Tribal myth mixed with an inbred defeatism that said *death is enough*. Let's die and be remembered. Let's teach the children to die, the mothers to accept their sacrifice as something glorious. Let's say that only God can judge, and so confound our judges. And let's ask God to not remember our failures, just our faith. Faith, hope and murder. And now it's the same on both sides.'

'So what's your basic premise?' asked Georgia.

'That it eventually dawned on Yeats that the myths most important to his nationalistic friends were hollow, artificial things – and that in spite of the genuine rage that underlay those myths. But he couldn't get the message across, the message being that myths proper – the myths of a people – are universal constants that always transcend their origin and incorporate something shared by humanity as a whole. Do you understand what I'm saying? I'm saying that real myths are about birth, coming of age, sexuality, death, and the cycle of the seasons. I'm saying that they are about the process of rebirth and renewal, the quest for meaning, the conflict between rationality and irrationality. And about the relation of man to nature and the cosmos. Such myths resonate and open out into the invisible, the numinous, the sacred. They do not contract and lead a people into insecurity, blindness, prejudice and hatred. George Russell – a not so befuddled mystic as some would like to think – said it best early in 1916. He said, "The gods are never so turned away from man as when he ascends to them by disorderly means." He was trying to tell us that hatred ought never to be made the basis of personal or collective myth. You simply can't ever be free if you hate other human beings. If you hate something, you're not free of it. And if you hate something with the full force of your being, then the hated object blocks out everything else in sight. You end up distracted from the values you cherish most. That's the price you pay – and it's a heavy price by any standard. So we have to make a distinction, a careful distinction between myths secular and myths sacred – particularly when the secular ones are dressed up in holy guise. And at the same time we have to be astute enough not to lose sight of the political realities, and the fact that we live in a hard-nosed world. Yeats managed to find that balance for himself. Even Russell's mysticism took on muscle in the end. And Louis MacNeice brings us bang up to date with the whole damned issue. The problem is, it's never been spelt out clearly enough for either the men with lava in their veins, or the softly spoken, wily apologists from Westminster to really understand. That's what has to be done now. Especially now.'

'This is what the book's going to be about?' said Drummond.

'It'll be an attempt to get some of these things across.'

'Then you've done more than change tack,' said Georgia, remembering the original intention.

'I've changed,' said Kevin Murray. Then with a smile he looked straight at Drummond and added, 'I had no choice.'

They talked on for another three-quarters of an hour, the question of Ireland's past, and of Ireland's future, taking on substance beyond that of documentary or newsreel. Drummond listened mostly, enjoying the man's mercurial wit, his precise and often lyrical way of talking. Then quite suddenly Kevin Murray was on his feet saying he would have to go, that he had thoroughly enjoyed the evening and hoped he hadn't bored anyone with his diatribe on Ireland. Yes, he would get a taxi and collect his car in the morning, but walk a little first to clear his head. He shook hands with Drummond, pecked Georgia on the cheek and received a little hug. When she returned from seeing him off she was laughing.

'Quite a fella,' said Drummond.

'A gem.'

'I felt quite inadequate.'

She smiled down at him, turned dreamily away toward her chair, but remained standing.

'You know some interesting people.'

'Some of them are interesting.'

He looked up at the standing woman. 'Known him long?'

'A few months. We met at Broadcasting House. He was giving a radio talk.'

'On Ireland?'

'Probably.' A terribly serious look from Georgia. 'He's also a recognized authority on Celtic poetry.'

'I'd never have guessed.'

'Another drink?'

'A small one.'

She poured him a whisky and handed it to him, asking him quite without conviction to tell her about Duval's lecture.

'I don't think I could. Not now.'

'Why not?'

'All that stuff about Ireland's knocked it completely out of my head.'

'You must be able to remember something!'

Staring at the carpet he patched words together. 'Free will. Choice. That kind of thing.' He looked up, tried to smile. 'You name it, he spoke about it.'

'That's not terribly explicit.'

'He covered a lot of territory.'

'Think.'

'I'll tell you about it some other time – it's been a heavy day.'

'As you will.' She turned away abruptly.

'I'm terribly, terribly sorry,' he said back, putting on his best English accent, 'for not remembering every word of it.'

'I didn't expect it word for word.' Down into her chair she went, to stare at him. 'I just thought from the way you sounded on the telephone that you'd have a lot more to tell me than that.'

'I did, then.'

'Why not now?'

'Because it would be a waste of time.' He paused, and they stared at each other. 'You're still thinking about Ireland and Kevin Murray.'

'That's hardly my fault; he's been here for last three hours. It's up to you now.'

'I can't *be* a Kevin Murray, Georgia.'

'I don't want you to be a Kevin Murray.'

'I suspect you do.'

Her eyes widened in anger. 'Allow me to know my own mind, Ian!'

'It's what's at the back of your mind that bothers me,' he replied, nailing her with a look. 'I seem to disappoint you on a regular basis.'

A sigh from Georgia. 'You obviously want me to admit that I'm in the wrong whether I'm in the wrong or not.'

'I've never been lucky enough to meet a woman who would willingly admit to being in the wrong,' he said evenly, astonishing her further. 'You've all had one thing in common – the knack of covering your verbal tracks so expertly that the apology always seemed due from the other person.'

'That's sexist nonsense!'

'No. Merely an observation I've had the rather doubtful privilege of making more times than I care to remember.'

'Don't equate me with Patricia; it isn't fair!'

'Then stop acting like Patricia!'

'I do not –'

'You've been playing games ever since I arrived.'

'Games?'

'The basin and the cotton wool for one.'

'I was concerned for you!'

'A little bit, perhaps. But not a lot. I think it would have suited your sensibilities better if I'd staggered in here sodden with blood. But I didn't. I walked in with just a little bruise on my forehead. That's all.'

'Kevin Murray comes from the same kind of background as yourself.'

'I don't doubt it – but he's an authority on Celtic poetry.'

'That's childish!'

'It's the fucking truth!' he roared back, startling her. 'You were out to stick the knife in me a moment ago, and you succeeded. *You must be able to remember something*, you said. *That's not terribly specific*, you said. And then you asked me to *think*, damn it! Did you know what you were saying? I hope not.'

She stared at him, shocked by his vehemence.

He pushed himself up out of the sofa and stood before her uncertainly, not looking at her.

'What in God's name is the matter with you!'

'Inadequacy,' he replied, fixing her with a look.

'You've no reason to feel inadequate.'

'I did a moment ago.'

'You think –'

'You were out to get me for some reason.'

'I was nothing of the kind out to get you!'

'You couldn't stop yourself. You wanted to hurt me.'

'I didn't *want* to hurt you. I was just angry with you.'

'Why?'

'I don't *know* why!' She drew breath, searched in herself and found something. '– I think I wanted you to hurt as much as I was hurting.'

He waited, watching her face.

'– You're treating what's happened between us as if it means nothing at all. An *arrangement* you called it.'

'You want more?'

'I don't know what I want, but I sure as hell know what I *don't* want!'

Quite suddenly she was only Georgia Patton, and it scared him. He fumbled for words and found himself saying, 'The last couple of months have been absolute hell for me, Georgia. I had a breakdown. Almost went under.'

'I find that hard to believe.'

'It's the truth.'

'Why didn't you tell me?'

'It was something I had to deal with by myself.'

'At my expense?'

His anger flared again. 'I needed time to think! I still need time to think!'

'About what for Christ's sake?'

'Every bloody thing!' The words came out slowly to start with, gathered momentum and became a torrent. 'It isn't *you*, it's *me*! Just *me!* I'm being confronted with things at every turn that I don't understand. I don't seem to understand anything! Nothing at all! And up until a couple of hours ago I couldn't even see the point of *trying* to understand. What was the use? Why should I bother my arse trying to understand things when nothing was worth the attempt? Not worth a button! The whole world not worth a fucking button! Can you see what it is I'm trying to say? I simply couldn't see the point of making any kind of effort. There was no reason to. The world was in a mess and it was going to stay like that. I was in a mess and there was nothing I could do about it. Then up pops Duval and I suddenly realized that I'm not the only one, that there are millions out there thinking and feeling the same way as I do, that I'm not alone.

'And tonight, just a couple of hours ago, I began to realize that I'd never properly thought about anything in my whole life. I'd taken everything for granted. Other people. Myself. The world. Listening to that Frenchman made me feel sick to the gut. Ashamed. Stripped. Then I walked in here and listened to an Irishman talk of Ireland and the Irish, felt his concern for a country and a people at war with itself, and realized that I didn't care a damn about anything or anyone.

'And I'm not saying that I suddenly want to be a bloody nationalist! I'm saying that I'm without passion, that I can't feel anything because I'm fucking numb inside. That's what I'm saying, and as I'm saying it I can feel it, actually feel it in here.'

He rammed a fist into his stomach to drive the point home.

'And then I hear you asking me to explain what Duval said on that platform with the same goading tone that Patricia used so often, the same invisible sneer at my lack of formal education. It allowed her to feel superior, gave her the chance – intellectual snob that she was – to believe that she had everything tied up. The whole world tied up in a neat little bundle. Everything in its place. History. Psychology. Religion. Science. You name it and she had it packed away and pigeonholed, just as you've got Yeats and O'Casey and Christ knows how many other poor bastards pigeonholed in your head. So she felt safe, just as you feel safe. But I'll tell you something, Georgia, nothing's ever *that* safe! We don't understand what we think we understand, and we know hardly anything about what we think we know. You're just as lost as I am, but unlike me you've been led to believe that knowing and remembering things is enough. Well it bloody well isn't enough! Your fancy schooling and your inbred manners and your careful allusions to this and to that don't make you any better than I am – and I'm *nothing*!'

He was visibly shaking, visibly overcome by his attempt to explain. Georgia stood white-faced and stared at him.

'So there it is,' he said, exhausted by what had poured out of him, by what he had glimpsed as he tore the barriers down.

After a silence, Georgia said, 'I'm sorry, Ian – I didn't realize.' She wanted to hold him, but was afraid.

'I think I'd better go,' he said.

'Why can't I move?'

'Because you're afraid of the same things I'm afraid of.' He smiled at her, and began to turn away, but what she said next stopped him in his tracks.

'Don't leave me!'

'Why?'

'Because I know if I let you walk out of that door I'll never see you again.'

'Would that matter?'

'Yes. It would.' She controlled her voice. 'I'm not completely stupid.'

'No one is,' he replied.

Chapter Seven

They spent the whole weekend together, almost idyllically, except for one brief moment when everything again threatened to crush him. But quite perfect, otherwise. He could not remember Georgia being so cheerful, so much herself. By Sunday afternoon he too was completely relaxed. A long walk on Hampstead Heath, and an equally long talk, brought them even closer together. Sitting now at his desk preparing for his meeting with Edouard Duval, Drummond found himself remembering the silkiness of her body, the feel of her breasts, the black of her pubic hair against pale skin, the taste of her. And to think he had almost refused to stay, had almost walked out on her because he could not believe in her need for him. But her need for him had turned out to be quite genuine when the last moments of silliness were swept aside. So much silliness between them, pushing them apart, pulling them apart in more ways than one. So many things to be forgotten, or explained. So much hurting because Patricia's ghost had not properly been laid to rest.

A real attempt on both of their parts as they walked, and talked, to understand one another. A superb winter's day, misty on the horizon, and cold. As much as they could bear spilled out and digested, shared for the first time. And always more to say, always more, and eventually without effort. Even some of his dreams described in detail. Georgia shaking her head, glancing at him as he moved back into that nether world of nonsense and terror. Immediately dismissed by himself as meaningless, but not convincingly – too much in his face as he spoke for such a quick dismissal. And such a strange atmosphere generated as they left the parkland and forced their way through a thicket of leafless, gangling saplings, and climbed up on to Spaniards Road. Almost as if time were standing still, and they were passing through it, and not it through them.

But he was back in time now, as he sat at his desk trying to concentrate on what should be said to Duval and his colleagues that very afternoon. Scribbled notes to lock the sentences into his head. The blue folder gone through yet again so that its wealth of detail might be fresh in his mind and available when required. And the problem of when to introduce the fact that he had been twice attacked, and that he suspected those attacks of being somehow related to his being offered the Katharsis account. What would their reaction be to that, he wondered. For it was highly unlikely that any competitor would go to such lengths, particularly such violent lengths, and that could only mean that Katharsis itself was being viewed by someone as a potential threat. But a threat to whom? Why should an advanced training procedure for therapists cause such consternation, cause him to be so brutally targeted?

There was little doubt that he was a target – that those who had him in their sights were quite willing to maim him to communicate their disapproval. The police were stumped by the whole affair, but had confirmed 'professional' criminal abuse both in his apartment and at the office. And now there was the additional factor of his having been attacked a second time – by hooligans admittedly, and on one of London's darker streets – immediately after attending one of Duval's lectures. Not just an attempted mugging that little episode; more probably an encounter with inept thugs hired to further intimidate him. Which meant in turn that he had been followed that evening, that he was being watched, and that it was only a matter of time before they again caught him off guard. Not the most satisfactory situation to find oneself in, he realized, as he sat there. Then suddenly he was answering the telephone and involved in another little mystery: someone without an appointment was demanding to see him, and would not give a name.

Intrigued, Drummond said, 'What does he look like?'

'Small, with thinning grey hair,' said the receptionist, trying not to be too obvious in her surveillance. 'A bit on the tubby side, but well dressed.'

'English?'

'For sure. Talks like an old-style BBC announcer.'

'And he won't give a name.'

'Refuses point-blank.' She added quickly, 'And cocky with it.'

'How do you mean?'

'Polite, but arrogant as all hell.'

'You'd better explain that it isn't possible for me to speak with anyone unless they have an appointment – particularly with someone that won't give their name.'

'I've gone almost blue telling him that; he just won't listen. Keeps saying that you'll be more than interested in hearing what it is he has to say, but won't say what.' She again added her tuppence-worth. 'It's the damnedest thing I've ever had to deal with!'

'Send him up.'

'You'll see him?'

'It's either that or have him thrown out and start a rumpus. Which would you suggest?'

'Don't tempt me!'

'Send him up,' he said again. 'I'll soon get rid of him.'

But he knew even as he replaced the receiver that he was obeying a command; the little man was an emissary of some kind. That angered him. At the same time it forced him to control his anger so that something might be learned.

The knock eventually came, and the man entered smiling. 'Mr Drummond,' he said, extending a hand.

Drummond ignored the gesture, remained seated. 'You are?' he asked.

The smile broadened. 'Who I am is totally irrelevant. It's –'

'Not to me it isn't. You can't just walk in here off the street without credentials.'

'I already have,' was the startling reply.

'What do you want?'

'Nothing. I've simply come to warn you.'

'About what?'

'Edouard Duval, of course.' Turning, the man without a name drew a chair away from the wall. 'May I?' he asked belatedly. Before Drummond could reply, he settled himself into the chair and said, 'Duval's an occultist of the very worst type – I take it you're familiar with the term?'

'Yes, but –'

'No buts about it, Mr Drummond. Edouard Duval is a *very*

dangerous man, perhaps one of the most dangerous men ever to have appeared on this planet.'

'That's a preposterous statement!'

'It's the truth, unpalatable as it may seem.' The brown eyes studied him for a brief moment. 'There is such a thing as evil incarnate you know.'

'I think I've heard quite enough,' said Drummond, his distaste obvious. 'You'd better leave before I call the police.'

The man looked huffed. He sighed and sat back into his chair as if addressed by a tiresome adolescent. 'You really must listen to what it is I have to say, Mr Drummond. It's for your own good. Duval intends to use your company to accomplish a quite devilish scheme. And I do mean *devilish.*' He sighed again, continuing unabashed. 'There's almost no adequate language available to me with which to describe his intentions, his *plans.*'

'Which are?'

'Social and spiritual disruption on an unimaginable scale.'

'That's somewhat different from what I've been told.'

'Exactly the reverse, I would imagine. And that's why I'm here. Duval has fooled a lot of people with his clever double-talk, and he's got to be stopped. This outlandish therapy technique of his is a cover for something almost unspeakable – you wouldn't believe some of the things he advocates. His techniques are drawn from things like shamanism and witchcraft. Even voodoo. And he's a devotee of tantric yoga, and all that that means. All of his therapists are trained in tantric yoga.'

'It's been explained to me as a synthesis of ideas drawn from psychotherapy, philosophy and religion.'

'There's nothing of true religion in it! It's a hotchpotch of occultist practices disguised as a therapy.'

'How do you know all this?'

'Because he's written quite blatantly about such things in the past, and extolled their virtues in lectures and broadcasts. And he is himself a practitioner. He's into all kinds of meditation and the good Lord knows what else. If you knew some of the views he held, you'd disassociate yourself from him immediately.'

'It isn't a crime to meditate, from what I've heard.'

'That rather depends on what you meditate on.'

'Go on, tell me.'

'Spirits. He allows himself to be possessed by spirits.'

'You believe in spirits?'

The smile returned. 'We're not discussing what I believe, Mr Drummond. We're discussing what *he* believes.'

'Have you been to any of his seminars?'

'No.'

'Then how can you properly judge?'

'Because I have eyes of discernment.'

'What does that mean?'

'That I'm guided by the Holy Spirit.'

'Ah! I see. You're a Christian of some sort. I saw quite a few of you on the march recently.'

'Do you know why?'

'You've obviously got grievances.'

'More than that, Mr Drummond.' His smile verged on the beatific. 'It's simply time to take a stand. Time to unite.'

'Against what?'

'The common enemy. Evil.' A melodramatic pause. 'I only wish I could fully explain what that means. But I can't. It's far too complex a subject, and you wouldn't be receptive. But there are things afoot that will eventually convince you, astonish you into accepting what I've tried to say about that Frenchman. You won't have *that* look on your face then.'

'What kind of things?'

'Events, Mr Drummond. Unbelievable events.'

'Here in Britain?'

'Everywhere.'

Drummond stared at the man, wondering what it would feel like to wake up with his perception of things, his belief system and unbudgeable conviction that God took sides. 'Can you be more specific?' He waited, but received only a shake of the head. Then came the question uppermost in his mind. 'Would you care to explain how you came to know of our involvement?'

'We were informed.'

'By whom?'

'I can't say.'

Lifting the telephone, Drummond dialled a double digit and sat back; he kept his eyes on the little man's face. 'Sally? Get me Detective Sergeant Spencer. I'll hang on.'

'There's no need to involve the police.'

'I think there is. You see, I was attacked on Friday evening immediately after attending one of Duval's lectures. It was a set-up. I think you may have had something to do with it.'

'Never! That's not how we function!'

'Someone was trying to scare me off, but they blew it. And you've spent the last few minutes trying to do the same thing, in your own way. There has to be a connection.'

'Please, put the phone down – I'll explain.'

'Sally? Cancel that call. Thanks.' He replaced the receiver. 'So?'

'The information on your involvement came by letter weeks ago.'

'Have you still got it?'

'No. It was destroyed.'

'Why?'

'. . . We always destroy them. That's the rule.'

'The rule?'

'Each letter ends with the injunction that it must be immediately destroyed.'

'Who are these letters from?'

'They aren't signed.'

'You don't know who they're from but you accept what they say without question?'

'They're written by someone who understand the signs, by someone who loves God.'

'What signs would these be?'

'The signs the Bible tells us will appear before the end of the world – the end of *your* world.'

'What's your name?'

'I don't think that's –'

'Your name!'

'. . . Peter Thwaites.'

'Why did you turn up today, Peter?' Drummond consulted his watch, looked back at the man and added, 'You know damned well I'm meeting with Edouard Duval in a couple of hours' time. Don't you?'

'I was told it was urgent, that's all.'

'Told? By whom?'

'Someone telephoned me this morning, anonymously.'

'How else?' Drummond laughed outright. 'First a bunch of letters, now a mysterious telephone call. What next, I wonder?'

'I've done nothing unlawful.'

'Of course you haven't! That's not how you *function*, is it? You prefer to waltz bold as brass into this office and expect me to believe that a potential client is a fleshly incarnation of evil. Have you any idea how that sounded to an ear like mine? Or didn't you give it any thought? Did you just assume I'd go along with whatever you said?'

'I prayed for you.'

'I'll bet you did! I think I'd pray too if I were about to embark on such a stupid exercise!'

'What I've told you is the truth.'

'No. Not the truth, Mr Thwaites – *your* truth. There's a difference.'

'The tru –'

'You're obeying blind orders, damn it! You're being used. Someone is playing games and you're nothing more than a pawn.'

Thwaites shook his head adamantly. 'We're *all* onto the Frenchman,' he said back. 'The Christian community right across Europe knows what he's up to. It's common knowledge. And now he's here in Britain to personally establish yet another offshoot of his damnable organization. But it's not going to take root here, Mr Drummond. We'll stop him somehow!'

Picking up the blue folder, Drummond opened it, searched through it and found the article describing Duval's success in speaking to Salesian priests and Church of England clergy. He handed the folder to the little man without comment, waited for a response.

'Typical!'

'These people aren't slouches. I don't think even Duval could fool them for more than a few minutes.'

'You don't understand what's going on. The established churches are basically secular in outlook, and the Roman Church in particular is nothing more than a business. Its pomp and splendour spells that fact out beyond contradiction, as does the Church of England's. The Vatican's nothing more than a political machine, and the Church of England wants to be part of that machine at all costs. Both parties want to consolidate their power base – even at the expense of a few doctrines. And it would surprise you how many priests and clergymen are into the same practices as Duval. Mantras. Meditation. Yoga. Trance-inducing states they laughingly call *prayer.* They're all into it. And none of it is of God, Mr Drummond – it's of the Devil. So of course they respond to what he has to say. That doesn't surprise me in the least!'

'You're saying they aren't really Christian.'

'Their intelligentsia are completely corrupted.'

'All of them?'

'So many of them it hardly matters.'

'So it's up to people like you to put the world straight, eh?'

'It's our spiritual duty.' Thwaites rubbed at his hairline in exasperation. 'Duval's going to become the central focus of all of this. Can't you understand that? He's going to use you and every other means at his disposal to propagate his hellish doctrines. And as one would imagine, he has of course got bottomless financial resources. Have you asked yourself where the money's coming from? Have you asked yourself *anything* about this man? I doubt it very much. I think you're more interested in what you're going to make out of it all, the hundreds of thousands of pounds you're going to rake in by turning a blind eye to what he's actually up to. You've accused me of obeying blind orders, but it's you who's going to be doing the obeying. That's why I had to come here today, stupid as it may seem to you. You're the key to the whole thing getting off the ground in this country. Those who supplied me with the information are well aware of that fact. What you have to understand is that it isn't some kind of conspiracy we're involved in, Mr Drummond. We don't go around beating people up to make our point as you seem to think. We're just ordinary people, good Christian people, and we're fighting to save what's left of the Christian faith in this supposed democracy of ours.'

'Money,' said Drummond quietly, 'is not my only concern in life. I don't expect you to believe that, but I can assure you that it is the case. If I detect anything untoward in what my client is doing, or intends to do, then I'll withdraw immediately. No agreement has been arrived at yet.'

'Then I suggest you challenge him on the issues I've raised.'

'I'm in no position to challenge anyone on such things. I don't know anything about them. But I've got eyes, and I've got ears, and I'm thorough in what I do. So you'll just have to trust to Providence that I'll do the right thing.'

'There's no alternative, is there?'

'None. I suggest you leave the whole thing in my hands.'

Peter Thwaites got to his feet without being prompted. His

earlier smugness had completely vanished. 'How long will it take you to reach a decision?'

'Could be couple of weeks. Longer. There's a lot of ground work to be gone through with an account this size.'

'May the Lord guide you.'

'I'll take any help I can get,' said Drummond.

The room into which they were shown was filled with raw November light. There were no curtains, just full-length white muslin screens which seemed to intensify the light and spread it throughout the room evenly. They were on the upper storey. The four large casement windows facing out onto the street had had their panes burnished for the occasion, and there was a smell of freshly dried paint, as elsewhere in the building. A large and rather dull-looking mahogany table surrounded by a cluster of straight-backed chairs dominated the room's centre. But it was what lay under it that drew Drummond's attention. On the floor, and singularly out of place, lay an intricately designed Persian carpet; it looked as though it might fly off any second and take the whole gaunt assembly with it.

Drummond had only a split second in which to register all of this, for in the foreground, towering above his two companions like an emaciated Goliath, stood Edouard Duval. He reminded Drummond of a picture he had once seen of General de Gaulle – and like the General's, Duval's face remained virtually expressionless during the initial greetings and introductions.

'As you can see,' he said haltingly, 'things are as yet somewhat spartan. My apologies.' Then noticing Bill Everton in tow, he gave a little bow of recognition.

First to be introduced was Aretino Lefèbvre, the diplomat identified by John Eglington as part of Duval's board in Paris. He was as small as Peter Thwaites, but well-built, and had a shock of immaculately-cut silver hair and pale blue eyes set in a squarish, almost Germanic, face. He also had the kind of grip one did not associate with diplomats. Then there was Dr James Fisher, psychiatrist and consultant physician to Katharsis in London. According to Duval, this stringy individual in a dark grey worsted suit was also consultant psychiatrist to terminally ill cancer patients in one of London's major hospitals.

'Which one?' asked Drummond.

'Bart's,' the man replied crisply.

'Dr Fisher has been doing research in biofeedback,' said Duval. 'His work is well known.'

Drummond nodded sagely and waited for an explanation. It came. Duval said that in biofeedback the mind was given the chance to take voluntary control of the body's involuntary systems. By way of example he said that patients with severe heart conditions could be taught to control their heartbeat, and there was even the possibility of cancer patients being successfully trained to stem the spread of their disease. Dr Fisher was apparently trying to find the mind-link in spontaneous remission, and was preparing a paper outlining some of his most recent findings for the *British Medical Journal*.

'Sounds exciting,' said Drummond, looking from one man to the other. 'What are the chances of success?'

Dr Fisher smiled. 'Reasonably high, now that Monsieur Duval is involved; he has been most helpful.'

'May I ask in what way?'

'Principally in the defining of the questions that have to be asked. If a question lacks coherence, then the answer to that question must necessarily be equally incoherent.'

'You've known each other long?'

'Only since March.' The psychiatrist smiled at Duval and continued. 'A chance meeting for which I will always be grateful.'

Aretino Lefèbvre said suddenly, 'We've put together quite a team of specialists, Mr Drummond. You'll eventually meet some of them.'

'I'll look forward to that,' said Drummond.

There was a moment of silence. Duval broke it by saying, 'Shall we be seated?' They moved towards the table, split automatically into two groups, settled themselves and waited for Duval to open the meeting. All a shade too formal, Drummond thought, adjusting his body to the chair's austerity. But they were of course dealing with Frenchmen, and the French loved formality. It annoyed him that he had no French, that his schooling had not stretched that far.

'Gentlemen –' Duval delivered his opening remarks, greeted the advertising men for a second time, reiterated what he had said to Everton about his organization's requirements. Then to Drummond's astonishment he added, 'We of course put the whole exercise into the hands of one of the best advertising agencies in Paris – Peyrefitte's. It was they who identified Drummond Advertising as one of the most . . . suitably creative agencies in London. Which is to say that you have been thoroughly vetted and checked, your performance over the last few years analysed and compared with other agencies' both large and small. Nothing has been left to chance. Drummond Advertising has an excellent creative profile – perhaps even better than you know.'

'I'm flattered to hear that,' said Drummond, one of his prime questions having been answered straight off.

'You would of course be working in conjunction with Peyrefitte's. An operation of this size has to have central focus. And there will also be a sharing of ideas, the formation of a creative pool upon which everyone can draw.'

'That's a unique concept,' said Bill Everton, glancing at Drummond. 'Can't quite see how it could work.'

'Ideas – spark off ideas,' said Duval, momentarily at a loss for a word. 'And we would wish a certain continuity.'

'The only problem I see with that,' said Drummond, latching on to the point about continuity, 'is that what works for the Dutch, or the French for that matter, might be quite unsuitable for the English – the British.'

'A sharing of ideas, not a dictating of word formats. There would be no form of creative censorship – that would rather defeat the purpose of choosing agencies with creative flair. All I'm suggesting is that a little guidance will sometimes be necessary, and that where one person comes up with a particularly good idea, an effective and tasteful idea, that idea will be offered to every other agency for evaluation and use. Do I make myself clear?'

'It's an unusual way of doing things.'

'It could make any one agency famous throughout Europe overnight.'

Drummond didn't say anything, he just gave a little nod of the head and began to chew over what that could mean within the terms of prestige. It was quite a carrot. A calculated challenge to get the best out of everyone concerned.

Aretino Lefèbvre spoke up at that point. 'I have something here that might help put the whole thing into a general perspective,' he said, producing a neatly bound sheaf of papers from a small attaché case. 'Along with much that is technical, you'll find a complete breakdown of our requirements, a series of basic guidelines worked out by Peyrefitte's for the formulation of all publicity materials, and a statement of philosophy describing in precise detail the aims and aspirations of those affiliated with Katharsis.' He pushed the sheaf of papers across the table. 'I think you'll find the work already done quite helpful.'

Drummond glanced at the document with interest, noted its apparent thoroughness, and handed it on to Bill Everton for scrutiny. Then in conjunction with his chief executive, and with the assistance of the document supplied, they got down to the business of discussing the ins and outs of what was intended, the operation's scope, the forms of media to be involved, and last but not least the financial arrangements that would have to be set up through the banks. They went on like this for over an hour, having first inquired of Dr fisher whether there would be any repercussions from the Medical Association concerning the ethics of the operation. He assured them at length that everything was strictly legal and above board, and that there was nothing at all to worry about. Then Drummond asked the question he had been dying to ask ever since he arrived. He directed his question at the diplomat.

'Is the French government, in conjunction with other European governments, underwriting this operation?'

'I'm afraid I cannot answer that question,' replied Aretino Lefèbvre. 'All I can say is that my government is fully aware of my involvement, and does not object.'

'Is that an answer to my question in a roundabout way?'

The diplomat smiled, but did not reply.

Drummond kept his eyes on Lefèbvre for a moment, then turned his attention back to Edouard Duval. 'I attended your lecture on Friday evening, Monsieur Duval,' he said, aware of his own flat, policeman-like tone. 'It was fascinating. You said some very interesting things. You also said some very disturbing things. For instance, you said that we were heading for some kind of breakdown in the structure of Western society. An upheaval of some kind. You referred to this upheaval as an *advancing spiritual earthquake*. Do you really believe such an upheaval to be imminent?'

The philosopher stared back unblinkingly. 'Yes, I believe such an upheaval to be imminent, Mr Drummond.'

'You have evidence to uphold this view?'

'Yes.'

'Statistical evidence?'

'Yes, and quite beyond dispute.'

A frown formed on Drummond's face. 'Hasn't there always been a problem in interpreting statistical evidence?'

'Your colleague suggested to me when last we met that statistical evidence could not generally be trusted. I told him that the figures we possess are quite beyond dispute, that they have been confirmed by some of the finest analysts in Europe, and in this country. I'm afraid the progressions are too blatant for any kind of mistake to have been made.'

'Government analysts,' said Everton, remembering.

'So how long have we got?'

Silence.

'Twenty years? Ten?' Drummond looked from one face to another. 'Less than ten?'

'It could happen in as little as two, according to some forecasts.'

'Two? Social upheaval across the Western world within two years?'

'Less, if we're unlucky.'

Drummond shot a look of incredulity at the philosopher. 'What's going to happen? Do you know that as well?'

'We have a fair idea.' He marshalled his thoughts, and proceeded to stun both Drummond and Everton with a grocery list of descriptions. 'Mass hysteria such as hasn't been seen since the Middle Ages. Infectious hallucinations. A resurgence of magical beliefs quite beyond anything being witnessed at the moment. The democratic process used to place figures of cultic importance in high office. A fast deterioration of the Christian community into vigilante groups. A return of diseases believed to have been long since conquered, and an outbreak of diseases unknown to medical science. And the belief that such diseases are the hand of God striking down selected parts of the general community. Superstition run riot. Miracles at every street corner. An almost complete breakdown in law and order – a prejudicial *use* of law and order, that is. And general psychic collapse to a point where many individuals will not be able to tell the difference between reality and dream. Shall I go on?'

'All of that in a couple of years from now?'

'The initial build-up is already under way. All that's required is a series of triggers to set the ball in motion.' A weariness crept into his face. 'Incidents of unbelievable ferocity will act as triggers. The unreason produced will spread rapidly.'

'Why?'

'Because in general terms, Mr Drummond, we are at the end of our tether, and cannot escape our frustrations through war. Not this time.'

'You expect to function in the midst of such madness?' said Bill Everton.

Duval's reply again surprised both men. He said that Katharsis would be disbanded before the worst struck; it was their hope to have accomplished what they had set out to do before the point of no return was reached. This was possible because it was not their intention to treat the general public through the Centres presently being set up, but to train many thousands of therapists and release them into the society as fluid commando groups. Such groups would immediately enlist the help of those unaffected by the hysteria and set up therapeutic cells where those only partly affected could receive treatment. The Frenchman smiled quite genuinely at that point and said that the whole complicated edifice was of course nothing more than an up-dated version of the Resistance.

'You must be pretty sure of your techniques,' said Drummond, trying to digest the scenario presented. 'I'd have thought there was as much chance of your therapists' succumbing as anyone else's.'

'We're banking on an 85 per cent success rate.'

'What will you do, brainwash them?'

A tiny smile from the philosopher. 'Hardly. We will simply introduce them to themselves on a deeper level, Mr Drummond. That's all. They will each take it from there and work on their own.'

'You make it sound simple.'

'The process is simple, but the results are highly complex. We are complex creatures.'

'So why the emphasis on healing?'

Duval paused, blinked, but did not ask Drummond where he had got his information from. 'Not really an emphasis, Mr

Drummond. Physical healing is a natural by-product of the techniques we have evolved; it was one of those unexpected bonuses of our initial research, and a welcome one. We are still exploring the implications.'

'And that's where I come in,' said Dr Fisher. He put his palms together, and agitatedly communicated his next statement as if pained by something. 'Some very important work is being done here – *very* important work. I feel privileged to be part of it.' The man's controlled nervousness held Drummond's attention, reminding him of Dr Freeman's difficulty in expressing himself when talking of what he had learned in only a few minutes from one of Duval's colleagues. The words which followed further aligned the two men. 'A whole new perspective on what it means to be a human being, on what it means to be a living being, is rapidly coming into focus for all of us as a result of Monsieur Duval's efforts. My own patients are already reaping the benefits, and the theoretical work I'm engaged in has been substantially advanced by the Maestro's willingness to share his findings.' A pause in this little drama as Dr Fisher sought to round off his thoughts; then a final statement of allegiance curiously out of character with the man's aloof bearing. 'I can therefore say without hesitation that I fully support Monsieur Duval in everything he is attempting to do.'

Accepting the psychiatrist's assurance with a little nod, and a smile, Drummond addressed his next question to all three men. 'Why don't you just hand over your findings to as many people as possible? Wouldn't that be the most sensible thing to do?'

'And run the risk of starting a panic reaction that could bring the whole thing to a head before we're ready? No. I think not.' The speed of Duval's delivery, and the look of concern on his face spoke volumes to Drummond. 'We have as a matter of duty informed the French government of the dangers – but to be perfectly honest with you, we haven't quite told them everything for fear of precipitous moves on their part. Governments are quite unpredictable in how they choose to handle certain situations – they fear their own demise more than anything else. And they have awesome power at their disposal. So only Monsieur Lefèbvre has been fully briefed.'

'Aren't you taking a hell of a gamble blurting all of this out to us?' said Bill Everton.

'Can't you be trusted?' asked Duval, his expression conveying feigned innocence.

'Of course!' Everton's face reflected real innocence as he walked into Duval's trap. 'But you can't know that for sure.'

'I do now. You've just told me.'

'That –'

'Doesn't make sense? Perhaps not. But that is how things must be if we are to work with one another.'

It was a trick similar to the one Duval had used on the psychologist Rosemary Waters, and it threw Everton completely. But unlike Rosemary Waters, he fell silent, for he sensed profundity in Duval's manoeuvre.

Continuing as if what had been said about a breakdown in Western consciousness was a *fait accompli*, Drummond took the plunge and said, 'I suppose you realize you've got enemies – quite a few, if what I was told this morning has any truth in it.' He went on to detail Peter Thwaites' visit, and what had been said. The accusations tabled by Thwaites brought a sigh of frustration from the diplomat, but did not elicit a response from Duval. 'So it would seem that someone's trying to stir up trouble behind the scenes. Were you aware that this kind of thing was going on?'

'There have been indications,' said Duval; he clasped his hands in front of him and continued. 'The Christian fundamentalists simply cannot grasp the fact that the universe is a little more complicated than they themselves believe it to be. There's no room in their system of thought for either experimentation or exploration. God is on His throne, Satan is on the loose, and anyone who dares question that rather neat little scenario is automatically in trouble. And as we head towards the centre of the cyclone, and the pressures increase, this kind of thinking will spring up in the most unexpected quarters. For the truth of the matter is this: Christianity has for too long prided itself in being a complete revelation, a revelation to which nothing can be added, and from which nothing can be subtracted. This has resulted in a closed spiritual system which must by its very nature feed continually on its own original energies until there is nothing left but dead symbols. Fundamentalism is an attempt to renew those energies, but it is an attempt doomed to failure because it must necessarily regress and not progress, attach itself to already superseded spiritual ideas and make them appear to live through a huge investment of emotional energy. It's a very dangerous psychological state to be in, and the established Church, Catholic and Protestant, has only itself to thank for the monumental problems such groups spawn by their very existence. If the Church is to survive at all, it must break out of the spiritual double-bind it itself has created and sustained for almost two thousand years, and the only way it can do that is by being brutally truthful about its own limited system of belief.'

'You believe that's possible?'

'I believe that the Church has no longer any option, Mr Drummond. It either wakes up and shoulders its spiritual and intellectual responsibilities, or it dies by its own hand.'

'Knowing that doesn't quite remove the problem of how to deal with the fundamentalists ganging up on you. Or for that matter the faceless individuals intent on stirring them up. Have you any idea who those faceless individuals might be?'

'We're acutely aware of their existence.'

'Fine. But who are they? And why pick on Katharsis?'

It was Aretino Lefèbvre who replied. He said that what had to be understood was that certain groups of people were already sensing the approach of the breakdown to come, but that due to their belief systems they were interpreting what they quite accurately sensed as their own particular vision as what was about to be fulfilled. Each group was convinced that their vision – and their vision alone – would soon be accepted on a wide front as the most naturally beneficial paradigm. The sectarian fundamentalists saw themselves ushering in the new Kingdom of God, and the magical fraternity were just as convinced that their collective stance would become the accepted vision of the day. But some groups were of course a little more manipulative than others, more Machiavellian in their tactics, and it was one such group that was now attempting to harness and organize the fundamentalists against Katharsis.

'But why specifically Katharsis?'

'Because we are fast becoming a high-profile target. The work we are attempting to do challenges such people on just about every level imaginable – it did not take long for news of our approach to get out. And we have of course stepped on quite a few philosophical toes, not to mention political ones.'

'You're beginning to sound like the meat in a sandwich.'

A smile from Lefèbvre. 'I think they'll find the meat tougher than expected.'

Drummond blinked, wondering what the diplomat might mean by that. He turned his attention back to Duval and said, 'I've had a few problems of my own over the last few weeks. On the 16th of November our offices were ransacked for no apparent reason – I was attacked in my own home in the early hours of the same morning. The person who attacked me was a professional with a rather odd sense of humour: a picture postcard of the Arc de Triomphe was left propped up in the kitchen for me to find when I recovered. The card was addressed to me and had been taken from the letterbox a few days earlier. There was a rather odd inscription on the card, in Latin – I thought it was from a friend, but it wasn't. The attacker used it to make a point.' Including the others in his monologue, he continued dryly. 'On one level I was being informed that someone had easy access to my apartment, and I was being asked in a very round about way to think about that – it was obviously supposed that I had enough of a brain to realize what was being said to me. But on another level, my attention was being drawn to things French, particularly things Parisian, and at that moment in time I had no idea of the approach soon to be made on behalf of Katharsis by Monsieur Duval. Then on Friday evening, directly after your lecture, Monsieur, I was attacked a second time – unsuccessfully, I'm pleased to say – by two young thugs quite obviously hired on an impromptu basis. This either means that I'm being watched, and followed, or that your telephone invitation was overheard by someone in your employ and passed on. Then this morning, as I mentioned earlier, I had to sit and listen to the abominable Mr Peter Thwaites telling me in all seriousness that the purpose behind Katharsis was social and spiritual disruption on an unimaginable scale. Thwaites was informed of this meeting anonymously. Now I don't know how many people were privy to our arrangement, but considering what you've told me over the last couple of hours, I would suggest a tightening of your security on all fronts.'

The atmosphere of the meeting changed in that moment. Duval remained his impassive self, but the diplomat again exhibited anger and frustration. It was quite obvious to Drummond that the subject of 'security' had arisen on other occasions, and that there was some dissension between the two men on how it should be handled. Even Dr Fisher huffed and puffed a little. When things settled, Duval said that greater care would be taken in future, that they had tried to avoid a siege mentality, and that he was truly sorry that violence had so soon entered the picture. He then asked Drummond what had been written on the card.

'*Quos* something or other,' said Drummond. 'I'm afraid I don't have a copy.'

'*Quos Deus vult perdere, prius dementat*?'

A look of astonishment from Drummond. 'I think that's it!'

'Those whom God would destroy, He first drives mad.'

'That's what it means?'

'It's quite a well-known quotation, but I may of course have chosen incorrectly.'

'I think you got it in one.'

'But you have no idea whom it may have been from?'

'None,' said Drummond.

'Then it is perhaps synchronous.' The philosopher smiled. 'A coincidence. An unusual coming together of factors quite unrelated, but made to relate in time and space by a – quirk of timing. Some would think such a happening prophetic.'

'What's your opinion?'

'I simply do not know.'

Drummond smiled, put aside the factor of violence and tackled the next priority on his mental list. 'It was our hope that you might let us see something of what you actually do here,' he said, taking the reins again. 'Would that be possible?'

'It was our intention,' replied Duval, glancing at Dr Fisher, 'to put on a little demonstration of our techniques, but things did not quite work out as planned. My apologies.'

Drummond's disappointment was obvious. Straightening he said, 'That's a pity. I'd very much have liked to see . . . well, anything.'

The philosopher's expression changed from apology to that of interest. 'Then perhaps you would be willing to take part in a little experiment – a demonstration, with yourself as subject?' He added quickly, 'You have of course every right to decline.'

'What would it entail?'

'A standard procedure. We would induce a state of mind not dissimilar to that experienced at the entrance to sleep – which is to say that you would be balanced exactly between sleep and wakefulness. You would in other words be perfectly capable of discontinuing at any time.'

'I'd still be in control?'

'Exactly. We've called the technique *Protasis.* The word comes from the Greek and refers to an actual technique used in the ancient theatre of Greece to introduce the audience to the characters and plot of a play. In our use of the term, however, the word "play" takes on new meaning and significance. What the subject interacts with is a visual *replay* of something known to the self, but pushed to one side due to the pressures and distractions of living. It is in other words a *play of mind*; or if you prefer, the mind *at play* without restriction. I think you might find the experience quite fascinating.'

A ball of panic formed in Drummond's stomach. 'How do you bring about this . . . play of mind?'

'By the simplest possible means. Two of my best therapists will put their hands on your head and hum to themselves in a special interactive pattern. It's a kind of singing. It results in a special reverberative tone being set up which somehow changes the subject's brain rhythms. It's a very ancient shamanic technique. I discovered it when travelling in Central Asia some years ago. Takes about twenty minutes to set everything in motion.'

'And it always produces the same kind of experience?'

'Without fail.'

Drummond found what Duval was saying difficult to accept, but he knew there must be something in it for the man to be so certain of a result. 'Sounds odd,' he said, wondering if he should agree or not.

'Quantum theory is odd,' replied Duval. He laughed suddenly. 'In fact the whole universe is rather odd.'

'It's never seemed particularly odd to me.'

'Never?'

'Maybe I've been too busy to notice – too busy dealing with the real world.'

'Are your dreams of the real world?'

'They reflect the real world.'

'Are they in themselves real?'

'Of course not.'

'And therefore have no significance?'

'None.'

'You've never been disturbed by your dreams?'

'Only if I happen to have a nightmare.'

'And then?'

Unnerved by the fact that Duval seemed to be closing in on him with the accuracy of a guided missile, Drummond said, 'I just accept the fact that some dreams are totally crazy.'

'But on occasions you suspect that that is not wholly the truth, that you are perhaps avoiding something of immense subtlety. Correct?'

'Yes. But in the cold light of day I see that as succumbing to superstition in a moment of weakness.' He added inspirationally, 'Idi Amin thought his dreams were meaningful. He caused chaos in Uganda because of that belief.'

'Amin,' replied Duval, seemingly unperturbed by Drummond's stroke of brilliance, 'believed his dreams to be prophecies; he interpreted them only in that vein. While in power he constructed a terrible reality out of his dreams, consciously bent and distorted them until they fitted in with his insatiable appetites. But that was a problem brought about through conscious interference with dream structure. It was a literal, and therefore primitive, approach backed by paranoia and a thirst for power – the Christian fundamentalists are similarly literal in their interpretation of the Bible. In our approach, dreams and dream-like structures are not wrested out of their natural medium and forced to coalesce with everyday reality. They are allowed to speak for themselves in the intermediary world between sleep and wakefulness. Now it may very well be that a dream is pointing quite directly at something in the supposed outer reality, the awake reality, but we cannot ever be sure of what is being said to us if we interpret only from the daylight side of the line. Common respect for the deeper aspects of our own psychology demands that we meet our dreams halfway, that we stand without prejudice on the threshold of our dreaming and allow that which is sacred to speak to that which is profane. It is a form of deep contemplation, or meditation, and it can afford startling results.'

'You can actually induce this state?'

'It was an initiatory rite for shamanic apprentices – they were of course expected to eventually perfect "threshold sitting" on their own.'

Caught between his own insistence on some kind of technical demonstration, and Duval's apparently innocent proposal, Drummond laughed nervously and said, 'I'll take part on the condition that my colleague is with me at all times.'

'But of course.' A look verging on pleasure appeared on Duval's face. He suggested immediately that they break for coffee, instructed the psychiatrist to inform the appropriate therapists of their intention. Then he said, 'If you would prefer tea, or wine, that too can be supplied.'

'I'll stick with coffee,' said Drummond, wondering what the hell he had let himself in for.

The therapy room was large, inadequately lit, and quite cold. The only source of light was from a red bulb hanging naked at the room's centre – a bulb directly beneath which sat a straight-backed chair identical to those in the conference room. Drummond glanced at the chair, then at Bill Everton: the idea of sitting on that chair frightened him somehow. For the chair spoke of isolation, the red bulb and the light it cast of things – indecent? And on top of all this was the fact of not knowing for sure what it was that Duval hoped to accomplish – apart from prove that the technique was founded on some kind of psychological reality – and his own growing fear of revealing to all present some deeply buried and embarrassing aspect of himself in spite of the assurances given.

So it was with trepidation that he finally seated himself and listened as Duval delivered instructions in rapid French to the two young therapists who had followed them in. They were male, identical twins, casually dressed, and in their mid-twenties. Then with raised palms Duval indicated to the others that they should move back, right back into the shadows. The therapists automatically took up position behind Drummond, but did not speak.

'I suggest,' said Duval, turning back to Drummond, 'that you take ten deep breaths so that you can relax a little. But I want you to fill your lungs so that you cannot get any more air into them, then empty them completely. Do you understand?'

A nod from Drummond.

'Please start.'

A look of approval from the philosopher as Drummond took his first deep breath and exhaled. 'Excellent!' Duval began to move back slowly, counting the breaths out loud, constantly encouraging Drummond. When he reached the limit of the light's efficiency, he stopped. 'Five . . .' Straightening to his full height, he stood like a soldier on parade. 'Six . . .' The therapists brought their hands up and stationed them a few inches above Drummond's head. 'Seven . . .' His arms folded tightly into his body to ward off the chill air, Bill Everton stared at the scene in disbelief. 'Eight . . .' A start to the humming which quite surprised Drummond and almost caused him to look over his shoulder. 'Nine . . .' The low, reverberative sound washing through him as he completed the breath cycle. 'Ten . . .'

The therapists brought their hands into contact with Drummond's head as Duval closed his eyes; their humming changed pitch in that moment, dropped, but immediately returned to the original level. Drummond had the distinct impression of becoming suddenly heavier, then lighter. Another change in pitch, only sustained this time, the two young men expertly alternating their breath patterns to create an illusion of sound continuity. Then the humming swooped up to a much higher register and remained there, the previously detectable breaks disappearing completely – at least, that's how it seemed to Drummond, as he sat there, the warmth of the therapists' hands producing an effect not unlike that of a knitted skull-cap pulled down to the brow: a cap within which the sound of his heartbeat was curiously amplified. His eyes closed involuntarily as he listened to that sound, became fascinated by the regular beat of that giant pulse over and above that of the other sounds being emitted. He could not remember ever having heard the beat of his heart so clearly, so – overwhelmingly near. It was all-encompassing and all-absorbing. It seemed to fill his mind and suggest sleep, invite him to descend into a welcoming darkness and allow all his cares and fears to float off into a gentle oblivion. Another change of pitch interrupted this siren-like beckoning. Then, quite unexpectedly, there was a tailing off into total silence.

Should he open his eyes and take a peek at what was going on? A smile on Drummond's face as he sat there, his heartbeat continuing to sound in his skull, the silence developing into an almost tangible stillness. He kept his eyes shut and slowly became aware of a lovely amberish glow radiating from somewhere behind his head – an amberishness which reminded him of something. He searched his memory without success, felt the presence of what he had forgotten nudge at him, but failed in his attempt to consciously identify it. Then again quite unexpectedly the therapists picked up on the sound they had allowed to tail off into obscurity, and the amber glow blazed out in response. The sound of his heart became drum-like in that moment, changed to that of a giant bird beating its wings as it descended into the therapy room – to tear him to pieces? He could see the huge talons and beak in his imagination, the cold eye of the bird staring down at him as it descended, air-breaking itself into strike position. Someone coughed and he immediately incorporated the sound into the scene.

No fear in him as the giant bird – an eagle? – reached him and began to tear his head apart with its hooked beak, its talons resting on his shoulders. His head was quickly and painlessly consumed, along with his shoulders and arms and upper trunk; yet he felt quite intact, and knew that his being digested was an act of friendship on the bird's part, a releasing of himself from himself, from his fears and secret agonies, his insecurities and his immaculately manicured surface notion of what it meant to be a human being. Nothing of him left eventually, nothing at all.

Silence.

A silence and a stillness beyond imagination striated with channels of memory which drew him this way and that until he was again aware of that curious amberishness, that soft play of ambered light radiating out as if from a setting sun upon which he had turned his back.

An amber sunset?

There had been an amber sunset in his dream the night he was attacked. It had tinted the rooftops of the houses, softened their extravagantly carved and garishly painted exteriors. He could remember the smell of the streets. He could remember the warm, silky air through which he had seemed to glide, or swim, as he tracked down the house with its frontal staircase of stone. A contrived nonchalance. The streets ought not to be – ought not to have been so empty. He was being watched from behind those shuttered windows, his every movement silently relayed, perhaps with a nod, a raised eyebrow or the backward flick of a hand, to other interested parties. Of this he had been certain. For he could feel presences and detect infinitesimal changes in the density of the ambered air as he swam-glided towards his destination. Their fear had betrayed them. He could smell their fear, sense their excitement and breathless fascination as they noted his progress. But there had been nothing – was nothing of note in his movements to alert them to the fact that he had penetrated their scheme and was already engaged in the task of outwitting them; and that in spite of their clear advantage. It was still possible to accomplish the deed, deftly and swiftly execute it in their very midst without their even realizing that the blow had been struck, that their confidence was not only mistaken but laughable.

But first there would have to be a moment of magic, an illusion of powers released, a veritable disappearing act through which a momentary confusion could be sown. He stopped, spun slowly but with gathering speed so that his monk's cloak might billow out, and out, to form a cone. And from out of this cone, having perfectly gauged angle and distance, he slipped from light into shade, leaving the gyrating garment to fall flat and empty on the street's uneven surface . . . A man of shadow . . . winging his way toward . . . with a surety of movement which delighted and exhilarated him . . . invisible even to himself . . .

Perplexed and genuinely alarmed by what he was witnessing, Bill Everton watched Drummond toss his head from side to side as if looking at, or for, something. And still the therapists held onto him, their hands following his every movement, their eyes fixed on Duval, their pursed lips continuing to produce those eerie notes. The philosopher's physical stance now verged on the extraordinary. He had buckled outwards from the middle, taking on the shape of a strung bow; it seemed almost as if he were suspended from wires – singing wires. Whereas to Drummond, caught as he was between two worlds, everything appeared to be quite normal – doubly normal. He was sitting on a chair remembering the end of a dream he had forgotten, and was on the point of discovering the identity of the man he had been hired to kill. It was exciting and totally absorbing, the images and sensations so real he had to work at remembering that it was only a dream. By sheer trickery and effrontery he had talked his way into the house and was now stepping into the room where his victim waited. And the fact that it was a dream, and that he knew it was a dream, was allowing him the exquisite freedom of carrying out the dream's self-evident purpose without fear or hesitancy. The man would die. He was determined that the man would die.

Everything suddenly went haywire.

As the man turned towards him, someone yelled out and Drummond reeled back shocked by the fact that his quarry had been warned. He glanced around fully expecting an attack, but there was no one else in the room. So where had the voice come from? There was just himself and the man in the white robe standing at the window with his arms held defencelessly apart. If he were going to kill him it would have to be done now, and quickly. He moved in, but did not deliver the fatal blow due to further disruption: the collapse of Edouard Duval. As Duval toppled backwards, the two therapists deserted their patient, so breaking the link. Drummond's eyes opened immediately to stare at the scene in unbelief. The philosopher was a heap on the floor and the two young men were already by his side. Bill Everton was standing quite stationary only a few feet away, and Aretino Lefèbvre and Dr Fisher were rushing over to lend a hand. It was like stepping from one bizarre dream into another. He closed his eyes to reorient himself, and snapped them back open immediately – the other reality was still in place. With his eyes open there was Bill Everton within a few feet. With his eyes closed there was this other man staring at him blankly. All he had to do was keep his eyes closed and the man would die. Or keep them open and he would live. An outrageous thought formed in Drummond's mind. He could kill the man and escape from that house by simply opening his eyes. That was when he realized he was in trouble.

Duval returned to consciousness in the same moment, rallied his senses and directed the two therapists to attend to their patient. But as they ran towards Drummond, he got to his feet and backed away, knocking over the chair. The two realities had merged. There he stood for a moment, expressionless, an imaginary knife in his hand. Duval shouted something in French and the young men stopped in their tracks. Then with remarkable control Duval said in English, 'I suggest you speak to him, Mr Everton, he will perhaps respond to your voice.'

But there was no need. What Drummond could see suddenly evaporated, leaving him with consensus reality. 'I'm out of it,' he said, swaying a little.

Assisted by Aretino Lefèbvre, Duval got up. He was badly shaken by the incident. Dispatching Dr Fisher with a hand signal, he leaned heavily on the diplomat and waited for the diagnosis on Drummond's condition. Fisher examined Drummond's eyes with a slim pencil torch, checked his pulse, said that everything appeared to be normal. Duval had him double-check.

'What the hell happened?' asked Drummond, when Dr Fisher was finished with him.

'A disturbance,' said Duval, explaining nothing. 'The shock of it made me black out.' He drew breath, tried to stand on his own. 'I blame myself entirely. I ought to have explained that any sudden interruption could be dangerous.'

Drummond didn't know what to make of the man's statement. 'Will someone please tell me what happened?'

'Your colleague,' said Dr Fisher quite without Duval's forgiving tone, 'yelled out at the top of his voice. He apparently thought things were not quite as they ought to be.'

'I thought you were having a fit,' said Bill Everton, using an old-fashioned term. 'You were lashing about all over the place.'

'Purely reflex,' said the psychiatrist testily. 'The movements were dream movements and perfectly normal.'

'You call what was going on normal?'

'Merely motor nerves acting independently of the will under a stimulus from impressions made on the sensory system,' Dr Fisher bulleted back. 'It must surely have been obvious to you that we weren't in the least worried.'

'I wasn't looking at you!' said Bill, as angry as Drummond had ever seen him. He then pointed at Duval and said, 'And what I could see of him over there didn't exactly inspire confidence!'

Duval tried to defuse the situation. 'I quite understand what prompted you to shout out the way you did, and I accept full responsibility.'

'It was downright scary!'

The pieces having fallen into place, Drummond said, 'I wasn't really in any kind of trouble, Bill. I was dreaming. It was incredibly real.' He would liked to have added *You saved a man's life*, but thought better of it.

A long look from Bill Everton, followed by a gesture of unwilling acceptance. 'Okay, if you say so,' he said, feeling suddenly terribly awkward. He looked towards Duval. 'I'm sorry.'

The philosopher, standing now without assistance, delivered one of his General de Gaulle nods, and asked Drummond how he felt.

'I'm okay.' said Drummond.

'We should perhaps discuss what you experienced.'

Drummond hesitated, decided to decline the offer for Bill's sake; he could feel the man's agitation radiating out of him like heat. 'No, I think we'd better get back,' he said. Then for some unknown reason he added, 'It wasn't really a terribly important dream – just the usual kind of thing.'

'But you found the experience worthwhile?'

'Most certainly. Fascinating. In that respect, absolutely unique. I'm impressed.'

'And you feel no ill effects whatsoever.'

'None. I'm right as rain now.'

'Please ring me immediately if you sense *anything* untoward. Your system has been subjected to quite a shock, as has mine. Will you do that?'

'Of course. But I really don't think there's anything to worry about. Honest.'

'I have never doubted your honesty,' said Duval, with just a trace of a smile.

Chapter Eight

Georgia sat listening in the big armchair among the oatmeal cushions, her slender figure sprawled out, her face momentarily turned away from him as he spoke, her eyes taking in the immaculate sterility of expensive furniture chosen and arranged and stationed by Patricia with such maddening perfection: good taste become bad taste without anyone's noticing. A glance at Drummond, a shake of the head and a small expulsion of air from between lips still wet from her tongue playing on their surface as she tried to digest what she was hearing. Drummond sat in the chair opposite, whisky glass in hand, struggling to paint an exact verbal picture of what he had experienced during Duval's 'protasis' experiment. A dream become reality. A dream functioning momentarily as an alternative reality. Preposterous, all of it. And then the totally unbelievable to round the whole thing off – the realities mixed and shaken together like an explosive cocktail.

Not knowing what to make of what she was hearing, Georgia said, 'If it were anyone other than yourself telling me this, Ian, I wouldn't believe them.'

He smiled in response, went on to describe his feeling of panic when he realized that he was caught between the two worlds, that he had actually considered using the situation to kill his quarry and escape from that room. That had been the moment of truth, he said, the moment in which his mind had rebelled against what was happening within its own confines and he had clawed his way up out of that chair. Never, never in his life had he felt as he felt then.

She stared at him, unable to adjust to his insistence that he had experienced his dream as a reality indistinguishable from the reality now confronting them. She couldn't get to grips with that.

She accepted what he was saying because he was saying it – she had no reason to doubt him – but at the same time could not help rejecting the essence of what was being said because of its strangeness. It was all too strange for words, and words were all Drummond had at his disposal

'It surely wasn't that real,' she said, in search of an exact bearing.

'It was,' he replied starkly. 'I was in a completely different world and it was as real as this one.'

Georgia immediately corrected him by saying, 'It *appeared* to be as real, Ian.'

'Okay.' He smiled at her again, conveying the impression of accepting her definition by way of sufferance. 'It only *appeared* to be totally and utterly and incontrovertibly real. The man I had been sent to kill only *appeared* to be flesh and blood. The door handle and the door and the floorboards and the window and the stink of the place . . .' He exhaled with a kind of exasperation. 'I'll tell you something for nothing, Georgia – I was completely fooled.'

Georgia went straight for the central issue. 'I think the shock of Bill's yelling out like that has confused you more than you know. You've already admitted that you ended up not knowing which reality you were in, that they had collapsed into one another, that you couldn't tell the difference and had begun to imagine that you could affect the one from the other. Right?' She waited until he nodded in assent before continuing. 'Well, doesn't that explain why you think your dream was as real as us sitting here talking about it? The shock caused you to imbue your dream with a solidity and tangibility it probably didn't possess up until that moment. Okay, so I'm guessing, but I'd rather guess along those lines than accept the improbable notion of our dreams being some kind of alternative reality.' She began to laugh at the ridiculousness of it all. 'Whatever you say about it, Ian, it was a dream. That's all.' Ticking off the points she had made on her fingertips to drive them home, she then said, 'Of course that still leaves a couple of things unexplained.'

'Such as?'

'Why this protasis thing does what it does. Where the hell did he pick up a trick like that?'

'Asia.'

'That's what he said?'

'Something to do with shamans?'

Georgia almost choked. 'Was he being serious?'

'I think so. He's hardly ever anything else but serious.'

'Funny kind of philosopher if he's into shamanism.'

'You're not the first to have pointed that out.' He told Georgia about Peter Thwaites, about the letter and telephone call, and went on to mention the reaction of Duval and his colleagues to the suggestion that their security wasn't as hot as it ought to be. 'I don't think everything's quite sweetness and light in the Duval camp,' he added, remembering Aretino Lefèbvre's annoyance over the security leak and Dr Fisher's rather astonishing lack of patience and tact when dealing with Bill's *faux pas*. 'I think Duval's idealism gets in the way at times.'

'He sounds like an absolute oddball to me.'

'Not an oddball, Georgia – just odd in the way he handles things sometimes.'

'Shamanism?' she said, giving Drummond a look.

'It worked.'

As there was no way to argue with him on that, she said, 'He certainly seems to have attracted the right people.'

'I would imagine Lefèbvre was probably foisted on him by the French government, but Fisher's definitely a convert. You can hear it in his voice when he speaks.' He made a face and added, 'Can't say I like the man much.'

'So what happens next?'

'I've arranged to have a private chat with Duval on Wednesday. Just the two of us.'

'To what end?'

Drummond hesitated. '– There are a few things I'd like further clarification on.'

'I'd say that was the understatement of the year.' She tilted her head questioningly. 'You really do want to take this account on, don't you?'

'Wouldn't you?'

'You said yourself that it might prove professionally embarrassing.'

'I think it's going to prove more challenging than embarrassing,' he said back, examining his fingernails. He looked up. 'My instincts tell me that Duval's on the level, Georgia, and I don't buck my instincts. My instincts also tell me that I'd be mad to pass up on the opportunity of being associated with a set of front-runner ideas such as Duval's in the process of developing. Fisher's no mug. He's in there getting everything he can out of the situation. And if a man like that is willing to put his neck on the chopping-block, then there must be something pretty interesting going on.' Taking a sip of whisky, he completed his evaluation with something Georgia had overlooked, something which a Scotsman in particular could not overlook: two attacks on his person to frighten him off the Katharsis account. 'They aren't going to get away with that!' he said, glowering at her, his tone as dull as gun-metal.

'What does Bill think?' she asked, ignoring his Scottish bravado.

'He's licking his wounds from this afternoon and trying to be polite about the whole thing. Gave me a hard time when we got back.'

'He's against taking on the account?'

'It's just his Catholicism's getting in the way – and the fact that he lost face. He'll come round.'

'You haven't any qualms at all?'

'Only questions.' He put down his empty glass and seemed to search the air for his next statement. 'I've never been so intrigued by anything in my life. Duval's tapped into some very powerful stuff, and if what he believes about Western society is in any way true, then he's probably the only person in existence with the requisite skills and knowledge to help us get out of the mess we're heading for. It's a helluva scenario to be involved in. It excites me. And what I experienced this afternoon made me realize yet again that there's definitely a bit more to living on this planet than I'd thought. Up until a few days ago, I was of the opinion that being on this planet was a rather crass joke we simply had to put up with. I'm not so sure about that now. There are ways of getting below the surface. I'd hate to think in years to come that I'd walked away from the opportunity to find out what makes us all tick in such a fantastically silly manner – particularly myself.'

'You'll let me in on it if you find out?'

'I'll run an ad in *The Times*.'

They laughed, sat in silence for a moment, she looking away toward the fireplace, he staring at her as if at a stranger. No longer the problem of seeing her as a kind of sister because of her previous closeness to Patricia. He was free of that distorted and distorting idea now as he sat surveying the woman who had admitted to needing him. That had made all the difference. He had suddenly been capable of reassessing himself, of finding a more attractive portrait of himself within himself. Such a simple little thing, yet so bloody important when it came to functioning in the world as a human being. One of two reasons for him to feel something akin to contentment now as he sat there, empty whisky glass in hand, in that palace of smashed dreams where Patricia had daily exercised her cunning. Another life and another time, but still in his memory like the dream which had almost appeared more real than real. Ghosts were like that, he reasoned: they were so without substance that their ever having appeared at all gave them a false solidity and importance – Patricia the ghost still trying to undermine his confidence like the scolding voice of a parent internalized and allowed to rule the roost as a secondary conscience. But over and above this, Georgia's opening up to him. And on top of it all the sensation of well-being generated by Duval's crazy little experiment. It was as if a window had been flung up somewhere, and a fresh breeze was changing the air in a series of stuffy rooms. What a shame it would be if he allowed things to revert to their old greyness because of a lack of courage and resolve, if he ended up undermining Georgia and acting as Patricia's unconscious plenipotentiary.

'Are you sure you wouldn't like a drink?' he said, holding up his empty glass as if to remind her of what the words meant. She shook her head, said that she'd had sufficient wine over dinner, that she didn't really feel like drinking. He got up and went to the decanter, poured himself a small whisky and almost casually mentioned the highly distressing telephone call from John Eglington just prior to her arrival. 'Sophie's apparently in a bad way,' he said, having had no wish to spoil her earlier enjoyment of their elaborate Indian take-away. 'She's catatonic.' He paused to grimace. 'Out of it all completely, one might say.'

Georgia's reaction was one of shock; it took her a few seconds to reply. 'That's awful!' she said, staring up at him.

'He's at his wits' end. Blames himself for not having been with her enough. Blames himself for everything that's happened. Nothing I could say was of any help.'

'Is the child in hospital?'

'Yes. They brought her up to London.' A sigh from Drummond, and a wry laugh. 'I didn't know anything was wrong at first. He started off by saying that he couldn't keep a lunch appointment we had arranged, then suddenly launched into the real reason for the call. He wept as he told me, Georgia. It was devastating. I didn't know what to say to the man.'

She blinked her astonishment at him, lowered her head stiffly in a vain attempt to digest the horror of it all. 'It's too much for anyone to take in, Ian. He'll crack if he doesn't get support.'

'I'm meeting him tomorrow.'

'At the hospital?'

'No. In a pub.' He smiled. 'That's where most men go when they reach the end of their tether, Georgia. It's our tribal tent. If he wants me at the hospital, I'll soon find out.'

As if reprimanding herself, she said, 'I thought something like this might happen. That's why I suggested Freeman.'

'I can't imagine Freeman dealing with kids,' he replied, remembering the man's austerity. Then a terrible thought struck him – he had quite forgotten to mention Freeman to John Eglington.

'He's wonderful with them!' she said back, unaware of his sudden discomfort, and the fact that she was reinforcing it with her enthusiasm for the man Drummond had cast as religious fanatic in another of his dreams. The dream came back to him without warning and he remembered the figure standing at the altar, and the white robe, and the hands raised in adoration of a gigantic cross. How could he have forgotten that? The man at the altar and the man in the room were one and the same!

'What's the matter, Ian?'

He blinked at her and explained, remembering the monk's cloak on both occasions.

'Same man? Same form of dress?'

'Identical.'

'You're sure about that?'

'If there was any way of proving it, I'd put on a sizable bet.'

'What brought it back?'

'Something you said.' He hesitated in telling her that he had omitted to mention Freeman's name to Eglington, then blurted it out like a small boy to whom guilt was a new discovery. 'Sophie might not be in this mess if I'd remembered.'

'Don't be silly. You're now doing exactly what you told me John's doing.' She further dismissed his act of self-accusation by returning to what he had unexpectedly remembered about the other dream. She asked for details, adding that she had changed her mind about his offer of a drink.

Pouring the last of the red wine they had been imbibing earlier into her discarded glass, he handed it to her and returned to his chair, conscious of the fact that Sophie and her father had been awarded a secondary status. He then described what had been going on in his dream-cathedral, and tried to capture something of his own shock when he had glimpsed Dr Freeman's face. Georgia listened, fascinated, and questioned him. Glad at last to share his nocturnal journeyings with someone, Drummond said that almost all of his recent dreams had been of a similar calibre, revealing that he had held back on that fact as they walked on the Heath.

'You've obviously got it in for Freeman.'

'He got up my nose with all that Catholicism of his. You know how I felt when I left his place.'

He attempted to explain his reaction. 'There were a lot of incredibly religious people in the town I was brought up in. Christian fanatics, Georgia. They were like terrorists. They quite literally brainwashed their adherents until they could think of nothing else but finding souls to save. I think they would have quite happily cut people's throats if there had been any chance of bringing them to Jesus that way. I learned to detest them then, and it's never left me.'

'You sound quite evangelical about it.'

He threw back his head and laughed, acknowledging her point with a slanted look. 'They're all tarred with the same brush as far as I'm concerned,' he said, gearing himself up for the onslaught. 'And it doesn't matter about the variations. You can call your branch of Christianity anything you like, but it all boils down to the same thing in the end – power seeking. They're all into power in a big way, but they've managed to rationalize it over the last two thousand years into a neat little set of beliefs that make it appear to be the opposite of what it is. It's clever stuff, Georgia, and it keeps everyone in their place.'

'Freeman wouldn't agree with that.'

'Freeman's still inside the "belief bubble", Georgia. He never escaped. Doesn't want to escape.'

'Aren't we all inside a bubble of some kind?'

'For sure! But some bubbles have vicious interiors.'

Georgia began to laugh. 'I'm afraid I can't quite imagine a bubble with a vicious interior, Ian,' she said back.

'Try marrying the wrong man; you'll understand what I'm trying to say within the first month.'

She sucked at her cheeks and threw him a glance which suggested that she'd grasped what he was trying to say. Then backtracking she said, 'We seemed to have strayed a little from the point.'

'My Hammer film dreams?'

'Are you a closet reader of 12th-century monastic texts?' she asked, tilting an eyebrow at him.

'What do you think?'

'Then why dreams of that particular nature? I've never ever heard of anyone having a whole series of seemingly related dreams. I've certainly never experienced anything like that.'

'I don't know what the hell's going on,' he replied, grinning at her. 'Maybe I was an assassin in a previous life and it's catching up with me.' That appealed to him. 'That's got to be it,' he added facetiously. 'Probably explains why I was born into the back streets of Glasgow.'

She grinned back at him, and then asked when the dreaming had started.

'A few days after Patricia left me for darling Mike.'

'A reaction to that?'

'Probably.'

'And then the sluice gate opened.'

'Something opened up and I eventually shut down,' he replied paradoxically.

A sluice gate indeed. Dream after dream after dream, then a temporary blackout for a couple of weeks followed by another series of dreams which had further confounded him with the oddness of their content. An awakening to emptiness one morning, a magnified uselessness which threatened to empty him to the point of extinction. Nothing of any worth in his life that he could detect, no matter how hard he looked, just a scary vista devoid of all meaning stretching into the future: his life. And brought about by living his life through Patricia, through the auspices of silently delivered commands and looks, body movements and tiny sounds that had eventually severed his self-autonomy with hardly a word ever being spoken. Words too, of course, but nowhere as important as the signs visible and invisible to which he had unconsciously reacted out of fear: the fear – of releasing Patricia's hysterical nature and his own pent-up violence. And as she walked out of his life, the conundrum of her berating him for having no soul, no ability to love, when she had in fact usurped his soul, pinned it to her lapel and rejected his attempts to love her on almost every occasion. But not a total rejection. She had seldom said no to his physical advances, and generally appeared to warm to his verbal endearments – but certainly rejection when he got too close, when his blood and his feelings and his attempts at honesty momentarily overcame his fear and he dared approach the inner sanctum of her sensibilities. No mistaking her rejection then. An immediate distancing. An almost pathological freezing of her senses as she quickly drained herself of the desire to respond. Agony on his part. His vulnerability in such moments used against him until all passion died and they were left emotionally stranded and without hope. A kind of bitterness at the bottom of it all – an embittered mind exacting a terrible vengeance on him for something long since forgotten.

'I don't know how I put up with it,' he said with a kind of astonishment as he pulled back the curtain and peeped into his life. 'I kept on giving in to her in so many little ways.'

A smile from Georgia. 'Patricia got her own way with just about everyone – everyone except me, that is.'

'She respected you.'

'But not her husband?'

'I think she was jealous of my success.'

'She got just about everything she wanted because of your success.'

'It was never enough. She was after something else and I couldn't supply it.'

'What?'

'Peace of mind, I think. She was a bit of a mess inside.'

'Maybe you should've stood up to her a little more often.'

'Arguing with her wasn't worth the effort. You could never win an argument with Patricia – at least, I couldn't.'

'Hadn't either of you ever heard of discussion?'

'Not possible. She interpreted everything said as a personal attack. I don't think I ever really succeeded in discussing anything with her. And I did try, God help me. You saw me trying to reason with her. It never worked. Generally took her about three minutes to decide that I was getting at her in some way.'

'I noticed.'

'But you could say the same thing ten minutes later and she'd accept it. I never understood that.'

'I wasn't in the bubble.'

'Exactly. You've got it.'

'I thought for some time that you were a bit of a coward.'

'I suppose I was, in a way. But when you live with someone day in and day out . . .' Another sigh from Drummond. 'That's why I spent so much time in that damned office, Georgia. I had to escape, be somewhere where I could function as myself. Be myself. Can you understand that?'

'A vicious circle.'

'Make your circle into a sphere and you've got what I was trying to say earlier.'

A lifting of the head, and a smile. 'It was fairly obvious that things weren't exactly . . . stable. I was glad to get away from the two of you at times.'

'Your being here was sometimes an embarrassment.'

'I was aware of that. I was always expecting you to blow your top, but you never did. I concluded eventually that you must have a mistress.'

'Not a mistress.'

'You had affairs?'

'A couple of short-lived things. I was very discreet.'

'Did Patricia suspect anything?'

'I don't think so.' He spread out his legs, stared at his glass and added, 'It was the only way I could keep my sanity.' A look. 'Can you accept that?'

Her reply absolved him, but with reservation. 'Not someone in the office, I hope.'

A quick shake of the head from Drummond.

'Office things are always so messy.'

'I'm not a fool.'

More than simply discreet, he could now admit to himself. Afraid. Rendered so unsure of his sexuality by Patricia's disguised frigidity that he had been forced to buy his sex. A trip to Shepherd's Market where high quality was ensured. An hour spent wandering round and round looking at the neatly typed and sometimes flowerily inscribed adverts on the doorposts. Lessons and 'special tuition' offered in just about every language imaginable by 'fully qualified' young ladies with names like Zelda, Penelope, Princess Marcia and Clarissa. The most improbable situation he had ever been in in his life. His finger raised to press on the white china centre of a highly polished brass doorbell with the name Fagina above it: Fagina's specialty was apparently Serbo-Croat. What would she look like? That had been his greatest concern as he stood there waiting for the door to open, having found the courage to summon an inhabitant. And then the moment of moments: an elderly woman with far too much make-up on drinking in his appearance and ushering him into a deeply carpeted narrow hallway laden with horse brasses and other similarly oriented knick-knacks. Fagina would be with him in a minute. Would he like a drink? A wait of about three minutes and then Fagina the Serbo-Croat teacher standing before him in a creamy silk dress. Quite tall and well tanned in spite of the fact that it was winter. Black hair and dark eyes. Excellent bust. Almost an aristocratic mouth. His own mouth dry as he was led into the most unlikely tutorial room ever witnessed by a student. A fixed price for a fixed deed, but 'extras' available if he were interested. The first of three visits before he decided that his virility was no longer in question.

'I fully expected a telephone call from you when she left.'

'I was too scared.'

'It crossed your mind?'

He nodded, grinned at her boyishly. 'Getting it together with you would have been the . . . perfect vengeance.'

'You eventually succeeded.'

'I succeeded? It was you who seduced me! Remember?'

She controlled a smile, and stared at him. 'I didn't intend to seduce you. I just wanted to know what you were really like, on your own. And the only way I could find out was by inviting you to dinner.' She raised her eyes to the ceiling in mild protest. 'I had of course already heard how awful you had been to live with.'

'I thought you were just being kind, giving me the chance to talk it out and all that.' It was only when we were halfway through the meal that it began to dawn on me there might be the chance of actually sleeping with you.'

'We drank quite a lot of red wine.'

'And I still didn't have the courage to grab you.'

'You were out of practice.'

'I felt like a seventeen-year-old.'

'You had the ardour of a seventeen-year-old when you got going.'

'Was I that clumsy?'

'You weren't at all clumsy, just in a hurry.' She added smilingly, 'It was like watching a highly-mannered but starving man tuck into a three-course meal.'

'Oh God!'

'Don't mistake me, I enjoyed our first night together immensely.'

'Then I disappeared.'

'For weeks. Can you imagine what I thought?'

'I was busy falling apart.'

'And then you turned up with that story about having the flu.' She eyed him with mock distrust. 'I didn't know what to think.'

'You seemed to accept it.'

'I had no choice, had I? It was either go along with what you said or call you a liar.'

'I couldn't bring myself to admit that I'd cracked.'

'Did you really crack?' A frown. 'It generally takes more than a couple of weeks to get over a breakdown.'

'Maybe it was more of a seizure than a breakdown.'

'Describe it.'

'Sheer and utter emptiness.' He dipped towards what he had experienced, a series of totally inadequate sentences forming in his mind. He articulated them like a bored actor. 'The bottom fell out of my world and I fell out along with it. Nothing seemed to matter any longer. I felt totally isolated in my head.' He paused, blinked at Georgia and tried to go on, but his words seemed shorn of conviction and he despaired of getting anything across. 'I just about drank myself into oblivion. I'll tell you, it was touch and go whether I got out of it or not.'

'Sounds like a bad case of depression.'

'It lasted for over two weeks.'

'Overwork?'

'More than that.' He struggled to capture something of what he had been through, and touched again on what he had said on the Friday evening after Kevin Murray's exit. 'I found that I just didn't believe in anything any longer, that there wasn't a damned thing worth believing in. That's what I meant when I said that I felt utterly empty. It was a helluva feeling, Georgia. I couldn't even raise the energy to wash my face.'

She remained silent.

'Yet at the same time everything was flooding in. And I mean *everything*. There was stuff coming back to me from years ago. Little things. Things you'd think shouldn't matter – but they did bloody matter, it seemed. Everything mattered, but at the same time everything was meaningless! I couldn't handle that. There was no sense in it.' A sour laugh. 'That's when it began to dawn on me that I'd been asleep for most of my life – that I didn't care about anything, that I didn't know what the word 'care' actually meant! But simultaneously meaningless . . . Can you appreciate what I'm saying?'

'I think so.'

'A contradiction in terms that I couldn't resolve no matter how hard I tried.' The muscles of his face contracted as he grappled with what he was trying to say. 'A meaningless world filled with meaningless people all trying their damnedest to be meaningful!'

'You still think that?'

'I no longer know what to think. All I know right this minute is that Duval seems to understand something about the whole bag of tricks and I want to know what he knows. That's why I'm so interested in what he's up to. He's got his finger on the pulse of the thing, Georgia, and even the priestly Dr Freeman knows it.'

She shook her head and sighed, looked away for a moment and distractedly examined bits of the room. Then, looking back, she said, 'Freeman would have a field day with what you've just told me.'

'I don't doubt it, but there's no way in the world you could ever get me to consult him.'

'Why not?'

'Because at heart he's still a priest.'

'He's also a first-class analyst.'

'Do I have to repeat what I said earlier?'

'You can't classify Freeman with the fanatics you were talking about, Ian. He's a highly intelligent man. In fact I can't think of anyone better qualified to deal with those dreams of yours. You can't rely on Duval.'

'Duval's a pretty smart cookie.'

'Sounds to me as if he's playing with dynamite.'

'What happened this afternoon wasn't his fault.'

'You're perhaps not being as objective as you ought.'

'I'm following my nose. My nose says – go for it.'

'That's doesn't sound like the Ian Drummond I used to know.'

'It isn't him talking,' he said back, aware suddenly of the change in himself. Then with a smile he added, 'I don't think there's much of that particular man left, Georgia.'

Eyes closed, Edouard Duval sat as if asleep on one of the chairs in his third-storey hotel room. But he was in fact in a highly alert state, a state of deep contemplation within which his mind viewed the happenings and events of the day without comment. It was a ritual with him, a daily seeing into his life which allowed him to survey and positively alter his attitudes without suffering either guilt or shame. For during his contemplations he would open himself up to what existed in an act of self-sacrifice, an act of letting go whatever prejudicial thoughts might have accrued as he interacted with the world as 'happening' and 'event', with the men and women who instigated those happenings and events. Some would have said that he prayed, if they had known, but because never a word was spoken in his mind, and there seemed to be no one present in the exercise, this would have been a misnomer, a calling out of ignorance of something by a name other than what it really was. If asked, he would not have denigrated prayer but would certainly have suggested that prayers formed by the ego and thrust out into the universe like wedges often verged on being more magical than spiritual, more an exercise in manipulation and escapism than in a true acceptance of one's own inability to love. And he would have made no apology for using that particular word. He would have said that 'love' was not in any way a weakness or a naïvety in the face of what the world offered, and demanded, but rather a lamp which illumined the mind and allowed it to function freely and without prejudice. He would probably have been quite technical about it all, explaining what he meant in rigorous philosophical and psychological terminology, but the spirit with which he would have said it would have more than cancelled out the apparent didacticism of his words. For behind that virtually unsmiling face lay a loving nature, a kind of void from out of which life itself seemed to pour on occasions, and only the mentally hijacked were unaware of it.

This man, this walking anomaly in intellectual terms, this philosophically anarchistic individual who constantly challenged his peers with notions often viewed as idealistically suspect, was suddenly on his feet and moving across his hotel room floor with the speed of a panther, his senses having alerted him to danger. And his senses were in no way misguided, for as he reached the safety of a buttress, and moved behind it, the hail of bullets which entered the room from the adjacent building all but demolished what furniture there was and reduced the place to a shambles. There was instant uproar. Screams from beyond the shattered window suggested casualties on the street as a result of ricochets. Then within what appeared to be seconds, the howl of police sirens filled the air.

Duval did not emerge immediately; an old canniness took over, and a stoniness. He counted slowly to twenty, reached for the light switch, then carefully made his way to the window, immediately checking the building opposite for activity. Nothing. The whole building was in darkness. Only one open window in the façade, and in exactly the right position. At least three pedestrians sprawling and bawling on the pavement from the sheer madness of it all. A crowd gathering now. A police car jammed about forty yards away, the constables racing toward the scene on foot.

Sheer madness.

A heavy-calibre automatic weapon used from that distance?

The sound of running feet in the corridor.

'Monsieur Duval!' The door handle spun erratically. 'Monsieur!'

With a shake of the head, Duval turned, walked slowly to the door, and unlocked it. The manager's face was ashen.

'Are you all right?'

He smiled tersely, switched the light back on, and stood aside.

'Jesus!' the manager said.

When the police arrived, they stood in the middle of the room staring at the mess, and at each other, and up at Duval with a kind of amazement. 'You shouldn't be alive,' one of them said.

'I was very lucky.'

'I think we'd better find somewhere else to talk,' said another. Then, with a puzzled look, he added, 'You're a bit of a cool customer, aren't you?'

Duval said nothing.

'Happen often, this kind of thing?'

'Not since Herr Hitler's attempt to run France.'

'You're a Frenchman?'

'I have that honour.'

'Name?'

'Edouard Duval.'

'A resident of Great Britain?'

'Merely visiting.'

'Ah,' said the officer, staring at him. Then with a glance at the others he added, 'Be better if you came down the station, Mr Duval, considering what's happened here, and the fact that you're – an alien. Okay?'

'Whatever you say.'

The officer conjured up a smile. 'Let's go, then.'

They bustled him out of the building and into one of the police cars almost as if it were he, and not some other, who had shot the place up; the waiting photographers had a field day, Duval's great height making him not only an easy photographic target, but an object of some strangeness. Towering above his escort of three, the Frenchman sailed out into the chaos of the street and straight onto the front page of every newspaper in Great Britain. An irony, some would have said, if the man's plans had been known. But for Duval in that terrible moment, as he was hurriedly and so suspiciously herded towards the police car, a more than obvious attempt by a quite ruthless enemy to make him the centre of unsavoury publicity. They had never intended to kill him, merely highlight his existence in the nastiest possible fashion. And as he would now be forced to play the academic innocent when being questioned by the police, the authorities too would begin to ask questions – for no one is the subject of an assassination attempt without good reason, particularly a philosopher. It was a clever ploy, but it was equalled a few days later by another almighty IRA blast in central London. Incomprehensibly, one newspaper – a rag of the lowest ilk called *The Mercury* – tried to link the incidents using the most circuitous reasoning.

Drummond almost choked when he glanced at the first of his morning papers and became aware of the attempt on Duval's life. His reaction brought Georgia out of the bedroom in a rush. Standing together in the hallway, they read the introductory lines in *The Guardian* describing the debacle on Tottenham Court Road; it left them speechless. A hotel room at the Burlington virtually demolished by automatic gun fire. Three pedestrians struck down as they walked innocently home. Traffic chaos on Tottenham Court Road as police quickly cordoned off the area. Then came a series of questions couched in a puzzled tone. The attempted slaying of an out-of-favour crime boss by an ambitious minion? asked the writer. No. Another terrorist attack to drive home the vulnerability of our hard-working politicians? No. The IRA tracking down a supergrass as he/she waited to be shipped across the world and given a new identity? No. The targeted individual had been a visiting French philosopher by the name of Edouard Duval. Monsieur Duval had quite miraculously escaped injury and was now back at the same hotel, the attempt on his life being, as he himself had later said, 'an obvious mistake on the part of some crazed killer.' The article then supplied a potted history of Duval's philosophical career, mentioned the publication in 1975 of a highly controversial book entitled *The Making of a New Philosophy for the Twenty-First Century*, spoke of his reputation in France as an 'intellectual trouble-shooter', and revealed that during the Second World War he had been awarded both the Resistance Medal and the Croix de Guerre for outstanding service to his country. A mistake indeed. Perhaps a bungled assignment by some newly formed terrorist faction, the writer suggested. Either that, or the first indication of a hit-list composed by savage ideological purists bent on removing all thoughtful opposition to their aims. A photograph showing Duval coming down the steps of the hotel flanked by police helped bolster this otherwise weak and pointless exercise in journalism.

'I wonder what Thwaites' reaction will be to this,' said Drummond, scanning the different headlines.

'What's your first move?'

'Find out what the hell's going on.' Going straight to the telephone, he looked up the number for the Burlington and dialled it, knowing that he probably wouldn't get through to Duval. He was right. No incoming calls for Monsieur Duval were being accepted, the receptionist said with a kind of relish. The telephone rang the moment he put it down. It was Bill Everton. Yes, he'd seen the papers. No, he hadn't spoken to Duval. Yes, he'd be out for the rest of the day.

'Where will you be?'

'Either at the Burlington, or Katharsis headquarters.'

'Anything I should be attending to?'

He detailed two appointments he had had for that afternoon and an interview with a journalist from *Campaign* magazine that would have to be cancelled; then, just as he was about to hang up, he remembered an urgent letter that had to go out. Georgia listened as he rattled off what that letter should and should not contain. 'Sorry to land you in it, mate,' he said, thankful that there was an Everton on the other end of the line. 'I'll ring you this evening. Okay?'

'Yup. Watch how you go.'

When he turned toward Georgia, she said, 'It's turning into quite a story.'

'You'll have to sit on it. You realize that, don't you?'

She nodded at him and smiled.

Following an idea that had struck him earlier, he said, 'When did you say you were going to Paris?'

'Mid-December.'

'Any chance of going sooner?' He smiled at her tersely. 'Like tomorrow?'

'You want me to nose around?'

'I'd like you to find out everything there is to know about Duval, Lefèbvre and Katharsis. There'll be a more than decent fee in it for you.'

'Sounds good.'

'You'll do it?'

A nod from Georgia. 'How long have I got?'

'One week. Ring me here each evening at six sharp.'

'Pity you couldn't come along.'

'I think I'm going to be rather busy.'

'Doing what?'

'My own kind of research. It isn't every day one of my . . . potential clients hits the headlines in such a spectacular fashion.'

They stood looking at one another. 'Be very, very careful how you handle things, Georgia,' he said, doubts about what he had suggested already flooding in.

'I know what to do.'

'Take the line that you're just following up on the Duval story because you think a couple of quid can still be screwed out of it. Sound mercenary and keep the whole thing as light as a feather. And for Christ's sake, don't mention my name to anyone. Not anyone!'

'Got you.'

'And take your mobile phone; no calls from your hotel. Ring me each evening, at six. On the dot. Okay?'

She dipped her head in acknowledgment, glanced at her watch. 'Might as well strike while the iron's hot. I'll go over this afternoon by Eurostar.'

'Up to you.' He smiled at her enthusiasm. 'Want some cash?'

'It would save me the hassle of going to the bank.'

He made to leave the kitchen, but stopped in the doorway as something else occurred to him. 'No fancy hotels, Georgia,' he said warningly. 'Don't draw attention to yourself.' He looked apologetic. 'Sorry it's got to be like this. I'd love to . . .'

'Fuck me in Paris?'

'That too.' He laughed, went to his study, and came back with five hundred pounds in new notes. 'All I've got in the house,' he said. 'Enough?'

She laughed. 'It'll do for starters.'

'I don't want anyone to think you've been put up to this. You're just a freelance journo trying to cash in on the tail end of an already dying story. Right?'

She smiled at him again, shook her head in bewilderment. 'I'm seeing a side of you I've never seen before.'

'I'm just being careful. Don't want you to get your skull cracked on my behalf.' He looked suddenly pensive. 'I probably shouldn't be involving you in this way.'

'It's what I'm good at. I didn't get where I am pussy-footing around.'

That was certainly true. It was one of the things that had early on made her so fascinating to Drummond – a woman with a good mind and the ability to use it effectively. Patricia had also had a good mind, but she had lacked the hard edge necessary for its exploitation. Brittleness of mind was no substitute.

'Know anyone over there who might be able to help?'

'There are a couple of people who could probably point me in the right direction.'

He hesitated to tell her her business, but felt it necessary to stress again how careful she ought to be. 'Don't confide anything of what I've told you to anyone because of past friendship, Georgia. You know nothing. You're starting from square one and hoping for a break. That's all.'

She stared at him for a moment. 'Okay.'

He caught her by the arm as she moved past, drew her in and kissed her lightly. She responded with a fervour that surprised him. Then with a laugh she turned away to get dressed, leaving him half-aroused and again in two minds about the whole escapade.

The rotund and balding manager of the Burlington eventually conceded to Drummond's demand on being assured that he was a solicitous friend and not a journalist of any sort. And when it was confirmed by Duval on the telephone that Mr Ian Drummond was in fact welcome, the man's politely obstructive attitude immediately blossomed into a form of intimacy. Taking on the task of personally guiding Drummond to the third floor, the manager indulged in a monologue about the incident in room 96, stating latterly that the bullets had been gouged out of the wall with such little finesse by police experts that it looked as though Duval had been shelled rather than shot at: the room in question was now locked and out of bounds. Then to Drummond's surprise, the man changed tack and unburdened himself of a problem resulting from the whole extraordinary affair. 'Exciting as it's all been,' he said, blinking, 'it's also been a catastrophe for this hotel as far as bookings are concerned.' He stopped suddenly and looked at Drummond in a desperate kind of way, blocking any advance. 'Can you appreciate my position, Mr Drummond? We've had eight cancellations since the incident, and no fewer than six of our American guests have already paid their bill and left. We could be ruined inside a week if Monsieur Duval doesn't –' Unable to articulate the words of dismissal, the manager fell silent. Drummond said, 'You want me to suggest that he find somewhere else to stay. Is that it?' An embarrassed nod in return. 'Okay, I'll see what I can do.' The manager audibly sighed with relief, delivered himself of a minuscule bow instead of speech, and they were again on their way.

Duval welcomed Drummond with his usual stiff formality, thanked the manager, closed the door quietly behind them, led his visitor into the bedroom and said, 'You'll forgive me if I continue packing. I'm returning to Paris for a few days.'

'That's probably a good idea,' said Drummond, having taken in the less than plush surroundings of Duval's tiny suite as he passed through. There had certainly been no money squandered on fancy accommodation. 'You'd be lucky if they let you stay on here under the circumstances,' he added, watching the man pull open a drawer and reach into it. 'And getting into another hotel might prove a little difficult right this minute.'

'Exactly.' Duval stood for a moment, folded shirts in hand; he looked a little haggard after his ordeal, but was still ramrod straight. 'That, however, is not my primary reason for leaving, Mr Drummond,' he said, continuing with his task. 'There are things that have to be attended to in Paris, and I'm the person best qualified to deal with them.'

'Call me Ian,' said Drummond.

Duval dipped his head slightly, but did not turn.

'Things related to what happened here last night?' asked Drummond.

'Yes.'

'You've got some idea of who's responsible?'

Duval's reply shook Drummond. 'I know exactly who's responsible.'

'You told the police?'

'No.'

'Why not?'

'Because it's something that will have to be dealt with in another way.'

'How?'

'Through . . . discussion.'

'Discussion? Someone tried to kill you last night!'

'I think not. The idea was to frighten me and highlight my existence at the same time. They succeeded with their latter objective.'

'Oh, come on!' said Drummond, unable to accept what he was hearing. 'They sprayed your hotel room with bullets!'

'When only one bullet would have been sufficient.'

'There are three innocent people in hospital, Monsieur Duval. One of them is in a critical condition. Are you trying to tell me it was all a game?'

'Games are their specialty.'

'Whose specialty, for Christ's sake!'

The philosopher did not immediately reply. He leaned heavily on the edge of his suitcase and thought for a moment, then said almost wearily, 'If I divulged that to you, you would be in danger of losing your life.' A glance at Drummond. 'It is, I think, better that you remain ignorant.'

Drummond stared at the man's elongated back, became suddenly aware of the weight being carried by those narrow shoulders. Should he press him further? Should he put his own life in danger for the sake of satisfying his curiosity? That was when he fully realized that he ought not to have involved Georgia, that her turning up in Paris with no conception of what she was walking into was just about the craziest thing anyone could do under the circumstances. He had sensed it all along, but had hidden the truth from himself. If she started digging in the wrong place, asked the wrong questions of the wrong people, then the chances were she could end up a sacrifice merely for the making of a point. It terrified him to think about that – and that in spite of the fact that he had only asked her to check up on Duval and Aretino Lefèbvre. But he had known all along that she wouldn't stop there, that her journalistic instincts and her contacts would inevitably take her deeper and deeper still. It also made him realize that he had acted with gross selfishness. He had suppressed his earlier doubts simply because it had excited him to be involved in such a caper. But more than that, he now admitted to himself as he stood there staring at Duval's back. It had also been his hope that she might return with information on those responsible for the attacks on himself. That had been his secret motive – pride had been at the root of it all. He shivered as that thought struck him. Maybe Patricia had been right all along about his having neither soul nor feelings in any proper sense. Maybe he really was as empty as he had felt that morning when he awoke and all light had been banished from the world. Maybe . . . He stopped the flow of his thoughts as they dragged him towards the black mirror of his fear, produced his mobile phone and asked Duval quite abruptly if he would mind him making a call.

'Of course not.'

There was no answer from the Hampstead flat.

'I'll have to go,' he said quickly, edgily.

'Is something wrong?'

'No. I've just got things to attend to, like yourself.' Finding Duval's stare disconcerting, he added, 'I take it this means that our little chat will have to be postponed.'

'Only for a few days. You'll be informed the moment I return.'

Drummond hesitated. 'Can I ask you one question before I leave?'

'Yes.'

'What makes you think you'll be able to . . . discuss what's happened with such people?'

Duval's reply was immediate and surprising. 'Because, strange as it may sound, Mr Drummond,' he said, continuing to use Drummond's surname, 'the people concerned are highly intelligent and amenable to words.' The merest tinge of a smile touched his face. 'The worst kind of madmen are the reasonable ones, and France has had its fair share of madmen.' He added, 'I know that that cannot possibly make sense to you, but that is how things must be, I'm afraid.'

Not knowing what to make of the man's statement, Drummond said, 'You know how to contact them?'

A nod.

'Then why don't you have them arrested? Stopped?'

'If it were possible, I would.'

'Why isn't it possible?'

'That is something you might work out for yourself, with a little thought,' he replied, and again that tiny smile disrupted the contours of his mouth as he prepared himself for the kind of delicate dismissal the hotel manager had found impossible to deliver. 'Thank you for coming to see me, Ian,' he added softly. 'I appreciate your concern.'

Drummond drove straight home, telephoned Georgia *en route* and was lucky enough to catch her. She listened patiently to what he had to say, questioned him thoroughly about Duval, but would not agree to cancelling the trip because of the supposed dangers.

The people behind the shoot-up were obviously unbalanced, she said, but if Duval felt he could talk to them in spite of what had happened, then there was still the chance of a damned good story without her being in any kind of danger. And Duval was going to be in Paris himself, she pointed out. It was perfect. Sensing something of what she had in mind, Drummond argued that he hadn't suggested the trip so that she might come up with a damned good story but for purely practical reasons. All he had asked her to do was check out the background of the leading figures in Katharsis where they were best known, on home territory, not take off on some harebrained piece of investigative journalism that might end up with her being either maimed or killed. He reminded her of what had happened to him; he said that he would never forgive himself if anything happened to her, anything at all, and finally admitted that it had been his deep-seated need for revenge that had probably sparked off the whole ludicrous idea in the first place.

'I'm afraid my ulterior motive was completely conscious.'

'What do you mean?'

She laughed guiltily into the phone. 'It was my intention right from the start to go beyond your brief, Ian. The whole thing's dynamite! It's a gift that someone like me can't turn away from. You must surely be able to see that.'

'I think dynamite is probably the appropriate word,' he said back, realizing that she had the bit between her teeth and that she had no intention of letting go. 'The whole situation's getting far too complex for my liking, Georgia. And downright dangerous. There's obviously a lot more going on than I was first led to believe, and I really can't imagine where it's all going to end up.'

'In print, as far as I'm concerned.'

'You can't use anything told to me in confidence by Duval.'

'No need to. It'll be more than sufficient if I find out who launched that attack on him.'

'On your own? In Paris?'

'I know the city well. My French is fluent. I've got some very good friends over there.'

'Sounds like anything I say isn't going to change your mind.'

'Not on something like this,' she said back quietly, adamantly. Then she said, 'I'll ring you with anything of interest tomorrow evening at six as arranged. Okay?'

'Where will you be staying?'

'Somewhere in the Algerian quarter, I'll let you know exactly where when I ring. Bye. Be back before you know it.'

Chapter Nine

PARIS, CITY OF symbols and signs. Napoleon's Paris where many of the streets were named after battles. Victor Hugo's Paris where the hunchback of Notre Dame swung from being literary legend to that of filmic hero. The Paris of Sartre and Cocteau, those beetle-browed intellectuals who sought something approaching ultimate truth in philosophy, poetry, film and novel. And where Peter Abelard had astounded his ecclesiastical masters in the 12th century with the idea that knowledge came only from experience interpreted by logical thinking. This idea, put forward by Abelard in the Cathedral of Notre Dame at a time when thinking was predominantly governed by scholastic Church dogma, had resulted in the revolutionaries' renaming Notre Dame the *Temple of Reason*. There had even been a feast of 'The Goddess of Reason' celebrated there, complete with dancers from the opera. Subconsciously aligning themselves with Abelard, Parisians had ever since prided themselves on 'speaking their minds', and it was on this built-in trait that Georgia now intended to capitalize as she left her hotel early the next morning and headed for the offices of a small, but widely read, magazine where speaking one's mind – in the form of gossip – had been raised to the level of an art form.

'You have returned!' The editor, a lanky southerner with perpetually sad eyes sat bolt upright in his chair as Georgia sauntered in. 'I thought I would never see you again after what happened last time!'

'Don't be silly.' She kissed him on both cheeks, drew back and smiled at him, sat on the edge of his desk and squinted at what he was working on as she spoke. 'How have you been? Stumbled on any juicy scandals I should know about?'

Simulating a gun with two fingers, Paul Paquel pointed them at his head and sighed that he was considering getting out of the business altogether. 'I mean it this time, I really do,' he said, looking at her tragically. 'Gossip is not what it used to be, Georgia. We almost have to invent it now.' He threw up his arms in exaggerated despair. 'No one seems to be enjoying themselves any longer!'

Paquel had immediately slipped into English, but even then his Toulouse accent was detectable.

'You're all getting lazy, that's what it is.'

'The good life melting our marrow?' He laughed without looking happy. 'If only that were true.'

In Toulouse, as a youngster, Paul Paquel had won his way into the best school, the Lycée Fermat, but had found that his face did not fit. Born the son of a worker, he had been virtually shunned by his middle-class classmates. And because the French literature he was taught had not reflected the problems or feelings of his own background, he had early on become an intellectual drop-out with an addiction for American black culture. He had found that he could identify more easily with the blacks in America than with the polite middle-class French culture held up to him for admiration. In spite of such drawbacks, however, he had managed academic success, become a reporter on the *Dépêche de Toulouse* newspaper, and eventually landed a plum job in Paris as reader for the prestigious publishing firm of Gallimard. But not for long. His accent and his attitudes and his difficulty with the mythology of all things Parisian had proved too great a stumbling-block; he had resigned his post within the first year. For revenge, perhaps, he had immediately founded *Le Miroir*, and with an eye for the ridiculous and the prejudicial, had used the lives and spoken sentiments of prominent Parisians to good commercial effect.

'You've taken on extra staff. Things can't be that bad.'

'Little sharp-eyes.' He coughed suddenly, reached for his packet of Gauloises as if they were a remedy. 'Everything is so specialized nowadays.' He lit one and sat back, inhaled, and coughed again. 'And I don't seem to have the energy I used to have.'

'You're getting old.'

'Ah! A terrible truth. Even my wife has noticed.'

'I was only joking.'

'I'm fifty-four! My life is all but over!'

'Not in Paris it isn't.'

Paquel smiled, gave a little nod of acceptance. 'Have you got time for a little . . . breakfast?' Georgia said that she could spare an hour, that being taken out for breakfast had been her sole reason for turning up so early. 'Huh,' he said, the heavy lids of his eyes drooping further. 'You expect me to believe that?' He slipped on his jacket, went to the stand in the corner of his office and retrieved his coat. 'I have a cold,' he said, the Gauloise dripping from his lips. 'I must keep warm.'

They went into a café on the Rue des Abbesses, not far from the entrance to the Métro, ordered coffee and a little something to eat, and began to talk. Georgia did not immediately ask the question she had in mind, but asked instead if he had managed a visit home during the summer. Paquel nodded, smiled with a southerner's satisfaction at the memory of being with his own people for four delicious weeks; it was Georgia's way of softening him up. For if Paul was in love with anything, it was with the Languedoc and the wine-growing peasantry from which he originated – the civilization of the vine, as he called it. When speaking of the Languedoc he would wax poetic, sometimes lapsing from French into Occitan to confuse and bemuse his audience; he was also a leading member of the Occitan regionalist movement, and preferred to speak of himself as an Occitan, and not as a southerner. After some 20 minutes of conversation about the Languedoc, Georgia decided it was time to make her move.

'I presume you've heard about the attack on Edouard Duval in London?'

'But of course!' Paquel's eyes strayed a little too quickly to a passing waitress, but returned. 'It was the headline in most newspapers yesterday morning. Everyone was talking about it.'

'Everyone?'

'Just about everyone in Paris.'

'And?'

'And?' he repeated innocently.

'Hear anything . . . unusual?'

He drew breath and shook his head.

'Nothing?'

'Nothing of importance.'

'Are you interested professionally?'

'I could be persuaded.'

A smile from Georgia. 'Like to tell me what you think is going on?'

Paquel stared at the white plastic of the table for a moment, touched the rim of his cup with a finger. 'This is not the kind of thing you are . . . usually attracted to.'

'I'm branching out.'

'Why? Have you stumbled on something?'

'You could say that.'

'May I offer you some advice?'

'Of course.'

He took on the air of an elder statesman. 'May I suggest that you forget what you have discovered and go back to what you know best. I speak as a friend.'

'It's not in my nature to walk away from a good story, Paul.'

'You are perhaps out of your depth.'

'I learn quickly.'

An almost fatherly look from Paquel. 'What have you found out, Georgia?'

'You expect me to tell you that without an arrangement?'

A laugh. 'What did you have in mind?'

'I'll come back to that,' said Georgia, playing her game carefully. 'Just tell me what you've heard on the grapevine.'

'You know as well as I do that you get nothing for nothing in this business.'

'You've obviously heard something interesting.'

'– I may have.'

'I knew if there was one person in Paris to pick up on this story, it'd be you.'

He looked straight at her. 'The others let you down?' he asked.

Georgia said nothing, sipping at her coffee. Then, looking up, she said, 'What's going on, Paul?'

A shrug from Paquel. 'Who knows? It is a very strange business.'

'Come on. I've done you favours in the past.'

His reply was quick and a little disconcerting. 'I am probably doing you a favour now by telling you nothing.'

Digesting that remark, Georgia said, 'It'll be your fault if I get my head knocked off before I even start.'

His mouth hung open for a moment. 'That's unfair!'

'I suspect it's the truth.'

Turning away suddenly, he snapped his fingers and ordered more coffee. Then quite anxiously he said, 'You have put me in a very awkward position, Georgia. If I tell you what I have heard, you will continue with your investigation. If I do not tell you what I have heard – the same.' He brought his wrists together, formed an agitated bird with his hands and tried to get his point across. 'Either way I will end up feeling responsible.'

'Thanks for your concern, but it's my neck.'

'And you are quite possibly asking me to wring it!' he said in a ferocious whisper. 'Do you understand what I'm saying?'

'I understand what you're saying, but not why you're saying it.'

'You intend to pursue this matter?'

'All the way.'

'With or without my help, eh?'

A nod from Georgia.

Paquel showed his exasperation by flapping his hands. He then laid them palms-down on the table and started to speak – but the waitress appeared in that moment and he broke off instantly. She smiled at Paquel, glanced at Georgia, and placed their fresh cups of coffee carefully on the table. He paid no attention to her this time. Putting his arms behind his chair, he clasped his hands invisibly, taking on the appearance of a prisoner under interrogation; it was most appropriate, Georgia thought. But the moment the girl returned to her place behind the counter, he leaned forward and said, 'Okay. I'll share what I know with you because of past favours, because of my little ... indiscretion when we last met. But I expect something in return – something of comparable value.'

'That cuts both ways,' she replied, the memory of how she had had to defend herself against his rather drunken advances again fresh in her mind. 'In fact I claim the right to tell you nothing if what you have doesn't measure up to expectation.'

'What you have is so good?'

'What I have is highly complicated.'

'You'll tell me everything?'

'That depends.'

'On what?'

Georgia paused, stared at the man she knew so well. 'On your swearing that you won't just take the material and run.'

'I am your friend! Truly!'

'You're also a journalist, Paul, and I did rather hurt your feelings the last time I was here.'

A sigh from Paquel. 'I was drunk, Georgia. I fully admit to behaving abominably. You have my word both as a friend and as an admirer that there will be no trickery.'

'On your mother's grave?'

'On my mother's grave.' He laid a hand on his heart and straightened as if on parade. 'Okay?'

A nod from Georgia.

'So what have you got?'

'You first, Paul.'

He smiled, leaned forward after checking that there was no one within earshot, and delivered himself of a quite outrageous statement that took Georgia completely by surprise. 'Digest this if you can –' he said, enjoying his moment of power. 'Would you believe a return to monarchy in France within the next five years.'

Georgia blinked. 'A monarchy in France?'

'That is what I said.'

'You're having me on.'

'You asked me to tell you what I have heard – that is what I have heard. And I have it on good authority.'

'I don't understand.'

'I don't think anyone does. But that is what is being whispered in the city in all seriousness. Believe me.'

'How does a scenario like that fit in with Duval being shot at in a London hotel?'

'They are apparently connected.'

'How?'

'I do not know how! I just know that they are.'

She blinked at him. 'I can't see how France could ever return to being a monarchy.'

He delivered himself of another Gallic shrug. 'France has shown herself to be capable of just about anything,' he said back, alluding obliquely to past goings-on in the antipodes. 'It wouldn't surprise me in the least if I woke up one morning and found that we had . . . *created* a king for ourselves.'

Georgia began to laugh. 'It's got to be an idea invented by crackpots, Paul. It has to be!'

'Perhaps.'

There was a silence. Georgia broke it by saying, 'So where's the danger for me in all of this?'

'Your innocence is what puts you in danger.'

'Anything else I should know?'

'That rather depends on what you have to tell.'

'What I've got is a highly complex story that doesn't make any sense.'

'I'll be the judge of that.'

She hesitated. 'There's a condition, I'm afraid.'

'You wish also to impose a condition?' He fabricated a sigh. 'Isn't my mother's grave enough?'

'Of course,' she said quickly, grinning at him. 'But I think it would be a good idea if we did more than merely swap information . . . I also think we should pool our resources and work together on this one.'

Paquel hesitated. 'That is a . . . pleasing possibility.'

'You agree, then?'

Another sigh. 'I think I'd better, for your sake.'

'Then here's what I've got,' she said, selecting her bait with care and betting heavily on her instincts, 'but for God's sake keep what I'm about to tell you to yourself. I'm really sticking my neck out on this one.'

Drummond lifted his mobile phone in the same moment as it summoned him; he had been sitting waiting for the call, trying not to think about little Sophie sitting rigidly in her hospital chair. Georgia said immediately that she was fine, but that she'd had a hectic day and was only just in the process of returning to her hotel after spending the whole afternoon in the *Bibliothèque Nationale*. He was to get a piece of paper and note down what she was about to say; it would save time later if he did some independent research and they were able to discuss their separate findings when she returned. There then followed a short grocery list of things to look into (mostly historical), plus a curious injunction to check out the logo for Saba Petrol, France's leading petroleum company. Drummond wrote the words down and stared at them. He tried to question her about why she was interested in Saba Petrol, but was told that she herself hadn't as yet had time to make sense out of what she had come up with. If there was any truth in what she had heard, she said, there was the distinct possibility of her handling one of the biggest stories to break on Europe since the Second World War was announced. He asked what she meant by that, and was given Paul Paquel's snippet on a returned monarchy for France within five years. Then suddenly the line went dead and he was left listening to the eerie purr, wondering what had happened. Switching off, he waited, but she did not ring back. So he rang her, but there was no reply from her mobile phone. Having no hotel name or number, he sat dejectedly staring down at what he had written, trying to beat down a sense of panic:

> Merovingian kings
> Protocols of the Elders of Zion
> Flag of Lorraine
> Crown of Charlemagne/Habsburgs
> Check out logo for Saba Petrol

He had also hurriedly scribbled *Possible return of monarchy to France within five years*. Now where the hell had she got that from? He shook his head in bewilderment, scanned what he had written, and decided to engage a professional researcher first thing in the morning to speed things up. After three more attempts to contact Georgia, he gave up, poured himself a large scotch, switched on the television and tried to banish the thought that things had already gone terribly wrong the other side of the English Channel. Scanning the piece of paper carrying his curious scrawl, he pondered what the *Protocols of the Elders of Zion* might be, and what role the logo for Saba Petrol might have to play in the whole business. He then began to wonder if Georgia had flipped her lid, but knew that she was too much the professional to be easily fooled. There had to be something to the questions she was asking.

The programmes ploughed on relentlessly, advertisements punctuating and sometimes puncturing what appeared – two of the ads had been created by Drummond Advertising. By ten-thirty, after innumerable attempts to contact Georgia, he decided that bed was the only sensible place to be and irritably switched off the set. A tangible silence filled the apartment.

Unease on two levels as he prepared for bed.

He slept fitfully, chased down narrow streets by a foe intent upon removing him from the face of the Earth. But when the moment came, and he found himself cornered, a quite remarkable thing happened: a young girl suddenly appeared, stepped between him and his attackers, and with outstretched finger caused them to fall back in disarray. In one moment a young girl standing there, radiantly beautiful; in the next his mother in her old coat complete with shopping bag staring down at him and shaking her head. He awoke from that dream sweating, fell back into sleep, and underwent what he later described to Georgia as the most horrific dream experience of his entire adult life.

A cave. He was standing near to one of the walls, his attention trained on a hole in the floor from which streamed a dazzling light. Afraid, but curious, he moved toward that hole with the intention of looking into it – but so fearful did he become as he approached, that he ended up crawling towards it on his hands and knees, knowing that what he was about to see might be too much for his mind to assimilate. And it was as he feared, too much. Lying flat out, his fingers on the edge of the hole itself, he looked in and down and immediately panicked: a bottomless tube of intense, blue-white light, bubbling and heaving and reaching up threateningly. His nerve gave out. He crawled back and away from that hole, fearful that it might draw him down into itself, and was on the point of standing up again when something grabbed his ankles and began to wheelbarrow him back towards the edge with irresistible strength.

His forearms acting as resistant runners, he twisted this way and that to dislodge whatever held him, but found to his horror that there was no one there, just his torso and legs magically suspended, held there by an invisible power intent upon his destruction. A dream from which he awoke sitting upright in bed screaming like a child after a nightmare. Yet another vigil in the kitchen with black coffee as companion. He eventually concluded that both dreams were somehow related to his having witnessed Sophie in her cataleptic state. Her 'helplessness' had horrified him, and he now seemed to remember that the radiantly beautiful girl in his first dream bore a striking resemblance to Sophie's mother.

A pot-pourri of nonsense – but no less terrifying for that.

And on top of it all, the memory image of Sophie caught and locked in her numbing silence, her father kneeling by her side in a state almost as bad as her own.

'Sophie? Can you hear me, Sophie?'

Drummond standing helplessly on the sidelines.

'Sophie?'

Words of encouragement from the nurse carried away from that place as if from the lips of a prophet. A lot of whisky consumed before and after the event as John Eglington fought to hold himself together.

'You have to keep thinking of your other kids.'

'I'm trying, God help me!'

'You're all they've got.'

Sick to the stomach as he drove home to wait for Georgia's telephone call; another couple of whiskies downed while he mindlessly read the evening paper, turned the pages and scanned the often brutal headings with only a rudimentary reaction to what was going on in the world. Then the shock of turning yet another page to be confronted by a quite extraordinary full-page advertisement. It was one of the craziest things he had ever seen, and given half a chance he would have mentioned it to Georgia.

> THE WORLD HAS HAD *ENOUGH* – OF HUNGER, INJUSTICE, WAR. IN ANSWER TO OUR CALL FOR HELP, AS WORLD TEACHER FOR ALL HUMANITY, THE CHRIST IS NOW HERE. HOW WILL YOU RECOGNIZE HIM?
>
> Look for a modern man concerned with modern problems – political, economic and social. Since July 1977, the Christ has been emerging. He is not a religious leader but an educator, in the broadest sense of the word, pointing the way out of our present crisis. We will recognize him by his extraordinary spiritual potency, the universality of his viewpoint, and his love for all humanity. He comes not to judge, but to aid and inspire. Watch and pray for the signs that will accompany his full emergence.
>
> **WHO IS THE CHRIST?**
>
> Throughout history, humanity's evolution has been guided by a group of enlightened men, the *Masters of Wisdom*. They have remained largely in the remote desert and mountain places of Earth, working mainly

through their disciples who live openly in the world. This message of the Christ's reappearance has been given primarily by such disciples trained for His task for over twenty years. At the centre of this 'Spiritual Hierarchy' stands the world teacher, known by Christians as the Christ. And as Christians await the Second Coming, so the Jews await the Messiah, the Buddhists the fifth Buddha, the Muslims the Imam Mahdi, and the Hindus await Krishna. These are all names for one individual.

*

His presence in the world guarantees there will be no Third World War.

So watch and listen for the Christ in your midst
Search your heart and prepare to
Serve Him.

Someone had spent an enormous amount of money to have such an advertisement appear in a national newspaper. It was idiotic. After the initial shock of reading such rubbish, the advert and its contents would be relegated to the dustbin and deserved oblivion. Only the Churches would react. The general public would shrug off such patent nonsense and go on with their lives as if it had never appeared. Intending to amuse Georgia with the advertisement's lunatic announcement, he had carefully removed it, folded it neatly in half and placed it within reach of the telephone – but it was not to be. She had produced her own lunatic findings, and for reasons unknown communication had ceased.

But there was no memory now of that advertisement as he sat in the kitchen sipping coffee, his head a fuzz-ball inside as he plucked up courage to return to bed and the possibility of another nightmare. Sometimes he got away with it, his sleep empty of dreams after a strong coffee. Sometimes he wasn't so lucky, the underworld of his psyche demanding that in some fashion he complete whatever journey he had started. There was never any telling which way it would go.

He awoke five hours later feeling much as he had felt five hours earlier – abominable. He washed and shaved, and eventually dressed, still aware of the greyness of his face in the bathroom mirror, the puffiness of his eyes, the lines that seemed to deepen and darken when his sleep was interrupted and he had to flee from his own messed-up psychology. He looked so old sometimes – so *bloody* old! In just a few years he would look older than his father had done before he died. That was an incredible thought. Older than his father both numerically and physically. The son catching up and passing the father's age and continuing until the father became son to the son! That stopped him in his tracks for a moment, made him think seriously for the first time in years about the man who had sired him, the man who had passed on the little he knew about the world and then passed away in an oxygen-tent fighting death with everything he had. What was it his mother had said? *He went out clawing the air and cursing because death was stronger than he was.* He had never forgotten that; it was about the only profound thing his mother had ever said. An unfinished life. Forty-nine years of age when he so unwillingly gave up the ghost – a difference of only six years remaining between them now. And the sudden thought that he might not manage to cross that magical threshold and complete his own journey, that it was somehow indecent to be older than one's father. Stuff and nonsense, of course, but nonetheless there at the back of his mind as he reached for his car keys and headed for the front door. Six years. What would he do if he knew for certain that he had only six years left?

Another stint at the *Bibliothèque Nationale* the following day furnished Georgia with the basic materials considered important by Paul Paquel. He had refused to fully discuss anything with her until she was thoroughly familiar with certain aspects of French history (the early Merovingian dynasty in particular), and had arranged to have a meal with her at a small bistro not far from her hotel. Mentally weary from six hours of research, she returned to her rosebud-besmattered hotel room, showered, changed into some fresh clothes, called Ian on her repaired mobile phone, and before leaving the hotel jolted her memory by quickly reading through the more obviously important of the photocopies she had made. One hour later, armed with her findings, and confronted by a steak on a wooden platter, she questioned the man who had demanded such a tiring exercise.

Paquel, elbows on the table, his chin resting on his knuckles, listened intently as Georgia fathomed her way through the intricacies of the Merovingian period and eventually alighted upon what she considered the crux of the whole matter – namely, the Church's usurpation of the right to create kings, oil instead of blood having eventually determined kingship.

'You have it,' he said back, delighted with her efforts. 'Anointment with oil replaced blood, and the Church became the most powerful institution in the Western world. In 800 Charlemagne was proclaimed and anointed Holy Roman Emperor, and in that moment Rome became not only the seat of an empire that embraced the whole of Western Europe, it also became the principle spiritual and secular authority throughout Europe. As you are already aware, a pact was signed with Clovis in 496, and the title of 'the new Constantine' conferred. But with Charlemagne it was different: he was created Holy Roman Emperor by the pope's authority alone, an authority founded on the ritual of anointment elevated to that of a divine inauguration. In the past, anointment had only been a ceremonial accoutrement, a symbolic gesture, but it now became a literal act which conferred divine grace upon a ruler. Blood was now subservient to oil. And there had of course been the convenient discovery of a crucial document a few years earlier called the *Donation of Constantine* – a document known today to be a forgery concocted by the Church itself. The influence of the *Donation* was enormous.'

'The *Donation* is a forgery?'

'Most certainly. It was supposed to date from Constantine's alleged conversion to Christianity in AD 312, but it was more likely fabricated around 754 as the first major step in a plan to consolidate the Church's position in Europe. Think about it. According to the *Donation*, Constantine handed over his imperial symbols and regalia to the Bishop of Rome, so making them Church property. Then what does he do? He declares the Bishop of Rome to be both Vicar of Christ and emperor in the one breath. Whereupon he stands back and twiddles his thumbs while the humble Bishop of Rome works out what to do next.' A wry laugh from Paquel. 'It didn't take him long to make up his mind. Acting immediately as emperor, the bishop-become-pope is said to have returned the imperial regalia to Constantine, who from that moment wore them with ecclesiastical sanction and permission.'

'A nice move.'

'And a telling one. As from that hypothetical moment, the Bishop of Rome exercised supreme secular power as well as supreme spiritual authority over the whole of Christendom. In one fell swoop he had become a papal emperor with the power to create and depose imperial crowns as he wished. Without the *Donation of Constantine*, the Church could never have claimed the right to meddle in high-order secular affairs. It was a brilliant move. As from that moment she had the power to make "sacred" whomever she pleased. And with the help of a little ceremony called "coronation and anointment", she perfected that right. The coronation of Pepin III couldn't have taken place otherwise.'

'You've lost me. I only got as far as the assassination of Dagobert II.'

'Okay.' Paquel cut off a piece of meat and forked it into his mouth, chewed at it with relish, washed it down with a little wine and continued. '. . . Pepin the Fat had Dagobert assassinated in 679. Right? But strictly speaking, that wasn't the end of the Merovingian dynasty. The lesser branches continued as helpless pawns for another three-quarters of a century, their power usurped – often because they were very young – by the Mayors of the Palace. Pepin the Fat was followed by his son, Pepin II. And Pepin II was followed by his son, the rather famous Charles Martel – Martel is one of the most heroic figures in French history. Martel died in 741, and about ten years later his son, Pepin III, Mayor of the Palace to King Childeric III, sought the Church's support in his attempt to claim the throne. There was simply no energy left in the Merovingian bloodline, and the Mayors of the Palace were running the show anyway. The pope, as you can imagine, was delighted with the idea. He could now flex his apostolic muscles and create a king, not merely go through the procedure of recognizing one – Church oil was about to take precedence over blood. It was too good a chance to miss. The Church came out in Pepin's favour, and by dint of a trumped-up apostolic authority – backed by the convenient discovery of the *Donation of Constantine* one year earlier, and by the ritual of anointment now elevated to the level of a holy transferral of "sacred" power – ordered that Pepin III be created king of the Franks without delay. Backed by Rome, Pepin deposed Childeric and had him confined to a monastery. He also had his sacred hair removed to deprive him of any residue of "magical powers" that might remain in the already weakened bloodline. Childeric died four years later.'

'Sacred hair?'

'It was believed that like Samson's, their hair contained their *vertu*, the essence of their power. Like the ancient Nazarites, they refused to have their hair cut. They were also said to be capable of clairvoyant communication, have phenomenal longevity, and to carry a red birthmark shaped like a cross either over their hearts or between their shoulderblades. They were called the sorcerer kings, and were believed to possess miraculous healing powers.'

'Quite a bunch.'

'Superhuman powers in abundance.'

'And then came Charlemagne.'

'And the final card in the Church's royal flush.'

'How do you mean?'

An animated look came into Paul Paquel's eyes. He pushed his plate aside and leaned forward conspiratorially. 'I mean, Georgia, that the Church completed its fabricated right to control the creation of kings by tricking Charlemagne into becoming what he did not wish to become – Holy Roman Emperor. His coronation was rigged. Contemporary accounts show that the whole thing was a piece of ingenious engineering. Charlemagne was lured to Rome and persuaded to attend a special mass. While seated in the cathedral, the pope placed the crown on his head from behind and declared him Emperor of the Romans without his being able to do a damned thing about it. And it's recorded history that Charlemagne wouldn't have entered that cathedral if he had known what the pope was planning to do For in that moment – and it's thought that Charlemagne was fully aware of the implications – the Church betrayed its pact with the Merovingian bloodline, a pact supposedly irrevocable and forever. And that is perhaps why Charlemagne immediately married a Merovingian princess, as had the usurper Pepin III. They seemed to regard the Merovingian throne with superstitious awe, and probably felt that the only way they could legitimize their position was through a direct link with the Merovingian bloodline. Anyway, the situation immediately after the crowning of Charlemagne was that Rome became the seat of an empire that embraced the whole of

Western Europe, an empire ruled only with the pope's sanction. The full hand had been dealt.'

'You're saying that the Church used both Constantine and Charlemagne for its own ends – history has been deliberately falsified by the Church to tend its own survival?'

'Yes, that is exactly what I'm saying. And I'm not alone in that observation. But what you have to understand is that Constantine used Christianity just as much as Christianity has subsequently used Constantine. He was hardly the "good Christian" that later tradition suggests, but he wasn't averse to using Christianity for his own ends. In the name of unity and uniformity, he collapsed Christianity, Mithraism – the other major cult of the day – and the cult of Sol Invictus into one another until the distinctions between them became almost invisible. He tolerated the deified Jesus as the earthly manifestation of Sol Invictus, and at the same time gave the statues of Sol Invictus his own face! He was, in other words, a consummate politician with an eye for the main chance. Sol Invictus was everywhere from the royal imperial banners to the coinage of the realm. The Church survived because it was an almost indistinguishable part of a religious triumvirate. It fused itself with the state religion, and Constantine supported its orthodox beliefs as just another reflection of Sol Invictus.'

'Then it took over.'

'Eventually.' Paquel looked away, successfully caught the waitress's eye. 'The Council of Nicea in 325 was the beginning of the end.' He looked back, delivered one of his hang-dog smiles, lifted the small menu lying flat on the table and glanced at it casually. Having decided on some titbit, he closed it and said, 'As you know, it was the Council of Nicea which defined the authority of the bishops and arrived at the date for Easter. From there on, power was concentrated in ecclesiastical hands, the worshippers being relegated to a secondary position. That's when they decided that Jesus was really a god and not just a prophet – that he'd been a god all the time and they just hadn't noticed. It was a big day for Jesus. He joined Sol Invictus as a god, and Christianity suddenly took on the aura of a real pagan religion with possibilities – St Paul must have been proud of them. But the point is this. As a god, Jesus could more easily be associated with Sol Invictus, and that must have pleased Constantine a great deal. As convenor of that Council he certainly held them to it. Those who didn't agree quickly found themselves either dead or in exile. Before anyone could blink an eye, the Bishop of Rome was ensconced in the Lateran Palace, and about six years later new copies of the Bible were commissioned by the state to make up for those destroyed by the Emperor Diocletian a quarter of a century before. The Church was on its way, an unparalleled opportunity for a little editing having been officially put into its hands. As custodians of orthodoxy, they were now in a position to revise, edit, rewrite and generally fiddle with what remained of the sacred writings. And as they already had permission to confiscate and destroy works that challenged orthodox teaching, they were in a position to change the whole face of Christianity in any way they liked. And that is exactly what they did. Everything, as I've heard you say, was up for grabs. So it's no surprise that of the five thousand extant versions of the New Testament, not one pre-dates the 4th century. From there on it was plain sailing, so to speak.'

'You've certainly done your homework.'

'I became interested some months ago.'

Georgia stared at her friend for a moment. 'Right. Okay. I think I've understood everything you've said. But I still don't understand what the Merovingians have to do with it all. You yourself said that the Merovingian dynasty came to an end with Dagobert II, that the cadet branches weren't important, and that through trickery and fabrication over a number of centuries the Church made it impossible for the Merovingians to continue as a royal house. So what's going on? How can anyone in their right mind think there's the possibility of returning a monarchy – I presume it would have to be a Merovingian monarchy – to France within the next five years?'

'Theory has it that Sigisbert – Dagobert's son – didn't die. He's believed to have escaped the slaughter at Stenay.'

'Says who?'

'There have been articles to that effect in the French press for some months.'

'Written by?'

'The names are unlikely to be real. They certainly don't sound real.'

'So where does Duval fit in?'

'Now there's a question.'

'You seemed to think yesterday that there was a definite connection.'

'I believe there is. I believe the rumours.'

'Why?'

'Because in his own funny way, Duval's a monarchist. He's written on the subject once or twice.'

'Are you saying that he's suggested that France should return to being a monarchy?'

'No. He simply wrote about the symbolic importance of monarchy – some time ago, I should add. Not quite the same thing.'

'You realize of course that none of this makes sense. If Duval's some kind of monarchist, why should those who wish to see a monarchy returned to France try to kill him? It's a self-defeating argument.'

'I do not know. Perhaps he has angered them in some way.'

'Who, Paul?'

'If we knew that . . .'

'Why should they be so scared of a philosopher?'

'That's why we're having this conversation, Georgia, and why I agreed that we should work together. There is a mystery to be solved.'

As the waitress moved towards their table, Georgia changed tack and said, 'What's so important about the Saba Petrol logo?'

'Have you seen it?'

'I've glanced at it,'

'It's fascinating.' Paquel stopped talking the moment the waitress reached them, passed the menu to Georgia for scrutiny. They ordered, and were again left to themselves. 'The Saba logo,' he then said, linking his hands behind his chair and rocking back slightly, 'is composed of a silhouette of a Merovingian king holding a lily and a circle. Within the circle there is a bee. Now why a major petroleum company should choose to promote their product with such a logo is rather mysterious. I've checked it out as best I can, but have got absolutely nowhere. What I have discovered, however, is that the lily is directly associated with Dagobert II, and that the bee was held sacred by all Merovingian kings. For instance, King Childeric's tomb apparently contained no fewer than three hundred miniature bees made of solid gold. And when he was crowned emperor in 1804, Napoleon made a special point of having those golden bees affixed to his coronation robes. Why, I ask you? May I suggest that Napoleon, like Pepin III and the great Charlemagne, was for some reason still in awe of the vanished Merovingian dynasty. Now if Napoleon felt the need to look over his shoulder in the early nineteen hundreds, then there is a fair chance of there being something about that ancient dynasty of kings that no history book has ever recorded – something so important that it makes the possibility of Sigisbert's descendants displacing the present Government less foolish than it sounds.'

'What, for Christ's sake!'

'*That,* my dear Georgia,' said Paquel, having captivated her attention, 'is what we have to find out.'

Chapter Ten

Aretino Lefèbvre placed his glass carefully on the huge ornamental mantelpiece, turned to warm himself, and again quickly considered the possible outcome of the Maestro's hurriedly arranged meeting with Tristan Lacroix. 'You know he won't listen, so why bother?' he said, staring down at his friend. Duval did not immediately reply. He sat as if in communion with some unseen adviser, his glass of wine lying untouched on a beautiful 16th-century occasional table. Tired out by two days of constant travelling (there had been so many people to meet and talk to), and only too aware of the responsibility he carried for their organization's future, he felt singularly alone. And he knew Aretino was quite correct in his assessment. Lacroix wouldn't listen. He would just laugh at him and again make his damnable offer. 'But Bertrand is in agreement with the move,' added Lefèbvre.

'Bertrand is sometimes too much of an optimist,' replied Duval.

'He's a good man, and loyal.'

'It's his romanticism that worries me – he has read too many novels, I fear.'

Lefèbvre laughed, reaching again for his glass. 'Good men are difficult to find. And he is after all in agreement with you.'

'Good men in positions of *power* are difficult to find,' corrected Duval. He paused. 'I sometimes wonder if it is good men – whether they possess power or not – who will bring this situation to a satisfactory end.'

'What do you mean?'

'I mean that I am not fooled by my own idealism, or by the apparent idealism of our benefactors. I mean that I am sometimes as guilty of pessimism as Bertrand is guilty of optimism.' Duval's face contorted into something resembling a smile. 'The historical facts are plain enough to read – it is not the "good" who generally rearrange history, Aretino. History is generally rearranged by those with a will ruthless enough to use the *Zeitgeist* to advantage. Goodness has seldom outranked self-interest.'

Lefèbvre made a small movement with his head, the burden of a thousand reports to that effect coalescing somewhere in his mind. Then almost innocently he said, 'But you also believe in . . . miracles.'

'I believe in miracles,' replied Duval, as if quoting from the Creed. He closed his eyes and added softly, 'But in my scheme of things, miracles are not *visitations.*' His eyes clicked open again. 'They are things created out of ourselves as we respond to the world as mystery.'

Lefèbvre sipped at his wine. 'How is the young lady who visited you in London doing?'

'She is well – quite well.'

'Then we can match their magic on any level.'

'Huh!' said Duval.

'You know what I mean.'

'Yes, I know what you mean. And you are correct to call what they are involved in "magic"; but not even by inference what we are involved in.'

'It's just a word like any other word.'

'Words, as you very well know, are power. They have to be handled carefully, Aretino. What we are involved in must never be even loosely equated with what they are involved in, with what they believe. You cannot mix magic and miracles and remain the same kind of person. We are involved in miracles of body and mind, miracles for the very reason that they defy reason and throw us nearer to a more open-ended appreciation of ourselves. That is the difference between what they do and what we do. Our miracles are grounded in the mystery of what we are as human beings; their supposed miracles are projected away from that intrinsic mystery and placed in some hypothetical space beyond that of the human. Their vision is, in other words, *non-human.* And, as history has shown us, often *inhuman* for that very reason. That is the crux of the matter. There is nothing hypothetical about being a human being. We exist. And because we exist, we can say without fear of contradiction that our "agent" exists, our deeper and more profound self. Whereas their "agent" is nowhere to be found but in their magical imaginings, their dualistic projections, their fanatical insistence that some disembodied power works through them. That is a form of madness, and it leads those who hold it to undervalue human life.'

'They still manage to do what I'd call miracles.'

'Not miracles, Aretino – acts of wilful magic. They are magicians. And like the magicians created by the Church, dress accordingly, only in secret. To "match" their magic, as you suggested earlier, would be to run the risk of being nothing more than a Moses at Pharaoh's court. We have better things to do with our time.'

'We may have no option but to match their magic, eventually.'

'I will not play magician.'

'Those you have trained may not be so squeamish.'

'That is the risk we take in unleashing forces that can disrupt the personality. We had no option in that sense.'

'They aren't going to hold back one iota of their power. You know that.'

'I know that they are carried away by the dream of ultimate power.'

'They will soon have the means to make that dream a reality.'

'Yes, they will soon have the means.'

'And they have the ferocity of will to see it through.'

'That too.'

Duval glanced up at Aretino Lefèbvre and said, 'The body's immune system often weakens, but it seldom gives up entirely. It fights to the end through acts of perpetual sacrifice. That is what we must do.'

'And the boys?'

'The boys understand. They know what to do if anything happens to me. They are prepared.'

Lefèbvre nodded slowly, stared at Duval. And then he said: 'I still can't understand why you're bothering to meet with Lacroix.'

'I have something to say to him.'

'He won't listen.'

'He will hear the words; that is enough.'

'It won't make any difference.'

'It will to me, Aretino.'

Dr Freeman rang around nine. Intrigued by the man's insistence that they meet, Drummond reluctantly agreed again to visit the little room in Moscow Road. Over coffee, the reason for the priest's concern soon became apparent.

'You were ordered to attend?'

'It was couched as a request.'

Drummond took the packet of cigarettes he had battled against buying from his pocket quite without thinking and extracted one. Then he glanced at Freeman, realized by the man's expression that he had committed a solecism, and reinserted it without bothering to ask permission.

'So what did your papal nuncio have to say?' he asked, his mouth dry, his throat contracting.

'Quite a lot, but not enough as far as I was concerned. An official car was sent and I was hurtled across to Belgravia as if someone's life depended on it, then made to wait three-quarters of an hour to remind me that I wasn't important. The interview itself only took about half an hour.' Freeman shook his head at the memory of it all. 'I was told straight out to cut my links with Katharsis and Duval. He didn't beat about the bush. Duval was described as being involved in things *he did not properly understand*, those who believed in him as a set of *gullible individuals who would soon regret their allegiance to both the man and his distorted vision*.'

'Didn't say much for your intelligence.'

'Ah, but the best was yet to come. I was then informed that a specially convened panel of Vatican psychiatrists had pronounced Duval a *probable* schizophrenic. You can imagine my reaction to that. I said immediately that I did not understand what was going on. Why was the Vatican concerning itself with such an issue? That's when the whole scenario became quite ludicrous. I was told that *that* was no concern of mine: the less I knew the better. It was simply expected that I would obey the injunction to cut all ties with Duval and his organization because I had once been a priest. I should be grateful. The Church was looking after my long-term interests.'

'You believed that, of course.'

A smile from Freeman. 'I said that I would consider what was being asked of me, but that I would require more than an *in absentia* decision by a panel of Vatican psychiatrists to make me believe Duval was schizoid. As a man of reason, I expected to be furnished with the reasoning of reasonable men, I could not just be expected to obey what to me was an unfounded assessment because I had once been a priest. I also said that the convening of such a panel was the most ridiculous thing I had ever heard of.'

'That must have delighted him.'

'It gave him the chance to make a rather interesting suggestion – a suggestion I now realize to have been the sole purpose of the meeting from the very beginning. It was said that they had hoped that I would accept their findings and bow out of the picture without protest, but as I obviously wasn't going to do that, then I might perhaps be interested in assisting them with their evaluation of Duval and Katharsis. I could of course not expect to be immediately enlightened as to why they were investigating the Frenchman and his associates, but with a little patience everything would eventually fall into place.'

'They want you to play spy?'

'They want me to report on everything that's going on at the Islington headquarters, on Duval and everyone closely associated with him. I said I would think about it.'

'What are you going to do?'

'Pretend, of course.'

'To what end?'

Freeman smiled and said, 'I've been doing a little checking through a friend of mine in Rome, Mr Drummond. It seems that the man I spoke to does not exist.'

'As a nuncio?'

'More than that. He simply doesn't exist at all. There is no such person on record.'

'You're sure?'

'My friend is very reliable – he's a cardinal.'

'Did you tell him why you were checking up?'

'No. I just asked him to have the most recent files checked.'

'And there was nothing?'

'He drew a complete blank. I was obviously dealing with an imposter – a highly rehearsed imposter, I might add.'

'A trained actor?'

'Either that, or someone in the Vatican is playing games. That is also a possibility.'

'Now you're saying he could have been for real.'

'Only in the sense that I don't think I could have been fooled by an actor playing the role. He had the natural authority one equates with such a post, and the bearing. It takes years to turn out individuals like that. They're a race apart.'

'They obviously attended to the details.'

'Scrupulously. Everything was as it ought to be. I didn't suspect a thing.'

'You mentioned being picked up in an official car. Anything untoward there?'

'Nothing out of place that I can remember.'

'So what made you check up on him?'

'I wanted to find out which of the Vatican factions he belonged to, who his friends were, his rating on the ambassadorial scale. I could have gleaned a great deal from such information.'

'Could there be a connection with the attempt on Duval's life?'

'I very much doubt it – the spirit of the Borgias has long since been transformed into simple political cunning. And why go through such a charade if it's your intention to remove the subject from the face of the Earth two days later? No. The fear behind the person I dealt with was not the kind of fear that transforms itself into physical brutality overnight. It was a fear grounded in *uncertainty*.' Freeman paused. Then quite distantly he said, 'Monsieur Duval has certainly upset a lot of people.'

'You obviously don't think he's round the twist.'

'I can only judge him by the quality of his work.'

'What he's doing is a bit strange at times.'

'You've witnessed him at work?'

'I took part in a little experiment.'

'And?'

'Mind-boggling.' Drummond again reached for his cigarettes, but stopped himself this time. 'He can induce some extraordinary conditions.'

'Are you referring to the technique called Protasis?'

'You've been through it?'

'Once.'

'What did you make of it?'

'I thought it remarkable.'

'Is everything he does as powerful as that?'

'Protasis is described merely as a "loosening mechanism", a first stage, or step. What is yet to come is anyone's guess.'

'You've started the training course?'

'Yes, I was eventually accepted.'

'Eventually?'

'I found the hours of preparatory contemplative silence difficult to handle. I'm a thinker by nature and training, and a doer, not a contemplative. In Duval's system "thinking" is secondary, not primary.'

'Yet he himself is a thinker.'

'A creative thinker *par excellence*, and with a classical base. But he seems to rely more on being . . . *empty* than on being full. It is a great gift, and a difficult one to master.'

'Why the long periods of silence?'

'It helps heal the breach between that which "thinks" and that which "knows".'

'I don't know what you mean by that.'

'Then you have the answer in your grasp. It is within the state of "not knowing" that the answer resides. The state of "not knowing" is the creative state; it is the cauldron of discovery and transformation.'

'If you say so.'

As if to drive the point home, Freeman said nothing for quite a few seconds. He just sat there, perfectly still, his eyes curiously defocused. Then quite suddenly he roused himself and said, 'How is my friend Georgia?'

'She's in Paris checking up on Duval and Katharsis – on my behalf. At least, that's what she was supposed to be doing. She seems to have got sidetracked into some related business through a friend. I was waiting for a call from her when you rang.' He again felt his hand twitch in the direction of his pocket, but stopped it from actually moving this time. 'She's been having trouble with her mobile phone.'

'She's very capable.'

'Very,' said Drummond.

'May I ask you a personal question?'

Drummond knew what was coming immediately. 'If your question is are we lovers, the answer is yes.'

'But not in love?'

For a split second Drummond did not know how to reply. He drew breath, blinked and glanced at the man. 'I would say we were in love.'

'I felt . . .' The priest hesitated. 'I couldn't determine the nature of your relationship when we last met. There was an ingredient of distance in it which I found difficult to fathom. It was almost as if you were both . . . afraid. Afraid of being recognized as belonging to one another.'

'That was a pretty astute observation.'

'And now?'

'I think we've found out where we're at.'

'And where is that?'

Drummond was again at a loss for words; he began to feel edgy. 'We've talked about it,' he said at last.

'And?'

'We're much closer now.'

'That's good.'

Another silence.

'We aren't teenagers.'

'No.'

'I'm a little older than she is.' A glance from Drummond that spoke volumes to the priest. 'She was also my ex-wife's closest friend. It's been awkward at times.'

'I can imagine.'

An affirmation from Drummond. 'I really *do* love her.'

'Does she know?'

'Yes, of course.'

'You've told her?'

Drummond's eyes brightened with anger, but he managed to control himself. 'I'm not one of your patients, Dr Freeman,' he said evenly.

Freeman's apology was immediate, and quite real. 'I'm sorry,' he said, looking distinctly uncomfortable. 'It's just that I've come to think of her as a daughter – the daughter I would have liked to have had. She's very special to me. I don't want to see her hurt.'

'Nor do I, I can assure you.'

A direct and searching look from Freeman, followed by a lowering of the eyes. 'Please forgive me my impertinence, Mr Drummond.'

Responding immediately to the man's sincerity, Drummond lightened the situation and said, 'First time I've ever been asked to give a priest absolution.'

A smile blossomed on Freeman's face, quite transforming him.

'It could be said that we are all priests in disguise. In fact such a thing has been said.'

'I'm afraid there's not much of the priest in me.'

The ex-priest suddenly removed the formal barrier he had erected between himself and the advertising man by saying, 'Georgia deserves a love that is whole, Ian.'

'I agree.'

Their eyes met and held for a moment, and Drummond wondered if Dr Freeman was perhaps just a little bit in love with Georgia himself. It was quite possible. Dismissing the thought, he returned to their original subject and said, 'I'd like to be kept posted on what happens next with your fake nuncio.'

'You'll be the first to know.'

'I wouldn't spread it around too much.'

'I have no intention of . . . spreading it around. Only one other person will be informed.'

'Who?'

'My friend in Rome, of course. He'll be more than interested, I'm sure.'

'You can trust him?'

'Oh yes. He's my brother.'

Tristan Lacroix, a man late in years and of diminutive stature, ushered Duval silently into his Paris apartment. The little man's expression was a mixture of fatherly patience mixed with something akin to a loss of confidence in a son – and that in spite of the unlikelihood of the son. Pleased, yet displeased, to see his towering guest, Lacroix stood aside and allowed Duval to pass into the confines of his exquisitely decorated hallway where mirrors with finely wrought surrounds dominated the walls. He had a fetish for mirrors. The two men did not speak until Duval stood in his spacious lounge, the very lounge where the philosopher had eloquently disassociated himself from Lacroix and his many influential friends many years before. Moving to the large picture window which afforded a magnificent view of the city, Duval stood staring at the moving lights, muted sounds floating towards him like whispers in a gallery, the whole expanse of Paris speaking the same words as the little man would eventually speak.

Lacroix said suddenly, 'You're a fool, Edouard. You can't win. And you must realize by now that you will never sway me with your rhetoric.'

'I'm well aware of that.'

'Then why come here?'

'Because I have something final to say to you.'

'Then speak, and be done with it.'

Duval turned from his reflection and viewed Tristan in the flesh. It was a silly name for an old man. It was a young man's name and Tristan was in his seventies. Yet it suited him by definition, for in the ancient myth Tristan had been an arch-romantic, and this Tristan was no less beguiled, indeed besotted by a romantic ideal which fascinated him to a point verging on madness. And like the Tristan of old, this old Tristan was equally capable of the Grand Deceit – the deceit of mouthing truths while practising lies.

'You are caught in the role of artificer, Tristan.'

'Artificer?' Lacroix chuckled to himself. 'You've always had such a strange way with words. Are you trying to tell me that I am the Devil in disguise? A Joycean devil perhaps? Or is it a reference to Coleridge, or Blake?' A smirk from Lacroix. 'I've never really understood your fascination with these . . . foreigners. Although I must admit, they do seem quite impressive when translated into French. Brings them alive, one might say.'

'You are without conscience.'

'I've never had much use for conscience, Edouard. It's a highly overestimated brain function disguised as a moral force. That must surely have occurred to you by now.'

'Two people are in hospital because of you. Both are in a critical condition.'

'You think I had that done on purpose?'

'It was to your benefit.'

'I'm not a barbarian!'

'You didn't give the order for someone to shoot at me?'

'Certainly not! I was horrified when I read about it.'

'But it was sanctioned by someone in your employ.'

'I . . . regret to say, yes. They have of course been stripped of rank and punished. Of that I can assure you.' Lacroix's expression changed from plausible regret to that of an embarrassed friend. 'The younger ones are a little too zealous at times. Terribly modern.'

'And well equipped.'

'You can hardly say that on the basis of one silly incident.

I haven't got an army.'

'Such people congregate like seagulls, Tristan. They're magnetically attracted to a situation like this. You may already be losing control.'

'I think not.' A smile from Lacroix. 'Nothing like that will ever happen again.'

Duval thrust his hands deep into the pockets of his coat, keeping his coal-black eyes on Tristan Lacroix's face as he spoke. 'It's obviously your intention to destroy my credibility as quickly as possible. Correct?'

'You've left me no choice! In my position you would do exactly the same thing. It is after all a species of war we are engaged in.'

'Are you conscious of being mad, Tristan?'

The little man's tone became gun-metal hard. 'If I'm mad, then you too were once mad.'

'It was a rather beautiful game then. A dream. I eventually realized that it was not a game, that the dream could be made into an actuality – a terrible actuality.'

'It's the answer, Edouard. Why can't you accept that?'

'It's a Utopian nightmare. You'll unleash hell on Earth.'

'Hell will have already been unleashed – it is we who will bring it to heel. Don't you see? The New Jerusalem will be ours for the creating, and such a wondrous thing does not drop out of the sky of its own volition! We'll have the opportunity to do everything you've ever hoped for, and more. Much more. The whole of Western society will be united spiritually and secularly for the first time.'

'I believe it to be madness.'

'Only because you want ultimate perfection – there's no such thing, Edouard. This will be the nearest thing to perfection that has ever appeared on the face of the planet. We'll do our best, our very best to keep everything under control. But you know as well as I do that it will be a time of extremes, a time of excesses. We won't be able to control every little aspect of the puzzle until things begin to settle down.'

'The whole edifice will run out of control and confound you.'

'It can't, Edouard. We are *chosen* for the task! That is irrefutable, and you know it.' Coming quickly across the room, Lacroix gripped Duval by the arm and manoeuvred him back to the window. 'Look out there,' he said, pointing. 'Look at it all! It's yours for the asking. If you want it I'll give it to you on a plate. Imagine! Paris on a plate! The whole damned country on a plate for that matter!'

'I prefer things the way they are.'

'That's a lie!'

'I prefer it the way it is to what you're offering.'

'Only because you think too much and have become afraid. Fear has weakened you, disabled you.'

'I've stopped thinking. I'm empty.'

'Nonsense! No man stops thinking. Thinking is the breath of life!'

'I'm finally empty.'

'Of thought?' A cold laugh from Lacroix. 'An illusion, my dear Edouard. The human mind cannot be emptied of the human mind – there is always a remnant of the self left to bedevil even the greatest acts of self-sacrifice. I'm surprised at you.'

'I am truly empty, Tristan.'

'History rebukes you.'

Duval's reply made the little man blink. 'It is true that all history speaks of artifice, but only because history is a snake biting its own tail. There is certainly no escape from artifice during such an act.'

'You're saying that you've stepped out of the historical process. That is not possible.'

'I'm empty.'

'Who is empty? You're talking to me. Answering. Formulating arguments. That is not to be empty. The basic principle of human life, Edouard, is thought allied to self-consciousness. You are quite obviously conscious of self. To believe for one moment that you can escape from consciousness of self is utter folly! Thought is artifice. Mind is artifice. Even self is artifice. There is therefore no escape from artifice. No escape from image or idea. And in turn no escape from self. We're stuck with that until death claims us.'

'Being empty is not a featureless state, Tristan. Reality is seamless.'

'I'm afraid I don't have the time to discuss the finer points of mystical experience with you. I'm more concerned with why you're here – and I know why you're here. You're here because you want me to change your mind for you, only you can't admit that to yourself. You know deep down that we can't be stopped, that we have to do what we have the capacity to do. And if you came back to us, Edouard, it would be a dream made all the richer. David needs his Jonathan. Come back and help us transform dream into a glorious reality!'

'No.'

'You revelled in the dream once.'

'I woke up.'

'You mean you deserted the ship when it needed you most. You'll never be forgiven for that.'

'Your manipulations eventually sickened me, Tristan. I realized suddenly that you were quite without scruples. All true conscience was dead in you. The dream had taken over and become an obsession – a dangerous obsession.'

'An obsession shared,' replied Lacroix softly, hoarsely, 'with some of the most brilliant minds France has ever produced. Don't ever forget that.'

'There is no soul in it.'

'I'm a pragmatist; you are a babe in arms. You really are! You haven't got the stomach for real life. It grieves me that those people were hurt during that piece of nonsense in London, it really does, but that is the price we sometimes have to pay when attempting great things. You had become a pain in the neck, and something had to be done about it. You brought the whole thing on yourself. Which is to say that it's as much your fault that these people are in hospital as it is mine.'

'So you did order the shooting.'

'Of course not!'

'What did you order?'

'A focusing, nothing more.'

'I won't stop opposing you.'

'Your . . . abilities are no match for *his* gifts. You are one man, Edouard, whereas we are many – and time has all but run out. Almost everyone that matters is already with us.'

'What makes you think you have the right to do this thing?'

Lacroix's reply was immediate. 'Capacity and the desire to straighten out this continent once and for all time. The potential has been there for centuries – things just never came together.'

'We also have the capacity to annihilate ourselves. Should we also be allowed to do that simply because it exists as a potential?'

'What we're about to do can hardly be equated with that kind of madness.'

'There is a difference between annihilation and total subjugation of the mind?'

'Harmony of outlook is not subjugation.'

'Harmony without a vestige of freedom is ultimate subjugation.'

'It will spring from within the people themselves, as you well know.'

'In response to a manipulated archetype.'

'In response to the *king* – the King of Kings.'

'Don't you mean an idea run crazy?'

'Our spiritual heritage brought alive.'

'But founded on a lie, Tristan – a lie! That is what I have come to remind you of – that at root it is all a lie.'

Lacroix turned away abruptly, shook his head and stood belligerently with his back to Duval as he spoke. 'You'll have no option but to accept the truth of the Order when it confronts you in person.' He turned again and faced what had once been his star pupil with an expression of contempt. 'Even *you* will have to bend the knee then,' he said, his eyes shining with an unnatural brilliance.

CHAPTER ELEVEN

AS EXPECTED, Bill Everton's fears concerning Duval eventually tumbled out. He'd given the whole thing a great deal of thought, he said, and believed that Katharsis should be dropped for the hot potato it was. Immediately dropped. And not just because Duval had hit the headlines in such an extraordinary fashion, but because common sense dictated such a move – warning bells had been ringing since square one. What he couldn't understand was why Drummond was still undecided when it was perfectly obvious that the Frenchman and his strange amalgam of associates were into practices of a thoroughly bizarre nature. He was well enough aware of what was going on in the world to appreciate at least some of the unusual advances in psychology, but knew in his heart that what he had witnessed during the Protasis experiment had nothing whatsoever to do with psychology as it was presently understood – even in the *avant-garde* realm. And Dr Fisher couldn't be used to illustrate the profession's more sober and substantial side, for Fisher himself was known as a bit of a weirdo – Bill had taken the liberty of having him checked out, and the result had not been at all flattering. There was a rumour going around that the distinguished psychiatrist was about to get the chop from Bart's Hospital for therapy procedures thought both incomprehensible and possibly dangerous to the welfare of his patients. Now if that didn't spell out t-r-o-u-b-l-e for Drummond Advertising, then nothing did. Fisher was supposed to be the Katharsis watchdog, the consultant brought in to ensure that the therapy being taught was sensible and beyond reproach.

Ordering coffee, Drummond gave instructions for them not to be disturbed for at least an hour, lit a cigarette, and began to enlighten Bill as to what was going on behind the scenes – but not before tackling some basic issues. The first thing that had to be understood, he said, swivelling his chair to the left so that he wasn't facing Everton directly – a move designed to relax Everton a little – was that the therapy procedures practised by Katharsis were for real. The Protasis experiment had worked only too well in his own case, in spite of a hiccup or two, and Dr Freeman – a man of considerable experience and dedication – was fully convinced that Duval had formulated perhaps the most powerful therapeutic procedures ever known to the profession. Secondly, it was almost certain that the French government was backing Duval and his elaborate scheme, and they wouldn't be doing that if the man was a charlatan, or if his prognosis on Western society was without validity. That rather terrifying fact had to be kept in the forefront of one's mind at all times. It was perfectly true that something extremely odd, if not a little frightening, was going on at the same time – the attacks on himself, Drummond Advertising being broken into even before Duval appeared on the scene, the Burlington Hotel shooting, were without question disturbing – but basically everything pointed to Duval's being in the clear, the forces working against him a powerful, but obviously subversive, group yet to be identified. They were certainly in the thick of something political, something highly complex, and there was a nasty element in the background that could not be ignored. But apart from 'fear of reprisal' there was as yet no fundamental reason for them to bale out and allow some other agency to reap what would eventually be considerable financial rewards – that also had to be kept in mind. And the fact that Peyrefitte's of Paris were the coordinating agency for the whole extraordinary exercise spoke more than positively in Duval's favour. It confirmed the probability of government backing, for Peyrefitte's was the agency presently handling the French government's electoral programme. When placed along side Aretino Lefèbvre's involvement, that fact alone spoke volumes.

'The possibility of reprisals doesn't worry you?' said Everton, astonished.

'Of course! But I think they're now more interested in Duval than in us. It's him they're after. Think about it, Bill. They'd have to systematically disable all of the agencies involved to halt the process – doesn't sound likely to me. Better to nail Duval through adverse publicity than go in for that kind of madness.'

'They tried to kill him!'

'Highlight him.'

'They didn't intend to kill him?'

'I don't think so.'

'They blasted his room to pieces!'

'And he was sitting in that room, yet they missed. Highly unlikely, don't you think?'

'Plain lucky if you ask me – got the luck of the devil, that one.'

Drummond did not much care for the analogy.

'We could end up in a right old mess.'

Stubbing out his cigarette, Drummond said, 'I'm well aware of that. That's why Georgia's in Paris right this minute checking everything out for us first-hand. I hired her on a professional basis. We'll soon know exactly what's going on.'

'How long has she been there?'

'This'll be her third day.'

'And?'

'And she's doing fine.'

'Meaning what?'

'That she's doing her job, and doing it well.'

'You're not exactly telling me very much.'

'I don't know the details myself yet. But she's got her finger on the pulse, you can be sure of that.'

'So what's she actually said?'

'That she's probably on to the biggest story of her career.'

'In relation to whom? To what?'

'The people behind the shooting. She's closing in.'

'Sounds dangerous.'

'She isn't taking risks, Bill,' he said, hoping against hope. 'It's purely a fact-finding tour.'

'What if they latch on to the fact that she's snooping around, or that she's connected with you?'

'She's a known journalist; asking questions is her job. There's probably a bunch of journalists over there all doing the same thing right this minute.' He hadn't thought of that before; it relieved him somewhat. 'She'll be back in a couple of days and we'll be able to wrap this thing up once and for all.'

'The whole thing stinks to high heaven as far as I'm concerned. I can't see it working out in our favour.'

'Life stinks most of the time, Bill, yet we go on.'

Everton said nothing for a moment; he just stared at the Scotsman. Then he said rather quietly, 'You really do enjoy a fight, don't you. Right up your street, all of this.'

'I told you before – I won't be intimidated.'

'Meaning that the rest of us will just have to put up with whatever happens?'

'Only for as long as it takes Georgia to come up with the goods.'

'And if what she comes up with still doesn't clarify the situation?'

'. . . I don't think that'll be the case. She's very bright. And I have the feeling Duval's about to take us into his confidence.'

'That'll be something!'

'We'll soon know what has to be done.'

Shaking his head, Bill Everton said exactly what was on his mind. 'I have the terrible feeling you're going to drag us through this one no matter what surfaces. It's in your face, the tone of your voice. You want more than anything else to believe that Duval's on the level. But does that matter? We could lose everything. Everything!'

Ian hesitated, realizing that Bill was right, that he was indeed driven by his belief in Duval to put everything at risk. 'I don't believe that will happen, Bill. It's true that I'd like Duval to come out of this squeaky clean, but I'm doing everything I possibly can to prove the opposite of what I think and hope will be the case. I can't be fairer than that.'

Everton shook his head in disbelief. 'How long is this going to take?'

'A few days at most.'

'Will you drop Katharsis on the basis of reasonable doubt?'

'I'd like to think we can do a little better than that. We should know for sure one way or the other.'

'With something so obviously political, that might not be possible.'

Fully aware of what Bill Everton was getting at, Drummond said, 'We'll have to cross that bridge when we come to it.' He added by way of defence. 'I haven't flipped my lid, Bill.'

'No, but you've changed. You're not the man I went into partnership with.'

'We all change, Bill.'

'True. But we can't assume always for the better.'

'You do think I've flipped my lid.'

It was Everton's turn to hesitate. '. . . I just think you're – vulnerable, that's all. Looking for a truth of some sort. A *big* truth. You think Duval can deliver that truth.'

Ian said nothing.

'That's unlikely in my book.'

'Why?'

'Oh, I don't know. It's just a feeling I have.'

'Then we're on exactly equal terms,' said Drummond.

Peter Thwaites' passion boiled over as he spoke to his little group of spiritual henchmen. He was in his element. The opportunity to whip them up into a spirit-filled condemnation of Katharsis and all it stood for delighting him, energizing him, and producing in him a spate of near-hysterical language designed to bring out their hatred of the Devil and all his works. For in Thwaites' estimation (an estimation supplied to him by others) that was Edouard Duval's origin – he was of the Devil. It was after all the *end of days*, that time in the history of man when God would again reveal himself directly, and the ultimate battle between good and evil would be fought in the plain of Jezreel. All the signs were there. God was emerging in the consciousness of man and the great Apostolic revolution was already under way – the stage was set for Armageddon. It was all so obvious. Everything was breaking down. There had that very week been the worst outbreak of terrorism ever witnessed in Europe and in the United States – no fewer than five passenger aircraft blown out of the sky, plus the virtual destruction of three military installations – one British and two American – on home territory; the IRA were continuing to refuse British overtures; and fundamentalist Islam was on the warpath as never before. The signs were everywhere: earthquakes, false Eastern Messiahs, portents of the coming destruction intuited by believers of all nationalities, a great religious revival in the brewing that would undoubtedly overtake the innocent masses and transform them into a great and terrible army. The supposed elite in their fancy robes would be deceived, but those with the Cross of Christ in their hearts would don their battle armour and fight with Christ Himself at their head – it was rumoured that He was already in their midst, His glory veiled, His identity known only to a select few. And according to those who knew, Duval was the Devil's smooth-tongued prophet, the snake's forked tongue, the liar of liars, the axle of Satan's chariot. Having memorized these metaphors, Peter Thwaites now used them to drum the seriousness of the situation into his little band of God-struck helpers – Duval's Islington headquarters were the target, a small protest rally the first barrage against that citadel of hell.

It was quite obvious to Georgia that her friend Paquel had struck gold the moment she walked into his office. He was almost smiling. She said immediately, 'Okay, spill it. What have you found out?'

Leaning on his desk in a kind of crumpled way, he eyed her sleepily and said, 'I talked with someone very interesting this morning. He was most helpful. Came up with all kinds of information.'

'Who?'

Paquel sat back again, smiled, pushed his thumbs into his waistcoat and was suddenly overtaken by a yawn. Trying to speak through his open mouth, he said disjointedly, '. . . I'm not at liberty . . . to say who my informant is.' He brought the palms of both hands to his face for a moment, recovered and apologized. 'It appears that there is a certain professor of history at the Sorbonne who probably knows what we want to know. In fact it was suggested to me in all confidence that this man may in fact be directly involved – a suggestion I took to mean, because of its tone, that he *is* involved.'

'Your friend is very well informed.'

'He moves in the right circles.'

'The name of the professor?'

'Lacroix – Tristan Lacroix. Seventy-three years of age, but looks only fifty, so they say! A tiny specimen, but a marvellous brain and still in complete control of his faculties. So much so, in fact, that he is still lecturing. They can't get rid of him. Wouldn't dare get rid of him, from what I've heard.'

'You're working up to something.'

'Correct. Lacroix belongs to an organization called the *Hieron du Lys*, a historical society purportedly founded during the 19th century for the study of French history. Has quite a following. It's more than that of course. It's actually a thinly veiled secret society, only it's not really secret because it's lawfully registered – like all the other secret societies in Paris – with the police.

'Lys – lily!'

'Interesting, eh?'

'And he's obsessive about history.'

'Got quite a following for his ideas.'

'Which are?'

'Among other things, that France will never again be a great nation until she returns to being a monarchy.'

Georgia began to laugh. 'That's rather blatant.'

'Are you familiar with the word *hieron*?'

'No, but in this context I can guess at what it means.'

'It's not a French word. It comes from the same root as *hierarchy* or *hieroglyphic*. In this context it implies an organization or structure with specifically sacred connotations – almost synonymous with *church* or *temple*. But not in the sense of a building, more in the sense of a . . . congregation. But a congregation rigidly hierarchical. The other synonym would be *order* – as in a monastic order of some kind. Like the Templars perhaps.'

'The Order of the Lily.'

'Try *Sacred Order of the Lily*. That might be a little more accurate.'

'I'm still surprised by the fact that people go in for such nonsense.'

'More than you would ever believe – particularly in Paris. It's exciting. It is being young again. Everyone likes to have a secret, Georgia, but *being* a secret is even better.'

'Lilies seem to be the favourite flower around here at the moment.'

'It would seem so. Saba Petrol certainly seems to have a liking for them.'

'Not to mention old Frankish kings.'

A droll laugh from Paquel. 'Could be that they are trying to tell us something, eh? Either that, or we are dealing with a series of remarkable coincidences. And as that is always a possibility in this strange world of ours, we will have to tread very carefully.'

'What are you going to do about Lacroix?'

'It's already done. I've taken the liberty of hiring a private detective to keep an eye on him – someone I can trust. We should know quite a lot about Monsieur Lacroix within the next few days.'

'That's a good move.'

'There's one thing more – the most important thing of all. According to my informant, Edouard Duval has known Lacroix for many years. Duval taught philosophy at the Sorbonne before the war; he and Lacroix were apparently very close. They were also in the Resistance together – actually functioned together from what I can make out.'

'And now?'

'It seems that they quarrelled over something a good few years ago. Lacroix is known for his quick temper.'

'To the extent of being real enemies?'

'It could be.'

'Are you saying that it was Lacroix who arranged the shooting in London?'

'I'm saying nothing until I have proof. I would strongly advise you to do the same.'

'I'm not that silly.'

'Of course not.' An actual smile from Paquel. 'So now all we have to do is wait.'

The little band of protesters drummed up by Peter Thwaites – no more than fifteen souls armed with home-made banners – started off their siege of the Katharsis headquarters during the Friday evening rush hour reasonably enough, but it was not long before their banner-waving antics turned into something a little more direct. Their shouted slogans, lost in the din of heavy traffic and utterly meaningless to the swarm of pedestrians hurrying home, quickly turned into an assault on the premises themselves. The fragile sticks of wood from which hung God's indictment of Duval and his organization were being used to beat at the double entrance door. It was hardly a serious attack, and those inside the building had no fear of the door's giving way, but when the first stone was thrown, and one of the large upper-floor windows shattered, it was decided that the police should be informed. From there on in chaos ensued. Much to the surprise of the police – three confident constables who thought they'd seen everything – Thwaites' followers, by now in a kind of frenzy, refused to respond to common sense and stood their ground. A radio call for assistance produced six more constables, and by the time the local inspector got to the scene, all were fully engaged in what quickly became known as the Second Battle of Upper Street, the first having been on behalf of a young black man found dead in the police cells many years before. Twelve of the fifteen were jailed as a result of the evening's handiwork, and Peter Thwaites was eventually identified as the ringleader.

Oblivious to what was going on in Islington as he spoke to Georgia on his mobile phone, Drummond detailed his conversation with Dr Freeman in response to the question *what's happening your end*, then listened equally amazed as Georgia reported what she had learned about Tristan Lacroix, the little historian with the voracious appetite for all things French and monarchical. She decided to hold back on the *Hieron du Lys* for the moment, knowing that she couldn't possibly explain the significance of that rather innocent flower without delivering an impromptu history lesson.

'Sounds to me like we've stumbled on to a real bag of snakes,' said Drummond, supporting the phone with his shoulder as he pulled a cigarette out of the packet on the little table with his free hand. 'I'll collar Duval on that one the minute he gets back. God knows what's going on there.'

'I'd love to be a fly on the wall when you mention Lacroix to him.'

'And I love producing rabbits out of the hat when people least expect it.' He laughed suddenly, sourly. 'And to think I tried to fob Bill off this morning. Yes, we had an eyeball-to-eyeball. It was touch-and-go for about half an hour. I thought for a moment he was going to challenge me flat out. I decided in my wisdom that I'd better keep Freeman's news to myself for a few days.'

'What was his gripe?'

'That I was being irresponsible. Seemed to think that I'd take on Katharsis at any cost.'

'He said that?'

'More or less. I don't ever remember seeing him like that before; he was really scared.'

'Do you blame him, Ian?'

'No, I suppose not. I've been a bit pushy recently, a bit one-eyed. Haven't really consulted him the way I ought.'

'You never ever really have. You've always led; he's followed.

He doesn't have your . . . confidence.' She added quickly, 'I suggest we have a round table on all of this when I get back. Maybe you should hang fire on Duval.'

'You could be right. How about we include Freeman? He could have quite easily kept that stuff to himself.'

'He's obviously worried, like Bill.'

'Can you blame him? It isn't every day one is summoned by a fake nuncio who probably isn't a fake, if you see what I mean. Must have been quite a shock to his Catholic sensibilities.'

'He knows the kind of things that go on. He's no fool.'

'I'm looking forward to the next instalment.'

'I'll bet.'

Reaching for an ashtray, Drummond said, 'You're going to end up with one hell of a story – could make you famous overnight.'

'I don't think anyone'll believe it. It's too much like fiction run riot.'

'And I suspect we don't know the half of it yet.'

A stifled laugh from Georgia. 'If it gets any more complicated I'll have to invest in a more powerful program for my laptop to handle the variables!'

'You're enjoying every minute of it, you know you are.'

'Just wish you were here with me; Paul's face isn't the most –' The line went dead.

'Damn!' said Drummond. He switched off; waited.

His phone rang out and Georgia was back on line.

'Sorry about that,' she said. 'Still playing up.'

'Get it fixed. Who is Paul?'

'The man doing most of the work. Journalist. Runs his own magazine – *Le Miroir.* The Mirror. Knows everyone and everything that's going on in Paris. You'd like him. He's very droll. It was he who put me on to the historical materials. Which reminds me, have you managed to get into that yet?'

'I will as soon as my researcher comes up with the goods. I wouldn't have known where to start. Important?'

'Very, from what I can make out. What about the Saba Petrol logo?'

'Nothing so far. I've got someone in the office looking into that one. It'll probably take a few days to track down the brain behind it. Not that I understand why you want to know. What's the significance of a king in silhouette holding a lily, and a circle with a bee in it?'

'I couldn't begin to explain, Ian,' she said, laughing a little. 'I'll put you fully in the picture when I get back.'

'When are you coming back?'

'Probably Monday. But if things hot up I'll hang on – at my own expense if necessary.'

'No need. You're doing me a big favour. Just put in the bill.'

'*Okay . . .*'

He said suddenly, surprising himself, 'Love you, Georgia. I mean that.'

She paused, her thought processes freezing. Words tumbled out before she could stop them, 'A girl enjoys being told things like that.'

'I'm glad,' he said back.

She rang off soon after and stood staring out of the window of her hotel room, his little overture holding her there, her mind zeroing in again and again on the tone and quality of his words rather than the words themselves. Then, turning away from the now dark and deserted street, she stared at the single bed on which lay a quantity of history books and her copious notes, realizing that Drummond perhaps meant more to her than she was willing to admit. Only once had she come close to articulating her true feelings, but by some verbal sleight of hand had managed to avoid saying what he had just said. She had said instead, and even then not directly, that she needed him, that she didn't want to lose him, but had been unable to find the courage of commitment. And quite miraculously, the anger had immediately gone out of him, almost magically – an anger which only seconds before had caused him to rail at her middle-class privilege, accuse her of game-playing and indict her (along with the whole female species) as never quite knowing their own motive for things said and done. One minute a raging male with an ancient chip on his shoulder, the next a caring human being to whom grudges in the face of human need took second place. She hadn't known what to make of that – it had thrown her completely.

Love you. I mean that.

Said so quietly, so carefully she was inclined to believe it was true. And over the telephone!

She stood stock still, a young girl's flutterings in her stomach, the beginnings of an unavoidable certainty undermining previous disappointments. Then quite involuntarily the words formed, and she heard herself say: '*Love you too. Mean that.*'

The Upper Street police station didn't quite have accommodation for an influx of 12 guests, and by ten that evening they had four more, a fight having broken out in the jazz cellar of a nearby pub. Sharing a cell with two of his followers, Pastor Peter Thwaites of the Holy Ghost Church of The Last Days reminded them of St Peter's stint in Herod's dungeon, and of how God had sent an angel to deliver him, and of how astonished Peter had been when in the angel's presence his chains had fallen off and he had been delivered safely from the hands of his captors. It was not at all clear what Thwaites was hoping for as he sat there, Bible in hand, but it was certainly heartening to think that like themselves, the great apostle had also had to put up with a few hours in a draughty cell. And then with relish Thwaites got down to the business in hand. He read two carefully chosen verses of Scripture to drive his point home. 'And then shall that Wicked be revealed,' he intoned, eyeing them slowly, 'whom the Lord shall consume with the spirit of his mouth, and shall destroy with the brightness of his coming. Even him, whose coming is after the working of Satan with all power and signs and lying wonders.' There was no doubting what he was getting at this time, or to whom he referred.

A warmth crept over them, and a certainty. They were doing God's will. The Spirit of Truth was in them, and with them and they could take no wrong turning. They began to pray in their usual fashion, and the din they made set off the others like fire-crackers – so much so that a constable was sent down to shut them up. But they couldn't shut up. Something had been loosed in them and it would not go back in the box.

It was a new thing they felt, and powerful. Even Thwaites was startled by it.

'We had a visitation of the Holy Ghost,' he said later in archaic language, remembering their spiritual drunkenness and his own inspired deluge of words as he knelt on the hard grey concrete. 'We have been bequeathed the fire of God to rout evil and usher in the Kingdom. The Lord be praised!'

'Amen!' they chorused back, their eyes glassy with joy, their expectations at fever pitch.

'It's up to us now,' he added, changing from minor prophet to that of a spiritual Oberbärenführer in God's elite battle corps. 'Be strong in the Lord, brethren. Hearken only to His word.'

And again they prayed, and were wrapped around by that terrible certainty which made some of them faint clean away.

Chapter Twelve

Duval returned from Paris early on the Saturday morning, in the middle of a finely-grained snowstorm, the particles greeting him ferociously as he disembarked, an east wind raking them into miniature drifts on the already iced tarmac. He had been informed by telephone of the assault on the Katharsis building late the previous evening by a highly agitated Dr Fisher. Thirty-five minutes later he was heading away from the airport and speeding toward London in the back of a private car, the details of Peter Thwaites' siege and the subsequent battle with police graphically relayed to him by the elder of his twin therapists. Staring out at the whitened landscape as it slid smoothly and silently by through the swirling blur of crystals, Duval again felt the approach of that terrible loneliness which sometimes afflicted him as he listened to the tale of the world through mouths either wise or foolish. What a sad tale it generally was. And how much more sad it would become if he failed in his task – if the dark gods of the tribal psyche were again loosed and set up in a high places. So much to lose, even in a world where values were threadbare and vision was scoffed at as an aberration. So much to lose. And capable of being lost in the twinkling of an eye, in the time it took for a few arrogant men to enact a terrible drama on the stage of human history – the drama of the *Sacred King* – a known internal event again made external. The innocents would automatically rally to the king's banner, be seduced by the king's own seduction, accept and applaud the irrefutable evidence offered by Lacroix with gasps of relief and wonder. They would rally to that dread image as surely as a bee rallies to a flower's nectar, for they were already succumbing to their own creative madness, and were almost ripe for the plucking.

Lacroix did not understand the creative aspect of that burgeoning madness. He assumed it to be what it appeared to be, and no more – a psychic breakdown. Argument was futile. There was perhaps a glimmer of hope in that, but only a glimmer. For although the transition in human consciousness was toward unimaginable change, a strong pattern such as Lacroix's could very well derail the whole terrifying surge toward psychic reappraisal for a century or more. The species might never recover, its sensibilities being bound early on to the reversed psychology of a little man with a gigantic ego. But it would finally be someone other than the little professor of history who would turn the trick and win the hand. Ultimately that was in the immaculately manicured hands of the man chosen to be king – he to whom even Lacroix bent the knee. And there were so many others involved, so many who unwittingly carried responsibility for the coming nightmare because they longed to actualize the dream of ultimate authority through sacred dictatorship. It was the wish of children to whom freedom had become a burden, the demands of life a terror. And involved was much more than a resuscitation of the French monarchy – much more than that – more the unleashing of an embryonic god, a being of false light carrying the double title of Emperor and pope – an eagle with two heads.

Who would believe such a thing possible, until it happened?

He had been as honest with Ian Drummond as he possibly could, but could not let the advertising man in on the whole story until he committed both himself and his organization to Katharsis without reserve. That would take almost an act of faith under the circumstances, and was highly unlikely. The Scotsman was a pragmatist. Only the intervention of the benign gods could change his nature. There was always that possibility of course – the benign gods could never quite be discounted in any situation. They were always watchful. Tilting his head infinitesimally in acknowledgment of their constant vigilance, Duval smiled to himself and slowly returned to being empty, surrendered thought for snow and closed his eyes.

Little Sophie had not in any way recovered: she was still blankly catatonic. In the presence of a doctor who was also a psychiatrist, John Eglington sat stroking his daughter's hands and talking to her in a soft voice, trying to lure her up from the depths with sweet-talk. But there was no response. She was locked fast in her own fear. Again horrified by the apparent hopelessness of the situation, Drummond remained on the sidelines, his face a piece of carved stone. And while the father talked and the doctor watched, he found himself unsuccessfully willing the child to move. Nothing. Not even the tiniest movement imaginable to inspire hope; not even in the eyes. Almost an hour of this before John turned away and struggled to his feet, tears welling up, his head moving disjointedly as he fought to control himself. A glance at Drummond as he swam toward the swing door and the heartless corridor where they had earlier been made to stand and wait.

'It's okay, I'll look after him.'

The doctor suggesting that the child's father see a doctor. Something about sedatives. The sound of the swing door batting backwards and forwards as he walked smartly up that corridor in pursuit of his friend, not wishing to run for fear of making the man feel foolish.

'John!'

The figure halted abruptly in flight, the head half-turning. Drummond caught up and grabbed the man around the shoulders, marching him through the remaining passages and out of the building. They were greeted by an icy wind, and slush, by a sky heavy with snow.

'Let's get the fuck out of here!'

'The car's over here.'

No pub this time. Straight back to Drummond's apartment for lunch as previously arranged; a large whisky consumed by both men the moment they arrived; a silence to match the silence of the snow now falling mushrooming between them. And then quite suddenly John Eglington saying that it was not his intention to wear their friendship thin with his personal problems – that he was grateful for what Drummond was doing, but that he wouldn't burden him with further visits to the hospital. It was too much to ask of anyone, too painful.

'What the hell are friends for!'

'Yes, but there's a limit to what anyone can absorb.'

There was no arguing with that; it was a truth. Drummond said, 'You know where to find me if you need me, John.'

It was acknowledged with a glance, and a smile.

They talked on about this and that, turned full circle, and were again faced with the horror of a small child traumatized beyond belief. Drummond was relieved to have cigarettes in his pocket. Back to 20 a day already. No headaches so far. He lit one.

A statement of fact from Eglington. 'I've come to hate her for what she's done to Sophie. I really mean that.'

Drummond took a breath and said, 'Hate isn't the answer, John.'

'There aren't any fucking answers.'

Said in a perfectly measured tone.

'. . . Perhaps not.'

The man visibly grappling with his thoughts, searching in himself. Then more terrible words rattled out into the room. 'It must have crossed her mind that the kids would find her first.' The life draining out of Drummond as he sat there, not looking at his friend because there was nothing sensible that could be said. 'Why couldn't she have killed herself in the car?' Eglington took a breath, battered on insensibly. 'We could all have accepted a car crash, in time. But to . . .' Looking away for a moment, he then added a mystery to the mystery, 'You know I haven't dreamt about her once since it happened. Not once. Isn't that odd?'

Lifting the bottle of scotch from the floor by his chair, Drummond offered it. The empty glass held out immediately, the hand steady, the eyes not so steady. An acute awareness of every move made distancing Drummond, surgically separating him from himself and from the man upon whose face his eyes momentarily alighted. 'It wasn't my intention to get drunk again.' The feeling growing in Drummond that he could ease himself up out of his physical shell and tiptoe away, leaving John in the presence of no one. He continued the descent instead, forcing himself to be available.

'Life's an absolute bastard sometimes.'

'Life was pretty good – that I remember. The kids. Marjorie endlessly reading her books. Going away for weekends . . . I didn't know anything was wrong, Ian.'

'There was maybe nothing wrong, in the sense you mean.'

'Nothing?' An incredulous look.

'Nothing that you should blame yourself for.' Eglington's eyes were fixed on him. 'We can all get mighty depressed at times . . . I've had a few bad moments myself, I can tell you.'

'You're still here to tell the tale.'

'Yes, but it was a near thing on one occasion. Bloody near. I haven't been the same since.'

'You seem the same to me.'

'Not quite the same . . . not quite.' An uncomfortable thought struck Drummond. 'Don't misunderstand me, John, I'm not claiming difficult territory for the sake of it, or to sound superior. I'm just saying that it can hit you for six when you're least expecting it, and that some people don't survive.' He paused, starkly aware of the truth in his own words. 'A hell of a lot of people don't survive you know.'

'But why didn't I notice? She must have been yelling it at me.'

'Probably not. We have a habit of keeping these things to ourselves. They embarrass us. None of us like to be thought of as inadequate. I know I didn't. It's the old Japanese thing of not losing face pushed a few steps further. You can't ever appear to have tired of life, not of *life*. Simply not allowed, old son.'

John's expression seemed to softened a little. He said haltingly, 'I . . . I think I felt it in her. It was like something slowly draining away. Hardly noticeable even at the end.'

'And then suddenly there's nothing left – not a damned thing. You're capable of just about anything in that moment.'

'That's how you felt?'

A grimace from Drummond. 'I consider myself very lucky to still be around.'

Eglington quietened further. They sat musing on what had been shared; two men with very different memories of the same woman – the woman who had broken the code of *life at any cost*. That was how Drummond saw it. The repercussions of Marjorie's death were horrific, there was no denying that, but it was perhaps the breaking of that code more than anything else that had so shattered Eglington. Suicide was the ultimate taboo because it seemed to unravel the very fabric of creation; it was a slap in the face for the mystery. You had to hang on, and on, and on, and never allow the sheer ridiculousness of it all to get to you. It just wasn't the done thing – life was meaningful. We all knew deep down that it was meaningful to be alive, a privilege and a gift to wake up in the light, or in the night, and know that we existed. Self-conscious life was the crux of the mystery. It was also, however, the crux of our despair – we didn't know what it meant. And there seemed to be no way of answering the perennial question. No way at all. We could talk our bloody heads off in whatever disciplined fashion we wished, and the result was always the same: a blank wall of cosmic indifference grotesquely draped in our own verbiage. But as Freeman had pointed out, our *not knowing* was also the cauldron of discovery and transformation, and as such the very basis of our creativity. So on the one hand our 'not knowing' seemed to unravel creation, but on the other endlessly reconstituted it out of the silence of despair. Just being alive was a tricky business.

Having sensed something of the complexity they were all involved in, Drummond said, 'What are they actually doing for Sophie at that hospital?'

'Doing?' A perplexed laugh from Eglington as he returned to the present. 'I've got no idea really. There's apparently not much they can do.'

'Have you had a consultant in?'

'Yes, of course. I got in one of those Harley Street chaps. All he did was confirm the diagnosis. It's got something to do with hysteria.'

'That's all? He didn't treat her?'

'He said he couldn't do any more than was already being done – that he knew the psychiatrist in charge of the case and that he was first-class.'

'Mind if I make a suggestion?'

'No, of course not.'

Drummond couched his words carefully; the last thing he wanted to do was raise John's hopes, then see them dashed. 'I've stumbled on a therapist who's apparently very good with kids,' he said, hoping that Georgia's estimation of her friend's skills was accurate. 'Might be worth having him look at her.'

'I'd give the local witch doctor a try, if we had one.' Eglington said quite without humour, and instantly contradicted himself. 'Is he properly qualified?'

'Fully.'

'Have you got his number handy?'

'You want to phone him right now?'

'Of course!'

Producing his pocket diary, Drummond opened it at the appropriate page and handed it over. He decided that it was probably better to leave unmentioned Freeman's background and peripheral involvement with Katharsis for the moment. 'I'll talk with him first, if you like. We've got to know each other quite well over the last few weeks.'

'How did you come to meet?'

'He's a friend of Georgia Patton's – do you remember Georgia? Freelance journalist. She was a close friend of Patricia's, not that that would probably mean very much to you.'

'Yes, I know who you mean. We've met.' Eglington glanced at the neatly inscribed name and address, then he looked up and said, 'She put an excellent story together for our supplement a few months ago on the Paris fashions. Impressive piece of writing.'

A smile and a nod from Drummond. 'That's the lady.' He retrieved his diary and made for the telephone. 'There's just the chance he might have a couple of tricks up his sleeve that no one else's thought of,' he said, remembering the priest's curious antics as he cured Georgia's headache. 'He's that kind of fella.' Dialling the number, he waited. 'Might have a patient with him now – he seems to work night and day.'

But as luck would have it, Dr Freeman didn't have a patient. He was in fact spooning a plate of tinned tomato soup into his mouth when the telephone rang. Drummond got straight to the point, delivered himself of the basic details, and asked the man if he could help in any way. Freeman was reticent. Catatonia was one of the most difficult conditions to handle, particularly in such a young child, and he himself had no experience in dealing with such cases. Twisting the therapist's arm, Drummond then asked if the experimental techniques they had recently been discussing might be of any use. Yes, there was that possibility, but as a mere trainee Dr Freeman felt himself in no position to try out such a radical assault on a child's psychology. Duval would have to be approached directly on that one – he might be willing to help given the circumstances. Having got himself into an awkward situation, Drummond quickly terminated the call wondering what to do next, but not before asking if anything else of interest had happened since they last spoke. Nothing so far, was the reply.

'Can't help, can he?' said Eglington, when Drummond put the phone down.

'He hasn't ever handled anything like this, and it's apparently quite unusual in a young child.'

'So they keep telling me.'

Drummond returned to his seat contemplating the suggestion that he approach Duval directly; it hadn't occurred to him to do that. But the more he thought about it, the more sensible it seemed. Reaching a decision with characteristic speed, he immediately began to explain why he had thought Dr Freeman such a good bet in the first place. Eglington listened without comment, a frown riveting itself onto his face as the advertising man jumped from a detailed description of Georgia's headache being removed to that of the general effects of the Protasis experiment. More than a little astonished by what he was hearing, John Eglington eventually broke in and questioned Drummond, his mind trying to grapple all the while with the sheer oddity of what he was being asked to accept.

'Could you have been hypnotized without realizing it?'

'Not a chance, as far as I'm concerned. And Freeman's been through it as well – he'd have picked up on that one.'

'Then I don't know what to say. What you've described is extraordinary.'

'It blew my mind, I can tell you that.'

'What I'd like to know is why someone emptied a full magazine in his direction? Any ideas?'

'We'd all like to know the answer to that,' said Drummond, with a laugh. 'Right this minute your guess is as good as mine.'

'But you think he's on the level?'

A nod from Drummond.

'You think he might be willing to help?'

'He might, because you're a friend of mine. I'll certainly ask him when he gets back from Paris if you want me to.'

'Do it,' replied Eglington flatly. He smiled suddenly. 'We've got absolutely nothing to lose, Sophie and I.'

Neither have I, thought Drummond, the situation inadvertently a perfect test of both Duval and Katharsis. He got to his feet and said, 'Lunch is in the fridge. I think we'd better get to it before the whisky gets to us.'

Drummond was watching the ITV news when Georgia's call came through. They greeted one another. It was snowing heavily outside, he said, glancing at the window. And he now had some information on Saba Petrol – just a snippet, but interesting. The young executive awarded the task had called around personally that afternoon with the details, such as they were. The logo for Saba Petrol had apparently been chosen to suggest the sheer Frenchness of the company. It had been in the form of a cartoon to start with, then changed into a more realistic image. The bee had been added to the interior of the circle later for two reasons: one, it subliminally suggested to the public the idea of Saba's product being a form of nectar; and two, it balanced the overall image and was aesthetically pleasing. For what it was worth, that was the story. Georgia said that she and Paquel would be taking a closer look at Saba on the Monday, and that she would now try to explain the possible significance of that logo in relation to Tristan Lacroix. She then rattled off the basic historical details and arrived at Lacroix's *Order of the Lily* hoping that her rather terse rendering of the whole complicated affair made sense.

'I don't think I quite grasped all of that,' said Drummond, the material a congealed mess in his mind, 'and I'm certainly not going to ask you to repeat it!'

Georgia laughed into the phone. 'I don't think I could even if you wanted me to. I'm just getting to grips with it myself. Paul's the expert; he's been beavering away at this one for months.'

'You obviously think there's a connection between Lacroix's organization and Saba.'

'It strikes me as highly possible. Doesn't it you? Could be their way of subtly conditioning the public mind.' She added thoughtfully, 'Quite draconian if it is.'

Drummond digested her remark and said, 'You're staying on?'

'Just for a few more days. It's beginning to get really interesting.'

'And dangerous by the sound of it.'

Another laugh from Georgia. 'Paquel's training me in invisibility; he's a first-class snoop.'

'Don't forget what they tried to do to Duval.'

'That,' said Georgia, 'is constantly at the back of our minds.' And then she said, 'By the way, I've tracked down a couple of very interesting articles on what I was trying to explain to you a moment ago about the Merovingian bloodline. One was in *Midi Lèbre*, the other in *Bonne Soirée*. The *Midi Lèbre* article goes as far as to suggest that the present Merovingian descendants include a *true pretender to the throne of France*, and the piece in *Bonne Soirée* involves a Catholic archbishop who's giving the present pope a real –'

'Shit!'

'What's the matter?'

Drummond stared aghast at the television screen. Telling Georgia to hang on, he bent forward and turned the sound up. The newsreader was again visible by this time and saying something about twelve people of the something-or-other Church having been arrested after a brawl with police in Islington's Upper Street. But what had attracted Drummond's attention was the unmistakable figure of Peter Thwaites in a previous shot being bundled into a waiting police van after a rather grotesque close-up; there was absolutely no doubting that it was he. It took a few seconds of listening before Drummond realized that the incident was already one day old. Describing what he had just witnessed to Georgia, he informed her that Dr Fisher was now on screen, and that the man was saying something about an attack on Katharsis by fanatical Christians with a totally distorted idea of present-day psychological procedures – it was sad to think that such individuals could still exist in society when so much money had been poured into education by successive governments.

It was a good tack.

Mesmerized by what he was seeing and hearing, Drummond continued to relay Dr Fisher's words to Georgia. The psychiatrist was rising to the occasion – in fact, he was verging on being eloquent. And then there was a cut and Duval was on screen, his sombre face and bearing adding a further solidity to Fisher's words. Drummond didn't know what to think for a moment. Then he realized that Duval was already back from Paris and that this was immediate, the rest having been a run-up to an interview with the Maestro himself.

'Duval's on!'

Georgia waited, straining to pick up the stray word or two. 'I can't hear properly,' she shouted into the receiver.

'Hang on!'

Duval's face filled the screen, his thin mouth articulating sensible things.

'I still can't make out what he's saying!'

Unable to hear the voice on the line – he was holding the phone out towards the television set so that Georgia could pick up on what was being said – Drummond listened to the Frenchman deftly blast those who had attacked the Katharsis premises in a string of tightly phrased statements; it was impressive stuff. And following hard on Dr Fisher's strongly worded overview, it came as a confirmation of the narrow-minded idiocy of those involved in the attack. And the accusation of his being involved in witchcraft, voodoo, and other practices of a magical and satanic nature was of course utterly ludicrous – the people involved had allowed their imaginations to run riot. Katharsis was dealing with advanced forms of therapeutic training which had simply been misconstrued by individuals of a superstitious bent. It was alarming and it was sad that such individuals still thought the way they did in the 20th century. It was certainly true that meditational procedures were being used, and that meditation was a technique originally developed in relation to Eastern forms of worship, but in a therapeutic context such techniques were used solely for the purpose of relaxation. Meditation and special breathing exercises were now practised in hospitals and clinics right across Europe to great effect, and it should be noted that many sections of the Christian church were also experimenting with similar procedures for purposes distinctly spiritual and uplifting. To view meditation as either 'magical' or 'satanic' was to exhibit total ignorance of what was going on in the world of science and advanced religious thought.

But the interviewer wasn't to be put off so easily. Mustering her armaments she rejigged her previous question and said smilingly that Duval and his organization for the training of advanced therapeutic techniques seemed to be evoking an unusual amount of violence and bitterness. She was of course referring to the brutal shooting at the Burlington Hotel only one week earlier. Three innocent pedestrians had ended up in hospital as a result of that rather bizarre happening, and two of them were still on the critical list. In the light of what had now taken place, would he care to speculate on why he and his organization had become the centre of such unsavoury attention? Duval asked if she were suggesting a connection between the two incidents. At a loss, she turned the question round and handed it back, whereupon he skilfully used it to terminate the interview and further dissipate the aura of suspicion and distrust she had worked so hard to create. Laughing to himself, he said that he thought it highly unlikely that good Christian souls would resort to the use of a high-powered automatic weapon on one occasion, and then follow it up with sticks and stones. There was quite obviously no connection whatever. The supposed attempt on his life had simply been an act of terrorism directed at the wrong person, those so severely injured, the unfortunate victims of that grotesque mistake. But that was not to say that those belonging to the Holy Ghost Church of The Last Days – a rather cumbersome title in his own opinion – had not attempted to ride on the back of that vicious incident for their own intellectually illiterate purposes. They may very well have thought their timing impeccable.

The interview ended on that note.

Putting the telephone to his ear again, Drummond said, 'Did you get all of that? It was superb! I wouldn't have believed either of them had it in them to –' That was when he realized she was no longer there: her mobile phone had again died on her. 'Get it fixed, woman!' he shouted into the dead receiver.

Knowing that Duval would be in the process of leaving the ITN studio at that precise moment, he went into the kitchen and prepared himself a snack from the leftovers of lunch, thinking all the while about the conversation he hoped to have with the man that evening if he were free. Allowing three-quarters of an hour to elapse, he went back into the lounge and dialled the Katharsis number. It was almost a minute before anyone answered. Yes, Monsieur Duval had returned, but he was very tired and was unavailable. Drummond persisted. The voice asked if he would kindly hold the line for a moment. He said yes, and waited for a further two minutes. Then quite suddenly Duval's voice sounded in his ear, and the old feeling of talking with someone from beyond the grave returned. Congratulating the philosopher on his TV performance, he quickly explained about Peter Thwaites and suggested that they meet right away – that had, after all, been their intention prior to the Paris trip. But if he were tired . . . To Drummond's surprise, Duval immediately agreed and set a time; he had apparently been contemplating exactly the same move only moments before. Going to the window, he stood for a moment staring out at the snow – he'd picked one hell of an evening to go visiting.

London was curiously silent. It was momentarily a blinded city, the snow flurry having reduced visibility and added uncharacteristic caution to both drivers and pedestrians alike. With the heater on full blast he drove carefully through the congested streets, conscious of the fact that he had Duval cornered, that everything now hinged on what the gangling philosopher said, or did not say, admitted, or did not admit. He'd know within ten minutes whether to bail out or go for broke. Then with a start he remembered what he had promised John Eglington, and belatedly realized that if Duval agreed to treat Sophie, and she recovered, then in spite of professional distrust he would be beholden to him for having cured the child and rescued the father from abject despair. But that possibility itself depended on how Duval measured up under questioning. He wouldn't even broach the subject if he either proved himself a liar or was unwilling to open up with a full and convincing explanation of what he was involved in. For if he lied, or continued with the game of half-truths, then any treatment offered would probably prove spurious in the long run – the Protasis experiment could have been a trick: perhaps a drug of some kind had been administered in the coffee prior to their departure from the conference room. That was an uncomfortable possibility; it hardened Drummond's resolve to get at the truth.

It took three sharp raps on the door before anyone answered. By the time they did, Drummond looked like a snowman. He laughed and shook himself like a dog, wiping the furry crystals out of his hair and eyes as they moved down the long entrance corridor and headed for the staircase which led up to the conference room. The young man leading the way had smiled at Drummond's appearance, but said nothing until they reached the first floor and walked another 20 yards or so down another equally dismal corridor to the back of the building.

'The Maestro will be with you in a moment,' he said, opening a door. 'Please wait in here.'

'Okay if I smoke?' asked Drummond.

'If you wish; there's no restriction this end of the building. I think you'll find an ashtray inside.'

As predicted, there was an ashtray. There was also a pile of magazines next to it on the low table, a row of tubular metal chairs and a square of cheap blue carpet. It was like paying a visit to the dentist. And it was none too warm. Drummond immediately lit a cigarette, and again tried to ignore the fact that the smoke was going down into his lungs, that his mornings would soon be filled with coughing again. Bloody things! Only a couple of stolen cigarettes per day for well over a month, and now back to it with a vengeance. The thought depressed him, the sight of the fine grey ash dropping into the glass ashtray driving home his stupidity for the umpteenth time. Georgia would be disappointed. He sighed to himself, glanced toward the door, listened, but there was no sound from the corridor.

His mind seemed to go blank in that moment, the stillness of the room and the sheer quietness of the building robbing him momentarily of time and place. He began to wonder if there was anyone there at all, if he had perhaps been abandoned to the same silence which had so disturbed Dr Freeman – Freeman the thinker. Not exactly a description he could lay claim to himself; his own thinking revolved almost totally around business and the business of making money. Well, someone had to do it. They couldn't all be Freemans and Duvals and devote themselves to the niceties of philosophy. The world turned on money, not philosophy. And it took a funny kind of brain to appreciate the kinds of things thought important by such people. They lived in a world of their own, a world of twisted meanings and arguments too difficult to follow couched in a language of their own making to keep ordinary mortals at bay. It was a closed shop unless one made an almost superhuman effort to break their specialized code of communication. He laughed to himself as the almost astonishing simplicity of his own profession came into focus – the profession whose greatest claim to fame lay in the fact that it had successfully sold itself as the greatest and most powerful product of all the products. That's why so many people instinctively disliked advertising: it proved just how vulnerable we all were on a minute-to-minute basis. It also proved that ideas – the beloved product of the philosopher – could be sold as readily as saucepans.

Having come full circle, he walked to the door and stuck his head out. Emptiness. Not even the occasional sound in the distance to create the illusion of having company. Where the hell was Duval? Why had he been left to wait in an unheated room when he ought to have been greeted immediately by the Maestro himself? The Maestro. What a stupid fucking title for a human being. He was a man just like any other man, and he was up to his Gallic ears in trouble. The sooner they got down to business the better.

Leaving the little waiting-room altogether, Drummond made

his way down the corridor, came to the top of the stairs and turned left; it was the only sensible direction in which to go: there were a couple of doors up ahead. Not knowing what to expect, he opened the first door. An empty kitchen. He retreated, closed the door quietly behind him and approached the second door. Listening for a moment, but hearing nothing, he turned the handle and looked into a room crammed with about 40 students sitting in absolute silence. It was a shock for everyone concerned, but nothing was said. Mumbling apologies, he backed out and closed the door behind him, turned, and found Duval standing only a few feet away.

'Are you lost?' asked Duval.

'Lost?' Drummond blinked. 'No, I was looking for you. I'm afraid you're waiting-room's too damned cold to hang around in.'

'Ah, I see.' He immediately explained his absence. 'I'm afraid a long-distance call came through just as you arrived. I had to take it.'

'No harm done,' said Drummond.

They continued down the same corridor, rounded a corner and came to a door marked Private. 'This is about the only civilized spot in the whole place,' said Duval, opening the door and standing aside. 'And we will have the benefit of a heater.'

The room was small, and obviously a place of study and retreat. An oak desk covered with papers and the odd book or two dominated one wall, while two leather armchairs and a standard lamp with a tasselled shade added warmth and a touch of informality. An old-fashioned Chubb safe (the key was in the lock) and a wooden filing cabinet with three drawers enhanced rather than detracted from the setting, and a Persian carpet not unlike the one in the conference room, but much older, completed the arrangement. There was also a slender window to which a patterned paper blind had been fitted. Closing the door, Duval immediately plugged in the heater and switched it on; a fan started up. He then suggested that Drummond remove his rather damp coat and be seated. The advertising man complied, draped his coat cape-like on the back of the nearest armchair and enquired as to exactly when Duval had arrived back from Paris.

'Early this morning. The snow made the landing quite tricky. Dr Fisher telephoned me late last night with news of the . . . attack. He was most upset. I thought it best that I return immediately.'

'You had a successful trip?'

'I would be hard pressed to describe it as successful, but it was certainly useful.' Alluding to the shooting, he added, 'I doubt very much that they'll resort to such strong measures a second time – that was apparently a mistake; at least so I was led to believe.'

Drummond frowned, tried to take in what he was hearing for a second time, but again failed. 'You actually spoke with the people who set up that outrage?'

'In a manner of speaking.' Duval eased himself down into the other armchair. 'I spoke with someone who assured me that he too saw the shooting as an act of barbarism, and that it was not at all what he had intended.'

'Not what he had intended?' A look of utter perplexity usurped Drummond's face. 'What on earth is that supposed to mean?'

'It means . . . that a zealous minion went beyond his brief: I suspect he was perhaps testing the authority of his superiors.'

Feigning exasperation, Drummond said, 'Who the hell are we actually talking about? Who are these people you're referring to?' He added sharply, 'Give me a name!'

Duval's head moved back on his shoulders fractionally. 'Their identity hardly matters at this juncture . . . Ian. It's more important that I –'

'I want a name,' said Drummond flatly, knowing that they had reached breakpoint, that he mustn't allow himself to be sidetracked. 'I think you owe me that.'

'And you will have it,' replied Duval quickly, almost imperiously, 'but not until I have explained certain things to you – things difficult to follow and for you perhaps impossible to believe.' He paused, looked away, drew breath and continued in a clipped fashion. It was quite obvious that he did not appreciate having such demands made on him, that he had a set programme of thought and did not warm to what he considered unwarranted interruption. 'But first I must tell you a story,' he said, laying his hands on his knees, 'an unusual story, a story which at first will seem totally unrelated to the happenings of the last week or so. But when you have grasped the rudiments of that story, and have had it set in a larger historical context, then everything else will fall into place. Will you bear with me?'

A nod from Drummond.

'Good. Then here is what you must know before being given the identity of those to whom violence and intrigue have now become second nature.' He composed himself, taking on the aura of a man about to reveal some terrible secret; it was quite a performance. 'During November 1964 an Australian journalist by the name of Donovan Joyce wrote to General Yigael Yadin seeking a permit to visit the Masada excavations then being carried out by the Israeli government – Yadin was in charge of those excavations. Thinking it an automatic courtesy that a permit would be granted to any visiting writer, he did not wait for a reply, but went straight to New York to arrange publication with William Morrow & Company. That done, he then flew straight to Tel Aviv, arriving at Lod airport on Thursday 3rd December. It is an interesting coincidence that today is also the 3rd of December, Ian, and that it is today that this story has to be told.' An actual smile from Duval before he continued, a smile meant to convey something of importance to Drummond. 'According to his own detailed report, Joyce was sitting in the lounge of the Dan Hotel one hour later having drinks in the company of a stranger named Professor Max Grosset; they had been brought together by the availability of tables. Conversing casually, both men volunteered information about themselves, Joyce describing himself as a writer, Grosset identifying himself as a professor of Semitic languages at an American university. Intrigued by Grosset, and excited by his own venture, Joyce talked about the book he intended to write and launched into an enthusiastic account of the Masada epic – only to discover later that the tweedy professor had been a member of General Yadin's specialized team. I'm sure you can guess Joyce's reaction to that. Not a little embarrassed by his own boyish enthusiasm, Joyce changed direction and mentioned that he had not yet received a permit to visit the site. At that point, Grosset turned unexpectedly into a prophet of doom. He assured the would-be historical novelist that he would never set foot on Masada for the very reason that he was a visiting writer. He then added quite perfunctorily that Joyce should catch the next plane home, and left a stunned Donovan Joyce sitting in the lounge as he headed for the elevator. This is exactly as Joyce tells it in a rather interesting book published in 1973.

'As from that moment, and as if in fulfilment of Grosset's prediction, everything went wrong for Joyce. On enquiring about his permit, he was informed by letter that General Yadin had not been in receipt of his application until the day of his arrival in Israel. As everyone was far too busy to show him around the site, it was suggested that he buy a copy of the *Illustrated London News*; he would find everything he wanted to know in that, the letter said. Fuming over the treatment he was receiving, Joyce went to Jerusalem the following day and telephoned General Yadin's home, but got nowhere. Still angry, he then kept an appointment he had at the Knesset with Menachem Begin; he felt sure that Begin above all would be able to overcome the Masada impasse imposed by Yadin. A former leader of the Irgun – one of Israel's underground armies during the war of independence – Begin was known as a tough customer, a man who detested red tape and got things done. And as expected, Begin was suitably astonished by the fact that Joyce had been refused a permit to visit Masada. Calling several MPs into the room, Begin swiftly outlined the situation. The solution agreed upon by all present was direct intervention by no less a person than the Prime Minister himself – Mr Levi Eshkol.

'But as it turned out, neither Begin nor Eshkol were able to break the impasse set up by General Yadin's department: it was almost as if he were single-handedly running the country in that point. And from that moment onward, Joyce becomes convinced that his apartment at the Dan Hotel is under surveillance by either the official Shin Beth – the Israeli Secret Service – or by some other less romantic arm of Israel's security force. Things then start coming to a head. Two more meetings with the mysterious Professor Grosset follow – one at the hotel, the other at Lod airport on the day Joyce is due to leave the country. At the first of those two meetings, Grosset confesses to being involved in the removal of a valuable scroll from the Masada excavation, a scroll of such importance that were it to fall into Israeli hands they would have it *incinerated on the spot.* At the second meeting, having shed what turned out to be a disguise, Grosset attempts to involve Joyce in a smuggling operation. It is apparently vital that the stolen scroll, referred to by Grosset as the *fifteenth scroll*, not be allowed to fall into General Yadin's hands due to its explosive nature – a $5,000 incentive is offered. Realizing that anything might be being smuggled out of Israel – drugs, diamonds, information of a military nature – Joyce demands to see the scroll and be informed of its exact contents before consenting. Grosset reluctantly agrees. The scroll is shown to Joyce in the men's toilet, and is estimated by him to have been ten or twelve feet long, the separate sheets of skin having been stitched edge to edge to form a roll. At first Joyce isn't impressed. Accusing him of being a philistine, Grosset eases back a loop of parchment to reveal neat rows of black lettering. "Hebrew?" asks Joyce. "No, Aramaic," states Grosset. He then tells Joyce that he has in his hands what is probably the most astonishing document ever written: a personal document or letter addressed to no one in particular, and therefore to everyone in general, and signed by a man whom many believe never to have existed at all. Joyce asks the obvious question, and is eventually rewarded with a name – *Jeshua ben Ya'akob ben Gennesareth*, the last Hasmonean Priest-King of Israel.'

'Jeshua?'

'Jeshua ben Ya'akob ben Gennesareth – *Jesus of Gennesareth*.'

Drummond's face remained expressionless, but his eyes conveyed shock. 'You believe this story?'

'I have good reason to believe it,' replied Duval, his tone as even as when he started. 'Grosset, and not Joyce, eventually managed to smuggle the scroll out of Israel, and someone of my acquaintance was allowed to read it a few months later; I have no reason to doubt that person's word, only his sanity.'

'The person whose word you accept is mad?'

'Not really mad; it would perhaps be more accurate to say . . . *obsessed with an idea*. But he is no one's fool when it comes to the evaluation and verification of such documents. He is more than qualified to do so. And outside of his normal discipline, I might add, which is history.'

Drummond would have loved to have said that man's name there and then, but decided to hold back a little while longer. Duval appeared to be speaking honestly and without subterfuge – but what in the name of God was he leading up to? What had the Donovan Joyce story to do with Lacroix's obsession for things monarchical? Keeping his tongue under firm control, he waited for the opportune moment to arrive, his mind trying to make connections between what he was hearing and what Georgia had already supplied on the telephone, albeit in a sketchy fashion. But it was some time before a pattern emerged, and when it did, he gasped at its improbability.

'. . . But the really important point is that this extraordinary document, apparently in Jesus' own hand, states that the writer is eighty years of age, and that he is the last of the Hasmonean kings – which is of course to say the last *Maccabean* king of Israel. And it should be remembered that it was this crime, the crime of being a king of Davidic descent, and therefore a direct threat to the political stability of Palestine, that caused Pilate to arrest Jesus, try, convict and sentence him to death – his very existence was a challenge to the Emperor Tiberius. Hence the written accusation on the Cross itself, *King of the Jews*, and the suggestion of the chief priests to Pilate that he write: *He said, I am King of the Jews*, and Pilate's continual reference to Jesus as *Messiah* and/or *King of the Jews* during his trial. Without doubt he believed himself to be a priest-king, and acted accordingly – hence the mockery of dressing him in royal purple prior to his being scourged, and the placing of a platted crown of thorns on his head. And it's highly unlikely that the supreme court of Judea, the Sanhedrin, delivered Jesus into Roman hands for blasphemy; the Romans wouldn't have been interested in such a charge. But a Jew claiming to be a king, and hailed as a king by the populace, obviously forced the issue – the Sanhedrin had no wish to see another bloody insurrection, and the Roman Governor of Judea was of an identical persuasion. It's ludicrous to believe that Jesus was delivered into the hands of the Romans for stating that he was the Son of God. A Jew of Jesus' obvious calibre could not have entertained such an idea. That is a preposterous notion foisted on Jesus by the Council of Nicea in AD 325 under the auspices of Constantine, and it has proved itself one of the most dangerous and pernicious of notions ever since.'

Continuing to play along, Drummond said, 'What you're saying at base is that Jesus did not die on the Cross – that he survived his crucifixion and ended up at Masada.'

'Exactly.'

'Fascinating. In fact, riveting. But why are you bothering to tell me all of this? I can't –'

'Because, as you will soon see, what I've told you of the scroll relates directly to everything we are presently involved in.'

'In what way?'

'The Hasmonean bloodline did not terminate with the death of

Jesus at Masada. It survived, and in another country. Jesus was a married man. The fact that he was married has been carefully excised from the historical record – but not completely. The scroll smuggled out of Masada by Grosset confirms that he was married, not celibate as the Church would have us believe. One can still find rudimentary evidence to this effect in the New Testament. When Jesus refers to himself as a "bridegroom", it is not by way of homily, Mr Drummond. 'Duval again paused. Then he said, ever so quietly, 'There was a child. Legend has it that soon after the crucifixion the wife of Jesus escaped from Judea by sea, and in the light of what we now know about Jesus, it is not at all surprising that she was hastily smuggled out of the country – the child's survival was of paramount importance.'

'That's – quite a story. You expect me to believe it?'

'I expect you to weigh in your mind whether it is more probable that Jesus was born of a virgin, walked on water, raised the dead, changed water into wine, stilled storms with an upraised hand, cloned loaves and fishes, remained celibate all his life when the religious climate of the time demanded that all Jewish men engage in the reproduction of the race, got himself crucified and rose from the dead, and was then physically translated into heaven and ended up in full accordance with everything the Church did in his name. Or that he was a man born to be king, a married man, a man who survived his own crucifixion and died in a suicide pact at Masada as a last heroic gesture of defiance and kingly disdain against an empire with a mentality equal to that of the Third Reich. A man whose wife was smuggled out of the country by friends so that her yet-to-be-born child might survive and some day return to his people. That, Mr Drummond, is what I expect you to make up your mind about.'

Drummond huffed an embarrassed laugh, throwing a look at Duval which intimated that he clearly got the point. 'You put that extremely well.'

'I have a professional responsibility to put things well. It is expected.'

'There's obviously more to come.'

'Yes.'

'Mother and child survived?'

'Legend has it that she was eventually washed up on the shores of Provence in a rudderless boat along with a small party. Yes,

Provence! It is said that this party brought with them the bones of the Holy Innocents and the head of James the Less, plus the Holy Grail – the *Sangraal*. We're told that she is *carrying* the Sangraal. I leave it to your imagination as to what that means in real terms.'

'You know who she was?'

'Can't you guess? Mary Magdalene of course. Her body is said to lie in the crypt of St Maximin's church in Aix-en-Provence; it was discovered there in 1279. Her cult still flourishes in the area.' Reading Drummond's expression, Duval added, 'You think that preposterous? It isn't really. Ships plied the oceans in those days almost as they do now. The Phoenicians were sailing to this island at the time of Solomon. What you don't realize is that there was a strongly established Jewish colony in southern France at that time, a colony attested to by modern scholarship. It was to this colony that the Magdalene brought her child.'

Struggling not to blurt out what he had learned from Georgia, and having instantly made the rather obvious connection between the Hasmonean bloodline and that of the Merovingian kings, Drummond said innocently, 'I was taught that Mary Magdalene was a reformed prostitute – a whore who saw the light. You seem to be painting a very different picture.'

'And as I know the picture I'm painting is accurate, the reason for her being interpreted a whore, or harlot, is self-evident. But the Gospels do not confirm that interpretation. In Luke's Gospel there is the story of Jesus' having supper with a Pharisee called Simon. As they dine, an unnamed woman enters and washes Jesus' feet with her tears, dries them with her hair, anoints them with a precious ointment. The Pharisee is appalled that Jesus should allow a "sinner" to touch him while he eats, but is sternly reminded that these acts of kindness and hospitality have not been offered by himself. It is correctly assumed that this woman was Mary Magdalene. Then comes a telling statement, for Luke has Jesus say, '. . . her sins which are many, are forgiven, for she loved much.' The implication that Jesus would have been polluted by her touch has led believers to think of her as a whore, not as a murderess, thief or liar. And the words *for she loved much* have been interpreted as a reference to sins of a particularly carnal nature. But Jesus' statement has been incomprehensibly distorted, for he states quite clearly, and quite grammatically, that the woman's sins have been forgiven *for the very reason* that she loved much, not that her sin is a result of her having loved much. Nothing more than imagination and prejudice have damned this woman in the eyes of believers. Western folklore identifies Mary Magdalene as a reformed whore, but the Gospels speak of her as being healed of 'evil spirits and infirmities' – a reference to no more than ill-health couched in the language of the day. Such is the power of tradition.

'But as I insinuated earlier, the conception of Mary Magdalene as harlot assists to distance her from Jesus as sexual paragon, and the only embarrassment suffered by the Church is that St John's Gospel awards the Magdalene a role of considerable significance, a role that totally eclipses Mary the mother – Mary the perpetual virgin and sexual mirror-image of her son. The mother of Jesus inexplicably disappears after the crucifixion, whereas the Magdalene is first to meet her supposedly resurrected Lord. And it is Jesus she meets – Jesus disguised as a gardener. There is no getting away from the fact that Mary of Magdala was closer to Jesus than any of the disciples. Both the apocryphal *Gospel of Mary* and the little mentioned *Gospel of Philip* afford Mary Magdalene a special place in the affections of Jesus. The Gnostic *Gospel of Mary* portrays her as a supreme initiate in the mysteries Jesus taught as priest-king, and the ignored *Gospel of Philip* tells us that Mary was *often kissed by him.* The Church views such writings as garbled nonsense totally lacking in validity, but not all scholars follow suit.'

'They'll never buy it!'

'Mr Drummond, they won't have any option. The Church has put off the evil day for centuries, but the evil day has all but arrived. I call it evil because it will tear the Western world apart and be a presage for acts of unbelievable barbarism in the name of a priest-king two thousand years dead, a man of flesh and blood and passion reduced through elevation to the rank of a god and now embedded in the consciousness of Western man as an archetype without equal. The Church succeeded beyond its wildest dreams, and it now has to pay the price for that success.'

'What exactly are you saying to me?'

'I'm saying that not only did the ancient Hasmonean bloodline survive the destruction of Jerusalem, but that it has also survived nineteen centuries of political machination in Europe, and is still with us.'

'Is that what Lacroix is up to?'

Duval's surprise was almost amusing. He gaped as if struck. 'What do you know of Lacroix?' he asked.

'Enough.' Drummond wetted his lips, continued almost nervously. 'I've had someone in Paris for the last week unravelling the whole mess with the assistance of a friend. They haven't done badly, I now realize.'

'They've spoken with Lacroix?'

'No, but they're having him watched – someone tipped them off that you and he were old friends, and that you had served in the Resistance together.'

'What else do you know?'

'That Lacroix is a rabid monarchist; that the idea of France's returning to monarchical rule is being rumoured in high places; and that there's been some rather interesting pieces of journalism floating around on the ancient Frankish kings.'

A shake of the head from Duval. 'I'm impressed, Mr Drummond. *Very* impressed. You are quite obviously a very resourceful man.'

'It's taken too many years to get where I am to just throw it away overnight.'

'Your next move is?'

'. . . That depends on the rest of your story. I still don't understand how this incredible change in things is going to be brought about. Fill me in on that, and I'll give you a decision before I leave this room.'

'We have almost reached the moment of truth,' said Duval, having taken a deep breath. 'The success of establishment Christianity as a moral breakwater against the chaos and anarchy of Western civilization is at an end – which is to say that its days as a *controller of crowds* is over. The chaos, anarchy and violence so obviously resident at the heart of our civilization is the direct result of the Church's unwillingness to properly instruct the people in the tenets of self-knowledge, direct them away from the letter of the law and allow a natural surfacing of the spirit of the law. The Church's disguised greed for power has ever got in the way of that, as has its erroneous belief that human beings are fundamentally evil and require saving by some external spiritual force. *That* is the crux of the problem, Mr Drummond, and we are now about to reap the reward of that mistaken allegiance to power, and the perpetuation of half-truths over the last two thousand years. The game is at an end, and millions are aware of that fact. So she has no option but to close ranks and consolidate what power there is left, leaving the few in her midst who truly understand the nature of the problem to bear the weight and responsibility of pointing the people in the direction of their own innermost being. She herself refuses to do that. She prefers, indeed has always preferred, to point to the artefacts of theological imagining and hope that the spiritual fear instilled into the masses will eventually return them to the fold. But it won't. Not this time. The edifice of so-called Western spirituality is about to be split asunder, and there will be no putting it together again in the old form.

'How will this be done? It will be done by Lacroix and the usurped bloodline of the Hasmoneans in a moment of unbelievable stress, a moment of psychic breakdown and widespread paranoia – the breakdown I described to both yourself and your colleague when we met in conference no more than one week ago. And so will be initiated the ultimate irony, the irony of a Church destroyed by what is probably a descendant of the very man believed to represent everything she believes and stands for. In that moment the stone will disallow the corner and the building will fall. But only to be immediately replaced with a hierarchy more ruthless than anything witnessed in the whole history of the Church, a hierarchy of individuals convinced of both their spiritual superiority and their divine right to abolish democracy and inaugurate a theocratic dictatorship backed by nothing less than a kind of god manifest in the flesh. Can you grasp that? Can you imagine the enormity of the thing I'm trying to describe, what the reaction of a half-crazed populace will be? The Church certainly can. And as we sit here she's battling for her life across the breadth and width of five continents! She knows all about it, has known for centuries that it was always a possibility, and she's now panic-stricken as that possibility matures by the minute into an imminent reality. The present pope is grasping at straws, battening down the hatches against liberalism and unwittingly setting the stage for the biggest take-over in history. For the man chosen as the Christian Messiah of the West, the returned Christ, will not only claim an emperor's crown – the crown of Europe – he will also sit on the throne of St Peter's as God's direct mouthpiece on Earth – the folly of infallibility stretched to its ultimate extreme. Is the picture forming? Can you see it? Feel it? Can you now see what I see?'

'It's terrifying.'

A sigh from Duval, and a longish look before he completed his entreaty. 'I think it must be fairly obvious to you by now that if you decide to take on this task, then with a number of others you will be in the firing-line – perhaps literally.'

'Yes, that has dawned on me.'

'You know what they're capable of.'

'Yes.'

'And your decision?'

A sharp laugh from Drummond, and a rhetorical statement as Duval waited for his yea or nay. 'Why in God's name does it always have to be me who has to make such decisions!'

'You wish me to answer that?'

'I doubt very much that you could.'

'I will try.' His smooth, long face was suddenly radiant with humour. 'I think it is because you are a natural warrior, Mr Drummond – and I mean that in the very best sense of the word. A warrior of the heart.'

'Or just a fool with a quick temper I think that is a little more likely.'

'In the past perhaps, but not now.'

'You wouldn't be trying to flatter me, would you?'

'And run the risk of releasing that quick temper from captivity? Never! I'm not that foolish. I will accept without protest whatever you decide.'

'For my sins,' said Drummond, wondering if he were himself perhaps even more mad than Tristan Lacroix, 'I'm in.' He added quickly, 'And I'm in whether or not you grant a favour I have to ask on behalf of a friend of mine, a friend whose wife recently committed suicide.' He explained, using all of his verbal skill to paint a picture of Sophie's need and her father's grief. 'If there's any possibility of your . . . new therapy's helping the child, I'd be in your debt for the rest of my life.'

'Then we are in each other's debt.'

'You'll do it?'

'Whatever can be done will be done.'

'That's marvellous!'

'But please do not build up the father's hopes; the child is very ill.'

'I'll keep the whole thing low-key.'

'Good.' Duval tilted his head suddenly, as if listening. Then he said, 'I sense that you have a question you would like to ask.'

'Has Lacroix got Grosset's scroll?'

'No. The scroll written by Jeshua ben Ya'akob ben Gennesareth is in the new Russia, I'm sorry to say.'

'Russia? Then why haven't they published it?'

Duval smiled. 'Governments aren't interested in truth. They are only interested in survival. Such a document will already have been used many times behind the scenes, and will be used many times in the future. Its existence need never be admitted.'

Chapter Thirteen

The next few days were hectic. Drummond told Georgia on the Sunday evening that she must return to London immediately, saying that he now knew everything there was to know and that there was no sense in her staying on in Paris. She tried to argue, wanted to know what he had found out, but was left unenlightened. He then managed to contact John Eglington, having phoned a number of times earlier without success. Dr Fisher would arrange to talk with the psychiatrist in charge of Sophie's case first thing on the Monday. Everything would hinge on that. Sophie would have to be taken out of the hospital for treatment. A grateful Eglington said that if Fisher felt there was the slightest chance of recovery then he would instantly remove his daughter from the hospital. Conveying Duval's warning that the skills developed were still experimental, Drummond asked Eglington to hold his hopes in check. The man bubblingly agreed.

Monday morning arrived, and Drummond put through a call to Peyrefitte's of Paris the moment he sat down behind his desk; he had spent what was left of the previous evening poring over a copy of the proposals given to him by Aretino Lefèbvre. Having identified the man he should speak to from the document itself, he was soon engaged in the business he understood best, thankful that his English was as perfect as Duval's. Yes, further materials would be sent immediately, but not by post – someone would fly over and deliver them by hand. A laugh from across the English Channel. So many things went missing in the post these days, one had to be careful. And immediately after that Bill Everton facing him across the same desk – the man chagrined at having been left out of such an important decision.

'You've taken it on, just like that!'

'I had no option Bill, believe me.'

'Okay. So tell me what the hell they're up to.'

An impossible task, Drummond realized immediately. He said, 'You're going to have to trust me on this one.'

'That's it? You expect me to just accept your word that everything's . . . tickety-boo?'

'Just this once.'

Bill Everton stared at Drummond unblinkingly. 'What's happened? Have you been made to sign the Secrets Act or something?'

A total silence from Drummond.

'What do you think I am – a fucking salaried manager? Is that what you think?'

'Of course not.'

'Then why are you treating me like this? I'm supposed to be your partner!'

Drummond did not know what to say in reply. He simply stared at Everton, willing him with his eyes to accept the situation.

'I won't have it,' said Everton. 'Either you level with me, or I pull the plug.'

The telephone rang at that moment and Drummond reached for it gratefully. It was Dr Fisher. Sophie was to be released that very afternoon into the good doctor's hands, returned to the hospital by four o'clock. Would he please contact Mr Eglington immediately and arrange for him to be there at one-thirty sharp. It might also be a good idea if he came along as well to keep the father calm. Could he do that? Drummond said yes, thanked the man for his efforts, and slowly replaced the receiver.

'Duval's going to treat John Eglington's kid.'

Bill Everton looked away for a moment; then he looked back and said, 'Your doing?'

A nod from Drummond.

'You think it'll work?'

'It's got to,' said Ian, his face expressionless.

Everton nodded slowly, and seemed to understand something. 'If he fails, it's over, Ian. Right?'

Ian dipped his head once in acceptance, watched as his partner headed for the door.

Sophie was in a wheelchair when she arrived. She was so pale it was frightening: a little girl caught in the clutches of a psychological dilemma from which, in strict medical terms, release was highly unlikely outside of a shock of similar proportions – so Drummond was informed later by an ecstatic Dr Fisher when it was all over and the child had been returned to her father like a mended doll. But hardly ecstatic as the ramp at the back of the specially seconded ambulance was lowered to street level. The man's face was a mask of severity and authority in that moment, only the eyes occasionally betraying the nervousness he felt. Standing in the doorway, Duval's gaze hardly left the child's face as the ambulance men lifted the wheelchair over the doorway's threshold and set it down again. Drummond, hands characteristically in the pockets of his coat, took it all in, aware of his own expectations and of the risks being taken by both Duval and Fisher. And all the while the father helping, gyrating around the little fair-haired being in her chromium chariot as she was wheeled by the psychiatrist to the therapy room, the ambulance men having been dismissed the moment they entered the building.

Closing and locking the door behind them, Duval said, 'She has a lovely name.'

No reply from Drummond until they stood together in the therapy room watching Dr Fisher station the wheelchair and its little occupant directly beneath the bare red globe. 'What *are* her chances?' he asked in a low voice, expecting Duval to again hedge his bets. But to his surprise the man said that Sophie had every chance of a complete recovery. Complete? A look of amazement from Drummond. 'That isn't what you were saying on Saturday!'

'I had to guard against the father, Mr Drummond. If he had believed for one second that we thought success probable, he might very well have mentioned it to others and drawn unwanted attention to our little exercise. It's one thing to succeed with a difficult case; it's quite another to say that you are going to do so before the event takes place.'

'How can you be so sure it'll work?'

'For the very reason that we're dealing with a child and not an adult. Adults create defences which are sometimes extremely difficult to penetrate. It's like trying to break down a wall – a wall of fear. They quite literally hide behind that wall and avoid being helped through the trick of building another, and yet another wall behind the first. Some patients are so successful in this that they appear to be living in a completely different reality. And in a way they are, for each wall deprives them more and more of the reality we all share. To compensate for this, they have to create a series of alternative realities to house their consciousness. Young children are quite different. They too may retreat behind a wall of fear, but they know too little of this reality to spawn alternatives in the way an adult does. So there is in fact only one, perhaps two, layers of fear to get through before the child begins to respond. There are, of course, exceptions to every rule, but they are extremely rare.'

'If it's so simple, why haven't they been able to help her at the hospital?'

'Because they're forced to work from the wrong side of the wall. To get behind the wall of fear requires depth psychotherapy and some extremely delicate physical procedures. A psychotherapy that does not reflect the patient's own depths must rely on chance – that is the case with most of today's psychiatric procedures. A patient visits a psychotherapist or psychiatrist for months, quite often years, and the person doing the treating tackles the patient's wall of fear and emotional contraction with the consciously constructed idea that *everything* ought to be made conscious. But only because human psychology as it has now come to be understood is equated solely with the daylight world. Everything has been made subservient to the idea that "personality" and not "soul" is of primary importance. The individual's personality is held to *be* the individual, the "soul" an unobservable religious notion of little or no significance. So it follows that if the personality begins to disintegrate, the person as patient is automatically thought to be in dire trouble. What a calamity! A body has been removed from the workforce and subsequently must be kept as far away from others as possible – it's far too distressing a sight for other personalities to bear in their supposed sanity. As from that moment, and contingent upon the patient's being consciously available, the fractured personality is trained to reject its own dark depths and respond only to the world of light, the world of reason and coherence, the world of questions and answers where the most profound experiences are dragged up into the light and made to fit into the world of conscious growth and maturity. But if, like little Sophie, the patient is not consciously available, then what can they do except keep her clean? You see there's no one there to treat. The person as personality has disappeared.'

'You seem to be –'

They were interrupted at that point. It was time for Duval to play Maestro. The same therapists were being used as for the Protasis experiment. One of them raised a hand in recognition of Drummond after having attracted Duval's attention. The philosopher excused himself, walked over to the two young men and issued last-minute instructions. Drummond glanced at Dr Fisher. He was making some point or other to John Eglington, who was nodding his head sagely and glancing at the little arrangement in the middle of the room. Both came over to stand with Drummond a few seconds later.

'Similar procedure to last time?' asked Drummond, more than a little excited at having been told that Sophie's recovery was virtually certain.

'Yes, similar,' replied Fisher in a distracted manner. 'But reversed, I believe.'

What the man meant by 'reversed' became immediately obvious – it was Duval who took up a position behind Sophie, the therapists who stood off to one side, a gap of some three yards between them.

John Eglington said, 'I don't understand any of this.'

Touching the man's arm, Drummond said reassuringly that there was nothing to worry about, that Duval knew what he was doing. He hoped he was right.

'But what exactly is he doing?' asked Eglington.

'It has something to do with the regulation of sound.'

'You've seen them do this before?'

'I was in the chair last time.'

There was a long silence; no one dared move. Duval eventually placed his right hand above Sophie's head. She was the perfect subject, locked as she was into physical immobility. But as before, it was the two therapists who started the humming. There was no making sense of it, and Drummond couldn't help wondering how such techniques had been developed, and why the little red globe was thought so important. It was all very eerie. He glanced at John Eglington. The man's face was a study in concentration. The first reverberative tones filled the therapy room. Standing gigantically behind the wheelchair, his hand barely touching the child's corn-silk hair, Duval watched the two young Frenchmen ease into their amazing vocal routine. After about 30 seconds they changed note and dropped back, only at once to surge higher and cleverly sustain the incredible sound emanating from their mouths.

Two, perhaps three, minutes of this elapsed before the introduction of a new register. His heart beating almost audibly in his chest, Drummond listened to the additional sound of the father's breathing beginning to labour as the sounds intensified and the atmosphere of that large room became charged with something indescribable.

Then, quite without warning, an almost alarming note was produced from those two highly-trained throats, and Duval's body immediately began to twist at the waist in the most extraordinary fashion. His appearance suddenly verged on the grotesque. A quick glance at Eglington by Drummond afforded him the realization that Dr Fisher was ready to pounce on the man at the first sign of interference. A sudden *Oh my God!* from Eglington as Sophie's body visibly lurched and the twist in Duval's body was accentuated. Then an unbelievable moment as the energies released began to shake Sophie like a rag doll and she burst out of her catatonia with a scream and crumpled where she sat.

Drummond held his breath in that moment, watched Duval right himself, scoop the child up in his arms and begin to rock her backwards and forwards, comforting her all the while in his native tongue until she quietened and her father found the courage to move. A few strides and he was there, the child immediately stretching out for him. It was an incredible sight.

Surprising Drummond, Dr Fisher said, 'Now you've seen what he's capable of with your own eyes. It generally takes a shock equal in proportion to that which triggered the withdrawal to bring about the kind of release you've witnessed today – either that or months of gentle coaxing.' He glanced at Drummond, and looked away again. 'That man could change the whole face of medicine if he so wished.'

'Isn't that his intention?'

A sigh from Fisher. 'No. His priority is the training of therapists to deal with hysteria and hallucinations. He sees the healing aspect merely as a fringe benefit, almost as a distraction. Refuses point-blank to train anyone else in the techniques. There's only a handful of therapists in the whole of Europe specifically trained in healing.'

'Why's that?'

'Because ultimately he doesn't think it terribly important.'

'It wouldn't do your cause any harm if he could pull off a few minor miracles.'

'Exactly my point – but he doesn't see it that way. In fact he refuses to discuss it.'

'Maybe he just knows his limits.'

'Limits?' A hoarse laugh from Fisher. 'I don't think there are any. I've come to the conclusion he's probably capable of healing just about every condition in the book – and I mean *every* condition.' The psychiatrist was visibly excited by his own thoughts. 'It hasn't just been hysteria-based cases like this one he's been successful with.'

'Meaning?'

'That his treatment of disease is just as successful. You wouldn't believe some of the things I've seen accomplished here.'

'Try me.'

Dr Fisher was suddenly reticent. 'I've said far too much already, far too much. Please forget what I've just told you.'

'That won't be easy.'

'Then whatever you do, keep it to yourself. If it got out –' He sighed again, stared for a moment at the happy little group in the centre of the therapy room, then terminated their conversation. 'I think we'd better join the others, don't you?'

John Eglington was ecstatic over Sophie's recovery, and the child seemed remarkably normal after her long ordeal. She was hanging around her father's neck when Drummond and the psychiatrist joined them. For some unfathomable reason Duval smiled at Fisher in that moment, reached out and touched him. Then to Drummond he virtually repeated Dr Fisher's injunction to keep what he had seen to himself – it was almost as if he had heard the man and was both confirming the point and making a point.

'I won't breathe a word of it to anyone,' said Drummond.

Putting out a hand, John Eglington said to Duval, 'There's no adequate way for me to express my gratitude, Monsieur. Thank you again.'

'Dr Fisher will return you to the hospital,' replied Duval. 'Please leave any explaining that has to be done to him.'

'But of course.'

They moved towards the swing doors in silence, exited, and made their way down the corridor in silence. Drummond was delighted. Sophie was well again and John's spirits were high. The man had been instantly transformed by the healing, his face at once losing the haggard hopelessness which had set in with Sophie's mental freezing. And in combination with that double success Drummond's trust in the Frenchman had become virtually absolute – there was now no doubting either the man's extraordinary ability or the sincerity of his purpose. Happy in himself for having been of use to his friend, he stood watching as father and daughter entered Fisher's cream Volvo and the door was shut carefully behind them. John waved to him in that moment, made a shrugging motion with his shoulders, laughed through the thick glass with obvious embarrassment at being bundled away before he could say thanks for a brilliant hunch. Then suddenly they were gone, and Duval was saying something about a glass of wine, and he was agreeing.

Georgia was already on her way home as Drummond turned back into the Katharsis building following Duval. The two young therapists had already disappeared as if they had helped accomplish no more than a routine happening. And the philosopher himself did not seem particularly impressed with his own genius. He stopped at a small office where a couple of young women were busy typing letters, said that he would be engaged for perhaps half an hour at most, and took Drummond into an adjacent room where a large map of Europe dominated one wall.

It was a bit like entering a military headquarters or a schoolroom. There was a blackboard, complete with chalk and felt duster, a flat table with a wooden pointer lying on it, and a dozen or so kitchen-type chairs arranged in two rows. Opening a large cupboard built into a recess, Duval then quite incongruously produced a bottle of red wine from a store of at least a dozen, and set it on a nearby table, following it up with a corkscrew and two glasses. Drummond laughed outright. He watched the man insert the corkscrew into the bottle and discovered on being handed the cork that the wine was an excellent vintage.

Coming straight to the point, Duval said, 'I was told a rather bizarre story last night by someone known to you; he was apparently a priest at one time.'

Drummond's attention moved from the bottle's label to Duval's face. 'Dr Freeman,' he said immediately.

'The very same. An interesting man. He has been contacted by a high-ranking emissary of the Catholic Church, an inquisitor of some kind, and asked to spy on me.'

'Yes, I know about that.'

'He was sent for again last night and asked for a decision.'

'And?'

'He caused a certain consternation by challenging the person concerned with fraudulent behaviour.'

'That must have gone down well.'

'He also refused to have anything to do with his machinations and demanded to know exactly who he was dealing with. He was told that what I was doing was of concern to the Congregation of the Doctrine of the Faith, that a special arm had been created to investigate both myself and my associates – which was of course another way of saying that the Inquisition was again functioning on behalf of Mother Church.'

'I thought the Inquisition was done away with a long time ago.'

'The Congregation of the Doctrine of the Faith *is* the Inquisition, Mr Drummond. It is the watchdog of the Faith. To be told, as Dr Freeman was, that a special investigative body had been set up by the Congregation of the Doctrine of the Faith was the equivalent of saying that the Inquisition had again been reconstituted solely to look into the proliferation of our therapeutic units across Europe. That did not make sense to him. He immediately suspected those he was dealing with of being part of a Vatican faction working well outside official channels.'

'Must be something like that.'

Lifting the bottle of wine which he had left to breathe, Duval part-filled both glasses and said, 'The situation is now immensely complicated. I thought at first that the group Freeman described must be a Church faction working clandestinely for the realization of Lacroix's theocratic nightmare, but I'm now of the opinion that the opposite is more probably the case. The man Dr Freeman dealt with as supposed nuncio must in fact be an authentic papal investigator charged with the task of ferreting out what is going on within the Church in relation to Lacroix, and charged equally with the task of deciding whether we can be considered suitable allies in the fight against Lacroix when the gauntlet is finally thrown down. The Vatican has quite obviously split into two distinct camps, one accepting as a *fait accompli* that Lacroix's dream of a theocratic dictatorship with Rome as subservient handmaiden is better than a Church totally destroyed, and the other fighting against such a heretical notion with the only effective tool it has at its disposal – the Inquisition in disguised form.'

'What did Freeman make of that?'

'He immediately wanted to know what it was that could cause such a split.'

'You told him?'

'Everything. He was suitably astonished.'

'I'll bet. What's he going to do now?'

'When everything is confirmed, act as negotiator with the Church on our behalf – we may have an unexpected and powerful ally fairly soon.'

'You'd work with the Church against Lacroix?'

'I think that is how the cards will fall, Mr Drummond . . . There is a certain humour in the situation, don't you think?'

'It surprises me that he accepted anything of what you had to say.'

'It was not an easy task.' A curt little laugh from Duval. 'It took some hours before he would accept what I had to say as even plausible. But he is of course a highly intelligent man, and very well educated. The pieces of the puzzle eventually fell into place. And he can of course check everything said through those he's dealing with – which leaves only the problem of Dr Fisher.'

'What's problematic about Fisher?'

'He believes too desperately in the healing aspect of the work we're doing, and is frustrated by my apparent disinterest. You see, he cannot understand my reasons for not exploiting our discoveries, and is trying to . . . force my hand on the issue. He would like me to work a miracle or two, show the world what can be accomplished through the alternative techniques we've evolved. But as everyone knows, a little knowledge can be highly dangerous if it is inappropriately handled. In my estimation any such demonstration would be inappropriate.'

'He said to me earlier that you could probably change the face of medicine overnight.'

'Yes, but only in as far as the medical profession responded without prejudice and took on the task of exploring the deeper aspects of human psychology. That is why it would not work. The medical profession is virtually incapable of responding to the kind of training that would be necessary to bring about such a revolution. For that is exactly what it would be – a revolution in both concept and procedure. They are not ready. Psychology is still in its infancy. Medical practitioners deal only with the most acceptable, and therefore the most limited, psychological knowledge available. Everything in medicine and psychology is bound by a theory of limitation, a strict adherence to laid-down scientific principles. And because those principles have worked extremely well over the years, no reason can be found to dispense with them. And why should they be dispensed with? Why should the attempt be made to incorporate what appears to be a magical conception of the human mind into modern medicine when it has been shown that all magical conceptions are quite without validity? It stands to reason that what I have to offer would be rejected, and those who did the rejecting would be perfectly within their rights. It simply isn't the time.'

'Only idiots would interpret what I saw today as magical.'

'We are all idiots when presented with things we do not understand.'

'I think I might be a little bit in agreement with Dr Fisher,' said Drummond. 'If you're right about the coming debacle, shouldn't you be handing over everything you know to the people best qualified to make use of it?'

'No, it would only further confuse things – and I can assure you that everyone will be quite confused enough without my adding to it. What you have to understand is that almost everyone will be affected by what you have so accurately described as the coming debacle. Doctors and psychologists and psychiatrists and scientists will not be immune. They too will succumb. Medicine as we now know it will all but vanish. There will be a return to medieval ideas, a resurgence of notions centuries old. Lacroix and his pocket-Messiah will be shown little resistance when the moment comes. His historical proofs of legitimacy will be presented to a populace in a state of high hysteria, and there will of course be minor miracles of healing to further validate those proofs – healings of a calibre similar to what you witnessed this afternoon. Fear and superstition and an astute tapping into the psychology of human beings will do the rest. Confusion will be quickly traded for religious certainty far beyond anything you could ever imagine. Millions will bow the knee without question; those considered slow in their reaction will be herded into special instruction camps where the truth can be instilled by other means. It will be a time of collective madness. Ian, it will be a time of visions and hallucinations and religious insanity. The initial announcement will probably be made on television with what appears to be the Church's blessing and the backing of all kinds of experts. Understand that, and you will immediately understand why I daren't play their game in reverse, be identified even now as having the ability to heal by such unorthodox methods.'

'I don't –'

'Allow me to explain. Such a move would only strengthen Lacroix's position and add an extra dimension to it. It would allow him to identify me as some kind of Antichrist. There is nothing Lacroix would like more than for me to make that kind of mistake – it would delight him.'

Having finally understood the point the philosopher had been trying to make, Drummond then tackled what he saw as the next major problem in accepting the whole unbelievable story. Choosing his words carefully he said, 'There's still something I don't understand – something else you'll have to explain, I'm afraid. Why are people going to accept this Messiah of Lacroix's? Okay, so they're in a very excitable state of mind – completely crazy if you like – but wouldn't it be immediately obvious even to people in that kind of state that if this miraculously-produced Messiah was indeed a descendant of Jesus Christ, then Jesus Christ himself must have been nothing more than a man of flesh and blood. Why should they go for that? I certainly wouldn't! It would mean their rejecting the whole conception of divinity taught to them for two thousand years!'

'It would be accomplished in a moment.'

Duval drank a little of his wine, savoured it, and continued in his highly controlled fashion. 'Very few people believe in Jesus as the Church has presented him over that period. They know deep within themselves that the story lacks authenticity – that it is part fabrication, part overt lie, part superstition and part political expediency. In their hearts they know that. And in knowing that, it will come as no surprise to be told by the Church itself that it has been mistaken in its overview – that the people have been misled through Scriptures tampered with, blocks of history eradicated, lives eliminated for daring to express the perfectly obvious – that Jesus was a man of flesh and blood, a creature of his own time, a man to whom passion was known. They will in fact welcome that news, accept it readily. For it will partly release them from a lie that has systematically undermined and eroded their capacity for a true spiritual life in every century since Jesus' demise at Masada. They will not have any problem with that. And I can assure you that similarly, Lacroix will not have any problem in convincing them, in spite of the cover-up of fifteen centuries, that Jesus is still the pivotal character in the world's spiritual history. How? By and through the fact that Jesus has become what we term an "archetype" or "symbol" of all things spiritual in the consciousness of human beings born within the Church's sphere of influence.

'But Jesus as God manifest in the flesh is of course an invented archetype, an archetype *legislated* into existence by the Council of Nicea under Constantine in AD 325. This is why it has sown endless conflict and bitterness when addressed as an irrefutable truth by those needful of certainty. It is Jesus as invented archetype who appears in the visions of the saints, which causes the appearance of stigmata, the mystical visions so eagerly sought by committed Christians. He has been made into an incredibly powerful symbol, and nothing will ever totally eradicate him as the only legitimate spiritual threshold in human consciousness until human beings learn to transcend their own limited belief systems. It is an ingrained conception that has been part of our psychological make-up for far too long to be just thrown aside by a feeble suggestion that Jesus the man had had a wife and children. That will be easily accommodated by those with the Second-Tier revelation ready at hand; a revelation backed by the massive breakdown of all human institutions – by the breakdown of the human will itself.

'Presented with what appears to be a modern miracle-working descendant of Jesus bearing an unmistakable birthmark in the shape of a cross, the psychological adjustment will be made and they will immediately respond to what is quite obviously the *Second Coming of Christ*. Very few will doubt that that is the case, and those who do will be separated out for special therapeutic treatment using techniques specifically developed for the purpose.'

Drummond stared at Duval for some seconds before replying. 'The full-page advertisement I saw in the paper recently is the start of it all, isn't it?'

'Yes. The public mind is being prepared for the coming onslaught. It doesn't matter that hardly anyone takes such a message seriously at the moment. The basic programme has been laid down and will be systematically built upon over the next few months.'

Drummond lifted his glass of wine and sipped at it, again showing pleasure in the vintage.

'It is from my own vineyard in southern France,' said Duval. 'I have it brought in to remind me of home.'

'It's quite excellent,' said Drummond.

'A fitting wine for warriors,' replied Duval.

Chapter Fourteen

For reasons that never became quite clear, but which produced chaos in the timetables of many travellers, Eurostar did not bullet its way under the Channel on the afternoon Georgia chose to return to London – some hitch or other brought the sleek beast to an embarrassed halt. Her return fare would be refunded, she was told. As a result, it took her just over six hours to get from Paris to her flat in Hampstead. A two-hour wait at Calais due to high seas and an almost blinding snowstorm added to the charm of the occasion, and there was even the rumoured delight for the passengers that they might not be able to leave until the following morning. The alternative of flying was precluded by the closure of the airport, and the storm's severity had grounded the usually robust hovercraft service. Even crossing by Stena *Lynx III*, the new and luxurious catamaran service which she herself had written about the previous year, remained uncertain right up until the last minute. But as luck would have it, the wind finally dropped somewhat, and the decision to make a dash for Dover was taken on the strength of weather reports showing a general easing of conditions. This supposed easing of conditions was not at all evident during the crossing, or when she eventually disembarked, and there were further delays as the rail and bus services to London coped with the inclement weather. Arriving at her front door bedraggled and exhausted, Georgia paid off the taxi she had been lucky enough to grab at the bus terminal, and searching out her keys, opened her front door and climbed the stairs to her little Hampstead flat with an audible sigh of relief.

Stillness and a slight mustiness.

Dumping her case and hand-luggage behind the sofa, she switched on the gas fire and headed into the kitchen to make herself a coffee, delighted to be home, and pleased that the precautions she had taken to ensure her plants' survival had again proved effective. It was six o'clock in the evening and already quite dark due to the heaviness of the sky, more snow being expected. She had noted the large patches of snow left over from Saturday's blizzard as she journeyed back to London from Dover, the tell-tale remnants of that sudden whiting-out on lawns and backyards as the bus entered the city suburbs and snaked its laborious way towards the terminal, the beginnings of the rush-hour chaos further slowing their advance.

How she hated buses.

A sigh and another look around at her collected bits and pieces to help orient her to the fact that she was again in her own home. Then almost frighteningly the stillness shattered as the telephone shrieked for attention. It was not Ian on the line. Paul Paquel's accented English filled her ear; he had been ringing at 15-minute intervals for over an hour. She explained quickly about the hold-up at Calais, sensing bad news, and was told that their private detective was in hospital with multiple fractures and a highly suspect loss of memory.

'That's *very* nasty of them,' she said, her anger evident.

'They've scared the poor devil out of his wits. He wouldn't even look at me, never mind talk.'

'What are you going to do?'

'There isn't much I can do.'

'Be *very* careful,' she said back, her perspective on the whole affair radically changed by what he had just told her. 'The friend I told you about has apparently wrapped the whole thing up this end, so there's no need for you to stick your neck out. I'll get back to you the moment I have the facts. Okay? Paul?'

'– Okay.'

She rang off soon after, turned and saw steam pouring out of the kitchen. When she returned to the lounge it was with the intention of telephoning Drummond, but the door bell rang in the same instant, and she found him on the doorstep. Welcoming him not quite in the manner she had envisaged as the big catamaran, in spite of computerized stabilizers, surged, plummeted, rocked and battered its way across the English Channel, she kissed him and unburdened herself of Paquel's news. Then stopping suddenly at the top of the stairs, she stood blinking at him.

A turning away in the same instant: double confusion wrought out of circumstances and her fear that she had perhaps read a little too much into his *Love you, mean that.* Did he want coffee? Yes. She made him one and contracted further, took up position in her chair and sat listening with an expression of utter disbelief on her face as he tried to explain what had been explained to him in such detail by Duval, interjecting regularly with queries to which he seldom had satisfactory answers.

It was tough going. What he had been told came out as a jumble. In a moment of exasperation he said that it did not matter how preposterous the story sounded, what mattered was what Lacroix and his immediate coterie of lieutenants believed either to be the truth, or what they held up as the truth while they forged a situation for themselves out of which others – millions of others – could be herded into a coherent army of convinced devotees. The whole crazy story might sound like a farrago of nonsense coming out of his mouth, but that did not mean that it was nonsense, merely that he was inept in the telling of it and that she ought to be making allowances for that at every step. That made her listen with a little more respect – in fact she smiled at him at that point, impressed with his honesty, with the courage of his attempt to make her understand what he had obviously accepted from Duval as a probable truth. But she refused to let him off the hook easily.

'Duval's obviously as mad as they are,' she said.

'You'll have to include Freeman in that,' he replied, knowing how she respected the priest's erudition and intelligence. 'And you'll also have to write off as deluded some very important people in the Vatican if you want to keep on believing that Duval's round the twist.'

'The Vatican?'

He described in detail Freeman's summons to Belgravia, the subsequent contact, and Duval's interpretation of the event. There was obviously a deal more going on than an attempt by royalists to restore the French monarchy in the form of an ancient bloodline. Then with a look he quite deflated Georgia by reminding her that she herself had described Freeman as a highly intelligent man, and that this highly intelligent man had apparently accepted what she rejected.

'It's just too fantastic.'

'Jumping about on the moon is fantastic, but it's been done.' He relented a little, having no real wish to make her feel foolish. 'Look,' he said, unconsciously producing his packet of cigarettes and lighting one, 'I'm as mind-boggled by the whole thing as you are, but I've never met anyone with their feet so firmly planted on the ground as Duval's are. You haven't sat and talked with him as I have – it's quite an experience. And what I once referred to as Freeman's little act of voodoo is nothing when compared with what I saw that bean-pole of a philosopher do only this afternoon; it took him only fifteen minutes to bring little Sophie out of a catatonic trance. Fifteen minutes! John Eglington walked into that therapy room a lost and shattered man, and waltzed out with his daughter in his arms. It was the most moving thing I've seen in my life – and the most remarkable.'

'That . . . doesn't constitute evidence for what he's told you, Ian.'

'Maybe not, but it strengthens his credibility as a quite remarkable therapist – and don't forget that dear Dr Freeman has admitted to being knocked for six by his ideas. Now he's not the kind of man I'd expect to be easily taken in on any level.'

'It's –'

'Take a look at this.' He took a piece of neatly folded newsprint from his inside pocket and handed it to her, watched as she opened it out. 'That appeared in every national newspaper in the country while you were away. I've never read anything quite like it.'

She scanned the words quickly, surprised him by saying that she had read the same ad in the French press, but had thought it nothing more than an expensive joke.

'Unbelievably expensive if they covered Europe as well,' he said back, aware of how astronomical the figure would have been.

'No one in their right mind would take a piece of crap like this seriously.'

'No one was expected to take it seriously, Georgia. That wasn't the purpose of the exercise.' The ash dropped from his cigarette onto the carpet in spite of an attempt to catch it. He apologized with a look, and continued. 'It's the equivalent of someone tapping you on the shoulder and ducking out of sight as you turn. It's just a device.'

Choosing to ignore the fact that he was smoking again she said, 'You obviously think this nonsense is for real.'

'What else can I think? It fits, doesn't it?'

She was silent for a moment. 'Did that researcher of yours ever come up with anything on the Merovingian kings?'

'It was promised for early this week. Could be lying on my desk now for all I know.'

'I was lucky enough to have someone who knew the territory help me,' she admitted, realizing that a researcher going in cold would probably have had immense difficulty in uncovering the really interesting stuff on the Merovingians, the mythology having been stripped out of the early texts as they were updated. 'They were quite a bunch.' She laughed uneasily and shook her head as what she had read of Merovingian wonder-working slotted into Duval's context of a direct connection between the ancient Frankish kings and the priest-kings of Israel. 'They didn't cut their hair, apparently,' she said with a look, 'and were said to have had a rather unusual birthmark.'

'A cross-shaped birthmark.'

She let out her breath, waited for him to continue.

'Duval mentioned the special birthmark in passing – said something about Lacroix's drummed-up Messiah having one. Go on.'

'. . . Either over their hearts, or between their shoulder blades,' she said, feeling distinctly uncomfortable with how the situation was shaping up. 'They were thought of as priest-kings, embodiments of the divine – like the ancient Egyptian Pharaohs. They were also believed to be living incarnations of God's grace.' She drew breath, and admitted what she had no wish to admit. 'The Church of the time seems to have recognized them as having the sacred right to assume kingship without coronation.'

Drummond said nothing, merely stared back as she again ricocheted away from accepting Duval's scenario in spite of her own supportive statements.

'It's just mythological nonsense, Ian. Duval is accepting mythology as literal history.'

'Something bloody odd was going on, Georgia.'

'That's for sure. But you can't really expect me to believe that the Merovingians were descendants of Jesus Christ, that that's how those stories came about?' She added irritably. 'I'm afraid that's asking far too much of me!'

'Only if you're still superstitious enough to believe that Jesus was *actually* God wandering around in Palestine. I don't believe for one minute that that was the case.'

'Then how come the Merovingians were viewed as divine? Where did that oddball conception come from?'

'From the simple fact that they were blood-related to the Hasmonean priest-kings and a bit unusual, nothing else.'

'That's your answer?'

'Oh come on, Georgia!' he said, his Scottish ire rising. 'What are you saying to me? You either accept that they were unusually gifted individuals schooled in their ancient origins, their ancient Jewish origins as priest-kings, or you start all over again to believe what we all damned well know is a lot of nonsense, that they were themselves divine because Jesus was divine! It's exactly the problem Duval outlined for me this afternoon. We're carrying a phantom Jesus around in our heads, a paragon, a kind of bloody ghost that never existed, and it's because that image is ingrained in our systems that Lacroix's going to be so incredibly successful when everything falls apart. What's been done to us since we were kids is going to reap a whirlwind.'

She stared at him, avoiding the issue raised by asking him what he meant by 'gifted'.

'In the same way that Duval's gifted,' he replied with exasperation. 'The Merovingians were quite obviously in possession of some rather unusual knowledge. Duval's stumbled on something of what they knew. And it would appear that Lacroix's pocket-Messiah is a bit of a natural in the same area, a healer of some kind. That's all there is to it.'

'*All* of the mainline Merovingians were said to have had the same gifts.'

'So?'

'The probability of that happening age after age must be billions to one!'

'Not if the old healing techniques were handed on as a kind of legacy from parent to offspring.' He smiled suddenly, realizing that he had probably articulated the answer they were looking for. 'I'm sure that's it. It wasn't that they had holy blood as such, it was that they were thought to be holy because of their odd historical origins and the fact that they were all trained in what appears to have been a kind of magic. That's got to be it. Something akin to Lacroix's Order of the Lily was probably invented to safeguard the Merovingian descendants when they lost power and the Church turned against them.'

'I find it hard to believe that they survived intact after so long.'

A laugh from Drummond. 'Why not? The only thing an aristocrat has is his or her name, Georgia, and they each make damned sure that the name they carry doesn't die out. That's the game they play century after century even if their name isn't all that important. But if their name happens to be really important – if it is, say, a mainstream royal house of Europe directly linked to the equally royal Hasmonean house of ancient Israel, and there's documentation available showing that good old Jesus was himself of that bloodline – then think of the lengths those bearing that name would go to to safeguard themselves from discovery if the time wasn't opportune for that revelation to get out! It would be the most highly guarded and looked-after secret of any age. Is it any wonder that the Church is peeing itself right this minute! If Joyce's scroll is for real, and Duval's prognostication about Western society falling apart at the seams within the next two years is really on the cards, then we're literally teetering on the brink of a revolution, involving the setting up of an empire that will completely upset not only the whole European power base and situate it squarely in France, together with a literal taking over of the Catholic Church at the same time because of the blood link with Jesus as Jewish Messiah and rightful Hasmonean king. If General de Gaulle were alive he'd be jumping out of his socks with excitement over that one! It would make the French not only the most powerful nation in the world, it would cause them to be viewed as chosen by God for that purpose beyond all shadow of doubt. And think of what that would mean in real terms. It would mean that the Christian revelation had been vindicated on the one hand, but turned arse-over-elbow on the other. Lacroix and his modern Messiah would have a mandate to do absolutely anything they wanted. Anything! It would be a reversed equivalent of the French Revolution in the 20th century!'

'I don't believe it could happen, Ian.'

'I'd like to think you were right.'

'It's potty!'

'You may not have noticed, Georgia, but the whole bloody world's potty.'

'Not to the extent that it would allow what you've just described to happen. We're not that mad.'

'Not yet we aren't.'

'That's Duval talking.'

'Not just Duval. It's also Dr Fisher and Freeman and Aretino Lefèbvre and God knows how many others talking, Georgia. It's the French government talking. It's the governments of quite a few countries talking, from what I can make out. And it would seem to be the Roman Catholic Church talking as well. The Western world's in a mess, and something's going to give way pretty soon. It always does. Think of what happened last time. Who would have believed that a people as civilized as the Germans could have fallen under the sway of a nutcase like Adolf Hitler? But it damned well happened. There always seems to be some bastard around with his head back to front when things begin to collapse in on themselves. And it's no different this time. Lacroix and his bonkers Messiah are waiting in the wings to save the world ... at a price. And it's pretty obvious that things really are collapsing – right across the Western world as far as I can make out. Have you ever known such uncertainty on so many fronts? The economies of some of the richest countries in the world are breaking up in front of our eyes. The bottom is falling out of world markets on a daily basis. It's high inflation and undisguised panic all round. And on top of all that there's terrorism on a completely unprecedented scale. Murder. Bombings. Hijackings. Assassinations. It's a bloody nightmare! And the Russians aren't sitting laughing at the West's collapse as they thought they would – their own collapse has already taken place and they now need the West to survive. So when Duval starts telling me that the suicide rate for adults and children is going through the roof, and that statistics gathered from all over Europe indicate a massive breakdown in the psychology of ordinary human beings in every quarter of the Western world within a couple of years, I don't find myself laughing it off as an absurdity. And when he tells me that there's a maniac in the bushes who's going to capitalize on that breakdown by appealing to our ingrained religious naïvety, I find myself more than a little prepared to believe him.'

They sat in silence for a moment. Then Georgia said, 'You're turning into a regular little philosopher yourself, aren't you?'

'I'm facing the facts, that's all. And I'm quite willing to put a large bet on Duval's estimation of things turning out damned near the mark.' He paused, decided against lighting another cigarette. 'He hasn't said one thing to me so far that doesn't make sense when it's honestly examined.'

'I'd like to hear it from his own lips.'

'That could probably be arranged. He's aware of your involvement.'

'Do you think he'd go for an up-front interview?'

'That would probably be pushing it a bit, don't you think?'

'How about an off-the-record chat?'

'It would be strictly off the record, Georgia. I don't think he would see you otherwise.'

She smiled at him, chewed at her bottom lip for a moment and said, 'I'd very much like to understand why a man like Duval accepts the stuff he's told you.'

'I'll take my chances on his convincing you inside an hour, if you're willing to listen with an open mind. But be prepared for a refusal, he may not have the time to spare . . . and you are, after all, a journalist.'

'An honest journalist,' she said back. 'You could perhaps mention that.'

Heralding the fast approach of Christmas, the snow began to fall again quite heavily. They came out of the supermarket and stood in the illuminated street for a moment admiring the gentle flurry, then turned left and made their way back to the flat, each carrying a plastic bag full of groceries. They had shopped in virtual silence, and were now walking in silence. Thinking. But not cantankerously. There was no tension between them – and that in spite of their earlier reserve, a reserve born out of they knew not what. It was a natural silence, almost an emptiness. But not the old emptiness. More a waiting. It was as if each were waiting on the other to explain something, perhaps divulge something. Up the stairs they went, closing out the night, and the cold. A spaghetti with a chillied meat sauce was what they had decided on. Dumping the plastic carrier bag in the kitchen, Drummond returned immediately to the lounge, removed his coat and automatically poured himself a large whisky – but not for reasons of fortification. There was no threat in the air. Georgia was humming to herself as she sorted out the groceries and placed them where she usually placed them, each in its own niche in the cupboard. She was very tidy, but not obsessively so. In fact, when compared with Patricia she was a fraction scatty, her so casually created surroundings reflecting a quite different kind of nature.

'Want a drink?' he asked.

A small, dry sherry was her preference. He poured it and handed it to her, and asked if he could help prepare the meal. She shook her head and smiled at him, saying that there was no need and that the kitchen was far too small for two. He returned to the lounge, stood at the back window and watched the snow slowly overcome the dampness of the earth.

'It's beginning to settle again,' he half-shouted.

She left what she was doing for a moment and joined him, standing by his side quite straight, drink in hand, staring out into the semi-darkness where the snow was only just visible.

'Nice, isn't it,' he said.

'The kids are always pleased.'

An image jumped into his mind, surprising him – the image of a hearse complete with shiny coffin in the back. His father's coffin. Snow. Inches of it hard-packed on the pavement as he rode by on his sledge with nothing more than a glancing realization that his father would never return. A council house by this time, and the luxury of an overgrown garden within which flower or vegetable had never grown. His mother inside handing drinks to relatives. A quiet murmuring that had driven him out into the snow to play, and a spitting anger at it all. The man who had endlessly cuffed him about the head locked up in a box and his mother glad to be rid of him, free at last, and only just able to contain her relief. All over and done with. Her very words when she returned from the cemetery and called him in for a wedge of steak pie and a dollop of mashed potatoes. Three metal pie-dishes on the table, huge to his eyes then, one with its upturned egg-cup showing, shards of pastry hanging from it, the kidneys visible among what remained of the gristly steak. Over and done with not at all, he now realized.

'I've got things to do.' She left him and went back into the kitchen, beginning to hum again.

He shook his head with a kind of amazement as the past continued to reinstate itself in the present. It was almost as if something were trying to get through, speak to him, inform him. He found himself listening, his breath momentarily suspended as that something approached and he caught the first glimmerings of a terrible truth – his father wasn't dead at all. He was alive and kicking, and living inside his son like a parasitic growth!

An exclamation of disgust.

'Say something?'

'– No.'

His father's face as clear as bloody daylight in his mind's eye, alive and propped up in bed with a welter of pillows behind him. And staring at nothing, it seemed for a moment. But not at nothing. At him. An image so clear and sharp he tried to blink it away, only to discover that it was fixed as if in a solution. Not just an image. A reality. The head turning away and the hand stretching out for the metal spittoon. The thumb elevating the lid and the harsh, wheezing attempt to gather the phlegm into a manageable globule. The dying man shielding the act with his hand as he looked on. Without feeling? A little boy's icy stare, harbouring not only hatred but a wish.

He began to topple in that moment, managed to correct the downward swing of his body momentarily by leaning heavily on the protruding surround of the window, then lost his grip and crumpled where he stood, his glass of whisky spinning away, his gasp bringing Georgia out of the kitchen in a rush. Unsure of what ought to be done, she yelled his name and tried to straighten his body out, slapped his face and loosened his tie, thinking he had fainted. But when after a few minutes he still hadn't recovered, she dived for the telephone and dialled 999, glancing back at him all the while, her heart battering in her chest, her legs only just capable of supporting her as she waited to be connected with the appropriate service. Then she was back kneeling by his side, quite at her wits' end as a further ten minutes elapsed and there was no change in his condition.

The door bell rang and she dashed downstairs to let in the two neatly uniformed ambulance men.

Not a word was said.

A bashing of feet on the staircase.

A heart attack diagnosed after a rudimentary check and Ian being lifted onto a stretcher.

Into the ambulance with him and the sound of the siren dinning above them as they sped away with only half a mile to cover.

A heart attack?

Left standing in a corridor to wait as they wheeled him off into the labyrinth.

She stood stock still for a moment and tried to digest the idea of his having had a heart attack, her senses still reeling from the suddenness of it all. Then turning slowly, she walked back up that corridor and sat down on a bench seat, the realization that he might die or be already dead causing her to inhale sharply.

Not possible.

But it was in fact only too possible, she eventually admitted to herself, and fear gathered in her inners at the prospect of losing him, of his being snatched away and of her being left to mourn without ever knowing for sure what might have been. It was a terrible moment. A seeing. A moment of unveiled terror. She began to pray, the words tumbling out of her mouth one after another in a poetic parade. But they stopped suddenly. Something in her woke up and yelled out that she was playing spiritual harlot, and the words dried up in the same instant. An anger surfaced. She damned herself as a silly bitch and hung on to his image. Prayed to him directly. Called on him. Shouted at him in the silence of her head. Then she began to cry, and her body doubled over with the pain of it all.

Drummond recovered moments later and found himself staring up into the faces of strangers. He was in an emergency room filled with gadgetry. A bearded man was looking down at him with interest. Two nurses were standing by, one with flaming red hair. He smiled up at them, blinked, asked what had happened, was asked in turn if he had taken any kind of drug – they weren't referring to medicinal drugs, he realized. He said that he had no interest in anything outside of what lay in his bathroom cabinet. But his mind began to work overtime in that moment, uncomfortable possibilities presenting themselves.

'You were dreaming,' the man said accusingly.

'How could you possibly know that?'

'Your eye movements. It's called REM sleep. REM stands for Rapid Eye Movement. You were at it when they brought you in and it's being going on all the while.'

'So?'

'Not usual. Odd, you might say.'

Drummond remembered dreams that had been nothing like dreams, re-enactments of the past that now astonished him with what they had divulged. He then remembered Georgia and asked about her.

'There's a young lady waiting in the corridor,' the nurse with flaming red hair said.

The bearded doctor gave a nod and she left the room with news of his recovery.

'Am I . . . free to leave?' asked Drummond.

'Not immediately,' replied the doctor. 'I suggest at least an overnight stay for observation. You feel okay?'

'Like new.'

'Headache?'

'No.'

'Any blurring of vision?'

'Nope.'

The man frowned and said, 'I'll be quite frank with you, Mr . . .'

'Drummond,' said Drummond.

'. . . I don't quite understand what's going on here, Mr Drummond. Ten minutes ago I'd have placed a sizable bet on your having been on a drug-induced trip that backfired, but I don't know what to think now. If you aren't on anything, then I can only guess at a small brain haemorrhage.'

'That sounds serious.'

'Not really. There's no reason to fear that it will ever happen again.'

'You mean that?'

'I wouldn't say it to you unless I meant it. Just something that happens. No need to worry about it at all – if you aren't on drugs.'

'That's nice to hear.'

'But if you are on drugs, then I would worry if I were you.'

'I'm not, I can assure you of that,' said Drummond, knowing that there was a possibility that the blood test would prove him a liar and Duval a charlatan in spite of his success with little Sophie. He pushed that thought away and said, 'How long before I can speak to my friend in the corridor?'

'Soon,' said the doctor. He added, 'Your pupils were dilated. They're quite normal now.'

'As I said, I feel fine.'

The result of the blood test arrived a few minutes later. It was negative.

'My apologies, Mr Drummond,' the doctor said.

They transferred him to a ward after an X-ray and Georgia appeared; it was pretty obvious that she had been crying, her eyes were still puffy. She hung onto him for a moment, let out a sigh and stared at him for a second or two before admitting that she had feared him dead. He pulled her back in against him and whispered that he wasn't that easily got rid of, knowing now that something very odd had happened, something related to Duval's unease when the Protasis experiment was interrupted by Bill's outburst.

But he felt fine now, and the experience had not been a bad one; In fact it had been of considerable value – memory and dream were perhaps not all that far apart.

'What's the diagnosis?' she asked.

'A *small* brain haemorrhage,' he said, smiling at her.

The worry returned to her face immediately.

'They're wrong.' Another smile and a little laugh. 'It wasn't a brain haemorrhage, Georgia. It was a kind of journey, a journey into the past to when I was a child.'

She frowned at him. 'I don't understand what you mean.'

'A journey into memory. A going back. A reliving of the past as if it were the present. I'm not having you on. Really. It wasn't a dream.'

'Sounds something like the other experience you described to me.'

'Exactly.' He drew breath and looked away, stared across the ward at an old man's face barely visible above the bedclothes before continuing. 'The whole thing started while I was standing at the window looking out at the snow. I went back in that moment to when I was ten. And it wasn't just remembering. It was like watching a movie, only I was in the movie. My father was propped up in bed as I am now, and very sick. I was standing at the foot of the bed watching him cough his lungs up. It was the actual incident. Everything came back to me. My feelings. My anger. My . . . dislike for the man.' He corrected himself immediately. 'I hated him, actually. He was very violent towards me. Cuffed me continually about the ears with the flat of his hand for the smallest misdemeanour. But when he got really sick and wasn't able to lay into me, I got the upper hand. I was well and he was sick, and he needed me for little things. It was a get-me-this and a get-me-that and get-out-of-my-sight kind of situation. But he couldn't enforce his will the way he had been used to doing, with his hands, and I turned into a kind of insolent jailer when my mother wasn't around. I did what he asked, but he knew damn well from my looks and my movements that he had lost power – that I had gained control.'

She digested that as best she could and said, 'The son overcomes the father. It's natural. It happens to all of us in one way or another.'

'Elijah's mantle passed on by default in my case,' he replied, the words popping into his mouth. 'An angry father and an angry son and a mother caught between them like a football.'

'I was referring to the process of growing up.'

'And I'm referring to my picking up on my father's frustration. That's why he was so angry most of the time – frustration. Hemmed in with a wife who'd never read anything more difficult than an Agatha Christie novel, and a son the picture of his mother both physically and emotionally. I was one big disappointment to him. Every time he looked at me he saw her, and only her, nothing of himself. And he was dying, and he must have realized that as well.'

'What age was he when he died?'

'Forty-nine.'

'He was intelligent?'

'Very. Started out as a shunter with the LNER railroad and ended up general manager of their largest railhead in Glasgow. Had a gift for figures. Could draw like you wouldn't believe. Read everything he could lay his hands on.' A laugh from Drummond. 'And you should have seen his handwriting. Copperplate. That's how they discovered him. He wrote down the contents of the wagons on the shunting tickets in copperplate handwriting. Can you imagine their surprise?'

'Where did he learn copperplate?'

'From his father. His father was a stonemason by trade, and a good one. Good stonemasons not only carve stone, they also write on stone. My father's first promotion was writing up ledgers for the railhead stores department – that's when they discovered he could count as well.'

A shake of the head from Georgia.

'But an impatient man,' added Drummond. 'Wanted to do everything at the one time and ended up doing nothing, because of his health. A bloody shame!'

'You really hated him?'

'I did then, primarily because of his impatience. If I asked him a question and didn't immediately understand the answer I got my ears boxed. And I mean boxed. Sent me right across the room on a couple of occasions. I was scared to open my mouth eventually.'

'He obviously wanted you to succeed where he had failed.'

'Yes, I suppose so – but he expected me to be as fast at picking up on things as he was, and I couldn't because he never gave me time enough to think anything through. So I'd start crying, like my mother, and the reward for crying was a cuff round the ear. Always a cuff round the ear. Then my mother would get in between us and the rowing would start. I was obviously her son and had her brains, her softness of nature, her inability to understand complicated things. I was, in other words, stupid. I believed that for some time.'

'Then he died.'

'He was in a sanatorium by that time, in Edinburgh. I only saw him at weekends. I'll never forget those weekends. It was a different world. Acres of mown grass and little trees. Willy-wagtails feeding from the patients' hands. Long low wards filled with healthy-looking men – they really did look healthy. The steamed food did it, apparently. Everything they ate was either steamed or boiled, for some reason. And so quiet. Took us a couple of hours to get there every Saturday.' He smiled again and continued. 'He caught up on his reading then. Had nothing to do all day but read, so he read. I can remember looking at the books, wondering what they were about ... I can still remember one of the titles.'

'What was it?'

'The works of Flavius Josephus.'

'The Jewish historian.'

'Yup. Liked to argue the toss about history with anyone willing to take him on.'

'An interesting man.'

He nodded, observed the white counterpane, its folds and crevices, the chromium bedrail and beyond it the other chromium bedrails. 'He was buried on New Year's Day.'

A silence set in and she broke it by saying, 'This is what you were . . . reliving?'

'Frame after frame after frame – it was like watching a bloody movie, only I was in the damned thing.'

'And?'

'And . . . I've forgiven him, for what it's worth.'

'You've hated him all these years?'

'Blanked him out of mind might be a better way of expressing it. But yes. Because of hate.'

'That's amazing.'

'It also feels good. Really good.'

'You've shed the mantle?'

'Yes, I think so. At last.' A sigh from Drummond. 'And I learned something else, Georgia. Something very important – that none of us is normal. Not one of us. Never have been and never will be. There isn't any basic denominator. We're plonked into this crazy world carrying crazy genes, and we do the best we can with whatever notion of normality happens to be around. No guilt required if we see things that way, just the necessity to be on our toes. Aware, if you like.'

'Of what?'

'Of the fact that we aren't living our own lives most of the time, that our identities are composite creations – bits of this and bits of that with only a glimmer of something at the core, whatever the core might be.'

'A little negative, don't you think?'

He laughed, reaching for her hand. 'Not bad for someone supposedly in the throes of a brain haemorrhage, eh?'

The immediate reality reinstated, Georgia said, 'What happens now? How long are they going to keep you in here?'

'Until tomorrow, as far as I know. Overnight observation was what I was told.'

Her earlier expression of concern returned. 'What if it really was a brain haemorrhage, Ian? Have you considered that?'

He blinked at her. '. . . I suppose it is a possibility, but I don't believe that it was.'

'I've never been so scared in all my life . . . I really did think I was about to lose you.'

'Advertising man dies aged forty-three.'

'Don't joke about it. You were unconscious for ages.'

'How do you think I felt when I woke up in hospital? It was quite a shock.'

'. . . I understood something too.'

'What?' He watched her face, waited.

'That I was scared of losing you, as I've said.' She hesitated, braved the moment and allowed the words to come. 'That I loved you. Needed you. I almost went crazy in that corridor when I thought . . . If you had died, I don't know what I'd have done!' She gave a little hiccuppy laugh and added almost by way of retraction, 'Pure sentimentality, of course.'

Drummond continued to stare at her. Then reaching for her other hand he drew her across him without a thought for what anyone in the ward might think. 'I'd almost given up on ever hearing you say anything like that,' he said in a whisper. 'Do you know what you're saying?'

'Uh-huh.'

'You really want an old bastard like me?'

She rolled to the side a little and looked up at him, laughed and said, 'Are you terribly old?'

'Old-ish,' he replied, astonished by the innocence of her expression, 'but in good working order.'

'Then you'll do,' she said, her voice breaking ever so slightly, 'for a while.'

She left the hospital soon after and walked back to her flat in spite of the heavily falling snow, her coat collar turned up, the lapels doubled inward and buttoned for the first time, her hands dug deep in the pockets and pushed against her body to help retain heat. The streets were almost deserted; everyone had fled home or into the cafés further up the hill to watch the snow overcome the dampness of the streets and slowly build on itself flake by flake. She trudged on toward the lights, wondering if Drummond's assessment of what had happened to him was in any way accurate, or if some terrible truth about his condition would be found in the X-ray. A brain haemorrhage was only too possible at his age, considering the amount of fatty food he pumped into himself. And the bugger was smoking again, which suggested tension. She smiled to herself, laughing wryly at the thought of what she had taken on, and turned into Willoughby Road where the parked cars now sat like dust-sheeted armchairs. A few minutes later she was in her flat and on the telephone, her mounting worry having driven her to track down the Katharsis number and speak with Duval about what Ian believed to be the cause of his sudden collapse. But getting to the man proved more difficult than she had anticipated. A male voice with a French accent informed her that Monsieur Duval could not be disturbed. He was working with a group of students at that very moment.

'It's imperative that I speak with him immediately,' she said back. To both drive the point home and gain her listener's full attention, she repeated what she had just said in French and added that she was a personal friend of Ian Drummond's.

'Your name is?' asked the voice.

She gave it and further explained the urgency of the situation, waited impatiently while someone was sent upstairs to fetch the philosopher to the phone. After what seemed an age, a deeper, and more resonant voice came on the line. It was Duval. She apologized for interrupting him, introduced herself, quickly described what had happened and forwarded Ian's interpretation of the event against that of the doctor who had examined him. It was all very confusing and worrying. He had talked about going on a journey into his own past, and seemed to accept the oddity of the situation without question. The chances were he would probably discharge himself in the morning even if the verdict was a brain haemorrhage. To her surprise, Duval said immediately that Drummond's interpretation was probably the more accurate of the two, for what she had described was a known result under certain experimental conditions. It was a most interesting development, and an unexpected one. Someone would be sent to assess his condition within the hour. Then to her surprise he changed the subject abruptly and said that he looked forward to meeting her, that he understood her to be interested in what they were trying to accomplish, and that he had been more than a little impressed with the quality of the information she had gathered on Mr Drummond's behalf after only one week in Paris.

'I would like very much to meet you too,' she said back, seizing the opportunity. 'You realize of course that I'm a journalist?'

'I was not aware of that.'

'But as a close friend of Ian's, everything's under wraps for the moment. I have no intention of breaking the story until things are, well, less delicate.'

Some seconds of silence greeted her statement.

'Are you still there, Monsieur?' asked Georgia.

'I was thinking,' he said back, as if taking one's time to think on the telephone were a perfectly natural thing to do. 'I was thinking that we might perhaps prepare the whole story for publication. Would you be interested in such an exercise?'

'I certainly would.'

'I do not mean in the form of newspaper articles; the issues are too complex for that kind of treatment. Perhaps a book would be more appropriate. Yes, a book.' He paused again to think, and astonished Georgia by saying, 'Do you have a good mind, Miss Patton?'

'I'm a professional journalist, if that's what you're asking.'

'That's . . . not quite what I'm asking. I'm asking if you enjoy the act of thinking.'

It was such an odd question that Georgia hesitated. '. . . I believe I do,' she said.

'Then we must talk. Soon. May I have your telephone number?'

Quite taken aback by the way things were shaping up, she read the numbers off the dial and waited for his next statement. He reverted immediately to their original topic and said that she must not worry about Ian's health. It was highly unlikely that he had suffered a brain haemorrhage. But their consultant physician would be immediately dispatched to the hospital to check on what had happened.

'Thank you. That's most reassuring,' she said back, wondering what Ian would think when Fisher turned up. 'Could you let me have Dr Fisher's diagnosis the moment he returns?'

'But of course,' said Duval. 'Goodnight, Miss Patton.'

Chapter Fifteen

To Bill Everton's delight, everything ran smoothly at the agency until the following Tuesday morning, seven days in all. Then to his dismay all hell broke loose and they were thrust into the kind of situation he had dreaded from the very beginning. Drummond was in his office working on the mountain of material the messenger from Peyrefitte's had delivered the previous Monday, and Bill had only just come out of the video room after a presentation to a new client, when Georgia appeared clutching a copy of London's most notorious newspaper and dumped it face-up on Ian's desk. Having met Bill in the corridor, she had swept him into Ian's office along with her, and now stood watching as both men digested the pernicious nonsense written not only about Duval and Katharsis but also about Dr Fisher. A large and quite distorted photograph of Duval, taken at the time of the hotel shooting, along with one of Fisher, dominated the front page. To Drummond's astonishment, there was also a small photograph of a grinning Peter Thwaites, gifted the title 'Reverend' for the occasion, and a rather sombre picture of Katharsis headquarters with a close-up of the front door and someone peeping out like a criminal. The banner headline read:

ISLINGTON BLACK WITCH-COVEN COVER-UP!

'We're even mentioned!' said Drummond, pointing to a paragraph Bill hadn't yet reached. 'It says here that we're . . . *aiding and abetting the spread of ideas and practices which the Church denounced centuries ago as devil worship*, and that . . . *in spite of being warned by the Reverend Peter Thwaites as to Edouard Duval de Chantillac's diabolical intentions* . . .' He stopped reading and looked across at Georgia. 'Edouard Duval *de Chantillac*?

That's a new one on me.'

'Obviously his full name,' she said back with a shrug. 'I would imagine he doesn't use it for the very reason that it sounds a little grand.'

'According to this he's into just about every bit of indecency ever invented.' He stared back at the page with disbelief. 'We're supposed to be ignoring the obvious because of the huge amount of money involved – the figure they've mentioned is preposterous! And they're questioning where his finance is coming from.'

'Nice little rag, isn't it? You've got to hand it to them for audacity.'

'But how can they hope to get away with it?' exploded Bill, to whom the *Mercury* was something he occasionally glimpsed on the newsstand, but had never opened in his life. 'It's lies from beginning to end!'

'Lies to us, but based on a form of proof as far as they're concerned,' said Georgia with a wry smile. 'I'll bet there's nothing in that article that they can't produce some kind of spurious evidence for. It's a difficult style of thinking to overcome in the courts for the very reason that most of it is speculation based on what could be construed as a *kind* of truth. They're totally unscrupulous, but they aren't stupid.'

'It's disgusting!'

'It sells newspapers by the million; they're in the business of making money. They're very good at it. So good, in fact, that not a few top journalists fear it could become the standard for all newspapers if we can't stop the decent ones from being gobbled up – quite a headache for those in Fleet Street who still believe in the old principles of reportage.'

'We have no way of fighting back?' said Drummond.

'Not really. Even if you got a retraction on what they've said about Drummond Advertising, it wouldn't change what they've planted in the public mind about Duval and Fisher and Katharsis. And if their sister newspapers take it up, which I think is more than likely, then what's been implanted will be reinforced.'

He digested that and read on through the mishmash of occult nonsense Duval was charged with either believing or practising, and came to the section on Dr Fisher where the writer suggested that this highly respected psychiatrist was engaged in methods of treatment at St Bartholomew's Hospital that were more in alignment with magic than medicine. The piece stated that Fisher's job was already hanging on a thread because of the nature of the research he was pursuing with public funds, and a patient was quoted as having had nightmares involving 'Satan' which she believed were the direct result of the unusual treatment she had received. The whole bizarre story was then linked to the attempt on Duval's life, and the suspicion that he was involved in drug-trafficking was tacked on for good measure.

Shaking his head and staring at the page before him, Drummond said, 'There's everything in here but the kitchen sink. The only thing they haven't suggested is that Duval is the Devil in person.'

'What's your first move going to be?' asked Bill.

'A writ for defamation. They aren't getting away with what they've said about us.'

'And then?'

'Carry on as if nothing's happened – it'll blow over in a few weeks if Georgia's wrong about the story being taken up and syndicated.'

'And if it is?'

'Then until something sensible's written we're on a collision course with the gutter press and the gullible public.'

'We'd have to bow out if it escalates.'

'I'll be *damned* if I will!' Drummond eyed Bill Everton ferociously. 'I don't give in that easily. You know that better than anyone!'

The man drew breath, glanced at Georgia and said, 'You might end up sacrificing the firm for the sake of an uncertain principle.'

'What's uncertain about it?'

'Duval's *actual* stance.'

'You believe this nonsense?'

'Of course not. But he is into some pretty odd stuff as you well know. Bloody odd at times.'

'*Odd*, certainly, but not diabolical, Bill. Duval's one of the finest and most intelligent men I've ever been privileged to meet. I won't let him down.'

His chief executive smiled uneasily. 'You've got a staff of twelve to consider, Ian. A reputation second to none. A mass of clients that our opposition would love to get their hands on. I really don't think you can be that dogmatic.'

'I'm afraid Bill's right,' said Georgia, surprising Drummond. 'If it comes to the worst you'll have to back out and leave Duval to sink or swim. It's common sense, Ian. I'm sure Duval would understand if it came to that.'

Drummond's reaction to such a suggestion was swift and unequivocal. 'There's too much at stake for us to back out,' he snapped back. 'Hasn't it sunk into either of your heads what the long-term consequences could be if we fail him?'

'Only if you believe all that stuff about the Western world collapsing into chaos,' said Bill, trying to take the edge off Drummond's statement. 'We don't really have any proof of that – just Duval's word, and the word of those who believe in him. He could be up to anything, for all we know.'

Looking straight at Georgia, Drummond said, 'I can't see how you could be of the same opinion, knowing what you know.'

'From the way you're talking, there seems to be a hell of a lot I don't know about!' added Bill.

'Quite a lot, old son,' replied Drummond. He turned back to Georgia. 'Whose side will you be on when and if it comes to the crunch?' he asked, his eyes fixed on her eyes. When she hesitated to reply, he said immediately, 'Don't you believe in him either?'

'It isn't a matter of whether I believe in him, Ian,' she said back, knowing that she would have to phrase her answer carefully. 'It's a matter of trying to determine whether the rather strange things *he* believes in make any sense or not. Okay, so he's been successful in getting Sophie out of her catatonia – but does that mean we have to automatically accept a mixture of 'shamanism' and 'sound therapy' as more sensible than what we've already got? If Fisher was playing around with that kind of stuff at Bart's, then it's no wonder he's for the chop. And if Duval has said half of the things he's accused of saying in that article-cum-exposé, then the chances are he really is bonkers in spite of his obvious intelligence. I've known a couple of highly intelligent people who went over the top and began to imagine they could work out the underlying secret of the universe. Really. I'm not kidding. They were fascinating and I liked them a lot, but they were in fact quite mad.'

'If Duval isn't for real,' said Drummond, drawing the strings of his argument together, 'why the orchestrated shooting and this supposed exposé to undermine his credibility? He was expecting something like this to happen. And it wasn't the Reverend Peter Thwaites who thought this one up. Someone supplied this mass of information along with a ground plan, and I've got a damned good idea who it was. Lacroix. It's too neat. The ideas roll along too easily. If we could pin Lacroix's name on this nonsense, then we could probably cripple the whole story and stop it turning into the witch-hunt it's intended to provoke.' He paused, looked at Georgia. 'We've got to stand by him on this one. He's worthy of it.'

'Paquel,' she said immediately.

'Your journalist friend in Paris?'

'Who better? He's got very good reasons for wanting to nail Lacroix.'

'Then Paquel it is,' said Drummond. 'I'll leave the details to you.'

Georgia returned to her Hampstead flat and phoned Paul Paquel immediately. He came on the line quite excited about something and she had to listen to his story before delivering her own. It was quite a story. Eight tonnes of Gestapo files on the Nazi occupation of France, kept in a secret-service vault, had been confirmed to exist by a former chief of the French secret service, Anton Triboulet. Triboulet had said that they showed 'men of substance' to have collaborated with the Germans while claiming to be members of the Resistance. The news had sent a series of shudders through French political quarters. Defence Minister Paul Détienne had announced a decision that Gestapo and Abwehr (German Military Intelligence) records should be handed over to the historical section of the armed forces, and had added that they would be available for inspection by both defence and prosecution in cases involving the Resistance.

Interviewed on television, the urbane Anton Triboulet said that when he took over the post of chief of the French secret-service in 1972, he had come across the eight tonnes of files and found that people of substance who had been, or had claimed to have been, good patriots and resistants had in reality been on the payroll of the Germans. Fernand Daniélou, French Resistance hero and President of the National Assembly, backed Defence Minister Détienne's decision to transfer the Gestapo files to the historical section of the armed forces, where they would be examined by a consultative commission of Resistance organizations. This decision had left a number of people quaking in their shoes.

'It sounds as if all hell's going to break loose,' said Georgia, saddened by the news; she had great respect for the French, and had no desire to see them tear themselves apart in a frenzy of recrimination.

They discussed at some length what the repercussions might be in political circles. Then Paquel remembered suddenly that it was she who had phoned him and said, 'So what is your news?'

Reading from an extra edition of the *Mercury* she had bought, Georgia outlined the accusations against Duval and said that it was quite obviously Lacroix's handiwork. If they worked on it separately, there was the chance one of them might pin Lacroix down as the source and blow the situation wide open. The newspaper she had in her hand was without doubt a rag of the worst ilk, but if given an even more explosive story they might well relent and use the second to displace the first and boost their circulation even further. It was a matter of fighting fire with fire, and the strategy must not be to take on the the *Mercury*, but to incite its editor to see the advantage of a reversal through supplying him with equally juicy material on the little history professor. But of course they needed proof that the story had come from Lacroix in the first place. Only with that beyond doubt could they then release information on his plans for a restored French monarchy within a couple of years and show him to have been engaged in a vendetta against an old friend. Duval's supposed diabolism would not only fade into insignificance when that story hit the headlines, it would completely evaporate and throw such a spotlight on Lacroix that he would be effectively tied from there on. It was a matter of using Lacroix's strategy against Lacroix. As things stood, Lacroix had the freedom to do whatever he wished to whomever he wished, but thrust him into a high-profile position and he would be shorn of much of his power. She added with a little laugh that they were in a tight position due to the *Mercury* feature, and that the angle she had presented was the only foolproof way she could see of fighting back.

'It is the waste of a very good story,' he replied, his tone intimating that he did not welcome the news.

'Don't worry about it. I'll only give them about a quarter of the story.'

'. . . I do not understand. What is a quarter?'

'Please trust me, Paul,' she said back. 'There's a damned sight more to this than even you guessed.'

Paquel paused. Then he said, 'You'll share it with me?'

'You shared what you had.'

'When will you share it with me?'

It was Georgia's turn to hesitate. 'The Merovingian kings aren't the end of the matter, Paul,' she said. 'According to Duval it goes back *much* further. That's really all I can say at the moment. Give me a ring if you come up with something.'

She replaced the phone, threw herself down into her cane chair and sat staring at the room hoping for an idea, but nothing came. Instead she grabbed at a novel she had been reading, opened it and read a few sentences. What she read did not help answer the question in her mind – but it did clarify something.

> *. . . in times of acute crisis, the public leans always to dictators and juntas as the sick man leans to the reassuring doctor, however incompetent he may be.*

She immediately began to appreciate what Drummond had already fully appreciated – that if Western society did collapse, Lacroix's New Age Messiah would have a field day rounding up his subjects for the kingdom. She read on and discovered that on the very next page this writer had more than summed up, in a work of fiction, the same terror Edouard Duval de Chantillac believed imminent. The author had his character write:

> *Psychic epidemics are no new phenomenon in human history. The germs which cause them lie encapsulated, like the anthrax bacillus, until conditions are ripe for their rebirth. These conditions are fear, uncertainty, the break-up of social systems too fragile for the loads imposed on them. The symptoms are as various as the illusions of mankind: self-mutilation of the flagellants and the castrate priests, the murderous fury of the sicarii, the sexual perversion of the witch-hunters, the methodical madness of the inquisitors who think to confine truth in a phrase and burn any contumacious fellow who dares dissent from their definition. But the effects of the disease are always the same. The patient becomes fearful and irrational, subject to nightmare*

terrors, addicted to pleasurable illusions – an easy prey to pedlars of nostrums, magical incantations, and the collective follies of the other afflicted ones.

Another coincidence? Georgia closed both the book and her eyes and sat in what was almost perfect stillness. What was going on? What was coincidence when it became more than mere coincidence? Why should she have decided in that moment of time to open that novel? Okay, so she had been reading it the night before. But it seemed almost as if she had been made to open the damn thing in order to read those damned words. Of course that was sheer nonsense. Coincidence was exactly what it was, coincidence and no more. That's why we called coincidence coincidence. She opened her eyes again, looked towards the window where a grey sky hung and thought of Drummond's weird dreams. Then to her horror the most incredible thing happened. A bird – quite a large one – appeared from nowhere and flung itself against the topmost pane so ferociously that it dropped to the stone sill below. Shocked by the incident, it was some seconds before she could move. When she did move it was to discover the bird quite dead, its wings flat out, its neck obviously broken.

'What in the name of God is going on?' she whispered, her eyes fixed on what only a minute or so before had been a living creature. Then more stridently, and as if expecting an answer, she said, 'Will someone please tell me what's going on!'

The demonstration led by Peter Thwaites, and on this occasion other non-establishment Church leaders, was highly controlled this time. In fact, there was hardly a sound from the hundred or so marchers as they made their way along Upper Street and converged on the Katharsis building. Inside, Duval and his assistants watched as the eerily silent mob moved into position and stood staring up at the windows, their placards spelling out what their lips had been disciplined to hold at bay. There was also a large Bedford van smothered in copies of the *Mercury* in attendance, and the van's secondary purpose became immediately evident when the snake-like procession halted and bunched up on itself. The back doors were flung open and someone inside began to throw out bundle after bundle of neatly tied-off newspapers. That was when the sheer genius of the operation began to reveal itself. Hardly had the bundles hit the street than their strings were removed and measured wads of newsprint were handed out into the waiting crowd of protesters for distribution – the *Mercury* had become a religious tract. And it was an operation even more refined than that. Each wad contained not just an armful of complete copies, but hundreds of front pages laboriously cut away to ensure each carrier maximum efficiency. Then as if adding faggots to a pyre, those carrying the wooden-stocked placards began to lay them against the walls of the old warehouse.

Within minutes of their arrival, the crowd had more or less dispersed to carry out their task of informing everyone within a mile's radius of Duval's evil purposes, their congregating at the front door of the Katharsis headquarters nothing more than a symbolic act. Only Thwaites and the other leaders remained behind, their intention to verbally enlighten anyone entering or leaving the building as to Duval's diabolical vision. For they believed him to be engaged in a conscious undermining of Christian values and beliefs, and saw only the intent to disrupt and corrupt the minds of those foolish enough to think the training practices offered beneficial in any way. Evil was not merely an amorphous process, it was identifiable as a being, and Duval came as close as anyone had ever done to exhibiting the cold-blooded cunning of that being loosed on Earth by God to tempt and try the souls of men for the purposes of salvation. Duval had set up his hellish kitchen not only in Britain but across Europe, and if allowed to continue would train thousands of men and women to magically subvert millions under the guise of a therapy conceived in the Pit itself. Nothing said would ever dissuade them from that point of view. They were guided by the literal truth of the Word and by the whisperings of the Holy Ghost to which they were privy during prayer. There was no doubting that at all. What they knew to be the Truth was the Whole Truth and Nothing But the Truth – all else was a mere approximation devised by Satan in the modern age to lead souls astray.

The substance of many of the placards was the source of Duval's massive finance and the fact that it could not be traced. Hundreds of thousands of pounds had already been spent acquiring properties in Britain and in Europe, and millions would be required to publicize the supposed Training Programme when the underlying plan was finally executed in full. National advertising campaigns which would touch almost every community across the Western world were presently being honed to a knife's edge by men to whom money was God, and those campaigns had to be stopped at any cost. 'Where is the money coming from?' blasted many of the expertly penned placards. Was Duval trading on gains made from drug-trafficking? Or was there an even more sinister source?

And things were no better inside Katharsis than out. The switchboard was jammed with calls of abuse and verses of Scripture being read aloud. A few students had turned up, some undaunted by the *Mercury*'s extraordinary feature article, others unaware of its existence until later in the day. But they were so few, and the tensions generated in the staff were sufficient for Duval to decide that the day's activities should be terminated. They would be contacted the moment things returned to normal. Given the ferocity of the attack, however, and the possibility that it might be sustained, it would probably be a week or more before they could resume their studies.

Running the gauntlet of preachers, both staff and students left the building hurriedly, leaving Duval and the twins as its only occupants. And having talked earlier with Drummond on the telephone about the *Mercury*'s vicious attack, and again when things began to hot up outside and it became obvious that Peter Thwaites had won the day's battle, the gangling philosopher waited for Drummond to arrive and whisk him away. For there was no Dr Fisher to assist on this occasion: he was at that very moment before a specially convened medical board to explain the allegation of unorthodox activities.

Double-parking the BMW, Drummond forced his way through the tightly knit group of self-appointed clergy and reached the big green-painted door. But as he knocked and waited for someone to unlock that door, and tried to ignore the ramblings of those around him, Peter Thwaites recognized him and advanced Bible in hand like a modern version of Elijah spotting an Ahab. 'And still you don't believe!' exclaimed Thwaites.

Drummond stared at the Church of the Holy Ghost's pastor fixedly, and in that moment saw something terrible in those little brown eyes – a kind of religious insanity for which there was probably no cure. But he had no time to answer. The door opened sufficiently for him to slide into the large vestibule, and shut behind him before he could even think of a reply.

'The vultures have gathered,' said Duval.

'We'd better leave immediately,' replied Drummond. He gave the Frenchman one of Georgia's most practised looks and added, 'Is it three for the road?'

'Just myself,' said Duval.

'Then let's go. If we move fast we'll be in the car and gone before they realize it's you. Okay?' With that said he unlocked the door quietly, glanced at Duval again, then opening it quickly walked through the small God-blinded assembly expecting Duval to follow hard on his heels. But when he reached the car and turned, there was no sign of Duval. It was in fact some seconds before the philosopher's elongated figure appeared. And it seemed that Duval was in no hurry. Standing on the worn step of his headquarters, a small suitcase in his right hand, he surveyed those gathered with an indescribable look. Then as if embarking on a stroll, he moved through the astonished little gathering and climbed into the passenger seat of the car without a single word being said by anyone. Drummond didn't wait around for the commotion to start; he gunned the car immediately and left Thwaites and his fellow fanatics to work out what had gone wrong with their vocal cords.

They cut down Canon Street onto Canonbury Road and doubled back along Essex Road to the Angel. Drummond said, 'Where exactly are we heading?'

'I'm not sure,' replied Duval.

'Where are you staying?'

'I have no place to stay.'

'You were sleeping upstairs – in that little room?'

'I've had no choice since the shooting.'

A glance from Drummond as they crossed the Angel's ultra-busy junction and headed toward Mount Pleasant. 'I think you'd better come home with me,' said Drummond at last, there seemingly being nothing else for it. 'There's a guest-room you can use until things quieten down.'

'That is most kind,' replied Duval without hesitation. 'Most kind.'

And so it was settled. They drove to Camden Town, to Camden Square, and Drummond found himself immediately embroiled in the philosopher's life more deeply than he could ever have imagined. For hardly had they entered the apartment than there was a telephone call for Duval, and Drummond was left wondering how the caller had known where to contact the Frenchman. Duval took the call in the study, but left the door open. The call was short, very short. Duval came into the kitchen where Drummond was percolating coffee and delivered some rather disturbing news.

'Our Centres in Europe are also under siege,' he said matter-of-factly, 'Everything has come to a halt.'

'Lacroix's been busy.'

'Yes. He is a very good organizer.'

'I'd like to wring his neck.'

A look from Duval which verged on what Drummond had witnessed as the man stood in the doorway of his headquarters and surveyed Thwaites' compatriots in hysteria. Then came the request that was later to change Drummond's whole conception of what he was involved in. 'It is necessary that I be driven somewhere this evening,' said Duval, glancing at the percolator which was now bubbling its contents up into the little glass dome. 'I would be much obliged if you could do that for me.'

'Of course,' said Drummond. 'Where do you want to go?'

'Hackney.'

'Time?'

'Any time will do.' The faint smile Drummond had become used to seeing asserted itself fleetingly on the philosopher's face. 'We must not be followed.'

'You expect to be followed?'

'I am under constant surveillance – on two fronts.'

Drummond digested that piece of information. 'The second party being?'

'– Friends,' replied Duval, his slight difficulty in choosing that word suggesting further complexity.

'What do you want me to do?'

'Arrange a suitable confusion so that we can reach our destination undetected.'

'We were followed here?'

'It is possible.'

Turning away, Drummond searched out coffee-cups and thought about how that might be accomplished. Then he said, 'I can see a way of doing it, but it would require involving someone else.' He added quickly, 'I'd ask Bill to help out, but I know he wouldn't want to be involved. And I don't think we should involve Georgia – Miss Patton.'

'Agreed.'

'Which makes me think there's only one person who'd be willing to help without my having to fabricate an explanation. Sophie's father. I think he'd do just about anything for you.'

'Most suitable,' said Duval, nodding.

'Right. Help yourself to coffee.' He was about to walk out of the kitchen when he realized that he hadn't explained to Duval what he intended to do. He said 'Sorry,' laughed to himself, outlined his quite simple plan, and waited for Duval's reaction. The man nodded and said that he thought it satisfactory, but suggested that he avoid using his own telephone – there was a strong possibility it had been tampered with.

'What makes you think that?'

'I would be most surprised if they had overlooked such an obvious source of information.'

'What about the call you just received?'

'There was nothing in it of use.' Duval changed tack. 'Is there some other telephone in the building you might use? A neighbour's, perhaps?'

The second neighbour he tried was at home and he was shown into a study as little used as his own. John Eglington listened intently to what he had dreamt up and said immediately that he would see to it – the man was fully aware of the mess Duval was in, having been informed earlier about the *Mercury*'s outrageous feature article by a colleague. The piece was already the talk of Fleet Street and beyond. His plan under way, Drummond hung up, thanked the neighbour for having allowed him to make his most urgent business call in privacy while lamenting the fact that his telephone had broken down when he needed it most, and returned to his apartment. He then donned his coat and made his way down to street level to initiate a charade designed to throw whoever might be watching off the scent. Getting into his car, he went through the motions of starting the engine, but engineered it so that the engine did not spring to life. After a minute or so of this, he released the bonnet, climbed out and appeared to check for a fault. Clambering back in he repeated the performance of being unable to get the car started. This resulted finally in his closing the bonnet, slamming the car door shut with obvious disgust and going back into the building.

'Now all we have to do is wait,' he said when back in the apartment. 'Coffee okay?'

'I'm sorry, I do not drink coffee,' replied Duval.

Duval rested in the short period prior to the taxi's arrival, leaving Drummond to his own thoughts sitting in the kitchen drinking coffee and wondering what their little jaunt to Hackney would reveal. Darkness fell and the taxi arrived at six and took them via Regent's Park and Great Portland Street to their destination – Broadcasting House. The entrance to this huge and rather formless building held Duval's attention for a moment; he stopped to stare up at the sculptured group of Prospero and Ariel before entering. In around four minutes he was back out on the street again, John Eglington having met and led them quickly through a series of corridors and out of the building by a side entrance. The journalist's old but immaculate Rover was parked only a few yards away from where they emerged. He handed Drummond the keys, pointed to where the car sat and was gone before anything could be said. They were on their way almost immediately, Drummond having taken about a minute to fathom which of the many extra switches on the dashboard turned on the lights. Then back up Great Portland Street they crawled, the car's powerful engine almost inaudible due to the attention John had lavished on it most weekends.

'I doubt very much that they're on to us,' said Drummond, glancing in the central mirror. 'What do you think?'

'Professionally done, Mr Drummond. I congratulate you.'

'Now all we have to do is get there,' he said back, knowing full well that the main route would be already congested with rush-hour traffic. Glancing again in the central mirror he then asked the pertinent question. 'Am I to meet these friends of yours? Or am I merely acting as driver?'

'They have agreed to talk to you.'

'Good,' he said back. 'May I ask who I'll be talking to?'

'I think it would be better if they explained that.'

Drummond drove on in silence for a few minutes before speaking again. 'Why didn't these friends of yours pick you up this afternoon?' he asked, conscious of the fact that he was pushing

Duval a little. 'If they could track you to my place without being spotted, they could surely have got you out of there without any problem?'

'I had no way of contacting them.'

'They could have contacted you . . . They eventually did contact you.'

'They could not run the risk of their presence being identified.'

'They took a risk in leaving this to me.'

'Not really. They said they had full confidence in you.'

'Why?'

'Because of your past military training.'

Drummond's reaction was immediate; he swung the Rover out of the traffic and into the first available side street, brought it to a halt, applied the handbrake viciously and turned to face his passenger. 'What the hell do they know of my past military training?' he asked raspingly.

The Frenchman's reply stunned him. 'The Intelligence Services are very thorough. When functioning at their best they leave very little to chance.'

'Intelligence Services?' The advertising man's stare was almost comic. 'May I ask which Intelligence Service we're dealing with?'

Duval stared back but said nothing.

'It's your lot, isn't it?' When Duval still refused to answer he turned away and sat with his back to the man, the fact that he was now probably involved in something highly irregular registering on him sickeningly. 'You should have told me,' he said at last, his tone intimating both disappointment and disillusionment. 'I had the right to know.'

'You have jumped to an erroneous conclusion,' replied Duval.

Drummond turned to look at the philosopher again. 'You're working in conjunction with our people?'

'I am not at liberty to say.' The Frenchman sighed and added, 'I could quite easily have given you some other explanation for your having been chosen to do this thing. I did not do so. I suggest you think about that.'

That was the truth. It made Drummond unsure again.

'Everything will be explained to you; that is the purpose of this meeting.'

'Everything?' said Drummond, wondering what else there was to divulge. 'I thought I already knew everything.'

'There are ramifications of which you are unaware.'
'I'm beginning to believe you.'
'May we continue?'
Drummond's reply was straight and to the point. 'I want to be assured that what I'm doing won't land me in prison for twenty years.'
'Prisons aren't always built with bricks and mortar,' replied Duval. 'Please trust me.'
In a bit of a quandary, Drummond turned away from the Frenchman and sat staring out of the windscreen. Then he said, 'I'm only doing this because it's you that's asking me to do it.'
'Thank you, Ian,' said Duval.
Digesting Duval's use of his Christian name, Drummond found his way back out on to the thoroughfare they had so abruptly left, checked his watch and began to weave his way deeper into the East End. He drove without speaking to Duval again, wondering if his decision were the right one. At a quarter past seven they crossed Dalston Junction, and with the aid of a small street atlas he had pocketed before leaving home, were soon travelling up Dalston Lane in search of Hackney Downs and the rendezvous point. No address had been given on the telephone; Duval had been previously briefed and given a code word designating the location. There would be a church on the street; they were to stop there and wait until contacted.
It was an unsavoury neighbourhood. The drab buildings, litter and inadequate street lighting reminded Drummond of the territory in Glasgow he had once wandered around so aimlessly as a teenager. They came to the top of Pembury Road and he spotted the church on their right. 'That's it,' he said, slowing and turning off onto Downs Park Road.
The street was totally deserted, but the church was lit up. Stationing the car as directed, he switched off the lights and engine and wound down his window a little; that's when he heard the singing. He sat listening, amazed by the quality of the voices, the sheer effortlessness of the harmonies being produced.
'Blacks,' said Duval, breaking the silence. 'It is obviously a black church.'
'They can't half sing.'
'Indeed.' Ten minutes passed slowly. Drummond stared around him, expecting someone to approach, but the street remained

empty. He settled back into his seat aware of the seconds drifting by, aware of the carols being brought to perfection by voices which were already perfection.

At seven-forty Duval said, 'Someone's coming.'

'Where?' said Drummond, glancing around.

'Very near,' said Duval. Unable to see anyone, Drummond looked at Duval – the man's eyes were closed. He was about to ask him what he was playing at when someone rapped on the driver's window with a knuckle and he spun back to see a face no more than a few inches away. Taken off guard, his body jerked to the side involuntarily, and in that same moment the driver's door was pulled open. The contact said nothing, merely jerked his head to signify that they should get out of the car. Drummond got out without a word, opened the rear door and stood like an attentive chauffeur as Duval eased his elongated frame out into the chill air. As the rear door slammed shut, the man jerked his head again and they set off along the street. The last house in a row of identical houses was apparently their destination. Pointing at the front door, their guide walked off without a word having been said.

Drummond stared after him, then up at what had once been an elegant Victorian residence complete with basement kitchen and servants' quarters. It was now in a state of total disrepair; what paint there was on windows and front door had flaked and cracked due to years of neglect. Two pockmarked pillars added to the theme of breakdown, and a dull red glow struggling out through ripple-glass suggested the possibility of other things. He unlatched an iron gate and they ascended five or six worn steps to the front door, searched for a bell or buzzer, but found none. He was on the point of knocking when a shadowy figure appeared in the hallway. He knew it was a woman before the door opened. She was dressed in jeans and a loose-fitting woollen jumper and was quite attractive. Not knowing what to say or do, Drummond smiled at her. There was no response. Standing aside, she let them pass into the hallway, and as the door closed behind them another opened and two men appeared. Drummond was made to raise his arms so that he could be frisked. They were then ushered into the room the men had come out of. The room had little furniture in it. A makeshift fire burned in the grate, and standing before that fire was a well-dressed man in his late forties.

'Mr Drummond,' said the man, advancing. 'So glad you could

make it.' The handshake was firm and positive. 'Sorry you had to be searched. It's a rule that has to be observed. Did you have any trouble getting here?'

Surprised by the man's affability, and as curious as all hell, Drummond said that things had worked out pretty well – that they had managed to give those following them the slip without much bother. 'Not that I ever saw anything remotely suspicious,' he added, registering their host's tailored appearance.

'They sometimes verge on being professional,' replied the man, smiling a little. He turned his attention to Duval, beamed at the philosopher as if at an old friend. 'Monsieur!' The hand shot out again and it was Drummond's turn to stand and watch.

Duval shook the man's hand and delivered one of his tiny bows of acknowledgment at the same time, but remained silent. Not knowing what to expect, Drummond waited to be illuminated. He did not have long to wait. The man turned back to Drummond and said, 'You're obviously wondering what the hell is going on, right? Who am I and what does all of this mean?' He laughed suddenly, as if at a joke, shook his head and again fastened his eyes on Drummond. 'This, as I'm sure you are already aware, is an Intelligence operation. But I'm afraid you're not dealing with British Intelligence, Mr Drummond – you're dealing with the Mossad'. He delivered another of his crinkly smiles and added, 'It was decided in Jerusalem only last night that you should be acquainted with the whole scenario.'

'I don't understand any of this,' said Drummond.

'You will, shortly.' The Intelligence Officer motioned with a hand that they should be seated, waited until they were, and began to explain in a tired voice what it was Drummond should know. 'Certain things have had to be left until now,' he said, continuing to stand with his back to the fire. 'Delicate things. As a result of information given to you – which, I should add, was never meant to lead you astray in your thinking – you've probably formed a picture not quite accurate in some of its details.' His smile was suddenly apologetic. 'That could not be avoided. You were told the truth, or something as near to the truth as possible at all times, but what you imagined that truth to mean was totally your own affair.'

'I'd be much obliged if you'd get to the point,' said Drummond, wondering what the hell Israeli Intelligence had to do with it all.

The Israeli's lingering smile faded. He began to articulate the essence of the situation in a carefully modulated tone. 'The point, Mr Drummond, is that the state of Israel is in danger. When the state of Israel is in danger we Israelis don't sit around and lament the fact. We act. That is what I am doing now, and it is what I've been doing since Monsieur Duval approached our government with certain . . . disturbing facts and figures. Now I know . . .' He stopped short. 'You have a question?'

'How did you get access to my military record?'

'Ah,' said the man.

'Are you working in conjunction with the British?'

'. . . Not exactly.'

'Then how did you get it?'

'We have friends in British Intelligence. They owed us a favour or two.'

Drummond gave the Israeli a nod and he continued.

'I know you're well aware of what the statistics supplied by Monsieur Duval suggest, but what you're perhaps not fully aware of is what they mean in political terms. What you have to imagine is not merely the collapse of Western society – a notion terrifying enough to any sensible person – but the simultaneous attempt to set up a new social, political and spiritual order spanning the whole of Europe, and based on principles dragged out of the Middle Ages. That's the more terrifying aspect as far as we're concerned. The nightmare of a Europe in political and social chaos is one thing, but a Europe under the control of a regime founded primarily on the bizarre notion of spiritual superiority is more that we Israelis can sit back and put up with. You see, in the scenario we envisage, the attitude of spiritual superiority based on the return of a Christian Messiah figure would quickly lead to a policy rejecting Israel as a sovereign state. And I don't think it takes much imagination to work out what the next move of such an élitist regime would be. It's our belief that Israel would be invaded and that our whole nation would again be dragged back into a form of slavery. Either that or they would simply set out to destroy us once and for all.'

'That sounds rather fanciful.'

'You think so, Mr Drummond? May I remind you that it's not so long ago that another regime with notions of superiority had a crack at the same thing. With the West in chaos and an accepted

Christian Messiah set up to instruct the masses on how they should think, feel and act, the result could only be slavery or extermination for the Jewish people – probably the Arabs as well. And there's another very good reason for believing that that would be the course taken – the fact that sectarian Christians around the globe are presently gearing up for what they term Armageddon. Irrationality mixed with supposed prophecy and a directive from him whom they will eventually consider the Messiah would produce an army of fanatics bent on fulfilling what is believe to be Old Testament prophecy concerning the Last Days. Give such people their head and they would make their damned prophecies come true with a vengeance. There would be no stopping them. They would descend on us like a plague of locusts and the whole of the Middle East would die defending itself against a fanaticism more murderous than anything ever witnessed on this planet. That, Mr Drummond, is the substance of our fear. And we have every reason to believe it more than a fantastic possibility, considering what we now know of certain people's plans and intentions for the near future. It is . . . on the cards, as they say, and we Israelis never ignore what is on the cards. We take everything into consideration. We weigh the evidence, no matter how bizarre it may seem, and act accordingly.'

Trying to grapple with what he was hearing, Drummond said, 'Isn't it more likely that they'll see Lacroix's Messiah as the Antichrist and tear him to pieces?'

'We've allowed for a reverse scenario in our calculations, but do not believe that it will come out that way.'

'And if it is in reverse?'

'We concluded that the end result would probably be much the same.' The Israeli smiled to himself, produced a packet of cigarettes and offered them to Drummond. 'Can you imagine what would happen?' He proffered a lit match. 'The Jews would be blamed for plotting a take-over of the Western world as in the *Protocols of Zion*. In that event, the hysterical masses would attempt to rid themselves of the insidious Jew by launching a final Holy Crusade. We believe that that crusade would include an invasion of Israel.' He laughed coarsely, squinting at Drummond. 'Do you see what I'm getting at? The only way we can win is to nip the bloody thing in the bud before it has a chance to take off.'

'You're the second person to have mentioned the *Protocols of Zion*. What exactly are they?'

'A blueprint for total world domination.'

'That sounds familiar.'

'The text advocates a many-tentacled hydra-headed conspiracy dedicated to disorder and anarchy, to toppling certain existing regimes, infiltrating Freemasonry and other such organizations, and eventually seizing absolute control of the Western world's social, political and economic institutions. And its anonymous authors declare explicitly that they have stage-managed whole peoples according to a political plan which no one as much as guessed existed over the course of centuries. It's quite a document. When the *Protocols* were first publicized, they were alleged to have been composed at an International Judaic Congress convened in Switzerland in 1897. This allegation has long since been disproved, but the *Protocols* are still being circulated as anti-Semitic propaganda in Latin America, Spain, the Middle East and even here in Britain.'

Only too aware that the man standing by the fire was a hard-headed specialist whose views had to be taken seriously, Drummond said, 'What did you mean when you said you'd attempt to nip it in the bud?'

'I think you know very well what I meant by that.'

'Assassination?'

'What else is there?'

A sigh from Drummond as he tried to accommodate the Israeli's point of view.

'We have no option. We no more like indulging in assassination than any other law-abiding democracy, but it is the only option left. We have to find him and stop him. Our problem is that we can't find him.'

'How long have you been looking?'

'Almost a year. It took us some time to properly evaluate the situation and make up our minds. There are Intelligence Units spread right across Europe hunting for him.'

'The other Intelligence Services aren't helping you?'

'In a small way, and quite unofficially. They think us a little paranoid.'

'That surprises you?'

'No, but it does depress me. There seems to be no way of

convincing them that there's a so-called Christian Messiah hiding somewhere in the bushes, and that the general situation in Europe is going to totally disintegrate in such a short period of time.'

'What about the French? The whole thing's going to take place on their doorstep.'

'We've been unofficially friendly with the French for many years, Mr Drummond, but the French government is split in the same way as the Vatican is split, and that has made things a little difficult.'

'The French government's split?'

'Oh yes. There's a very strong current in French politics that welcomes the idea of a returned monarchy – that is of course all the interested parties have been fed of the idea. But there are quite a few highly influential individuals who know exactly what's going on. They compose the upper echelon of the *Hieron du Lys*. The Sacred Order of the Lily is a hierarchical organization: there are something like a dozen other levels to the Order, each with its own officials, and numerous sub-groups, or Lodges, where the members are totally oblivious to what they are involved in.

Drummond digested that and said, 'A section of the Vatican wants Lacroix to succeed?'

'Assuredly.'

'I take it you know of Dr Freeman's little visit from those quarters.'

'Oh yes.'

'Care to comment?'

'There's not much I can say other than that they're running scared.'

'Doesn't that rather support my contention that not everyone will go along with Lacroix's little dream?'

'The bulk of people probably wouldn't go along with it if it were presented right this minute, but that's not how it's going to be done. Lacroix will wait until everything's falling about our ears before conjuring *le grand archetype* into physical existence.'

Flicking the butt of his cigarette into the fire, Drummond glanced at Duval. The man had sat in stony silence since their arrival, and seemed almost to be without identity. He looked back at the Intelligence Officer, and remembering something Kevin Murray had said when describing the plight of the Irish, surprised both Duval and the Israeli by saying, 'The whole thing sounds more tribal than archetypal.'

Duval rallied immediately. 'That is an astute observation, Mr Drummond.'

'The hollow myth,' added Drummond, borrowing from the same conversation.

'Indeed,' said Duval. 'And that is what the bulk of Western humanity will gladly accept when the moment comes. The early Jewish Christians in Jerusalem saw Jesus as a prophet in whom could be glimpsed the Messiah who was "yet to come", but with the destruction of that early community by the Romans, that idea was replaced by St Paul's radical theology of Jesus as "divine Saviour". That quite extraordinary notion was rejected by the original Jewish Christians in Jerusalem, and Paul's visionary version of Jesus as divine in his own right would not have become the established view if that early Christian community had survived. They were, after all, the ones who had known Jesus, lived with him, followed him, listened to him preach, who were aware of his strengths and failings. They knew he wasn't God in the flesh, that as a good Jew a notion like that would have been anathema to him. But they had witnessed a new strain of humanity in Jesus, a new consciousness, and it was this that Paul blew out of all proportion when declaring Jesus to be a saviour figure. The Jews were quite used to the idea of saviour figures, but they never thought of them as direct manifestations of God. As far as Paul was concerned, however, it was no longer Jesus' words that mattered, it was Jesus himself. He made Jesus himself into the spiritual breakthrough of the age, not what he taught. The Christ of history had turned into the Christ of faith.'

'A personality cult,' said Drummond.

'Just so.'

'And that brings us back to the Christian literalists,' said the Israeli. 'What I described earlier may have sounded like pure imagination, but I can assure you it isn't. The literalists have resuscitated the early hysteria of Paul's followers, calling it quite erroneously a renewal of the original Christian vision. The Church will eventually give in to that hysteria because the hollow myth of Jesus as God in the flesh is what the Church used firstly to initiate, and then consolidate, its grasp on spiritual and secular power. The Armageddon scenario being painted by religious fanatics like Thwaites fully supports our fear of a war in the

Middle East to end all war. You see, they believe that the decisive battle between good and evil will take place outside Jerusalem, on the Plain of Jezreel, to be exact, and that the Jewish nation will play a central role in the whole affair. There are of course thousands of interpretations – every literalist sect has its own variation. But they all boil down to certain agreed-upon basics: the armies of all-that-is-good will engage the armies of all-that-is-evil, and the good army will reduce the evil army to a river of blood. That is the substance of the Armageddon scenario, a river of blood. And it cannot be lightly dismissed when so many people are waiting for it to happen. The literalists are praying that it will happen. Some of them have gone as far as to say that the negotiated peace between America and Russia is pure heresy. It stands to reason, they say, that only the return of Christ can initiate a legitimate peace. Digest that one if you can! And the Armageddon scenario has reached a peak in the USA in that it has become a significant plank in the belief system of the enormously influential Christian New Right.'

Drummond said 'Christ' softly under his breath.

'And it isn't just a large slice of the American public that's fallen for such distortion. The same stupidity has infected their brothers in just about every other country you can imagine. France has her share of them, as has Britain and Germany and Holland and countless other countries. Even Australia has recently reported a dramatic growth in the acceptance of such ideas. It's a worldwide phenomenon. And in conjunction with the upsurge of mindless terrorism, suicides, meaningless killings and the Middle East's own literalist revival, it signals the very breakdown Monsieur Duval and his colleagues have shown to be a quite real statistical probability within a period of only two years.' He looked at Duval as if for confirmation, and returned to his subject. 'The fascination with Armageddon has spawned missionary movements to preach the gospel to the world's as yet unreached peoples, and the central theme of that gospel is the Armageddon scenario brought to a ludicrous interpretative perfection. They're so sure of themselves they're spending millions propagating their nonsense to speed up the whole process. I joke not. Vast amounts of money have been spent with the radio and television networks right across the Western world over the last few months in particular. They've started the countdown to

Armageddon, and are oblivious to the fact that in their hands the language of the Scriptures is being stretched and distorted beyond belief. Which is to say that the literalists are having a field day convincing the gullible and the afraid and the inadequate that their interpretation of supposed prophecy is the truth and nothing but the truth. It's a nightmare, and it's only just getting under way.'

'What will you do if you don't find him?'

'Fight, Mr Drummond. There won't be anything else for it.'

Pulling his own packet of cigarettes out of his pocket, Drummond offered them to the Israeli, who declined, and said, 'Is there anything else I should know?'

The man smiled, glanced at Duval and confirmed what Drummond already suspected – that it was the Israeli government who was financing Duval's immensely expensive project. 'In the event of our failing to locate the man we've code-named Masadan, it's our rather vague hope that Monseiur Duval's specially-trained teams will be successful in the production and in the nurturing of an underground sanity sufficiently strong to help what remains of our nation survive. We've learned to plan ahead. Attempt the impossible. Expect at all times to succeed in spite of the odds thrown against us. In this respect we're probably the hardiest nation in existence. And that's why you're here this evening, why you've been made aware of our existence and let in on what we're up to. Without people like yourself working at full creative capacity, we won't be able to set up the control systems necessary for even a partial survival of the hundreds of thousands of Jews scattered across Europe. The state of Israel may well go under, but a remnant of those Jews dispersed across Europe must be assisted to survive, whatever it costs us now. At least this time we can see what's coming and attempt to prepare for it.'

Drummond stared at the Israeli for some seconds. 'I think I've only just realized what all of this actually means. It's staggering.'

'Then consider yourself a wise man,' said the Israeli. 'Very few have either the imagination *or* the intelligence to grasp what you've just grasped.'

Chapter Sixteen

Dr Fisher arrived at Drummond's apartment during breakfast on the Wednesday morning with news of his indefinite suspension from Bart's Hospital. The psychiatrist was in a thoroughly agitated state, and Duval's surprisingly distant reaction to the man's plight did not help matters. Drummond's reaction was to overcompensate for the Frenchman's unsympathetic stance, and Fisher immediately involved him in an attempt to enlist Duval's support in the clearing of his name. The argument used was familiar to the advertising man – it was more or less what the psychiatrist had tried to get across to him as they watched little Sophie being rescued from her mental prison.

'All it would take is *one* demonstration,' said Fisher pleadingly. 'All this nonsense about my having practised some kind of spurious magic on my patients would be quashed if they saw with their own eyes what can be done through your new treatment.'

'It would not help,' replied Duval. 'They would not allow themselves to accept such procedures as valid.'

'How could they deny it?'

'They would not allow me near a patient. You know that better than I.'

'The father of that little girl would speak out on your behalf. I'm sure of that. Don't you think so, Ian?'

It was the first time Fisher had ever used Drummond's Christian name.

'. . . Yes, I'm sure he would,' Drummond said back.

'Why are the bulk of psychiatrists at this very moment denying even the possibility that Freud reneged on his own seduction theory?' Duval's look was stony. 'Can you explain that? It would seem that the psychoanalytic profession is itself involved in the suppression of a possible truth to avoid the problem of procedural adjustment. I suggest to you that the reaction of the medical establishment to any demonstration of our techniques would be identical. They would not be able to accommodate them for the very reason that they would call into question much of the standard thinking about disease. And that would necessitate the same type of major adjustment in procedure that their psychoanalytic colleagues have shown themselves singularly unwilling even to consider.'

Dr Fisher stared at Duval for a moment; then in a terribly controlled manner he said: 'That is your last word on the matter?'

'Yes.'

The ring of finality in Duval's voice caused the psychiatrist to turn towards Drummond. 'Perhaps you can convince him,' he said without energy or conviction. 'He listens to you for some reason.'

'. . . Would you like some breakfast?'

'No. Thank you, but no.' The psychiatrist turned back to face Duval. 'I believe you to be quite mistaken in this. Lacroix isn't going to hide his light under a bush when the moment comes.'

'The moment,' said Duval incomprehensibly, 'is more than that within which a deed can be accomplished; it is in itself a truth.'

The psychiatrist stared at him, frowned, turned away again, and without another word left the apartment.

As the door in the hallway closed, Drummond said: 'He's obviously a very worried man.'

'At least he knows for certain what it is he must do now.'

'What will he do?'

'I suspect he will contemplate betraying the best in himself for the sake of ambition.'

'You think he'll come out against you?'

'Not quite. He is more likely to seek the assistance of someone willing to put up with his ambition to be . . . a miracle-worker – which is to suggest that he may join Lacroix and allow himself to be mastered by an ambition greater than his own.'

'You really think that's what he'll do?'

'It is . . . *on the cards*, as our friend said last night.'

'You were pretty hard on him a moment ago.'

'He has been aware of the risks since the very beginning.'

Duval's body-language intimated that the subject had

completed itself, and that he had nothing else to say on the matter. They finished breakfast, talking for a further ten minutes about the situation in general as Drummond prepared to leave for the office. There would be no change in their plans, Duval said, sipping at a glass of apple juice. He was confident that everything would work out in the end, in spite of their little setback. Drummond smiled at that. Little setback? Lacroix had managed to close down virtually the whole organization in one move, but Duval seemed quite unperturbed by his success. Putting on his jacket, he filled Duval in on what he and Georgia had decided was the best plan of attack, and Duval listened intently. But even as he stood there articulating the words he had the feeling that the Maestro wasn't really all that interested in their scheme to reverse Lacroix's efforts and highlight the man's preposterous hopes for a returned monarchy. The impression given in that moment was of someone who trusted to fate and allowed the world to get on with its manic manipulations. Drummond assimilated that subconsciously and said that they would of course leave out the rest of the story. It would be quite enough if they managed to blow the lid off Lacroix's basic game plan. He then gave Duval a key to the apartment, said that he would be back around six that evening, and headed for the front door. But as he reached it, the telephone rang and he doubled back. Minutes later he was explaining to Duval that a quite incredible thing had happened: Dr Freeman had rung to say that he had been informed by an emissary of the Catholic Church that they were willing to back Monsieur Duval de Chantillac in whatever way might be required. It was felt that a great injustice had been done, and that it was the Church's duty to uphold the value of the work he was engaged in against the spurious opinions of those with too limited a view of both the Christian faith and the workings of the human mind. A certain bishop had been informed of this high-level decision, and would be willing to lend his name to any sensitively-worded statement of refutation being prepared in defence.

'Why do you think they've committed themselves in this way?' asked Drummond.

'Because they have little choice in the matter,' said Duval. 'The battle lines have been drawn within the Church itself, and those who wish to see her continue as she is have decided that an early move is necessary to galvanize and quickly shape public opinion.'

'You'll accept the offer of help?'

'But of course.'

Everton's face, when Ian burst in and broke the news, immediately betrayed an immense relief. 'That's . . . excellent!' he said, staring up at Drummond wide-eyed.

'I'd love to be a fly on the wall when this breaks, Bill!' he replied. Then thinking of what Georgia's reaction would be, he used Bill's telephone and dialled her number – but she wasn't there.

Imbued with new energy, he worked solidly for another two hours until it was time for him to leave for a filming session on the other side of London. With that behind him he drove back to the office, called Georgia again, and got through this time. She was amazed by the news and said that she too had had a certain success in interesting the *Mercury* in further revelations through a journalist friend who worked on the paper. She had played it very cool, she said, and knew that her reputation in the city as a crack freelancer would probably result in an approach from the *Mercury* within a few hours. She had set her bait well on the hook by naming Lacroix as the paper's source and had insinuated that the little professor of history was involved in something that would make the Duval story pale into insignificance when it broke. It was of course highly unlikely that Lacroix's name would mean anything to the *Mercury*'s editor, but if they were aware of their story's having emanated from France, the connection would seem sensible and they'd be on it in a flash. If there was anything at all in the paper's favour as far as they were concerned, it was its editor's willingness to consider the most unlikely connections and exploit them without conscience. Drop a name like Lacroix's into the mix, add a little mystery in the shape of the *Hieron du Lys*, and the stage was set for a riot of newsprint claiming inside information from sources that could not be revealed. Even if Paquel came up with nothing, they could probably rely on the *Mercury*'s daily need for raging headlines to overcome the problem of definite proof. She laughed and added that gutter journalism had its advantages, that her previous notion of supplying definite proof had suddenly hit her as virtually unnecessary, but that she still hoped Paquel might come up with a legitimate connection.

'You think you'll get away with it?' asked Drummond.

'Now that the Church is involved I could probably get away

with just about anything,' she said, laughing into the phone. 'Let me know the moment you get the name of that bishop. If that doesn't get them going, nothing will.'

They chatted on and she asked how his guest was faring. He said that he'd given Duval a key to the apartment, but that he had looked rather tired and was probably resting.

'I don't suppose I'll see you this evening then?'

'It's unlikely,' he said, wondering how Fisher would react now that things were about to straighten themselves out again.

He turned the key in the door of his apartment at six-fifteen, let himself in, walked down the hallway and glanced into the lounge expecting to see Duval seated there, but the room was empty. Calling out, he waited for a response, but the apartment was quite empty. He went into the lounge expecting to find a note, but there was no such note. Accepting the fact that Duval had every right to do as he pleased, but just a little annoyed that he had made no effort to acquaint him with his movements, he stood wondering if he should take it as read that he would be out for the rest of the evening. As they hadn't discussed what should be done about meals, the man had probably met up with the twin therapists he seemed to favour and booked a table somewhere. That made sense. It also made sense that he should now get himself over to Georgia's and spend a pleasant evening and not hang around waiting for the prodigal philosopher to return. By way of subtle reprimand he scribbled a note saying where he could be contacted. But as he pulled the front door closed behind him the telephone rang and he had to open up again. It wasn't Duval. The caller identified himself with the code-word *Masadan*.

'This phone's unreliable,' said Drummond immediately.

'We're aware of that, but it no longer matters,' said the voice. There was a pause. '. . . I've been instructed to tell you that Duval was picked off Regent Street at four this afternoon and bundled into a car. It happened so fast there was nothing we could do about it. We got the number, but of course it was a stolen vehicle.'

'What happens now?'

'We're working on that. Any idea what might have triggered them off?'

He explained about his call from Freeman, reiterated its

contents and heard his informant whistle to himself in surprise.

'We'll get back to you on this,' said the voice. 'They may contact you. If they do, I suggest you comply with their wishes. Oh, there's another thing . . . They've withdrawn their surveillance on you. Thought you might like to know that.'

The line went dead. Drummond stood, telephone in hand, focusing on nothing. Then quite suddenly his mind began to work and he thought of something positive that could be done. The phone went back into its cradle with a thump and he was out of his apartment and heading downstairs hoping against hope that what had occurred to him might prove useful. Aretino Lefèbvre was after all a senior diplomat in the French government with connections everywhere, and there was no doubting his devotion to Duval. If anyone could help, then it had to be Lefèbvre. But he in turn needed Georgia's help to get to the man, and this made him race the BMW almost recklessly all the way from Camden Square to Hampstead.

Georgia let him in, took one look at his face and immediately asked what had happened. He told her about Duval being grabbed as they climbed the stairs, and when asked how he had come by such information delayed his answer until he had a drink in his hand. Her reaction to the news of Israeli involvement was, as he had expected, total astonishment. 'I'll try to explain later,' he said, forcing a smile. 'What's important right now is that Lacroix has obviously panicked; that could be to our advantage. I don't think he has any immediate intention of harming Duval. He's too valuable. What I want you to do is to get me through to Aretino Lefèbvre if you possibly can. I'm sure he'll know what to do.'

'That might prove difficult. He could be anywhere. It's quite late.'

'*Try*,' he said back.

Half an hour later she was still trying. The Paris switchboard was quite busy and Drummond sat listening to her chatter on and on in French as they transferred her call from one government department to another. Most of the departments were already closed, for it was almost eight in the evening, and although eventually she made contact with the correct section after quite a run-around, and had a conversation with someone who ought to have known Lefèbvre's name, she drew a blank. But as luck would have it, someone passing through stepped into the breach and a new voice came on the line. Monsieur Lefèbvre? Ah. He was out of Paris at that moment and could not be reached. Georgia said that the call was urgent, that it was imperative that a Mr Ian Drummond speak with Monsieur Lefèbvre, and that if efforts were not made to contact him wherever he was, there would certainly be repercussions the following day. Something over and above the actual words used must have got across, for he said suddenly that it might after all be possible to contact Lefèbvre, and asked Georgia to hold the line. When he came back on about three minutes later it was to announce quite miraculously that the diplomat's location had been identified, and that if she would wait a further moment or two their lines would be linked. There was a series of clicks, then what had to be Lefèbvre's voice sounded in her ear and she handed the telephone to Drummond.

'Monsieur Lefèbvre?' said Drummond.

'Mr Drummond?'

They talked for only four minutes and Georgia noted that Drummond had not had to explain to Lefèbvre how he knew about the kidnapping – which meant that Lefèbvre hadn't bothered to ask what to her had been the all-important question. When Drummond put the phone down she immediately collared him on that point.

'He knows the Israelis are involved – his speciality is Israel. That only came back to me last night.'

'So what were you told?'

His smile was more of a grimace. He said that he needed another drink, that what he was about to say was for her ears only, and that it must not be passed on to her friend in Paris. She gave him a nod and waited for his explanation. It came out disjointedly as he fought for coherence, trying to verbally relive what the Israeli Intelligence Officer had said about the madcap fundamentalists invading the Middle East in an attempt to fulfil prophecies that weren't prophecies at all. Watching his face as he spoke, Georgia began to appreciate the monstrousness of the scenario and how it could be made into a reality by literalist interpreters like Thwaites.

'A holy *bastille*.' said Georgia.

'Exactly. And the Catholic Church itself coerced into accepting the whole shebang because she's never had the spiritual guts to fully admit her failings as a religious institution.' He delivered a caustic laugh and added, 'It would be laughable if it wasn't so bloody pathetic.'

He continued to describe the coming scenario, and she listened, knowing from what she herself had been taught as a child, that Israeli fears were not without a certain foundation. But unlike Drummond, she was aware of the Church's attempt to accommodate Vatican II and its basic premise of true community within the Church. The megastar pope had attempted during his whizz-bang travels to reclaim the countries of the world with a symbolic kiss and an often anything-but-gentle reminder of traditional values, but the growing division between the conservative and progressive laity heralded not a return to those traditional values, but a thorough questioning of old-style Catholicism and its replacement with a more community-minded attitude. Vatican II had put the cat among the pigeons, and if Lacroix's megalomaniac dream in conjunction with sectarian hopes for prophecy fulfilled could be stopped in its tracks, then there was a chance that the Church might re-establish its credibility and truly assist a world tearing itself apart for the sake of patently idiotic ideologies masquerading as never-to-be-changed truths. And when it came to such truths Israel wasn't exempt from criticism. She had quite a few fanatics of her own. There were cracked mentalities in Israel just as there were everywhere else, and if Israel wished to be taken seriously as a nation desirous of peace and stability, she too must put her own house in order.

As Drummond completed his rather topsy-turvy monologue, an image came into Georgia's mind – that of the present pope's face pressed against a dark cross. The image was from an old television programme showing the pope standing in the Colosseum in Rome during Holy Week. The ancient hymn *Stabat Mater* had been sung in a lonely unison, and a close-up of the pope's face had shown him to be quivering with emotion as Christ's walk from judgement under Pontius Pilate to crucifixion, death and burial was commemorated. That the man had been in a state of palpable fear had been obvious; and if what Duval and his Israeli friends believed was in any way true, then it was little wonder that the pontiff had been shaking in St Peter's shoes as he considered the future. The pope's frantic scramble from country to country made sense when viewed in this light; as did the draining of Vatican finances at a time when the Church ought to have been riding very carefully indeed. And the attempt to galvanize and hold the attention of 800 million Catholics and channel them back into the old mould when so many were hoping for a new and sensible freedom, strongly suggested a last-ditch stand by someone who knew that a great catastrophe was on the horizon. This was the question no one had dared ask the Holy Father as he descended and ascended like a mechanical dove – why is all of this being done? Was it merely an astute policy being put into action as some believed, a policy of 'I'll hit the liberationists with my presence and bring them to heel'? Or was the Church's very survival at stake as the countdown toward Masadan's appearance drained rapidly into the hourglass?

'You've given me the shivers,' she said, when he went on to describe the fundamentalists spending millions to sell their dangerous dream to as many of the gullible as would receive it.

'If they conjure that Messiah of theirs into existence at exactly the right moment, all hell's going to break loose.'

Drummond was well aware of what that hell might be like. Brought up in the backstreets of Glasgow, he had witnessed the ferocity of the Saints on both sides as they drum-marched *en masse* on the 12th of July. Most of the Protestant pulpits had screamed with invective on that particular day, and he had realized even way back then that, given half a chance, these convinced followers of Protestant eschatology would have torn their Catholic brothers to pieces if the law hadn't been there in force. It was true that many of the marchers on such a parade weren't Christians at all, merely half-drunk hooligans who liked to keep alive religious rivalries for the sheer sake of it. But there had been just as many good evangelical Christians among them for the obvious to become obvious, and he had never forgotten the look in their eyes as they strode, Bible in hand, behind the banners, the skirl of the pipes pumping the blood into their faces. Things had changed since then, it was believed, but many of the same hatreds still bubbled beneath the surface, and they were nowhere more visible than on a Belfast street when the boys in orange sashes caught the fever and exhibited their indoctrinated arrogance for the whole world to see. The American fundamentalists caught up in their thoroughly American Disney-type vision might sound strange when compared with the almost dour antics of their British counterparts, but much – if not all – of that surface gloss would disappear if they once believed they had the reins in their hands and there was no one to stop them bringing the ungodly and the heathen to heel.

The greatest danger of all was the releasing of that stated vision into a giant marketplace where the overall climate was one of psychological and social instability. The West was already in an observably unstable economic condition, and if the dam broke and the world markets crashed, the scene would be set for much more than another Depression. Terrorism would run riot in such a climate, as would the ideas of the superstitious and the magically-minded, and what remained of government and law enforcement would crumble toward an appeasement of any body of individuals strong enough to take the reins and promise even a semblance of sanity. That body of strong individuals, however, would not be the united fundamentalist sects testing their authority over a deranged populace, but the fundamentalist vision harnessed and redirected by the *Hieron du Lys* and turned into the greatest coup of all times – the setting up of a Theocratic United States of Europe.

Duval had eventually taken this picture and placed it in a strict political and psychological perspective for Drummond. Masadan would not only occupy a throne of political and secular power, he would also occupy the throne of St Peter as well. Under that supreme authority there would be an interlocking network of kingdoms or principalities connected by dynastic alliance and intermarriage – a kind of modern feudal system. But the actual process of governing would reside with the *Hieron du Lys* in the form of a European Parliament endowed with executive and legislative powers.

More important still was the increasing desire for a true 'leader', a benign spiritual figure in whom humankind could trust without fear of disappointment. Sated with materialism and aware of a profound spiritual hunger, the populations of Europe, North America and Russia were beginning to show their collective state of unrest. In fear of the world's ending because of the proliferation of deadly weapons, and confused by the story that a believable peace was an idealistic nonsense, they were fast moving into shock and experiencing the first tremors of psychic disability. And all because instinct had been betrayed and the human mind led toward a forlornness which was unbearable. Present to them at their lowest ebb a figure of immense charismatic power and apparent compassion, link that figure to the archetypal dream of a perfect society functioning within the confines of a predetermined plan in the mind of God, show proofs and evidences of this figure's being a blood descendant of Him who was edited into a perfect spiritual existence by the Church – and there was the basis for a dictatorship to end all dictatorships.

Being unable to remember all the twists and turns of what Duval had said, Drummond did not attempt to relay the philosopher's highly detailed statements of the previous evening. But he did get enough of his argument across to make Georgia appreciate the devilishness of the plan soon to be activated by Lacroix's deceptively powerful organization. There were, he said, quoting Duval, hundreds of important people involved, people highly placed in the French government, in industry and commerce both in France and outside France, whose dream was to rule like kings in their own right. Of these there was a nucleus of 144 individuals called 'directors' who would initiate the Great Plan when the moment came. They were evidently primed and ready to go about their duties even now, against the concurrent possibility that some series of outrageous acts of terrorism might trigger the whole thing off ahead of the expected time.

'It's like the plot for a Ludlum thriller,' she said, staring across at him fixedly.

'And we're sitting here twiddling our bloody thumbs,' he replied, reminding her of the uncomfortable fact that Duval had been taken and that they were impotent to act.

'Do you think he's still in the country?'

'Probably. I've got the feeling they won't be in any hurry to take him back to France.'

'They might just kill him and get it over with.'

'Perhaps.'

'You obviously don't think so?'

'I don't really know what to think, Georgia. We'll just have to sit tight and hope the Israelis come up with something.'

'Do you think they will?'

'I'm told they're the best in the business,' he replied unconvincingly.

They talked on about Duval and suddenly realized that a decision would have to be made about the *Mercury* article. Georgia surprised Drummond by saying that she thought they ought to go ahead – the basic premise of highlighting Lacroix's monarchical dream was still the best route to take. If the little history professor was fearful of his organization's intentions being pre-empted in the press, and particularly of the Church's willingness to exonerate Duval, how much more fearful would he be if they blew the story wide open and boldly accused him of having had Duval removed from the scene. He wouldn't be expecting that, and the *Mercury* would go for that one in a flash, she said, convinced of the soundness of her reasoning. The philosopher's chances of survival would be enhanced, not diminished by such a move. And if Paquel could be persuaded to make the same accusation in *Le Miroir*, then the ball would be again firmly back in their court. It would of course be a risky business, she admitted. Lacroix had already shown himself capable of panic and over-reaction. But they were now involved in a chess game of some subtlety, and an unorthodox move at this point might well throw their opponent into a state of further confusion. The media of both countries would immediately attempt to verify the story, and Lacroix would be reduced to defending himself at every turn.

After further discussion, Drummond accepted the strategy as sound. He left Georgia at ten o'clock and drove back to Camden Square wondering if Lacroix's people would attempt to contact him. He thought about what he would say if they did, and decided that agreement with whatever they asked would keep intact the necessary element of surprise when the story broke. Success depended on Lacroix's being taken off guard. With an expulsion of air from between his lips, he reached forward and turned on the radio, searched for some music, but was arrested instead by an Irish lilt and a manner of speaking he immediately recognized.

> *. . . Our reality has become fragmented and we must endeavour to reassemble the fragments into a coherent whole. Here, in Ireland, the fragmentation is even more extreme than it is elsewhere. This is because the myths in Ireland are more fragmented than they are elsewhere. Every man lives by certain myths – myth in the positive sense of 'scheme' or 'plan' or ' pattern' or 'hierarchy of*

values' – and it is thus important that people choose their myths wisely. It is important that we recognize the danger of limited, petty or 'tribal' myths – myths which reflect certain vested interests, which extol one or another 'cause', which emphasize one or another fragment at the expense of the whole. Such myths derive their energy from opposition – from manufacturing a scapegoat, who embodies everything about oneself that one wishes to disown. By generating conflict with this scapegoat, 'tribal' myths inflate themselves out of all proportion and begin to shape our lives – to romanticize violence, for example, to transform paranoia into virtue, to turn politics and 'political solutions' into surrogates for genuine spiritual values, for Mystery, for the Transpersonal. 'Tribal' myths stress the difference between men and, by so doing, drive men apart from one another.

There was more, much more. Then a presenter's voice told Drummond that he had been listening to Kevin Murray broadcasting directly from Ireland. Directly? Now there was a telling statement. Kevin had hinted at the possibility of his returning, and had apparently taken the leap. But he had done much more than that, it seemed. He had also grasped the nettle of his country's renewed problems and was attempting to make his fellow Irishmen aware of how those problems could be approached. He had, in other words, put his money where his mouth was and fully committed himself to what many would consider an impossible task –reconciliation of the warring factions through the articulation of a vision which differentiated between the archetypal and the tribal.

Shaking his head at the thought of this one man's lonely attempt to address his people and their utterly desperate plight, Drummond gave him a mental nod of approval and switched the radio off. Coincidence? What were the odds against his having caught that broadcast? He hardly ever listened to the car radio. It was just one of those crazy things – there was nothing else one could say. If asked, however, Duval would probably chunter on for an hour or more, linking coincidence to this and that, and the world would again cease to be the apparently simple place it appeared to be and turn again into a mystery.

That too was what Kevin had been talking about – mystery – and it was slowly beginning to dawn on Drummond that the mystery wasn't just a common-or-garden-type mystery, but a mystery with a capital 'M'. He had used Kevin's own words the night before when talking to the Israeli, and he could sometimes feel the capital 'M' mystery moving in on him like a presence, the sensation of being enveloped in some burgeoning truth registering on him when he awoke from one of his strange dreams. The dreams had more or less stopped now, but he suspected sometimes that they were still going on, and that he simply wasn't remembering them.

His mind jolted back to that moment when he had split into two beings and fought for his sanity, when by a man's fear-filled yell he had been delivered from committing a film-like murder somewhere in his own mind. A mystery indeed. And the dreams that had so threatened him stark and ineradicable in his memory. He swung the car round into Camden Square and brought it to a halt, switched off the engine and sat for a moment in the amber street light. Then wearily he pushed the door open and stepped out into the night wondering if he were again being watched.

CHAPTER SEVENTEEN

ARETINO LEFÈBVRE did not immediately contact Lacroix. He waited until the following morning and surprised him with a personal appearance. Paquel knew about the meeting within minutes, his new surveillance man having immediately recognized the diplomat and rung through with the news. Entering the apartment's mirrored hallway, Lefèbvre said angrily that he had just learned of Duval's abduction from Ian Drummond, and that he considered the Maestro's removal a precipitous and unnecessary act. Lacroix, unused to being spoken to in such a manner, was immediately petulant. It had been necessary to remove Duval because of a new development, he said, forgoing his manners and walking into the lounge ahead of Lefèbvre. Their hand had been forced by the fact that the opposing Vatican faction had promised moral support for their prime antagonist. If something had not been done, and done quickly, then an advantage difficult to overcome would have been gained within a matter of only a few hours.

'I think you should have consulted me on this,' said Lefèbvre, careful of his tone. 'I am after all in a posi –'

Lacroix's expression was one of blank amazement. '*I* need consult *no* one,' he snapped back arrogantly.

'That is of course understood,' said Lefèbvre, accepting the point with a nod, 'but I could have delayed any intended action by Monsieur Drummond with no more than a few words. I still can. He trusts me implicitly.'

'I was quite aware of that fact when informed of the decision.'

'It was not your decision?'

Lacroix drew air into his nostrils and turned away, staring at the window with his hands in the pockets of his immaculate suit like an informally arranged tailor's dummy. Then, looking back at Lefèbvre, he said, 'I too obey orders, Aretino, and I obey them without question.' His smile was sudden and condescending, his look searing. He changed verbal course and added, 'It may be necessary for you to go to England. We must know what they intend.'

'That's not really possible at the moment,' said Lefèbvre. 'My duties here are such that they cannot be abandoned. Awkward questions would be asked. I am not wholly a free agent you know.'

Lacroix laughed and stated a disconcerting truth. 'All I have to do is lift this telephone and you would instantly be at my disposal,' he said with a knowing look. 'That is all it would take, Aretino.'

'I believe it,' Aretino replied, now fully on guard. 'But I think such a move would be unwise, and I believe I could do no more by going to England than I could from here with the same instrument in my hand. Monsieur Drummond trusts me.'

'We *all* trust you,' said Lacroix, sustaining a distorted smile.

Lefèbvre's reaction was to laugh with mock embarrassment. He threw his hands apart in a gesture of defeat and carefully moulded his expression into that of a servant again mindful of his servitude. 'As you will,' he said, his eyes communicating both acceptance and good humour. 'Monsieur, I apologize for my behaviour.'

The little man's dismissal of the situation was almost regal. Content with the fact that his authority had been re-established, he appeared to give way to the diplomat's concern. 'Do what you think best and keep me informed,' he said, his tone and movements intimating that their meeting was at its end. 'But be prepared to arrange for Edouard's return to France within the next three weeks.'

'May I ask where he is being held?'

'You will be informed of that when the time comes.'

'I'll need time to prepare.'

'You will have all the time you need in that respect.'

Lefèbvre's final question produced unexpected gold. 'Why wait so long?' he asked with transparent innocence. 'Why not bring him back immediately?'

'Because an attempt is being made to modify his point of view.

Do you understand me?'

'By what means?'

'Ultimate means.'

'Drugs?'

'Nothing so primitive, Aretino. He is simply being subjected to the rigour of a mind greater than his own, a power which far exceeds his own.'

'They're together?'

A nod from Lacroix. 'It is the final gesture.'

'And if he remains adamant?'

'As I said, it is the *final* gesture. If it fails, he will be brought back and judged by his peers. There can of course be only one penalty for intransigence.'

There was no mistaking Lacroix's meaning, and Lefèbvre's instincts told him that retreat was the best part of valour in that moment. He had learned more than he had ever hoped from the interaction. Question the little man further and he would become suspicious. Attempt to wheedle the Master's exact location out of him and suspicion would turn into the realization that all was not as it ought to be. It was a dangerous game he was playing – had been playing for well over a year – and with a little luck it would pay off quite soon. And as it was a foregone conclusion that Edouard would reject the so-called Master's arguments, and quickly reveal himself immovable in the face of promises of power, wealth and ultimate authority, the decision to move him would probably be made within a few days.

'I await your orders,' he said softly, sickened by the very notion that the man he had grown to love and respect might be judged by someone like Tristan Lacroix. And he would have been further sickened had he known in that moment what Paul Paquel now knew – namely, that Tristan Lacroix's activities during the Second World War were quite other than as recorded in the official government records. A member of the Resistance he had certainly been, but his membership of that august body of men and women who had daily run the risk of imprisonment, torture and death, had been for reasons beyond any patriotic Frenchman's capacity to understand – *conscious betrayal*. Another set of records, those of German Military Intelligence (the Abwehr) now housed in the historical section of the French armed forces, painted a much fuller picture of Lacroix's wartime exploits.

Photographic copies of the principle documents pertaining to the man's direct dealings with the Gestapo had arrived on Paquel's desk that very morning – from a source unknown – and as Aretino Lefèbvre descended in the lift to street level, news of their contents and of the diplomat's visit to Lacroix's apartment was being voiced by a shocked Paquel to Georgia on the telephone.

Night, when it came to the island, was pitch-black and starless. A fierce wind, promising a storm of some proportion, whipped the bushes and trees surrounding the spacious, neatly thatched cottage where Duval was being held into a minor frenzy. Sitting motionless in a flower-patterned armchair by the unsecured window in his room, and bound only by his word that he would not attempt to escape, Duval contemplated the day's happenings in darkness. It had been an exhausting day, a battle of the will, and he knew he must carefully distil its content and allow the anger he had occasionally felt and accumulated to escape from his system if he were to endure another, and yet another, day of argument and deftly presented apologia for The Order.

Fourteen relentless hours had already been spent on the subject, and he now realized that the prime danger throughout it all had not been the lack of quality in some of his replies, but the quite hypnotic quality of the subject itself seeping into him like a refined poison. He was being slowly and methodically enveloped in an idea, swamped by it, and even though he rejected that idea, the *idea as a whole* was itself filling him up and taking him over – in spite of his success in verbally destroying much of its coherence and apparent irrefutability. He had caught himself warming to his subject as the hours rolled by, and had noted an actual sense of enjoyment as he delivered a particularly clever verbal blow and won an important point. The question was, had he actually won anything in that moment? Had not the ground gained almost immediately slipped away from him as he was forced to logically accept an indisputable series of observations about humanity as a whole, and the idiotic paths of supposed development and progress lauded by humanity as both inevitable and unavoidable? Because everything said was not ultimately related to the underlying pattern of take-over and subjugation, but often to basic truths accepted by all thinking men and women, civilized agreement had become a natural and frequent event in an otherwise clearly discernible field of perception distorted by power masquerading as compassion. Everything said could not be rejected, was not ultimately related to the suppressed desire for power – and in that intellectual fact lay a gaping hole into which, after days or weeks or perhaps even months of questioning and battling, he might inadvertently fall out of sheer exhaustion and the disabling honesty of his own wits. Like Pius VII closeted with the Emperor Napoleon, he was being slowly and methodically undermined and brainwashed by a group of people intent upon his conversion, and was conscious of pressures other than exposition and debate being directed at him as he counteracted again and again arrangements of thought and word subtly sliding towards a predetermined vision both invisibly vicious and disarmingly suasive in its appeal.

The truth of the matter was that they were not in the least concerned with whether they lost or won the argument, but with the fact that he was unconsciously digesting huge tracks of their reasoning hour by hour, and that when the crunch came it was those tracks of reasoning which he himself would neurotically accept as his own reasoned stance. It wasn't even a matter of dislodging and replacing what he presently believed, but of gently turning his thinking around until his own beliefs took on the quality of being secondary, their beliefs the quality of a primary vision. And during it all was maintained an almost undetectable vibration held steady by minds elsewhere, minds trained in the production of a seductive reverberatory wave allied to his own brain rhythms – he was being simultaneously verbally battered and psychically seduced.

He was also being flattered.

Inviting him again and again to rejoin The Order, they were attempting to imprint him with his own importance, calling on him like conscienceless sirens to throw himself into the arms of a false and deadly love. For their vision was of love dressed in the uniform of discipline, a love regimented and grey of texture, a love without tenderness or empathy, a love drained of its life's blood and replaced with a doctrinally concocted serum. Flatter him, they thought, and the weakest link in the chain of identity – personality – would automatically begin to work on their behalf. Personality always had its price, and his would react no differently from the many others already successfully processed and promised power without restriction. Not an idle promise, he realized, as he sat there waiting for the storm to break – for they would be in a position to deliver on their promissory note. And on top of it all there was the false security of having his word not to escape accepted as honourable and binding by their leader, the man's whose eyes sometimes blazed as he spoke, the man within whom a great darkness had taken root.

A triangle with its point downwards.

Three distinct processes were being brought to bear on him, hour in and hour out, with unbelievable cunning and precision. An inverted cone powered by discoveries identical to his own, directed by a mind equal to his own, a face the duplicate of his own. Only a few seconds of difference in their ages, and he the elder by a quirk of biological functioning. Twin babes carrying an unpleasant red birthmark between their shoulderblades disgorged into the world with a mother's anguished cry. And from that very moment an enmity separating them worthy of Jacob and Esau in spite of the bond of blood and flesh and symbol. A natural duality. The celestial and primeval twins separately encapsulating action and contemplation, ego and alter ego, darkness and light, sacrificer and sacrificed, artificer and creator.

He relaxed further, allowed the energy of the gathering storm to pass through him, placed his trust in the profound centre of his being and slowly – ever so slowly – descended into that centre and allowed personal identity to evaporate. A body in a chair in a dark room next to a window where the first drops of rain now registered like tears. Then a torrent as the heavens opened and the Isle of Wight was drenched, the heavy thatch again proving itself utterly impregnable.

And in that same moment, with Drummond sitting near by, Georgia dextrously moulded and edited Lacroix and his madcap organization's intent into a feature article for the *Mercury*. The bare story and no more. A king no better than a dictator for France, and a megalomaniac professor of history who had betrayed his country over and over again pulling the drawstring tight on the whole bag of tricks. The abduction of Edouard Duval de Chantillac brazenly broadcast, his abductor named and nailed, the intended *coup d'état* linked directly to France's ever-growing terrorist problem to side-step explaining the probability of social breakdown on a massive scale. And to end the piece, a verbal equivalent of a wax seal stamped with authority from the Roman Catholic Church for the man much maligned in the *Mercury*'s previous front-page article of 13 December.

'Done!' she said, slamming the last full stop into place. She swivelled round to face Drummond, smiled at him, her satisfaction with what she had accomplished obvious from her expression. 'All we have to do now is sit tight until the documents arrive.'

He blinked his tiredness at the dial of his watch, glanced up at her and said, 'I wonder why Lefèbvre hasn't called back. What the hell's he up to?'

'That's the question of the year . . . and not one I want to think about too much,' she replied, the fact of the diplomat's visit to Lacroix's apartment as much a mystery to them as the sudden and most timely appearance of the wartime documents on Paul Paquel's desk. So who was their mystery benefactor? Was it the same person who had sent the little postcard to Ian? 'Let's just hope he's as decent an individual as you seem to think he is.'

'I don't think I'll ever trust my assessment of another human being if he isn't,' said Drummond, hoping against hope that he was right about the man's basic integrity. Then with an enquiring look he said, 'When are you going to start writing the book?'

'. . . I think I've just started.'

'Let's hope Duval's around to read it,' he said back grimly.

The courier arrived at seven in the morning. Drummond signed for the fat manilla envelope and retraced his steps ploddingly, still half asleep. Georgia sat up in bed and watched him tear the envelope open, extract the photocopied sheets and lay them out on the bedcover. It was an unnerving sight. Scarred by time and the elements, and decorated at intervals with the official Nazi stamp, the blocks of thick black German type glowered up at them with a bleak authority, the sharply defined eagle with spread wings clutching its little swastika not only in the margins, but sometimes in the middle of the text itself. Drummond stared at the documents with a growing sense of horror, and in his mind's eye saw the fist of a ferocious officialdom slamming down to leave its menacing imprint for all future generations to ponder. He also wondered in that moment what Masadan's official stamp would be. A black cross within the outline of a lily? Or was the logo for

Saba Petrol perhaps the agreed-upon design? They had never been able to work out exactly what was going on at Saba, but it was fair to assume that the highest echelon of the company was in Lacroix's pocket.

'Your German up to translating this lot?' he asked.

She shook her head, said that the *Mercury* would find someone.

'What happens if they turn out to be forgeries?'

'It won't matter if they are – they'll have served their purpose by the time that's discovered. And the *Mercury* sure as hell won't question them, that's for certain.' She motioned with a hand toward the papers on the bed. 'Anyway, I don't think they are forgeries. Looks to me like just the kind of thing Lacroix would delight in doing.'

A coldness slid through Drummond, a chilling portent of the future related to the harsh blocks of grotesquely decorated black type he could not understand. There was so much he did not understand, so much, and he realized fully in that moment that his unthinking way of life was over, that he must properly take on board the responsibility of attempting to understand the basics of existence before he too was gobbled up in the psychic mess awaiting them all at Masadan's hand. He could sense the fatal attraction of such a character's appearing on the stage of history when all seemed lost, and having listened again and again to Duval as he so fluidly expressed the mysteries of the human mind, could now appreciate the truly disturbing possibility of the religious impulse being harnessed and directed in a manner quite beyond what could be intellectually anticipated. The mind was an unplumbed abyss where dragons still lurked, and with The Order's assistance those dragons would again be released into the light of day for all to perceive.

What a terrible moment that would be. A kind of controlled hysteria would reign, and 2,000 years of ingrained superstition would erupt as a pattern of mind against which none could stand. An army of ruthless inquisitors would be unleashed on the populace, those retaining a modicum of sanity a target for abuse and enforced conversion. The television and radio stations would broadcast the inane songs, thoughts and arguments of the Elite (this was already happening with monotonous regularity on some channels and wavelengths), and the courts would again become places where the non-conformist would stand trial and hear words of condemnation uttered by judges and juries turned lunatic. Such things were quite conceivable given that The Order would quickly take the whole existing system under its dark wing. And with a supposed descendant of Jesus lording it over the whole frightening edifice like a new Führer, the voice of reason and compassion would be drowned out by the dogmatic voice of the faithful at last become one in absurdity. Absurdity. The whole thing sounded absurd, but something of that nature was *on the cards*, and only fools and idiots could ignore the already well-established indications which daily heralded panic in the most unlikely quarters.

Wrenching his eyes away from the documents which seemed by their very presence to examine the mentalities of those who had so methodically created them, Drummond expressed his disgust for Lacroix and abruptly added that the quicker they got what they had to do done the better. He then left Georgia and went through to the bathroom to wash, stood for a moment staring at himself in the mirror, then reaching for the orange toothbrush designated his, set about the business of his ablutions. The water flowing from the tap prevented him hearing the door bell when it sounded, and he knew of the visitor's arrival only when Georgia came into the bathroom with the news.

'A young man to see you,' she said, shrugging. 'Very polite, but he won't give his name.'

'What does he look like?'

'Tall. Heavily built. Said he had a message for you from someone you met only recently.'

'Recently?'

'Your Israeli friend?' posited Georgia.

'Must have to do with Duval,' he replied, having reached the same conclusion. 'Tell him I'll be right out . . . and bring my clothes in, I don't like meeting strangers in a dressing-gown.'

She left him and returned with his clothes, went back into the lounge and waited for him to emerge. When he did so, it was to find the young man seated and chatting about the weather like any sensible Englishman thrust into strange company.

'You have a message for me?' said Drummond.

The young man got to his feet. 'Duval's been located, sir.'

Drummond smiled. 'Is he all right?'

'Yes. They seem to be putting him through a lengthy interrogation.'

'Where is he?'

'That's not for me to say, sir. Sorry. My orders are to take you both to one of our safe houses for a little chat.'

'Both of us?'

'Those were my instructions.'

'. . . Okay.' He looked at Georgia and she gave him a nod, left them together and headed for the bathroom. 'How did you manage to find him?' he then asked.

'A snippet of information was picked up in Paris. We got lucky.'

'Your people must have got pretty close.'

'Good field glasses have a decent range.'

'Of course.' He motioned that the young man should be seated again. 'So what happens now?'

'We'll move in the moment an opportunity arises.'

Drummond nodded sagely, reached for his cigarettes. 'Smoke?'

'I never acquired the habit.'

'Lucky you.' He lit his cigarette and inhaled. 'Same place as last time?'

'No. Golders Green.'

'That's handy.'

The young agent smiled.

'Been in the service long?'

'Two years. I'm still playing tea-boy.'

'You look as if you're in good shape.'

'I have to be.'

'I used to be in good shape, once upon a time.' Drummond laughed. 'Don't think I could run a hundred yards now if you paid me. I've grown soft.'

There was an awkward silence. Drummond broke it by saying, 'Why do you think they're interrogating him?'

The agent shrugged. 'Who knows?'

'Weren't you there?'

'There?'

'Weren't you part of the team that located him?'

'Me?' A laugh from the young agent, and a shake of the head. 'As I said, I'm still playing tea-boy.'

Drummond smiled, crushed the remains of his cigarette out and sat back into Georgia's cane chair. 'Bet you hope you have as much luck in locating Masadan.'

'Don't worry, we'll get him.' The young man looked up as Georgia passed from bathroom to bedroom, brought his attention back to Drummond and said, 'We'll have to play a few games when we leave here, if you see what I mean.'

Drummond nodded and said that he would be glad when the whole thing was over. He had never quite appreciated humdrum normality so much before.

The agent got to his feet when Georgia returned, stood waiting as Drummond helped her into her coat and struggled into his own. It was bitterly cold outside – there had been a heavy frost during the night. Down the stairs and out into the crisp air they went, the young agent leading.

'Any idea how long this'll take?' asked Georgia.

The agent glanced round at her. 'No more than an hour, I would think.' He continued on down the path, opened the gate and let them pass through. 'Our car's the white Celica,' he said, pointing a little way down the street. He looked around quickly and fell in behind them as they walked towards the car.

There was another man in the car, in the driver's seat. He started the engine as they approached.

When they reached the car, the agent moved forward, opened the door and watched as they slid behind the front seat into the coupé's rather cramped interior. Drummond glanced at Georgia and smiled, took her hand in his and pressed it reassuringly. The moment the agent was seated in the front the car took off. Turning left at the foot of Willoughby Road, they continued quite slowly up Willow Road and entered the maze of narrow streets backing Heath Street. After numerous twists and turns, they emerged onto Heath Street proper and crawled up the hill towards the Australian-looking Wheatsheaf pub, taking the left fork for Golders Green as Drummond fully expected. What he didn't expect, however, was the sudden turn off into Hampstead Garden Suburb. That was when the car really began to move.

'Damn it! They're onto us,' said the young agent.

They shot across the entrance to Wyldes Close – where a friend of Drummond's had stayed for some time – and continued down Wildwood Road at a quite startling pace. Drummond tried to look out of the back window, but the curve halfway down

Wildwood Road sent him careering into Georgia with such force that he feared she might have been badly hurt, her hand and arm twisted under him as was helplessly propelled to the right. Then just as suddenly they were both thrown viciously forward as the driver slammed on the brakes and wheeled the car screaming into Ingram Avenue, a short cut up onto Spaniards Road that Drummond knew well. Seconds later, having only narrowly avoided a collision with a red Volvo backing out of a driveway, they rounded the last of the tight corners and halted briefly before turning onto the main road and virtually bulleting their way up towards Highgate. That's when Drummond saw the other car and realized that – good as their driver was – there was probably little chance of shaking off their pursuer unless he collided with something or became bogged down in the now thickening traffic.

They slowed suddenly, shot cheekily past a stream of cars waiting for someone to turn off and scared the living daylights out of a driver coming down Hampstead Lane with at least a dozen cars on his tail.

'First right at the top!' shouted Drummond, knowing that Highgate at eight-fifteen in the morning was no place to be if you wanted to move around quickly. And as they rocketed up toward the zebra crossing and reached the turn off for The Grove, he yelled 'Now!' and braced both himself and Georgia for the sudden right-hand manoeuvre which, with a little luck, would carry them through onto Highgate West Hill where they had a much better chance of losing the black Honda now only some 30 yards behind. And that was when luck came down on their side. For not only was The Grove miraculously clear of traffic at that precise moment, they also managed to turn into it between two cars and cause the one behind to brake, stall, and come to a dead halt, so blocking the entrance to The Grove and allowing them a minute or so to vanish completely from sight.

The car slowed eventually, turned off into a side street, continued until they could not be seen, and stopped.

'Nice bit of driving,' said Drummond.

The man behind the wheel said 'Thanks' with a little laugh, glanced at his compatriot in the front seat and received a smile in return. Two, three, minutes passed, then Georgia formulated one of the most pertinent question of her life. 'Why suddenly start chasing after us?' she said, able at last to think clearly about the situation.

The agent who had collected them looked round. 'What do you mean?'

'I mean that they could have picked us up at any time. Why go in for such silly dramatics all of a sudden?'

The young man looked away and appeared to think for a moment; then turning full face he said, 'They may have thought they could get something out of a couple of Israelis.'

Georgia stared at the young man before answering. 'If it was *you* they were after, and not us,' she said frowning, 'then wouldn't it have been easier to grab you both while you were separated? Why wait? Why run the risk of being picked up by the police?'

'They're obviously amateurs . . . probably watched too many American cop movies in their spare time.' He grinned at his own words and added, 'Still, we were lucky to get away with it. They meant business.'

'I think we'd better start tracking for home,' said the driver, uttering his first full sentence. Then as if enjoying the articulation of words he added, 'Keep your eyes skinned for that Honda.' He switched on and they moved slowly away from the kerb, rounded the rest of the crescent they were on and arrived at a road called Holly Lodge. Turning left, then right onto Highgate West Hill, they proceeded back the way they had come and found themselves caught bumper-to-bumper in the rush-hour traffic. The driver said 'Fuck' and they carried on at a snail's pace behind a broad-beamed Leyland bus laden with passengers. Half an hour later they disengaged themselves from the madness and reached their destination in Golders Green.

Their destination turned out to be a dreary, part-furnished flat with steel-framed windows above some shops on the Finchley Road. As the door to the flat opened, Drummond's growing unease finally gave way to the same distrust Georgia had managed to communicate to him as they drove along in stony silence. Like persons momentarily displaced in time and space, the four of them stood for some seconds in the flat's almost empty front room before the full truth of the situation was voiced. The truth brought Drummond's anger bubbling to the surface. It also brought an automatic pistol out of the pocket of the fresh-faced youth who had so cleverly deceived them.

'I wouldn't if I were you,' he said, training the evil-looking mechanism on Georgia.

Drummond backed down immediately, palms up to indicate that he accepted defeat.

'Israelis!' Georgia said with disgust.

'What's the point of this?' asked Drummond.

The young man's smile could have been interpreted as one of innocence had it not been for the dark shadow of his thoughts. 'What would you do if you were me?' he said softly, his eyes straying to Georgia.

'I'll kill you if you lay a finger on her.'

'I don't think so.' The smile became a smirk. 'You didn't come out of it too well the last time we met.'

Drummond didn't say anything for a moment. Finding his voice he said huskily, 'That was you?'

'Yup. How long did it take for someone in your condition to come to? The rest of the morning?' The eyes moved to Georgia. 'You should have seen him. Naked as a babe and twice as useless.' Then came the boast that Drummond immediately latched onto. 'I could take you with one hand.'

'Try it,' said Drummond.

'Don't tempt me, fuckwit.'

'You're nothing more than a mouth.'

'You really think so?'

'I *know* so.'

'He's trying to bait you,' said the driver. 'Don't tangle with him.'

'He'll wait until my back's turned, like the last time,' said Drummond.

The young man's response was immediate. 'Take her into the other room. And take this with you,' he said, holding out the automatic. 'I'm going to teach our little friend here a lesson he'll never forget.' He corrected himself sinisterly. 'One he wouldn't forget if he had a future.'

'Don't be stupid,' said the driver.

'Don't call me stupid! Get her out of here and take this bloody thing with you!'

The pistol changed hands and the driver backed away, pulling Georgia with him. It was obvious he wasn't as confident a man as the other. 'For Christ's sake make it quick,' he said, reaching behind him for the handle of the door which led into the kitchen.

'Piss off,' said his mate, his eyes still on Drummond.

The door opened and closed, leaving them with their mutual anger. They removed their coats and jackets warily, threw them aside and stood facing one another like schoolboys about to settle a simple grudge – but Drummond knew damned well that it wasn't going to be like that. The youth facing him was no schoolboy, he was a trained fighter almost half his age and probably twice as fast. If he was going to come out of the bout alive and in one piece he'd have to disable the younger man in the first few minutes or, like Georgia, suffer dread consequences. It was a terrible realization. The voice of his old army instructor rang out in his head: *If you don't kill the bastard, then he'll bloody well kill you!* He had never forgotten those words. They had been dinned into him during basic training as they each learned the true meaning of war and stabbed and tore at one another with knife-shaped sticks and bare hands. Most of the old skills were still in his system, but he knew only too well that the reflexes which had once backed them had lost their edge.

Keeping his eyes on his opponent's face as they circled one another, and knowing that Georgia's safety depended on his every move's being made to count, Drummond emptied himself of thought and waited for an opening. It came sooner than expected and he moved in with a speed which took the younger man by surprise. He had expected the trim but obviously middle-aged advertising man to flail, not fight. Seizing the fingers so sloppily offered, Drummond twisted them back viciously, spun his opponent round and applied a headlock which might have finished the fight there and then but for a series of equally vicious countermoves. Breaking out of the hold, the youth spun away from him instead of following through as he ought to have done, his mind working overtime on the fact that this apparently soft individual was not as harmless as he looked. Knowing that he mustn't let up while his energy and strength remained, Drummond fought and blocked and jabbed quite successfully, but the other's more modern fighting techniques and superior strength robbed him each time of delivering the blow which could have ended it all. But the ferocity of his attacks and the street cunning he exhibited as they punched and pummelled at one another robbed the younger man's fight of its lethal edge, and he fast became wary of Drummond. In the end, however, none of it was enough to bring the bastard down. A strength and agility way beyond Drummond's own was draining his energies, and he knew it was only a matter of time before that superior strength and agility brought him to his knees. Knowing that he must end the fight as quickly as possible, and by any means available, he started to weigh up what the room itself offered by way of defence. That's when he noticed the old flat-iron in the fireplace and began to prepare a strategy of getting to it without his opponent realizing what he was up to. With that in his hand like an overblown knuckle-duster, he knew he could probably end the bout and still have enough energy left over to deal with the second man who wouldn't be expecting him to survive.

But how to get to it?

He had so far been taking the fight to his opponent at every opportunity, and had suffered punishment to both face and kidneys as a result. What he had to do now was slowly back-pedal his way across the room and draw the bastard after him, giving the impression of being more tired than he actually was. There was of course a great risk in such a manoeuvre. If he got himself flattened against the fireplace he'd be done for. And it would have to be a split-second decision, a ducking round and down and a perfectly timed upward delivery to either the solar plexus or the face. He began to actualize his plan, and a moment later received a blow to the head which almost knocked him unconscious while still on his feet. Reeling back, he tripped, fell, and found himself almost exactly where he wanted to be. Struggling onto his knees with a difficulty which was not exaggerated, he waited the second or two it took for the other to reach him, then grabbing frantically at the squat flat-iron, rammed it up and into the area of the man's genitals with all the strength he could muster.

The fight was over instantly, the youth's pain so intense he collapsed on top of Drummond and blacked out. Pushing the body aside, he got to his feet and headed across the room to the kitchen door. There he stood for a moment gathering breath. Then with a twist of the handle he burst in and threw the flat-iron straight at the astonished driver. It hit the man a glancing blow on the shoulder and he staggered back amazed as Drummond bore down on him like a maddened bull. There was no time to use the automatic. The Scotsman drop-kicked the driver and almost sent him through the thin plaster sheeting of the wall. The gun fell from his hand and skittered harmlessly across the floor. Georgia watched for a moment with sickened fascination as Drummond methodically beat the man senseless. Then, with presence of mind, she picked up the automatic and aimed it at the doorway fully expecting to see the other man lurch into view. No one appeared. Satisfied with the effectiveness of his own measured brutality, Drummond came over to her and gently prised her fingers away from the butt and trigger of the automatic.

Not a word passed between them.

He took the weapon from her and checked it, dragged the semiconscious driver through into the lounge by the collar of his coat and dumped him next to his groaning buddy. The youth had regained consciousness but was still in such agony from the blow to his genitals that he couldn't move out of the foetal position. Hunting around, Drummond found an old stocking and a piece of flex and quickly tied the men's legs together, having already sent Georgia to find whatever else might be used to secure their hands and keep her busy. She came back with a length of rag from under the sink and he completed the job after tearing it in half. The driver was so scared he actually held his hands in position while Drummond worked on them. Still moaning and bent double, the youth was more difficult to deal with, but when the automatic was jammed into his neck he quickly found the will to bring his hands into the open and let Georgia bind them.

'That's more like it,' said Drummond, pushing himself up and applying the safety catch. 'Are you okay?'

She nodded and stood up shakily, staring down with disbelief at what he had managed to accomplish before replying. 'I really thought we'd had it,' she said, a marked tremor in her voice. 'I couldn't believe my eyes when you came through that door.'

'There was a damsel in distress,' he said back with a smile. 'Did you think I'd leave her to the tender mercies of the dragon?' Thinking she might be about to faint, he stepped over the bodies and took hold of her, held her in close. 'You were fantastic,' he said, the image of her standing with the automatic pointed at the empty doorway having astonished him when he turned.

'I wouldn't have hesitated to kill him,' she said blankly, pulling back a little to look at him. 'The only fear I had was of pulling the trigger and of nothing happening, of the damned thing not going off for some stupid reason. Or of missing. If I'd pulled the trigger and missed and he'd kept coming . . .'

'Yeah, I know the feeling,' he said, nodding at her. 'I'm glad it didn't come to that.'

'. . . What happens now?'

'It's question and answer time,' he replied, certain in himself of the younger man's involvement in Duval's abduction. 'I suggest you go downstairs and wait in the car.'

She stared at him for a moment, then did as he asked knowing full well that he meant business and that he'd get the information he wanted by whatever means necessary. She had never seen such a look on his face before – never wanted to see it again. A cold, ruthless look. The look of a man with his will set to a purpose and utterly beyond deflection. If there was information to be had on Duval, then it would only be a matter of minutes before that information was generously shared. She sat in the car and waited, glancing at her watch and up at the window above the shops expecting to hear screams, but heard nothing except the din of traffic. And all around her life trundled on as usual, the preparations for Christmas everywhere evident. She smiled bitterly to herself and stared fascinated at a shop festooned with pagan Christmas trees, was suddenly wrenched back into reality by Drummond opening the car door. A glance told her that he had got what he wanted.

'Where is he?' she asked.

'Somewhere on the Isle of Wight.' He produced the car keys, searched out the one for the ignition and inserted it. As they moved away from the kerb he said, 'Duval was handed over to a second team after the Oxford Street pick-up. A place called Bembridge was mentioned during the swap-over. Bembridge is on the Isle of Wight.' Slowing, he waited for a gap in the traffic and did a quick U-turn. To Georgia's amazement he then said that he was going to have a crack at finding Duval himself if the Israelis didn't make contact within the next few hours. She began to argue and he held up a palm to stop her. 'I haven't got any option, Georgia,' he said, his determination visible in the set of his jaw. 'If he's half the man I think he is, they'll be forced to kill him – it's a matter of options all round.'

'It's a big island, Ian.'

'He's a big man,' he said back with a smile. 'Someone may have noticed him when they brought him in.'

She thought about that for a moment. 'What are you going to do about the two men in that room?'

'I think they're best left to the tender mercies of the Israelis. Don't you? No sense in calling in the police.'

'And if the Israelis don't surface?'

'Then they're sure as hell in for a bloody uncomfortable weekend.'

CHAPTER EIGHTEEN

THE MODIFIED Brute Bonanza carrying the small Israeli unit dropped onto the illuminated tarmac of the private airfield outside of Bembridge at ten past eight on the Friday evening. It had taken everything the overloaded plane's modified Avro Lycoming turbines had in them to battle the heavy wind conditions over the Solent. Five men alighted, each dressed casually and carrying a canvas sports bag. Moving in absolute silence across the wet and deserted airfield to where an old, but well maintained, Land Rover stood waiting, they wedged themselves into it and were driven off in the direction of Bembridge. An interested onlooker might have taken them for young businessmen over for a winter conference, or a band of Mormon missionaries intent on spreading the truth of the Golden Plates to Bembridge's friendly inhabitants – but they were in fact a highly trained hit team used by the Mossad when things got tough and deeds of a particularly nasty nature had to be accomplished.

It was a sad reflection on the democratic state of Israel that such units had to exist at all, but as a tiny nation subjected to permanent guerrilla warfare, the unit's existence had been rationalized on the grounds of expediency and self-defence. Forced to go it alone by the rest of the world and the supine attitude of the Western powers, Israel had no option but to retaliate with the same brutal precision as her enemies. Some of these unofficial squads had taken interesting titles for themselves such as 'The Avengers', 'Masada', 'Squad 101' (also sometimes referred to as Squad 1001 as a confusion tactic), the 'July Unit' and 'Wrath of God'; it was a *Wrath of God* unit that was now speeding its way toward Bembridge.

Summoned to the telephone in the early hours of Friday

morning by a thoroughly agitated Tristan Lacroix, Lefèbvre had been given Duval's exact location, a rendezvous point, and told to bring him out that evening under cover of darkness. The diplomat had immediately informed an Israeli agent waiting for the news, and set about the intricate task of arranging for a high-powered launch to cross the Channel and execute the little man's wishes, although not quite in the way envisaged. The reason given by Lacroix for such a hasty decision was that the philosopher had gone into a self-induced coma during the night, and everything attempted by way of resuscitation had failed. He had no detectable pulse, virtually no heartbeat, and had obviously decided to totally disengage himself from the situation out of fear of his twin brother. Faced with what he interpreted as a coward's retreat into mindless oblivion, Masadan had decided that the almost lifeless body of his brother should be returned to France. In possession of both Duval's and Masadan's location, Lefèbvre had also warned his Israeli contact that the rescue mission would have to be conducted with ultimate caution – they were up against a mind of unusual cunning, a mind capable of reaching out toward others in a most extraordinary and inexplicable fashion. And the dangers of confronting that mind should not be underestimated. Masadan wasn't an ordinary man: he was a genetic freak with the capacity to confound them psychically.

Lefèbvre rang Drummond at nine o'clock without success, then tried the other number given to him with the same result. At a quarter past nine, knowing full well that the Israeli team in London would be racing to follow through on the information supplied, he dutifully reported to Lacroix that the launch would be despatched for the Isle of Wight that evening, its exact time of arrival in the appropriate waters timed to be twelve midnight. Everything was under control, he said, smiling into the receiver.

But everything was not under control, not even in the sense Lefèbvre meant it. For having driven late afternoon to Portsmouth after a tiring two hours in the offices of the *Mercury*, Drummond and Georgia had caught a ferry for Ryde, and within three-quarters of an hour had disembarked and were on their way to Bembridge. He had argued vehemently against her coming along, but she had refused point-blank to stay behind, and he had eventually given in to her reasoning: two heads would be better than one when it came to the drudgery of inquiry – and she would of course stay out from under his feet if they got lucky and found out where Duval was being held. He had agreed to her coming along only on that assurance.

They checked into The Willows Guesthouse in the growing suburb of Lane End at quarter to seven, scoffed a quick meal, and spent the next two hours doing a tour of the hotel and pub bars in the hope of learning something useful. But on the question of strangers, particularly foreign ones, no one seemed to know anything, and they had all but given up when a quite elderly woman sidled up to them in the bar of the Royal Spithead and volunteered exactly the kind of information they were after. Someone had mentioned their plight, and yes there were some strangers – three to be exact – renting a lovely old cottage down Ducie Avenue. They had been there for a good few months and might very well be the 'friends' they had lost track of.

'Could you describe them for us?' asked Drummond.

'One is quite tall with black hair and very foreign-looking . . . The other's got fair hair and is about your height.' She added with a little smile: 'They're both very polite.'

'The fair one isn't foreign?'

'English.'

'And the third man?'

'*Very* tall,' she said, prodding high in the air with a hand.

'The third one sounds a bit like my friend,' said Drummond, giving Georgia a look. 'If he's French, it's probably him. Is he French?'

'I don't know,' said the woman, shrugging. 'He hardly ever comes out of the house. The other two take turns at the shopping.'

'He never goes into town?'

'Been seen in the garden a few times, that's all.'

'And he's really tall?'

'Tall as I've ever seen; a right bean-pole. I don't know how he stands being cooped up like that.'

Georgia came into the conversation at that point. She smiled and said, 'Do you mean by that that he's been here for some time?'

'About seven or eight months.'

Drummond's face fell. 'The tall one's been here for as long as that?'

'Could be longer.'
He sat back in his chair, disappointed.
'I hope you'll excuse me saying it, but they're all a bit odd.'
'Odd?' said Georgia. 'You said a moment ago that they were very polite.'
'Oh yes, polite, but they don't seem to like talking much.' She laughed to herself. 'It isn't that we're nosy . . . we just like to get to know folks a bit.'
Leaning forward again, Drummond said, 'They keep to themselves.'
The old woman nodded, staring at Drummond's bruised face wonderingly. 'To be frank, they give me the shivers.'
'Why is that?'
'It's the way they look at you.'
'How do you mean?' asked Georgia.
The woman thought for a moment, frowned to herself and attempted an explanation. 'They sometimes look right through me and out the other side . . . that's about the only way I can describe it. Cold. Know what I mean?'
'Doesn't sound at all like our friends,' said Drummond, sensing that they might be onto something after all. 'They're positively friendly.'
'Can't be them then,' she said.
'It was a bit of a long shot, asking around like this,' he said back. 'The people we're looking for may already have moved away, gone back to London. In fact they could be absolutely anywhere by now for all we know.'
Georgia came back in and said, 'I still think we should check these people out, Ian. If one of them is French he may have bumped into – Pierre.' She controlled the desire to smile and added, 'It's a small town.'
'What's the address again?' asked Drummond.
'Ducie Avenue,' said the woman. She added some directions.
Ducie Avenue, as it turned out, was quite near. If they turned left up the main road, then forked left again where the road swept round to the right, they would find themselves on a lane leading directly into the avenue. The cottage had a big thatch and deeply inset windows; it was on the right just before the turn-off to the shore, which was on the left. It was a *lovely* spot in summer, the houses in that quarter surrounded by extensive grounds in which

could be seen some of the best cedars and firs on the whole island. Drummond noted down the directions in his diary and offered to buy the woman a drink, but she declined. Having done her duty, probably more in the hope of learning something than from the desire to impart something, she said 'Goodnight' and trundled off towards the door, her little round body swaying from side to side as she walked.

'The only thing I don't understand is the bit about the tall man,' said Drummond. 'Sounds like Duval, but it obviously can't be him.'

'What are you going to do?'

'Check it out.'

They left the Royal Spithead soon after and returned to the guesthouse at Lane End, entering their room at exactly nine-thirty-five. Drummond immediately swapped his coat and suit for a pair of jeans and a leather jacket, then checked the automatic they had picked up and pushed it into his belt before applying the zipper. It was an American Colt with two safety devices, and he had thoroughly familiarized himself with it. Georgia stood watching and began to wonder why she had agreed to let him embark on such a mad stunt. It had been one thing to talk about it in London; it was quite another to be faced with the reality of the moment in which the deed itself had to be accomplished.

'I don't like this,' she said, staring at him.

'I'll be back before you know it.' He gave her a little smile, checked his watch and changed his tune. 'You can assume something's gone wrong if I'm not back by . . . eleven-thirty. Right?' He grinned, changed his mind and added, 'Better make that twelve o'clock – it might take a bit of time to find out what's going on down Ducie Avenue.'

'Be careful.'

'I'm learning to be *very* careful.'

'If it's the people we're looking for, don't for Christ's sake go in unless you're absolutely sure you can handle the situation. I don't want to have to take you off this island in a box.'

'I'm not an idiot.'

'No?' she said with a look.

He gave her a quick hug, kissed her, and was out of the room before she could say anything else. The door closed, and the silence made her look at her watch. Nine-forty. One hour and twenty minutes if she chose the eleventh hour in which to panic and recover. Two hours twenty if she could hold herself in check until midnight. She decided immediately to give him an hour and no more, went to her case and pulled out some old clothes, a pair of walking shoes and a strong-bladed butcher's knife in a leather sheath. She had taken it from the kitchen drawer without Ian's noticing. It wasn't much, but it was as sharp as all hell and had a wicked point. She shuddered just looking at the thing, threw it on the bed and began to undress.

Drummond was on Ducie Avenue by ten o'clock, having carefully parked the BMW for a quick exit from the Lane End guesthouse. He jogged part of the way, but was too stiff as a result of the fight and quickly slowed. Keeping to the right, he walked down the badly lit avenue and eventually saw the cottage nestled some 30 yards back from the road in its own grounds. It was quite large, and there was a light on in the front room. The curtains were closed. Glancing back to make sure there was no one else on the street, he hopped over a small fence and began to work his way through a grove of trees in the adjacent garden until he was edge-on to the cottage. The ground was wet and spongy, water-logged in places, and he cursed himself for not having worn heavier footwear.

The automatic slid out of his belt and into his hand. He checked it quickly in the dim light, flicked off the safeties and ran across the open space between the trees and the cottage, climbed the fence dividing the properties and reached the deep shadows of the big gable with its incredibly thick overhang of thatch. So far so good. With his back against the rough wall and the automatic held tight and pointed upwards he stood listening – but there was only the sound of his own breath easing out of his throat, the slow thump of his heart and the creak of leather. He stood there for some seconds wondering what to do next, then with great care made his way round to the front of the house in the hope that something might be heard through the lighted window.

Nothing.

Not a sound from inside the cottage. If there were people inside they were keeping unusually quiet. He slipped back into the shadows and thought about that, thought about what the old woman had said about the tall man's having been there for months. Then quite suddenly he felt utterly foolish, unnerved almost. A strange feeling swept over him, a kind of nausea, and he lowered the automatic and stood staring into the darkness, his will momentarily usurped by an overpowering negativity. Even his thoughts seemed to twist out of shape, become distorted, weave away from him into incomprehension. He swore softly to himself, shook his head, leaned his head back against the wall of the house, closed his eyes and applied the disconnector safety-catch on the automatic. What in God's name was he doing? Why was he standing in someone's front garden with a gun hanging from his fingers? He shook his head a second time, opened his eyes and stared down into the gloom at his feet as if looking for something lost, then turned slowly to his left and found himself staring straight into the barrel of a revolver. Obeying softly intimated instructions, he handed over the automatic to another man who suddenly came out of the darkness.

The revolver propelled him in the direction of the front door. The door opened and he placed a foot on the step, faced into the light, and saw what he thought was Edouard Duval standing in the vestibule. But it wasn't Duval. It looked like him, but the clothes were wrong, the hair thicker, the look on the man's face the wrong look. Another prod brought him within touching distance. The door closed behind them and he was shoved past the immensely tall figure and into the front room. Duval's look-alike followed them in. The man with the pistol turned out to be the fair-haired Englishman described by the old woman. He searched Drummond thoroughly and pushed him down into a plump armchair. The man who looked exactly like Duval stood watching like a schoolmaster waiting for an explanation from a wayward pupil. Drummond stared up at him, his mind working overtime. What in the name of God had happened during those few minutes? Something a little uncanny had taken place. The face that was Duval's face smiled suddenly, the thin lips curling back over perfect teeth, the small, coal-black eyes boring into him almost mesmerically. Drummond looked away, forced himself to look away.

'Your name is?' said Duval's voice.

He kept his eyes lowered and answered the question.

'How did you find us?'

'I got lucky.'

'There is no such thing as luck.'

'Whatever you say.'

The voice was suddenly impatient, the tone brittle. 'Explain immediately how you found us.'

A glance was enough to tell him that things could turn very nasty if he followed the impulse to try a facetious reply. Keeping Georgia out of it, he gave the rudiments of how he had pinpointed Bembridge, but couldn't resist adding that given the fact of his discovering the cottage so quickly, 'luck' had to be included in the equation.

'You are mistaken. There is always a motive in universal consciousness for whatever takes place, a *double* motive and a *willing* of events toward a preordained conclusion.' The look-alike then surprised Drummond with a fuller explanation of what he meant; he seemed to enjoy the sound of his own voice. 'When I say "double motive",' he added, 'I am of course referring to the fact that existence is governed by forces in apparent opposition, by a split in the divine nature. There is no disputing that, just as there is no disputing that evil can come out of good, or good from evil. Which is to say that good and evil sit side by side on the throne of existence and cannot be separated one from the other – they are, as someone has said, the two ends of the same stick. So to truly know God, one must fully explore the double motive of existence as it arises within oneself, explore it and know it in its fullness, live it out and not attempt to restrict the unfathomable desire which drives it. My dear brother has never quite grasped what that means, and it is obvious from your expression that you have never even thought about it.'

'You're Duval's brother?'

'Did you think me an actor?'

'I didn't know what to think.'

'I am the elder by a few seconds.'

'Really?' said Drummond, wondering why he was being given such useless information. 'I'm an only child myself,' he replied, as if chatting to a friend. 'And you're right: I haven't understood a word you've said.'

A little smile from Masadan.

Drummond trundled on, 'May I ask why you picked him up?'

'It was necessary that I talk to him.'

'You kidnapped your own brother so you could have a chat?'

'It was more of an invitation than a kidnapping. I was in a hurry. I needed to speak to him. Urgently.'

'You expect him to join you?'

'It is my belief that common sense will prevail.'

'Where is he? What have you done with him?'

'Done? I have done nothing at all; he is peacefully asleep in the next room.'

'You believe yourself persuasive enough to change his mind?'

'It is his unconscious wish that I change his mind.'

'You're saying he doesn't know his own mind.'

'Jealously can sometimes distort the finest intelligence.'

'He isn't jealous of you.'

'He covets the few seconds that separate us as a man covets gold.'

'You can't really believe that.'

'Why else do you think he has set himself up in opposition?' A little smile from the towering individual. 'But it is quite understandable. You see, like myself he has an innate sense of destiny and a desire to serve humanity, a desire to bring the world out of chaos and back into a state of order. But for reasons obscure he cannot find it in himself to accept that I too have the same desires, the same purpose and intent, the same right.'

'I'm . . . not following any of this. Are you saying that because he rejects Lacroix's pocket-Messiah he's on the wrong track?'

'The Messiah, as you call him, is in no one's pocket: I can assure you of that.'

Drummond huffed a laugh, 'That's not quite what I meant, but never mind.' He threw a glance at the man with the gun, looked back. 'You accept this Messiah figure without question?'

'It is his destiny to be what he is – the fulfilment of the Christian revelation.'

Drummond chuckled to himself, glanced again at the other man and realized that it would be madness to attempt anything with the pistol pointing straight at him. 'If you expect your brother to come round to your way of thinking,' he added, 'you really are fooling yourself.'

The coal-black eyes bored into him disconcertingly. 'There are things you do not as yet understand. And it is quite obvious that Edouard has been filling your head with all kinds of nonsense.'

'Ah, I see,' said Drummond. 'You're saying that that gun over there doesn't really mean anything, that I can get up out of this chair and walk out of here and nothing'll be done about it. Right?'

'I must remind you that you yourself were armed when you came here, that you would not have hesitated to do to us what is now being done to you. But you, of course, were on the side of Right, on the side of the Angels, as they say.'

'I was trying to help a friend, someone I respect because he's worth respecting.'

'And because of your belief in this friend you were willing to carry a weapon of destruction, and to use it as a tool to gain advantage and ensure success . . . Is that not so?'

'It isn't something I make a habit of,' replied Drummond, feeling the man's net of words close in on him. 'I haven't held one of those things in my hand for over twenty years.'

'I believe you. But I think you are rather missing the point. The point is that you chose to arm yourself, you chose to break the pattern of almost a lifetime and carry such a weapon because you felt the circumstances demanded it. And you were perfectly right to do so. If you believe wholeheartedly in something, then you have the right to defend that something in whatever fashion seems correct.' He paused in his argument, stared down at Drummond fixedly. 'Is it not a little self-righteous of you to deny others the same right of defence?'

'There was a man in London who would have happily killed me for no other reason than that he was ordered to do so,' said Drummond, articulating his words slowly. 'I don't believe for one second that that man believed in anything of value. The organization to which you belong hired that man, as it has hired other thugs to do its dirty work. If you're trying to tell me that what you believe is of value, then I want to know how you personally accommodate such tactics. I don't see how anything of value can be built on breaking into other people's homes, by having them beaten up on dark streets, or through attempting to remove them permanently from the land of the living because they don't quite see things the way you do. You talked about defence a moment ago, but what your people have been getting up to has nothing at all to do with defence.'

'Extreme situations sometimes demand extreme measures.'

'Against innocents?'

'No one is entirely innocent. We each carry the sins of the human species in our hearts and in our heads. The notion of Original Sin sprang from that realization.'

'So?'

'It is how we are; it is even how God is. That is why I said earlier that to know God one must fully explore the double motive of existence as it arises within oneself, explore it and know it in its fullness, live it out and not attempt to restrict the unfathomable desire which drives it.'

'You've got that pretty well off pat.'

'I have an excellent memory – please do not judge me on that.'

'God and the Devil on one throne.'

'If you like. The Devil is necessarily the other side of the coin of possibility, the creative drive in the divine mind. Without the Devil there would be nothing, nothing at all. No universe, no planets, no beings. So it could be said, and it has been said, that the world is his domain, that he is the creator of all substance, the generator of all ideas, the protector of all life. The realities are his creation; we are his children.'

'You seem to be more interested in the Devil than in God.'

'But it's *all* God. Without the Void, nothing of substance could exist. The Void generates substance in much the same fashion as we generate dreams. Reality is a dream. All of the realities are a dream. The Void supports and condones the realities it spawns through the act of spawning – and we too must condone and support those realities through believing in them *as if* they are real, through the populating of them with imaginative concepts born out of our own voidness. What you have failed to understand is that our dream is God's dream, a dream identifiable throughout history as a leaning towards order. God is chaos; the Devil is order. Consciousness is chaos; mind is order. And when society moves into chaos, then those of us in possession of true mind must immediately attempt to reinstate order. It is really all quite simple, once the basics have been understood.'

'There's one hell of a difference between order and dictatorship.'

'True mind does not have to dictate to anyone. True mind resonates with true mind in the same way as certain symbols resonate one with the other. All you have to do is find the right symbols, present them with finesse, and order will result. The human mind delights in order, welcomes it, strives always to attain it. Deprive the human mind of order and it crumbles automatically towards chaos. You must surely have noticed that.'

'I don't much fancy your kind of order, and I know for sure your brother doesn't.'

'My brother's fears are quite unfounded, as are yours.' Duval's brother smiled again, shook his head and sighed with a gentle exasperation. 'Western society is in chaos – I don't think even you would argue with that. The whole building is crumbling for want of true mind. Do you know why? I will tell you why. Because there is no Cornerstone. The foundation is true enough, the edifice sophisticated enough, but there is nothing to bind the stones together. There is a gap in the construction, and if that gap is not filled the whole edifice will fall. It may shock you to hear me say it, but Adolf Hitler clearly understood the nature of that missing component. He saw clearly that the Church was dead, that the symbols of regeneration belonging to that Church had lost their efficacy in the eyes of thinking human beings. And so he attempted to fill the gap, attempted to create a Cornerstone which would hold the building together for another thousand years. He almost succeeded.'

'You seem to hold Hitler in high regard.'

'I have always held intelligence in high regard.'

Drummond stared up at Duval's brother unblinkingly for some seconds. Then he said, 'What about your brother's intelligence?'

'My brother fails only in one respect: he is a sentimentalist.'

'And you intend to change him into a pragmatist.'

'I intend to extend his vision.'

'You'll never manage it, not with ideas like that.'

'You know very little about my brother – we share more than you would think.'

'Like what?'

'Blood. Blood is very important.'

'I don't think blood is going to be enough.'

'In the end it will be.'

'What are you going to do with me?'

'. . . That is something I have not yet decided. It was very foolish of you to attempt something like this on your own.'

'Who says I was on my own?'

'There is another?'

'Try "others".'

'I do not believe you.'

'Believe what you like.'

'Where are these . . . others?'

'Around.'

The unnamed brother laughed, looked at the man with the pistol, and said 'Do you believe him?'.

The man grinned, shook his head slowly from side to side.

'Neither do I. It is quite obvious that you only approached the problem the way you did because you were alone.'

'As I said, believe what you want to believe.'

'It is not a matter of belief; it is a matter of intelligence and sensitivity. There is no one out there. No one at all. I sensed you the moment you came within range, knew you as you stood there in the darkness. Then I disabled you, crippled you.'

'You expect me to believe such nonsense?'

'You know it to be the truth.'

'I know that you have an incredibly high opinion of yourself.'

'It is somewhat more than an opinion. Look at me. No, properly.'

'I don't fancy being hypnotized right this minute.'

'Look at me.'

Drummond glanced up with the intention of looking away again, but found that he could not look away. The man's eyes were suddenly alive, malevolently alive. A dark radiance swam out to engulf him and he cried out in alarm was for a moment caught in some baleful influence, then allowed to escape.

'Who am I, Mr Drummond?'

Drummond stared up into the man's face with a kind of horror. Then almost in a whisper he said: 'You're . . . Masadan.'

'So that is how they refer to me. How quaint.' The eyes that had dumbfounded him studied his face. 'I am He to whom every knee shall bow.'

Drummond rallied his composure as best he could. '. . . You can't seriously believe such a thing.'

'Intelligence is required to understand that statement – I am afraid you are singularly lacking in that basic gift.'

'At least I'm sane.'

'You think me insane?'

Drummond kept his mouth shut.

A smile from Masadan. 'The blood of the Merovingian kings

flows in my veins. Has Edouard instructed you in what that means?'

'He's mentioned the Merovingians.'

'And the origin of the Merovingian dynasty?'

A nod from Drummond.

'Then you know exactly who I am.'

'I know who you *think* you are.'

'You do not believe it?'

'I don't doubt that you believe it.'

'But you yourself do not believe that after so many centuries such a thing is possible.'

'It's . . . preposterous nonsense.'

'My brother believes what I believe.'

'I'm not sure that he does.'

'He has denied it?'

'He has disowned you and everything you stand for – that speaks for itself.'

'He believes in the bloodline nonetheless.'

'It doesn't mean to him what it means to you, I can assure you of that.'

'Perhaps not, but that does not change anything. I am what I am.'

'You're absurd,' said Drummond.

Masadan's reaction was immediate. His eyes took on a strange fixity, a quality of concentration so powerful that panic spread throughout Drummond's body like a flame. It was as if he had been physically struck. He was suddenly terrified, inexplicably engulfed by a feeling of vulnerability and fear so intense that if he had been able to move, if his body had been capable of responding, he would have cowered before Masadan like a frightened animal.

'Who am I?'

It was a rhetorical question. Masadan smiled, relaxed his hold on Drummond slowly, withdrew whatever it was he had mentally exuded.

The Scotsman felt physically sick as a result of the attack, feeling that he had experienced something grossly indecent. Glancing at the door behind which Duval was supposed to be sleeping, he said, 'The man in there won't let you get away with this.'

'Edouard? Edouard is powerless. *Utterly* powerless.'

'Then why are you afraid of him?'

It was a stab in the dark, but it found its mark.

'I fear *no man.*'

'And if the *second born* doesn't come round to your way of thinking?'

The little eyes darkened, became piercing again. 'Then destiny and the immutable powers will deal with him.'

'You'll kill him.'

'One man will die for the people – that is the Law.'

It was a good line, and well delivered, but Duval proved himself the greater master of timing in that moment. The bedroom door opened and he stepped into the room with the force of an Olivier. Masadan's words unravelled in the air, evaporated in the electric stillness generated by the philosopher's unexpected entry. It was a moment Drummond would never forget for as long as he lived. He looked back at the would-be Messiah's face and saw fear and anger battling on its surface. He also shot a glance at the armed bodyguard, but the man was a professional and knew instantly what was on his mind – he stepped back, his attention riveted on Drummond, both hands holding the revolver steady and at arms' length.

Regaining his composure, Masadan said. 'You are well rested, Edouard?' Then looking at Drummond he said, 'Do prisoners roam free?'

Duval advanced. He looked fresh and vital, and not at all like a man who had just awakened. His first words were to Drummond. 'You should not have come here,' he said.

'He is a *hero*,' joked Masadan. His next statement was incomprehensible to Drummond. 'And it would seem that he has the enviable power of waking the dead.'

The philosopher changed languages suddenly, speaking rapidly and with great force, his eyes dancing with indignation. Masadan's reply was almost casual, and in English. 'We will tutor him in the truth,' he said. He turned his attention back to Drummond. 'I think perhaps you may now be interested in the truth.'

His nerve bolstered by Duval's appearance, Drummond's reply was harsh and to the point. 'You wouldn't recognize the truth if it jumped you in broad daylight,' he said defiantly.

'It is said that the truth makes men free. Have you

no wish to be free?'

'Your kind of truth is a prison.'

'Truth is perfect bondage to the will of God – that is not to be in prison.'

'I don't believe in your God.'

'That is of no consequence. There is a *perfect* truth of which you are ignorant.'

'There's no such thing as a perfect *anything*,' said Drummond, his face screwed up with distaste.

'The will of God is ultimately perfect, Mr Drummond, and the will of God cannot be side-stepped. The stone rejected by the builders will be made the Cornerstone – you will come to understand and accept that fairly soon.'

'I wouldn't bet on it.'

'Enough!' said Masadan. He turned to his brother. 'We are about to leave this horrid little island, Edouard. Do I have your word –' He stopped short, turned his head to the side and stood listening for some seconds, his eyes almost closed, the fingers of his left hand curling into the palm and out again. It made Drummond think of a cat's claws being protruded and retracted. The eyes snapped open and he spoke. 'The reasoning in this is so foolish it escapes me. Did you think I –' The words in his mouth melted. He stared at Drummond as if to penetrate his skull and read the book of his memory. 'Why have them wait until now?'

'That's for you to work out,' said Drummond, trying to interpret the situation.

'There are perhaps four, maybe five of them,' said Masadan, addressing the fair-haired man. Then to Drummond he said, 'What did you hope to gain by this? You are helpless, and they too will soon be helpless.'

'I wouldn't bank on that – they're the best there is,' replied Drummond, the first inkling of who might be outside beginning to excite him. 'Now you've really got a fight on your hands.'

'You think so?'

'I know so.'

The disconcerting smile reappeared on Masadan's face. 'And *still* you have no conception of what you are dealing with.'

Drummond felt his confidence drain away. '. . . There's no way out of this one,' he said, more in the tone of a question than a statement. 'They've got you.'

'You are *all* fools,' said Masadan, turning away.

The five Israelis were in position; they intended to stay well back until the last possible moment. At ten past eleven, a woman was reported to be walking down Ducie Avenue in their direction. They watched her pass, watched her turn left onto the shore road and disappear. When she reappeared about a minute later, crossed the road, climbed uncertainly over the fence and began to worm her way through the grove of cedar trees towards them, a man was despatched to bring her down. He did so within seconds, knocking her virtually unconscious in the process. When she recovered, it was to find herself face down in the wet earth, her right arm pinned excruciatingly halfway up her back, the butt of a palm in her neck. There was the sound of someone else approaching, a short silence, words whispered in an unfamiliar tongue. A question was put to her in English. She tried to speak, but couldn't, the soft earth smothering her reply. The pressure on her neck was removed and she turned her head to the side, saw the dim outline of the other man kneeling very close. He repeated his question. She stared up at his blackened face and realized immediately who she was dealing with, said 'Shalom' and saw his mouth fall open in amazement. She then explained who she was and they let her sit up, staring at her as she quickly described how she and Drummond had come by the information that had led them to Bembridge.

'So where is he?' asked the squad leader.

She jerked a thumb in the direction of the cottage. 'In there, I think.'

He glanced at his companion, simulated a gauge with two fingers and said. 'Must have missed him by *that* much.'

'Thank God you're here,' she said, looking from one blackened face to another.

'I'd thank God later if I were you,' he replied. 'Masadan's in there.'

'. . . You're certain of that?'

'We have it on the best authority, the very best. It's their intention to move Duval out tonight. Should be doing it almost any minute now.' He had glanced at his watch as he spoke; he now reached forward and took hold of Georgia's arm to impress her with the importance of his next statement. 'Give me your word that you'll keep your head down and stay put?'

'Of course. I'm not stupid.'

'Whatever happens, *don't* change your mind. Stay put and keep your mouth shut. Do you understand?'

She gave him a tight little nod.

He stood up, signalled to his companion, and they moved off into the darkness leaving her with her thoughts. She watched them go, rubbed at her face and felt muddy grains slide this way and that. She realized suddenly that her coat was sodden with water and that she had lost a shoe. The coldness bit into her and she shivered. She eased herself up and stood with her back to a tree feeling utterly helpless, the foot without a shoe placed against the rough trunk, its numbness already evident. A twig snapped somewhere to her right and her breath caught in her throat. She listened with fierce attention for any further sound that might indicate movement, but could hear only the creak of branches and the sound of the wind as it swept across the garden in bursts. It began to rain in that moment.

The young Israeli's words suddenly hit home, and she realized that a new and dangerous element had been added to the situation, an element which scrambled predictions, an element which might well make the Israelis ignore the safety of those being held prisoner. Masadan was their primary target, Duval of secondary importance, Ian nothing more than a bothersome fly in the operational ointment. If they could get both men out they probably would, but as she stood there with the rain battering down around her, Georgia knew instinctively that that had already been classified as nothing more than a possibility. She didn't know why that had to be the case, why trained and well-armed men with a reputation second to none should think in such a way, but the injunction to *thank God later* had not been uttered out of modesty, of that she was certain. These men were afraid, and Masadan was the root of their fear.

It was thought unlikely that the front door would be used due to the position of the garage. The garage doors were open and it would have been the easiest thing in the world to have disabled the car that lay inside. But their briefing had demanded that they stay at a safe distance until the occupants emerged. A 'safe' distance had been estimated at between 20 and 30 yards. This had of course complicated things, and the squad leader had argued that a successful mission could not be conducted with his men so far back in the field at the moment of supposed interception. How could they gain the element of surprise when so much bloody territory had to be covered in the final seconds? But it seemed that there was nothing else for it. Masadan apparently had the ability to pick up on anything of a threatening nature within those approximate distances. Lacroix had boasted about this extraordinary ability, and had told Lefèbvre on one occasion that the Master could also create psychic disturbance in the mind of any would-be assassin. As there had been no time to consult expert opinion on such matters (there was a whole department devoted to psychical research in Israel), and Lefèbvre had been uncertain as to whether such an ability could be used against more than one man at a time, the worst had had to be assumed and the unimaginable allowed for.

But it was of course impossible to allow for the *unimaginable*. By definition the unimaginable could not be imagined, and the squad leader – a man of considerable intelligence – had nothing in either his experiential or intellectual repertoire with which to compare the situation. They waited, each man toying with his own thoughts, each with his eyes fastened on the cottage for any sign of movement, the rain continuing to make their vigil a misery, the conditions for assault more and more difficult. Obediently remaining at the spot to which she had been so unceremoniously dragged, Georgia hugged herself in an attempt to keep warm, her fears for Drummond's safety multiplying by the second. Ten more minutes passed with excruciating slowness. Then quite suddenly the back door of the cottage opened and someone stepped out into the night, the click of the old-fashioned latch being lifted piercing everyone to the quick. The figure ran to the garage because of the rain and disappeared inside. There was the sound of the car door being opened, and almost immediately the whirr of the starter. The engine came to life unwillingly, died, and was resuscitated. The headlights were then turned on full blast and the driveway was thrown into sharp relief.

Had the men squatting in the rain been able to see inside the cottage in that moment, they would have been surprised by the apparent lack of activity. Drummond was still in his armchair, the man with the pistol in exactly the same position as earlier,

Masadan and Duval standing within a few feet of one another. Then without warning something quite extraordinary happened. Masadan closed his eyes and Drummond felt a wave of something pass through him as the man's outrageous gifts were brought to bear on the Israelis. There was an immediate reaction. A shout was heard, then another. Georgia froze in that instant, turned to stare in the direction of what was quite obviously a situation of panic. The car came out of the garage. Masadan opened his eyes and smiled, but there was a strange look on his face and he did not speak from then on. Drummond was made to get to his feet and the whole party moved out of the lounge and into the tiny vestibule. The door opened to reveal the car already backed into position.

As they descended the short flight of steps, Georgia began to run towards the cottage; she could hear men crashing about on her right, and saw one of them fleetingly as he stumbled into view, and fell. She didn't stop. Driven by her fear for Drummond's safety, by a kind of parallel madness brought on by Masadan's attack on the Israelis, she raced through the trees in the direction of the sheen of light, reached the edge of the property and saw the small party approach the car. The yell she let loose in that moment stopped them in their tracks. Drummond spun round and struck out viciously at the man with the gun, sending him sprawling back onto the steps. Caught in a kind of psychic double-bind, Masadan stepped back and watched as Drummond beat the man insensible with a rapid series of punches to head and face. But there was of course the other man, the one in the car, and before Drummond could even turn he was levelling the seconded automatic at the Scotsman's back. That's when Duval acted. But in the same moment as he stepped into the line of fire Georgia screamed 'No!', and by means quite unnatural to her vaulted the boundary fence and came racing towards them. Distracted, the man with the automatic swivelled round, and in that same moment Drummond came out from behind Duval and tried to reach him. But there wasn't enough time. The gunman heard him coming, turned and fired, and Drummond went down with a bullet in his left shoulder.

The pain was so excruciating he blacked out for some seconds.

Georgia reached him without being stopped and fell to her knees. That was when Duval did something quite extraordinary.

He walked steadily towards the gunman, his hand held out as if expecting the man obediently to hand over his weapon. Not knowing what to do, the gunman backed off, the automatic raised threateningly. Georgia looked round, saw what was happening, saw Masadan's split powers of concentration waver and knew that she must act quickly. Her hand went into the pocket of her coat and she drew out the sheathed butcher's knife. Pulling the blade free, she turned. But as she made to get up, Drummond grabbed at her wrist. 'Give it to me!' he rasped. Taken aback by the fact that he was still alive, and that he was still functioning, she let him take the knife from her. As he struggled to his feet, Duval reached for the automatic and Masadan shouted to the man to kill him and be done with it. But the trigger was never pulled. Duval simply took hold of the gun's barrel and eased it from the hand that held it. Masadan immediately unleashed an attack on his brother, and in that same instant Drummond, knife in hand, moved in for the kill.

But once again it was not to be. It was almost as if some dark god were protecting its offspring.

Duval collapsed and Masadan switched his attention to Drummond. The effect was immediate. Drummond reeled back, managed to steady himself for a fleeting second, then like Duval, pitched forward. Still on her knees, and in a state near to hysteria, Georgia stared at Masadan, felt his evil permeate her, saw and felt him switch his mind back to its original endeavour like some conscienceless robot, and began to scream, and scream, and scream.

Drummond responded. Knife in hand, his left arm swinging uselessly, he struggled to his feet and advanced a second time. Masadan stared at him in disbelief, hesitated for a moment, then again directed his strange power at the Scotsman. But it didn't quite work this time – perhaps because he was tiring; perhaps because Ian was no longer really Ian, but somehow that other man whose business it was to kill. Driven by Georgia's screams, and by some other deep, dark force, he moved forward, forcing Duval's manic brother to back off. The terror so casually brought to bear on others now registered on the man's face. Again he lost control, and like any ordinary human being resorted to words, his palms held out in a ridiculous defence as Drummond closed in and the knife came within striking distance.

The knife slashed at the hands and they were quickly withdrawn, but not quickly enough. Blood spurted from both palms and Masadan squealed like a stuck pig as his juices spattered the footpath and fertilized the wintered flowerbeds. It was all over in that moment. His back was against the wall of the cottage and the knife was about to be driven into him. He crossed his hands over his chest to ward off the blow, his elbows dug in to protect the soft flesh of his stomach . . . but the blow was never delivered. Duval's voice rang out in that crucial second, and Ian hesitated.

Duval held out his hand for the knife as he had done for the automatic.

Drummond did not immediately respond. He seemed disorientated.

'Give me the knife, Ian,' said Duval ever so quietly. 'It is finished.'

Ian frowned, glancing at one brother, then at the other.

'The knife, Ian.'

When he eventually responded, it was because something in him lifted, like a curtain. Masadan stumbled towards Duval uttering thanks, his bloody hands held out to his brother in gratitude. Georgia didn't know what to think as the two men came together. Then she saw a sudden movement from Duval, and realized that he had knifed his brother in the solar plexus and was twisting the blade upwards, twisting and turning and thrusting it upwards to make sure it reached its mark, all the time holding his brother like a dear friend. And as they hung together in that deadly embrace, in that suspended moment of incomprehension and steely resolve, Ian and Georgia together saw Duval's body go into spasm, and watched horrified as both men sank, and fell. For the blade that found its mark in Masadan's body also found its mark in Duval's – not physically, but through that curious affinity which haunts the lives of twins.